HIGH PRAISE FOR WILLIAM BARTON AND
ACTS OF CONSCIENCE, WINNER OF A SPECIAL CITATION
FOR THE PHILIP K. DICK AWARD

"An intense and intensely pleasurable display of erudition,
writerly tact, and hard psychological realism ... fascinating."
—*Publishers Weekly* (starred review)

"A major artistic success for the talented Barton.... [His]
ability to weave disparate thematic threads together into
an intelligent and thought-provoking whole is impressive."
—*St. Petersburg Times*

"Barton generates a sense of genuine awe about the
potential of the universe."
—*Science Fiction Chronicle*

"Passion, war, and science: William Barton writes a mean
and astonishing tale."
—**Greg Bear**

"Full of event and spectacle."
—*Cleveland Plain Dealer*

more. . .

WHEN WE WERE REAL

WILLIAM BARTON

WHEN WE WERE REAL

A Time Warner Company

WARNER BOOKS EDITION

Aspect is a registered trademark of Warner Books, Inc.

Cover design by Don Puckey
Cover illustration by Chris Moore

Warner Books, Inc.
1271 Avenue of the Americas
New York, NY 10020

Visit our Web site at
www.warnerbooks.com

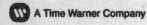 A Time Warner Company

Printed in the United States of America

First Printing: June, 1999

10 9 8 7 6 5 4 3 2 1

to
Anna Kavan
and
Cordwainer Smith

for the
taxonomy
of lost souls

There's nothing in life like loving someone .... It's all the difference between being dead or alive.

—H.G. Wells

CHAPTER ONE

Stories, they say, should always have happy endings. Only life is permitted to sputter out in a diminuendo of misery, dissolving through drab shades of gray before reaching some pointless fade to black.

When I was a boy, immersed in seemingly pointless study, I would read the biographies of the ancients and see that shadow hanging over every one of them. A man would be born, full of promise, would lead his famous life, fulfilling that promise, and then . . .

Well, you know.

Every biography is a tragedy.

The hero always falls.

The great man is always humbled in the end, no biography ever finishing up with "they lived happily ever after."

Those were the days before humanity emerged from its ratty little world, when *hope* was a word you used with utmost caution, associated with the profound fantasy that life might really *be* a dream from which you'd one day awaken.

Here at the other end of history, we know better.

We know, when a boy's done dreaming about his

Baedeker of wonder, he'll realize those shades of gray can go on and on, waiting for a daybreak that might never come. Sown to the dark between the stars, we live our open-ended lives, freed from the valley of the shadow out on all our ratty little worlds.

My ratty little world, the place where they made a gray little boy, anticipating a gray little man, where I dreamed a boy's grand dreams while reading those sad old tales, was called Audumla.

Down in the bayou country, down in Audumla's belly, well away from the habitat's endcaps and the settlements of the Mother's Children, you can see the decay a century's neglect has made. My father and I, when we visited the lowlands, would drive our cheap plastic boat down a wide, sluggish stream, tall, gray-green fronds of unnatural swampland vegetation blocking the view to either side. I would steer the skiff away from a long, iridescent blue oil slick, feeling the electric motor's soft vibration through the tiller, while Father sat between the thwarts, fiddling with his tinker's tools.

Overhead, you could see a long way, despite the haze. It was only hazy down by the ground anyhow, down where the air had gotten thick, most of the air-conditioning returns long ago plugged up, overgrown. The sky was still quite clear, though nothing like I understand it used to be, dark blue up around the brilliant orange stemshine, purple shading off into brown everywhere else. Beyond it, you could see the bare outlines of Audumla's other two habitat panels, between them patches of empty sky, where the stars would glimmer at night. Ygg's ruddy half-disk, almost hidden in the color of the sky, was peeking out from behind the edge of Panel Three like a hill of dull fire.

My father looked up from his hardware, an agelessly grizzled man with a lean, handsome face, big beak of a nose, pale blue eyes, and said, "Darius. How much farther?"

I steered the skiff to one side of a big flat mudbank that hadn't been here last time, feeling the current surge under us, catching a whiff of organic stink from the shore. "Just a couple of kems, Daddy. A few more minutes." Have I been down this stream a hundred times? I wondered. Probably not, but he's been bringing me here since I was a little kid . . . and I'm sixteen years old now. Maybe a hundred times after all.

"Good. Mrs. Trinket's baby won't wait."

Baby. Funny to think of it like that—but I do too; natural, I guess, coming out here with him, time and again, despite Mother's disapproval. He always calls me by my Timeliner name, the one he gave me, pronouncing it the old way, Dar-eye-us. Darius Murphy.

I like to have my friends call me Murph, and that makes Mother angry too. Dagmar Helgasson. That's your name. Your *only* name. The only kind of name a Mothersbairn *can* have. Mother won't let him near my brother Lenahr. Not since she found out about the name.

We came around a bend in the river and there was the Himeran village on a little hill beyond the bank, a sparse collection of packing crates set up where they'd cleared away the thicket. Beebee was waiting for us down by the shore, a tall, mirror-finish metal cylinder nearly two ems tall, standing on steel spiderlegs, waving assorted arms. You could hear him shouting, "Dr. Goshtasp! Dr. Goshtasp! Thank God, Dr. Goshtasp!"

Daddy muttered, "Just in time, I guess."

These trips down in the bayou country piss Mother off more than anything else. When I was very young, I supposed that marrying a resident alien—a Timeliner, no less, rather than a Mother's Son—had been her own act of youthful rebellion: Helga Rannsdottir, who hated her own mother just *so*, eloping in the night with a hooknose tinker.

It makes a pretty, romantic story for a boy to tell himself, dreaming in his bed. Something that makes his tale of the wonder years to come more plausible. I imagined them as adolescent lovers, daring the disapproval of the Mother's Children and . . .

So Helga Rannsdottir, turning up her nose at the Mother's Children and their arranged marriages, would show them all just what a *real* woman could do with a husband's Goddess-given talents.

Even if the wretch did believe his talents came from some silly, alien, *male* deity with the ridiculous name of Orb.

I can hear his tired voice now, remembered from when I was a boy, he never talks about it anymore: Not the Orb, Helga. Orb's just a symbol. Our souls emerge from Uncreated Time like everything else in the . . .

Then she'd screech about the Goddess' Truth. Sometimes throw things at him.

And, of course, one day I stumbled on the actual details, found some inkling of what it means to have an open-ended life, where you just go on and on, no matter what.

There and then, just as here and now, I followed him up the muddy hill, carrying the toolbox. You could see that Beebee, seniormost of Mrs. Trinket's fifteen husbands, was some kind of welding machine. Hard to say what his kind's job would have been, back when Audmula was a working industrial center called Standard ARM Decantorium XVII. Something out on the hull, judging from the grippers he had instead of feet. It made him limp, walking around inside, where there was only mud, grass, and loose rocks to trip over.

Those must have been good days for them, back before Ygg's ready resources played out. Bright days full of life and purpose and doing. I sometimes wonder if they miss it all, but they never talk about it, at least not in front of me.

When Ygg was finished off, Standard ARM found no profit in shifting its equipment to some other site—it's much cheaper to build new machinery *in situ*, so the mining tools were abandoned in place, not even told what was happening. Just one day the supervisors came no more.

After a while, they figured it out for themselves, cooked up some scheme to become an illegal service station, catering to the tramp freighter trade that was springing up in those days. Called the place Himera and let it develop quite a reputation as a den of iniquity. Maybe they'd've done all right for themselves, enough to buy all the supplies and spare parts they needed, but then Standard sold the joint to the Mother's Children, who soon turned the tramp starships away. Not a problem for anyone, what with the Centauri Jet and Telemachus Major being so close and all.

No problem for anyone but the Himerans.

And Mother, always angry because Dr. Goshtasp devoted so much profitless time to helping them stay alive.

Inside the largest packing crate, Mrs. Trinket was a big white enamel box lying on the floor, moaning softly in her best-little-girl voice. She looked something like a refrigerator, a refrigerator with four stumpy legs, four long, spindly arms, face of doll-like blue eyes and pursed pink lips mounted in the upper half of her breastplate, just above the spigots.

Lying on the floor now, she was surrounded by frightened husbands and excited children. Little Tillie the buffer's daughter, who'd never have reproductive organs of her own.

Maxine, a baby incubator just like Trinket, big eyes wide, taking it all in.

Daddy went to her side, obviously concerned about the state she was in, attached his diagnostics, and waited for his displays to come up. Hiss of exasperation. "Trinket, you sissy! When the call came, I thought you were dying!"

She whimpered, "Oh, Doctor. It never felt like this before . . ."

Daddy started plugging in to her other ports, making software disconnects at internal sensors, anesthetizing her. "Well, hang on, kiddo. We'll have a look and see what's what."

When the screwdrivers started to whine, Beebee flinched and averted his eyes.

When her access panel swung open, I felt like backing away, at least getting away from the powerful gust of . . . I don't know. Call it the smell of life that came out. I looked anyway, and there, in a womb made of bleeding raw steaks and heaving layers of rump roast, lay a collection of metal parts that seemed all angles and spikes and sharp edges.

Daddy said, "Well, shit. There you go."

One of the other husbands, an incomprehensible thing that seemed to be made mostly of gooseneck lamps, peered over his shoulder, blinked oddly this way and that from his seven or eight eyes, then crowed, "Beebee! I didn't know you had it in you!"

Beebee came forward too, edging nervously past me, and took a look. "My God! A baby welder!"

Trinket squeaked, "*Beebee?* You told me you ran dry *years* ago."

"Well . . . well . . . I'm sorry, Trinket. I *thought* I did . . ."

"You lying bastard! You just wait! You *see* if I ever—"

Daddy, laughing, patted her on the side. "Take it easy Trink. We'll have this critter out of you in five minutes."

I leaned in, holding my breath against the smell, and tapped him on the shoulder. "Uh, Dad? I think I'll . . . wait outside. If you don't mind."

He looked up for a second, giving me an odd, somehow disappointed look. Then shrugged and said, "Sure. This won't take long."

I stood out on the hillside, air much fresher here despite the surrounding swamp, and watched the children play, a bizarre assortment of kits and boxes and things that looked like they might even be hybrids between more than one sort of machine.

Years ago, back when we first started coming here, I used to play with Himeran kits. Play with them just like they were *real* children, friends and all. Well, the ones I knew grew up, went off to do whatever the hell it is abandoned hardware does when it grows up . . . Maybe I just don't want to think about it, now that my turn's come.

I looked away from the river, looked back up into the sky.

You can see the southern endcap from here, it's not that far. Rugged red hills rising up and up, becoming sheer red cliffs just before they disappear into the deep blue shadows around the axial port. All over the hills were the twinkling cities and towns of the Mother's Children. Towns, farmland, the gleaming silver of the new monorail lines we'd just put in, replacing the wrecked transport system Standard had left behind.

After a while, Daddy came out of Mrs. Trinket's crate, wiping bloody hands on some kind of rag, cottony stuff the Himerans always had laying around, came and stood beside me, watching the indigo shadows of dusk just starting to peep around the edges of our platform.

Finally, he said, "I always hate going home."

I felt a small pang, wishing he'd just fucking shut up. "Then don't."

He looked at me, then looked away, maybe wishing that, just this once, I'd sympathize with his bellyaching, and muttered, "So where the fuck else would I go, hmh?"

I shrugged. "Guess we better get started. She'll be pissed if we're late for supper."

Another long look. "Yup." We went back in to pack up his tools.

From the roofgarden atop Helgashall, on a grassy knoll some eight kems above the bayou country, you can see a long way down Audumla's axis, lowlands curving up to the right and left, stretching straightaway before you, two hundred kems to the northern endcap, tiny circle drowned in day by a glare of orange stemlight, little halo of bright freckles at night, faraway light from other Mothersbairn cities and towns.

Far below, on the panel where we'd just been, tall purple clouds were billowing up, twisted and sheared by Coriolis effects. Beyond, in the void between the panels, as the stemlight began fading away, stars were popping out, but Ygg's red ball was missing, having transited the nearest void, going behind habitable landscape. It'd be out again in a couple of hours, by the time the night was really black.

Woolgathering doesn't get anything done. I looked down into the freeze-frame, put my hands in the warm shimmer of the interface, and waited. Nothing. No inspiration. No desire to . . . finish. Graduation thesis is the last worthwhile thing you'll ever do. Why aren't you interested?

Nothing. The freeze-frame didn't seem to have any answers. Nobody gives a shit about the stasis-metric analytical conjunctions on gauge-dynamic metacontrols. I scrolled open the hopper and let it play at random, knowing it'd take me even further from getting the job done, but what the hell? Here, Standard ARM smugly announcing record profits from its big mining operation at Proxima, what they call the Glow-Ice Worlds. Attached adverts for new colonial positions just opening at Glow-Ice. Also at some frontier posting, way the fuck out by Altair.

Stock market surging giddily upward for the fourteenth straight year.

Profits up. Wages down. God's in his heaven and all's right with the economy. Aren't you glad?

News from the Centauri Jet. News from the Solar System, a full parsec and more from Ygg and Audmula. How's the refrain go? A billion-trillion datatracks and . . .

I stopped briefly in my favorite old atlas, a twinkle of jewels in a jet-black void. Here, solitary Sol, with its fine flat Kuiper disk and spherical Oort shell, home to four hundred billion human souls. There, Alpha Centauri A/B, its own cometary cloud distorted into a long, flat stream by the hectomillennia-long hyperbolic passage of Proxima, home to billions more.

And Audumla, just off the ragged terminus of the Centauri Jet, not far from Telemachus Major, headquarters of mighty Standard ARM. Always wanted to go there, a dreamable dream, only four days' travel from abandoned Ygg. A long look sideways at the pale blue sparkle of manhome Earth, picked out beside yellow Sol. Thirty-seven years by fast commercial starship? No. Never. An impossible dream.

Oh, sure, I've got the time, we all do, since things just go on and on, willy-nilly. But the dream of actually *doing* it . . .

I shut the freeze-frame, got up, and walked away. Two

weeks before I have to turn in my thesis, go to graduation, and then . . . then. Well, there is that.

Downstairs, in the Whitehall boundary of the *kemenatë*, the no-boys-allowed part of Helgashall, I stood in the doorway of my sister Rannvi's room, watching her, perched naked on the edge of her bed, painting her toenails black and gold. A startling, lovely young woman, incredibly unmarried at the age of twenty-two. Long, straight, golden-blond hair falling tousled around her shoulders. Deep, dark blue eyes. Rounded breasts with perfectly shaped pink nipples.

Once, wandering some far recess of humanity's civilization-wide, lightspeed DataWarren, I came across a small piece of fiction set against Mothersbairn society, obviously written by some ignorant tourist, fascinated by what he saw. All those women doing as they pleased, dressing as they pleased. All those men, seeing them. Seeing them and . . . the author's vitals seemed gnawed by what he saw, evidently wanted, and could not have. So his story portrayed a dark side to Audumla, to the society of the Mother's Children, a world of incest and violence and secret rape and . . .

Well.

A woman invites you into her body, at her convenience, at her need. A man knows never to ask. In his ignorance, blinded by his own unquenchable need, drowning in bloody fantasy, the author missed the real darkness in which we live.

Rannvi looked up from her pretty toes and smiled. "You can come in, Murph." She pulled her legs up on the bed, going cross-legged, motioning for me to join her. "Having a hard time, aren't you?"

I sat at the head of the bed, sprawled among her pillows, still looking at her, sights and visual textures, familiarity breeding no contempt. "I guess. It's . . . well. I never wanted this day to come. But it has anyway."

A slow nod, a pensive frown. "Have you . . . made your arrangements?"

"No. There's no one I can . . ." What? No one I can fucking stand? Is that it? "I don't know what to do, Rannvi."

She said, "She'll wait for me to make up my mind, getting angrier all the time. She won't wait for you."

"Doesn't she understand you *want* to keep on studying, try for a . . . well, a *career*?"

"Oh, shit, Murphy. No, she doesn't understand. 'A woman's work is Motherhood.' "

And "a man's work is woman's support." I know the Goddess-damned refrain. Embossed in fucking gold on the surface of my brain. "Why *doesn't* she understand? *She* broke with Mother's Children and Goddess. For a while, anyway. I mean, Daddy . . ." I said that, knowing by now that we both knew the truth, though we'd never talked about it.

Her voice low, Rannvi said, "It's still Motherhood, Murph." She struggled, breasts bobbing prettily. "I'll get maybe another year in school, if I'm lucky."

I've always appreciated that I'm Murph to her, not just Dagmar, Mother's Son. Some sisters are worth having. "Wish I could help . . ."

"But you're stuck a lot worse, I know. And I wish I could help . . ."

After a while, she got up and went over to her wardrobe, started picking through her clothes. Time. Time for everything. And nothing.

Being a middle child, I was left more unsupervised than either Rannvi before me or Lenahr to follow. Maybe that's why Daddy got so much of my time, in which to spoil me for the Mothers' Life. And why I got so much time *to* myself, in which to wonder and explore.

One day, when I was nine years old, I figured out how to unlock the hatchway to one of the household service panels, getting into the crawlspaces between the walls, a wonderland that was, at first, as alluring as anything in the Baedeker I'd imagined from the unfathomable universe beyond Audumla. And, when its novelty paled, I used it to get into other places I wasn't supposed to go.

Which led, in short order, to the attic.

All sorts of things were stored up there, mostly things that should have been thrown away, recycled, passed on, but people will retain the relics of their lives, just because they *are* relics.

We make a sentimental attachment to artifacts of the past, even as we put them away, knowing we'll never look at them again.

I spent a lot of time going through my mother's trunks, looking at her old clothes, out of fashion, out of date, though of course nothing was ever stained or frayed. I wondered why she would keep a box of colorful, silky underpants, neither wearing them nor discarding them.

Things like that.

And one day, I stumbled across a box of old albums, spending long hours poring over them, fascinated by what I saw. The one on top was full of familiar things, the things of the life around me, beginning with recent views that would spring to life in the air above its surface.

Fascinating to see my last birthday party, hear my own voice from just a few months gone, already seeming fantastically childish to a months-older me. Below it, a family picnic. Below that . . .

I watched with dull astonishment as my mother gave birth to Lenahr, smiling, naked, in a tub of bloody water as she strained and pushed and extruded him from the hair between her legs. Deeper in the album, beyond the part where I was a naked baby running about the yard, I saw myself so extruded, then Rannvi, then . . .

The album began with my mother's wedding to Father, Mother looking precisely as she did now, though dressed in . . . well, dressed in clothing I'd already found in one trunk or another.

The other albums held only mystery. My mother in an unfamiliar house, with an unfamiliar sky, sky apparently made of dark brown stone, hanging low overhead. She shared the unfamiliar house with an unfamiliar man and three unfamiliar adolescent children, two girls and a boy, all with stark, coppery hair. In time, deeper in the album, the children grew young, and I watched as, one by one, my mother gave bloody birth to strangers.

There were three albums like that, each beginning with a wedding.

The two middle ones were on the world with the brown sky. The oldest of the three seemed set on a skeletal habitat where the sky was always black, from which you could always see the stars. In that one there was a woman my mother called Mother, prominently featured in almost every scene.

Of course, you knew.

Audumla's not the only world the Mothersbairn own. You knew that. Out in the dark between the stars there must be a million little worlds. Since no one living on those worlds willingly dies, the worlds quickly grow full. And when they grow full, there's a call for volunteers: Go out, found a new world, start a new life.

When there aren't enough volunteers, they hold a lottery.

As I put the albums away, I wondered just who those men had been, and wondered about the children. What became of them? Were they my brothers and sisters, then?

I wonder if I would have liked them.

I was afraid to ask, knowing what'd happen to me if I was discovered to have been in the attic, messing among my mother's things.

Just a story, that's all. Put it with the Baedeker of wonder and move on.

I finished my thesis, bored as hell with the whole business of the rest of my life, turned it in, got my grades, and that was that. In a couple of weeks we'd have our ridiculous little graduation ceremony, proud parents comparing notes, not-so-proud parents pretending it didn't matter. In between we had a week off, and the members of my graduation cohort had a party, a little day trip to Mimir's Well, an old reduction transformer orbiting just outside Ygg's roche lobe that's been turned into a sort of park.

Ygg is huge in the sky here, and the park's main interpretive center is just at the tidally locked moonlet's subplaneton, infrastar hanging right over our heads, taking up almost a third of the sky, a frighteningly three-dimensional sphere more than two hundred thousand kems in diameter, holding maybe twenty jovian masses, well into the brown dwarf range.

Just a dull red disk seen from Audumla, a million kems out, lit by starlight, most of that from close-by Alpha Cee, ruddy from its own fading heat, hardly visible at all but for the greater blackness of the sky. There's a nightside, an umbra, the side away from Alpha, but that distinction's hard to make. Shadow. Something.

From here, though, just a few score thousand kem . . . band after band of swirling storm. Deep holes into the clear hydrogen air below, letting out light from Ygg's firehell within. Upwelling places that'd be sunspots on a real star, places where Ygg's magnetosphere was twisted . . .

"That's a fuck of a sight, eh, Murph?" Styrbjörn, skinny, blond, squinty-eyed, always smiling, the perfect Mother's Son. So long as the Mothers weren't around. So long as there was no one who would tell. Just not the son they thought they'd made.

"Yeah. Sort of makes you wish . . . kidstuff wishes. All that bullshit."

He shrugged. Grinned. "I dunno. I been on a few cloud-skimmer runs with my dad. I guess it's not for me." A long silence, while I thought about his father, a silent, frowning, black-bearded man who spent most of his time away from home, away from Audumla, away from his startlingly voluptuous blond wife and their six blond kids, Styrbjörn the youngest, flying an atmospheric ramscoop, bringing home the helium 3 bacon. "I've qualified for an apprentice-ship with the Mother's Trust, Murph. Information Sideband Specialist Trainee."

"And?"

Another long silence, then he said, "Sieglindë Smillas-dottir."

We were standing on the brow of a low hill, looking down at the interpretive center, broad greensward, oak trees and tall swaying pines, gaggle of graduates milling together around the pool and fountain, fountain water moving in low-G slow motion, catching an oily twinkle of domelight. You could hear them talking from here, voices blending together, the crowd like a single entity, dominated by the high, sharp voices of the girls. "When?"

"Harvest Moon."

"That's a little soon, isn't it?" Most people wait for Yule, even more for a traditional Beltane wedding. Gives the boys a chance to get on their economic feet.

Girlvoices yapping ever louder from down below, punctuated by the occasional inarticulate male grunt. Girls telling each other all about their wedding gowns, who was marrying whom, and, whisper, whisper, who was not. Whose boyfriend's got a hot job lined up and whose did not . . .

Strybjörn said, "We couldn't wait."

"No?" I looked back up at the sky, not wanting to see his face. A small blue spot had just come around Ygg's limb, climbing steadily toward us, swept along in the Midsouth Band's eight-hour rotation.

He said, "Whatcha gonna *do,* Murph?"

I shrugged. "Go into business with my dad."

A slow nod. "He spends a lot of time down in the bayou, I hear."

Right.

Long silence, then, "And?"

I looked at him. "And nothing."

He said, "Shit. Good luck, Murph." And then he grinned a sleazy little grin that made me want to poke him one. Good luck, haw, haw. Yer fulla shit, Murph. Tell me another one. "I, ah, got a couple of weeks before I have to start with the Trust, Murph. You wanna, ah, make one last, um, hunting trip?" He looked at me earnestly. "*You* know. Before, ah . . ."

I smirked at him. "Before we have to go be grown-ups? Sure, pal. That'll be . . . fun." Right.

A little later, after Styrbjörn'd gone back to fawn over his girl and strut for her jealous friends, friends with short, pudgy boyfriends, girls who'd be jealous 'til the fat boys started bringing home that famous bacon, while Styrbjörn was still only pretty, I found a flat, shadowy place on the backside of the hill where I could sit looking out over the old dump.

Lot of old stuff here. Crusty, long-dead industrial machines, things that'd never really been alive in the first place. Dinosaurs. Pieces of machines whose original form and function I couldn't quite conjure from a blend of imagination and technical knowledge. This place must've been something in its heyday.

In the shadow of the dinosaurs there were other, more familiar pieces of dead hardware. Over there, one of the gooseneck lamp things, sprawled motionless, glass eyes open on nothingness, empty, some of them smashed, become bits of glitter, mangled shards. A dead welder, just like old Beebee, limbs missing, featureless cylinder lying not far from the burst-open box of a smashed incubator. No sign of any meat inside, just bare metal walls, tangles of plumbing, feeder tubes, and circulatory conduits.

Mrs. Trinket loves her kits, loves her fifteen husbands with a heart as spacious as anything the likes of me could ever imagine. These ones here—

"So. Here you are."

I didn't turn at the sound of Ludmilla Nellisdottir's voice, just kept looking out over the ruin, picking out familiar shapes among the strange, wishing I could somehow will them all back to life. Thinking about death's a funny thing. Stupid. Like wondering where you were before you were born. "Hello, Luddy."

I could see her shadow on the ground beside me, most of the light that cast it coming from the interpretive center's little microstem, a bit offset, another shadow, tinted with indigo, apparently cast by the combined vector from Ygg and

Alpha Cee. When you looked closely, you could see the second shadow was . . . fuzzy.

"What are you doing, Daggy? I wanted to talk to you."

Daggy. Her main shadow, gray-black, showed the shape of a slim, pretty girl, graceful arms and shoulders, slim waist flaring to hips shaped just so, hips you could see would one day be just right for their main job. Long, sleek legs. "So talk." Not really interested in why I was sitting here looking at dead robots, just an opening gambit, followed immediately by her stated desire.

"Could you look at me? Murph?"

Murph? I turned and looked up at her. Smiled my goodboy smile. Ludmilla Nellisdottir, not quite breathtaking, but close enough, wearing a silk party dress woven from a thousand colors that clung to those just-so hips, looking down at me with something of a frown, but with a shine in her pretty blue eyes.

Silence then, the two of us just fucking staring.

Finally, she said, "We've been seeing a lot of each other this past year, Murph."

Murph again. I felt a slight burning in the pit of my stomach, remembering those dozen or so dates, especially the one to the senior prom, three weeks back. Not the only girl I'd been dating. Sure as hell not among the ones I'd gotten closest to, but . . . memories of laughter. Of having fun. Just a date. Just a date, Murph. Doesn't mean a thing.

She said, "I think we'd make a . . . pretty good team, Murph. You and me, I mean."

Why didn't I see this coming? Hell. Maybe I did.

"I heard you were going into business with Dr. Goshtasp."

I nodded. "My dad and I always got along. I like robots."

Sure as fuck better than being a Mother's Trust sidebander, anyway.

She said, "You know my family controls a lot of big contracts, Murph. Even some government contracts. If you wanted to, you could be a lot more than just a . . . tinker. A few years of hard work, maybe you wouldn't have to do any of the work yourself anymore. You'd hire people and . . ." She nodded toward the dump, with its pathetic dead sprawled all around. "Spend as much time as you wanted to . . . helping them."

Helping. I felt my heart go crunch in my chest. Imagined careful, oh-so-clever Ludmulla Nellisdottir watching me, trying to understand. What does Mr. Murphy *want*? Well, he loves the little robot trash, wants to *help* them, you see, and he's not *really* a Timeliner, just half a Timeliner's son . . . Maybe I would have said something bad then, but . . .

Ludmilla smiled, a bright gleam of perfect white teeth, stretched, seemed to work up her courage. Then she reached down, oh so slowly, and pulled up the silky hem of her dress. Nothing on underneath but her own lovely brown fur, fur just the same color as her long, lustrous hair. She smiled and said, "I know how you like to play gatesie, Murph. Girls can't keep a secret."

A pulse of horrid dismay filled my breast, imagining all the girls who'd opened their gates for me the last couple of years, just for fun. *Just for fun*. Whispering together, telling jokes, in the girls' steamroom, in long nighttime vidfests and slumber parties and . . . That Murph. Christ, he'll do . . . anything. Anything you want.

And coming into a pretty good job, besides.

Luddy moved her hips, striking a pose, showing me Goddess' Altar and Child's Gate all rolled into one, and said, "You . . . want to take me for a test drive, Murph?"

Test drive, I thought. That's what girls call it when they whisper. Rannvi told you that, years and years ago. Rannvi's the one who told you all their secrets, giving you an . . . edge.

And Ludmilla Nellisdottir standing before you now with her gate exposed, inviting you in, giving it her all, thinking that she's figured you out. I think if I could've spoken just then, I would've taken the Orb's Secret Name in vain. Women aren't supposed to humiliate themselves like this, not in front of a man.

She said, "I'm asking you to marry me, Darius Murphy."

Did my heart stop? I couldn't tell, heart flooded with an image of Ludmilla Nellisdottir following me around, getting me to go on all those fun, friendly dates. Making friends with all the girls with whom I'd played gatesie so she could figure me out, figure out what I wanted, paint me into a corner where what she had to offer was so good that . . . The silence stretched on too long, Luddy letting go, letting the hem of her skirt fall, closing the gate.

I said, "This is a hard time for me, Luddy. I mean, my whole future, the rest of my life, however long . . ." Her face seemed to crumble, eyes filling with a horrible shine of tears. "Wait. I'm not telling you no, Luddy." How could I say *no,* after what she'd just done?

Maybe that was the point of doing it.

I said, "I just need time to . . . think."

She said, "Oh."

That's it. Time to think. I need time to think.

But I could see I'd spoiled it for her, maybe ruined everything forever. All the work she put into this moment, all the planning, standing there with her dress pulled up, making her proposal of marriage. You'll be a rich man, Murph. You won't have to work. All your spare time, all the time I'm willing to let you have, can be spent with your beloved robots, Murph.

Imagine that.

How the hell do I tell her she got it wrong?

Dr. Goshtasp loves the robots, Luddy.

Me?

I don't fucking know.

In a voice faint with despair, she said, "Can I . . . sit with you, Murph?"

"Sure."

She sank down at my side, getting as close as she dared. Sat silent for a moment, looking out over the dump. Then she whispered, "Who were they, Murph? Tell me. Please."

Who were they? Like it really mattered. After a while, before the silence could get ugly, I started making up pretty lies. Fairy tales. The long result of time. Et fucking cetera.

Making things worse, in other words.

You do things for people who really love you, even if maybe you don't quite love them back, even if maybe you think those things are foolish. So, about a week after graduation, I went with my father to a Timeliner Firehall deep in the Audumlan wilderness, beyond the bayou country, back by the old, abandoned blocks of dormitories where Standard ARM's human workers and expensive optimods had lived, once upon a time. Went and knelt before the magus for my manhood ceremony, though I hadn't believed a word of this for a long, long time.

If ever.

Old America spawned the Timeliner faith, they say, part of that last great surge of religious ecstasy that also spawned things like the Mother's Children. Maybe even its direct counterpart, a religion to comfort men, men who must go sailing the dark skies, working for something, some goal never quite their own. Wealth of the corporations. Families of the women. Something to fill their empty hearts. Uncreated Time giving birth to the universe, manifesting itself in the universe it made through the agencies of Flame and Shadow, the personified forces of good and evil at work in all our lives, calling on human free will to decide between one and the other, evoked through the agency of Restitutor Orbis, called the Orb by one and all.

Nonsense.

The Firehall wasn't so different from a Mother's Temple. Darker. More shadows, cast into its many alcoves by the altar's Eternal Flame. A Temple is always clothed in green grass and garlands of flowers, red more often than not, symbolizing a Mother's Blood. The Firehall is made of gray stone and black iron. Walls lined with icons of the historical Archimages under whose guidance we wander through the Cavern of the Night. Just above the altar's Flame, the icon of Archimage Xerxes XII, Living Voice of the Orb, a vibrant, handsome man with white hair and beard above bare young muscular chest and shoulders.

Nonsense.

When I was a little boy, my favorite thing was the traditional statue before the altar, Restitutor Orbis, cast in the image of a heroic naked man, battling the Bull of Labor bare-handed, grappling him by the horns, dogging him down in the dust. If you look closely, you can see both Orb and Bull are experiencing a certain amount of sexual excitement.

Utter foolishness.

After the ceremony, my own and that of six other boys, whose words no one but a Timeliner can ever know, there was a little buffet, men and boys milling around, talking in low, sporadic voices, stuffing their faces, telling crude jokes, and laughing. Sometimes, talking to boys who come from Timeliner families, I feel a little jealous. None of these boys has ever been to a Mother's Service, ever knelt between the Goddess' legs and babbled out humbling prayers while little girls tittered behind their backs.

It seems like a wonderful dream, but I hear those families are hard to live in too, families where Timeliner mothers and sisters see their Mothersbairn neighbors going about their business, heads held high, and wonder if that's not the life for them.

Hard to be an alien, in any land.

So I laughed and stuffed my face and told gatesie stories to the other newborn men, like a good little Timeliner male. My father seemed proud of me then, smiling as he listened while I told tales about girls these boys all knew from school, girls who'd probably want me dead if they knew I'd told. The same girls, I guess, who couldn't keep a secret from Ludmilla Nellisdottir.

Walking out to the family flitter afterward, dusk already deep purple in the sky, stemlight fading away right on schedule, night forming up, three bands of bright stars arching overhead, my father breathed in the clean air of the empty wilderness, looking around at row on row of abandoned city block, and said, "Well, we'd better get going. Your mother will kill me if I don't get the flitter home on time."

In the world of the Mother's Children, Mothers own everything there is, no matter who does the work that pays the bills. I thought about what my life to come would have to be like, and couldn't think of anything to say, bitter words stilled just inside my lips.

He stopped, turned and looked at me, then said, "Is something wrong, son?"

Don't you know? Why not? You ought to know. You went through this yourself, even if you weren't really . . . one of *us*. There was a long, long silence, the two of us just looking at each other. Then, suddenly, I told him all about Ludmilla Nellisdottir, words coming out in a rush.

There was another long silence, my father frowning, not looking at me at all. Finally, he said, "I know how it is, Darius. But . . . gatesie's just a game for teenagers, you know that. Those girls will all get married now, and, you know, no adult woman, married or not . . ." More silence, then: "Your mother would never consent to a Timeliner marriage."

No. Not like the one she made for herself.

I said, "What the hell good would that do?"

Something tragic in his eyes then. "None. None at all."

"If I wait, work with you, just go on . . ."

He said, "After a while, you'll start to feel . . . too alone."

"I'm not afraid of that."

He gave me a long, sober look. "You will be, sooner or later." Hesitant then. "The Himerans . . . well, they're just never enough."

I think I must have given him a very dirty look then.

"I'm sorry," he said. And looked away from me. "We'd better get going." I followed him to the flitter and we went on home.

CHAPTER TWO

One last little stemshiny aside before life settles down and dreary. Styrbjörn and I took our airguns and bedrolls and camping gear, had Daddy set us down on a hillside in the backcountry beyond the old habitat blocks, where not even the bayou robots go, on a bright yellow morning, promising to come for us again in a few days, when we'd gotten this boyish nonsense out of our systems.

As we walked away, down into the shadow-dappled glades of an old park forest, the sky was an unusually clear blue overhead, soft, soapy azure, as if it had the texture of some of Mother's best jewelry, things I'd loved to rub with my fingers when I was little. We walked, feeling these things as part of last, stolen moments, beneath the boughs of wind-rustling green trees, among slanting beams of stem-light.

If I tried real hard, I could imagine myself walking through some Old Earth forest, imagine myself some before-time man from thousands of years ago, lanky and lean, hard and fit, long arms swinging by my sides, long legs striding effortlessly forward.

Smell the dust of the Fatherworld. This is the world that Uncreated Time made for Man before Man himself was made, before Goddess was made, before even Woman.

Walking in my imagination, I snickered softly to myself, remembering a day when I'd tried to talk Timeliner doctrine to a much older Rannvi, who'd grinned and asked me the riddle about the chicken and the egg.

I tried to listen for the sounds of the forest. I don't really know what sounds an Old Earth forest would make, only the sounds you hear in made-up datatrack adventures, the cooing of tropical birds, the howl of the monkeys, the incessant screaming of faraway predator cats.

In the stories we saw as children, stories from the unblocked Mothersbairn datatracks, it's always in that old-time world where the Mother's priestesses are still fighting their desperate rearguard action, defending the Sign of the Labrys against the Patriarchy's vanguard.

Ah, but for that damned volcano, the narrator's soft contralto whispers in your ear, the universe of today would be . . . different.

I stopped suddenly, listening, Styrbjörn a few paces away, puzzled.

"Murph?"

"Shut up."

Long, still silence. Then I heard the sigh of the wind again, the rustle of the leaves in the trees. The little crackle of dead leaves and pine needles on the ground as Styrbjörn shifted his weight impatiently. Finally, far, far away, a faint, almost inaudible whine. Whine as of a distant machine.

I caught my breath, feeling almost suffocated, then we started to walk again, and, as we walked, Styrbjörn began to talk, while I tried not to listen, tried to hold on to my dream. Where, in the dream, do we want to know about Sieglindë's family, about how cool his Mother's Trust job is going to be, about the house where he and his girl will be setting up, courtesy of her mother's familial wealth?

Test-driven her yet, Styrbjörn?

Well, no, but . . . a gate's a gate, eh, Murph?

Sure it is, pal. One gate just like another and another and another and . . . We came out of the forest then on the slope of a long, long hill, put here for Orb knows what reason when Standard ARM Decantorium XVII was newly built, eroded just a bit now, raw red earth showing between banks of tall, weedy, dry brown grass, long gullies forming up in the absence of gardeners. Little things, dark shapes buzzing around in the long grass, dull thrumming sounds, and a blur of transparent wings.

Styrbjörn said, "Oh, snappers already! Let's get a few." Good eating, almost time for lunch, and . . .

I swung the airgun down off my shoulder, where it'd been hanging by its canvas strap all morning, made sure the clip was loaded, pumped the barrel once, *ka-ching,* pressurizing the chamber, jacking in a pellet. Then we walked down the hill toward the snappers, mighty hunters closing in for the kill.

Styrbjörn, always impatient, lifted his gun and fired first, *pap.* Nothing. Snappers suddenly flying up, darting in all directions, confused. I called him an asshole, ran in among the dark, bounding shapes, listening to the sharp, shuddery buzz of their wings, picked out one that was too stupid to zigzag, and . . . *pap.* Faint kick of a recoil against my armpit, then the snapper tumbled, transparent wings become a jumble of broken plastic panes. *Pap.* A second one went down. Styrbjörn started firing again, standing beside me, but I didn't see if he was hitting anything.

When it was over, most of the snappers getting away, outrunning us in an expanding circle, disappearing into the forest, leaping to safety over the edge of the bluff, we'd brought down more than a dozen of the little critters, were walking around, gathering them up, filling our game bags. Not sure why the hell they're here or what they are, where they come from. Daddy thinks they're genengineered from a variety or arthropods, crustaceans—earthforms, as always. In any event, part of the complete, calculated ecology that Audumla must once have had.

Strybjörn picked one up by the leg, dangling it, watching clear yellow blood drip down off its wings, blood the color of fine, golden honey, and said, "Mmm-*boy*! This is going to be the best lunch we ever had!"

A night camped out under arching bands of brilliant stars, the intermittent, staring red eye of Ygg, bellies full of roast snapper, listening to the crackle of the campfire, the faraway, irregular rumble of the air-conditioning system, then, in daylight, we were up again, walking, talking, doing our best to revel in the splendors of nature. By midday, we got to our real destination, the unstated one that Styrbjörn'd been thinking of, I suppose, when he proposed "one last hunting trip." Like as not, my father knew what we were up to when he watched us go.

We popped out of the woods at the crest of a long, low hill, vista of valley sweeping away before us, sweeping down to a broad, turbid river that flowed in the direction of Audumla's axial spin, before rising again in the middle distance, turning back to green forest, then blue haze, upcurving landscape, a broad swath of empty sky, then the remote, mistily dangling countryside of the next panel.

Down by the river, down on the bottomland, was a little village, real houses, white-painted wood, red brick, lovely cedar shingles, houses arranged just so, each one in the middle of a perfect, symmetrical, jade-green lawn. Flitters parked in a parking lot inland of the village, a dozen or so shiny metal bugs glinting in the stemlight. People walking the streets of the little townlet, walking down along the river, walking in twos and threes, seldom alone.

I could feel Styrbjörn's excitement by my side, just from the way he caught his breath, from the way his step quickened when he caught sight of the place.

When we approached, as we passed by the parking lot, you could hear men laughing, men talking, oddly out of sync with each other, but making up a steady cadence nonetheless. And nowhere in all this, the rapid, high patter of talking women.

Beyond the clustered flitters, the sounds became more and more subdued, until finally, once we were among the houses, it was almost as if we were back in the woods, hearing the shush of the wind, the deep, liquid gurgle of the river. One or two men on the street that we could see, walking along, almost in a hurry, not looking at each other, not looking at us, sort of behaving the way men do when they're in a public toilet. You know.

We picked a house, almost at random, maybe the same house we'd picked, almost at random, the last time we were here, months and months ago. New Year's Eve, I think. As we came up the walk, the door opened and a man came out, face looking—I don't know, exhausted, maybe. Stopped short when he saw us, flicker of fear in his eyes, *Do you know me?* Then, not recognizing us, grinning a nasty little furtive grin. He turned and spoke to the small thing in his shadow before hurrying off, brushing past us, hurrying on up the street and away.

Where the man had been, a pretty young girl stood in the

doorway, slim, top of her head not even reaching as high as my chin, long, tousled light brown hair falling down around her shoulders, face serene and . . . looking at us with her eyes of glass. She smiled a warm, sincere smile of welcome, and said, "Come in, friends. We've been waiting for you."

I could feel Styrbjörn tense up at the promise he heard in her voice. She turned away, and we followed her, through the black hole of the open door, on into the dimly lit red room beyond. We dropped our gear in the corner nearest the door and waited.

There. A row of them, sitting silently on a red-padded bench by the back wall, nine little girls dressed in clingy silk robes. Not so little, of course. Tall. Slim. Featureless. Not so much featureless as . . . unformed. Not immature, no. Just . . . waiting.

They call these things allomorphs. Daddy says they started out a couple of centuries ago as therapeutic tools. Tools to fix the damaged psyches of human men and women. Men and women who were . . . I don't know. Not right somehow. Afraid of each other, I guess. It must have seemed like a good idea at the time, but it's too much work to fix yourself from the inside out like that. Easier just to submit to the needle, needle and knife, let them shoot you full of soul. Soul and well-being.

So the therapists gave up, Daddy says, threw all their allomorphs away, some of them just wandering off, so much abandoned machinery in the functional habitats of Piazzi, Kuiper, and Oort. Some picked up for scrap, most bought for their entertainment value. These here, they say, are part of a package deal the local Standard ARM management staff got when they first built Decantorium XVII.

As if on cue, one of the little girls, the one nearest the rightward end of the bench, stood, stepping forward in a whirl of white robe, pirouetting before us, sort of . . . expanding. As she whirled, her black hair grew longer, flying up in a circle of sheen, disappearing briefly as she pulled out of her robe, white robe flying to one side, crumpling up by the far wall.

There. There, in the Name of the Orb . . .

They say these things can become anything. Anything you want. Anything you could possibly dream. Maybe anything *anyone* could possibly dream. Certainly it'd have to be that way, if they were once used to heal those sick old men and women, men and women who might like . . . anything at all.

This one, here and now, dancing in the half-darkness before us, grew sleek as a fishpond seal, hips rounding out as she danced, waist nipping in, large breasts with huge dark nipples bulking up on her chest, face almost hidden in masses of lustrous, suddenly curly black hair, hair almost hiding those famous eyes.

Slick shine, as of flowing oil, suddenly appeared on the inside of her dancing thighs, and the air seemed to fill with a hard pull of . . . wanting. I heard Styrbjörn gasp softly by my side, saw him step forward a half-step out of the corner of my eye.

Whose dream is this, then? They say they can read your mind, the allomorph things, but it's not my dream. Not my dream at all.

When I turned and looked at my friend, he was looking at me, face screwed up in some kind of comic agony, silly desperation, and I could see an erection was already tenting the front of his pants. So much for *whose* dream . . . He said, "Murph. Do you mind?" Gesturing at the dancing thing.

I shrugged. "Be my guest."

He turned quickly away, having forgotten me, struggling

to get his chit out of a back pocket, handed it to the dancer, fumbling, almost dropping it. She slowed to a stop, smiling, took the wafer from him, put it briefly in her mouth, handed it back. Then took him by the hand and led him stumbling away into the darkness.

And me?

When the next allomorph came dancing forward, I stepped forward too, chit already in my hand. Put my other hand on her shoulder, stopping her before she could turn, before she could strip off the robe, before she could change. Stood looking for a long, empty moment into those fathomless eyes of glass.

She took my chit, still looking at me. Bit down softly, gave it back. I slipped it into my pocket again, wondering if Mother would know, when the charge appeared in the household accounts, that Einar's Total Glutton Pizzahouse, or whatever guise these things used, was really . . .

I can hear her now, screaming at my father, How the fuck could Dagmar and his friends eat *that* much pizza?

Dr. Goshtasp, wincing, murmuring, Well, growing boys, you know . . .

Growing boys, my ass.

The allomorph stood close enough for me to feel tiny budding breasts, surely having detected by now that I longed for neither men nor girl children, looked up into my face, and whispered, "What do you want me to be?"

What. Not who. I said, "Nothing. Not yet." Then I took her by the hand and led her down a long, dark hallway, led her past a score of open, empty bedroom doors and out the back door of the establishment. Led her out into the brilliant, clean midday stemshine.

* * *

I led her away from the house, away from the village, led her down the river and into the cool shadow of the trees, following a trail along the banks of a river red with mud, holding one small hand in mine, curiously conscious of delicate bone, of the cool stillness of her fingers. Something indefinable here. Something . . . utterly unlike the hands of real girls, held on so many dates.

Quick, fragmented memory of Ludmilla Nellisdottir, holding my hand as we walked outside, walked through the night, night of the promenade dance. Holding on to me, gripping my hand so firmly in her own.

I remember she stopped me in the darkness. Stopped me, faced me, looked up at me, waiting for that stolen kiss. Laughing softly to herself as we walked on.

Not at all like this thing's hand now.

Nothing from my little allomorph as I led her by the hand, deeper and deeper into the abandoned forest, led her up a steep trail away from the river and through the trees, until finally we burst from shadow and into the brilliant stemshine of a forest glade, acres of meadow stretching out before us. Quiet stillness and . . . No, those are not flowers.

Before us on the dark green grass, dots of yellow here and there, moving gently, though not to the residual breeze of Audumla's faraway air-conditioning fans. Thousands of pale yellow butterflies, clinging quietly to their stalks of grass, waiting for . . . something. Every now and again as we watched, one or another of them would rise up, fly for a little while, a delicate flutter of living color, then settle again, wings flexing gently, open, close, open again. Waiting.

Unbidden, the allomorph said, "Pretty."

I turned and looked at her then, as she turned to look at me, focusing on my face somehow. "Do you like pretty things?"

She glanced back at the butterflies, watched another one fly about for a while, following it with bits of crystalline glitter. Then she looked at me again, and said, "Who do you want me to be?"

Who, rather than what. You read me well, little allomorph. "I don't know."

She undid the tie of her robe and shrugged it off her shoulders, so that it fell in a pool around her slippered feet, stood still, watching me watch her. Maybe this is what they make for men who know nothing of themselves? That tender, innocent, barely formed face. Those budding little breasts. Narrow hips barely flaring from a slim, flat-bellied waist.

Featureless slit of a vulva, furred just enough to let me know her machinery understood I wasn't here to rape a child.

Nothing here of the Goddess, though. Nothing threatening at all.

Behind her, a whole section of butterflies lifted off in unison, whirling off the ground, spiraling upward like autumn leaves in a sudden wind, and my allomorph turned away, murmuring softly, as if to herself, a gentle whisper of delight. Nothing threatening about the flight of yellow butterflies. About yellow leaves helpless before the wind.

Nothing threatening in an allomorph's private joy at a nature to which she does not belong.

She turned toward me again, taking my two hands in hers, looking up into my face, standing close to me, so close my senses would fill with the pheromones she made just for me.

All at once, all around us, the butterflies flew, for no reason we could know, for no reason that could matter, blizzarding into the sky. I looked deeply into her fathomless, forever-empty eyes of glass, and then, fragile insects swirling around us like a storm of buttercups shining in stemlight, imitation light of a sun that was to me only a dream, I laid her down in the cool green grass and did what a man will always do with a compliant man-made whore.

Home again, finished, I thought, with boyhood things. Oh, yes, I know I can go see the nice little allomorphs anytime I want, just like all those other men, but . . . whose dream is that? Not mine, certainly. A young man may have a vision of what his life will be like, or he may not. I didn't, but hated to imagine myself married and dull, working, coming home, paying to see my children raised, sneaking away every now and then for a hopeless frolic with a thing.

Better than boyhood things, of course.

Keep telling yourself that.

Better than the household servants, the . . . silvergirls. Silvergirls, those almost silent, will-less, liquid metal humanoid things that serve in Mothersbairn households, humanoids on the feminine verge of androgyny, naked and sleek, nothing between their legs but a vaguely suggestive shaping of curves.

You see them all your childhood, as they dress and bathe and feed you, play with them after a fashion as they play with you. When you grow just old enough, it doesn't take a particularly clever boy to alter that play, discovering they'll more or less . . . do what you tell them.

Do what you say and not tell Mother.

If you're not clever enough, some other boy will snicker and tell you. You'll be horrified, of course, but then you'll start to think about it, lying alone in your bed at night and, sooner or later . . .

I used to have a favorite silvergirl, one I came to regard as my personal toy, but, one day, Mother came to watch as the thing gave me my evening bath, got a stony look on her face, and told me I'd have to bathe myself after that, ordering the silvergirl away.

Maybe I was eleven years old by then.

Just old enough, as they say.

When I was home, showered and dressed again, I checked my mail and found a note from Mother on my freeze-frame interface. It told me to dress for dinner guests, specified my powder blue semiformal dinner jacket, white ruffled shirt, and little blue bow tie. Dress, my boy, and be there on time. No indication as to who the dinner guests might be. As usual. No need for me to know. Just show up. Smile and be polite. Make chitchat. Don't spill steak sauce on your ruffles.

I dawdled anyway, poking around the DataWarren, finding nothing, as usual, staring moodily out my bedroom window at the long, dusky orange tunnel of Audumla, until just before dinnertime, wondering if this was a grown man's angst at last, or just more boyish silliness. Finally got into my suit and went downstairs.

Just get through the evening. Maybe there'll even be something to do later on. Hell, maybe Lenahr will dump chocolate milk in his lap like he did when Mother had the Priestess' Acolytes over.

Lenahr was already in the dining hall foyer when I got there, being fussed over by a silent silvergirl. My brother was the perfect image of a pouting boy spalled from Mark Twain's Sidney, clad in Mother's favorite blue and gold sailor suit, short pants showing his smooth red knees, robot making a futile attempt to retie his floppy bow tie, futile because he was a moving target.

I walked over, grinned, ruffled his straw-blond hair, and said, "Hiya, Lenny. How's it going?"

He looked up at me, all serious and owl-eyed. Then he said, "Fuck off, Doggie. Why don't you suck my ruby-red dink?"

Doggie. I wiped my hand ostentatiously on my pantleg and gave him one of those looks you give an asshole kid brother. "Lemme know when you grow one."

Lifted his middle finger, gave me an unusually evil grin. "Last chance, shitface . . ."

I think I might have wondered what the hell he meant, but Rannvi came hurrying down the stairs, dressed in a clingy siniform pantsuit of slick, iridescent silk, mostly blue, but with moving sheens of green, orange, and metallic red, covered to the neck with cloth, body nonetheless on perfect display. Her face seemed flat and white, mouth set hard, lips compressed into a pale streak. Eyes stony, full of anger, looking right at me.

"What the hell's wrong?"

Lenahr snickered, and Rannvi snapped at him, "Shut the fuck up, you little prick."

Good grief.

The double doors to Mother's Wing swung open and she came in, cutting off whatever might have been said next. Mother, dressed up *kretikai,* long, pleated red skirt sweeping the floor, already narrow, muscular waist further cinched in by a velvet-strapped girdle, underbodice turning her bare breasts into solid, rouge-nippled mounds, trailed by Father, dressed in a standard semiformal dinner jacket just like mine, but black, as if he were going to some kind of casual wake.

She said, "Well. On time *and* dressed up."

That wonderful sarcasm with which she'd so successfully

molded us all, that smooth face, even-toned complexion the best money can buy. Those wonderful sky-blue eyes I'd loved to look at when I was little, perfectly matching her favorite turquoise jewelry. Long, straight blond hair drawn back in a flowing ponytail mane. Ruby-red lips set in a tight little smile and . . .

I looked at Dad, wondering why the hell Mother was dressed up for a trip to the Goddess. *Restitutor Orbis*. Face full of tension, one corner of his mouth turned sharply downward. Eyes black like flint. And not looking at me, no matter how hard I willed the two of them to do so. They must've just had one *fuck* of a big argument.

When I glanced at Rannvi, she leaned close, seeming anguished, and whispered, "I'm sorry, Murph. If I'd known, I'd've told you."

I felt an odd little pang, and thought, Told me what? But, somewhere I think I already knew.

Mother swept forward, dining hall doors swinging open before her, flooding us all with light, opening on a room full of people, Mother holding out her arms to greet her old friend Nelli Torgunnsdottir. The two of them embracing, breasts wallowing all over one another. Beyond them, more of Mother's friends and associates. A young priestess with portable altar. A dozen or so girls from school, all in their party best, including some I'd gated for fun, laughter in all their eyes.

And there, dressed in Virgin's Veil, was Ludmilla Nellisdottir, face glowing with some glorious, otherworldly joy.

I guess, in another world, in another time, they'd've all screamed, *Surprise!*

I guess maybe I'm pretty stupid.

When I looked at Father now, he returned my gaze, stood

stock-still by my side, and said, "I'm sorry, Darius. I'm truly sorry."

Sorry. Wonderful.

As they led me forward, the silver organist began to play "Posting of the Banns," priestess lighting her candles, making her ritual announcements, telling everyone concerned that in six weeks, if nothing unwholesome turned up, Dagmar Helgasson would be sealed in holy wedlock to Ludmilla Nellisdottir, and that would be that.

Somewhere else in the house, I suppose, my so-called friends will be hastily assembling some kind of bachelor party. Barrels of sweet red ale. Some cheeky little pornoflick or another. Styrbjörn drunk, slobbering all over me, going, See buddy? Now we can go hunting together forever and ever, while our fuckin' *wives* do whatever they fuckin' want.

Sure, pal. Fulfilling my every dream.

They led me to the altar, led me to stand beside Ludmilla Nellisdottir, who stood oh-so-close, hip touching mine, and whispered, "We're going to be happy together, Daggy. I just know we will."

So. Banns posted and prayers said, symbolic white satin ribbon tied around our wrists. Ludmilla giving me what was supposed to be that symbolically chaste "first kiss."

Torgunn and Mother and all the fine ladies of the Motherhood heading for the banquet board, talking, talking.

My father standing silent in one corner of the room, looking down, as if at his feet.

Ludmilla led off by her friends to the Virgin's Retreat.

Me led off by mine to Final Night.

All I remember of the latter is a drunken, slobbering Styrbjörn asking me, "Hey, Murph. She give you any tongue for firstie?"

And remembering with a peculiar pang that she had, just a tiny flicker, the tip of her tongue briefly poking my lower lip. Earnest of intent?

And realizing that not one of my little friends was a Time-liner boy.

I imagined the Orb, astride his bull, looking down at me with scorn.

What are those words he's mouthing?

Mother's boy.

Sure.

That's me.

Eventually, the day came to an end. I went to my room, refusing to talk to anybody, went to bed, and lay there in the darkness, head spinning from too much liquor, looking out the window at darkness, at the Audumlan landscape, at the dark skyscape with its bands of stars alternating with bands of nothing at all.

After a while, Ygg started to show itself, edge of dim, sullen red sliding out of nowhere, slowly growing.

Well, you knew this would happen. Knew it. Knew it and did nothing about it, because . . . well, what the hell *could* I do?

No place to run. No hiding place.

Angry at myself. Angry with Father, with Rannvi, refusing to talk to either of them as I stumbled off to my room.

My room. What a laugh.

Nothing's mine. Not here. Not anywhere.

In a little while, I'll go live in Ludmilla's spanking-new house, and nothing will be mine there either.

What's going to happen to me? Life with Luddy. Life working with Father. Nothing will change, except I'll have to contend with Luddy's cunt every day and the girls won't come to me anymore.

Maybe one day, I'll have a son of my own, and we can go down to the bayou country together, visit with the Himerans, fix their little woes, play with all the cute little kits, and pretend . . .

Right.

Suddenly I was back down in the bayou again on a bright and stemshiny day, walking along some drytrack through the swamp, Father and I together, airguns under our arms, daypacks on our backs, fishing poles folded away in their cases, waiting for us to take them out and use them.

We could have flown the flitter in to the little lake Daddy'd found, but, as he said, walking in along the drytrack made it . . . nicer.

I remember the look in his face as he looked down at me. Looked down at his son. "Ah, this is the life."

When I walk the drytrack with my son, I'll have to remember to say that to him, make him . . . dream. Remember, because one day, after I betray his trust, he'll never look at me the same way ever again.

Will it be my fault when that happens?

What choice will I have?

Somewhere else in the house, my father would be sitting in darkness all alone, thinking his bitter thoughts, waiting for me to come for him and say it's . . . all right. It's all right, Dad. I still love you.

There was nothing you could have done.

I can get up right now and . . .

His room was empty when I got there, door standing open, door to my mother's suite closed and silent. Most likely, she's got him in there now, making him perform.

When I turned away, my favorite old silvergirl was standing in the dark hallway, looking at me, motionless. Maybe wondering if I wanted her to come play with me? Who knows what silvergirls think?

I went back to my dark room and lay down in bed again, looking out the window at full-blown Ygg, watching it transit the patch of starry sky, moving with the background stars at Audumla's rotation rate, waiting for it to set behind the next panel.

After a while, I fell asleep.

The next day, early in the morning, before anyone else had gotten up, I was breakfasting on the patio, watching Ygg fade as the stemshine blossomed, drinking strong black coffee, eating sweet, dry crumb cake, when Dad came out and stood by the hillside rail, looking out over the landscape. Not saying anything.

I was . . . I don't know. Angry still, I guess. But there *really* was nothing he could've done, and I could see how badly he felt about the whole business. Finally, I said, "It'll be better this way, Dad. I knew the rest of it, the idea that I could *ever* be anything other than what they said I was to be . . . Well. It was just a silly dream. Now . . . once Luddy and I get settled in, you and I can . . ."

He turned and looked at me then, and I saw with considerable relief that he could see right through me, understood I was being nice to him, making sure we could go on being what we'd been since before I could remember: friends. Saw his relief and mine, and beyond that a future in which life went on, more or less unchanged. Dr. Goshtasp and his intern, Darrayush. Mr. Fixit and Son, friends to every machine, everywhere.

And Luddy?

Hell, a gate's a gate, and what the fuck else was I going to do with my life?

Grow up. Be a man. That's all.

He made a weak attempt at a smile and said, "You want to go for a drive?"

Drive? I shrugged and said, "Sure. Why not?"

We got in the flitter and took off, to my surprise heading uphill through the heart of Lydia City, away from the bayou country, away from the old lowland habitats, abandoned city, Timeliner Firehall, whatever. Went under the monorail overpass and skirted the Knossian Beltway, following bright stemshine up toward the axial core. Finally, we got to a point where the gravity was too low and the topography too steep for the family flitter, boarding an elevator and going straight up the face of the red ersatz cliffs.

The elevator was a big one, a sliding glass room the size of Mother's dining hall, full of passengers, women, men, children, many of them with luggage piled around their feet. Mothersbairn, sure, but a lot of strangers too. What looked like a Timeliner couple from the cut of their clothes, the angular look of their faces. A group of young men in some unfamiliar uniform, red cloth, black boots, green trim, golden badges. A stiff, uncomfortable-looking fat man with a robot toolbox standing placidly by his side.

I looked at my father, studied the conflict in his face. "Dad? Where're we going?" No sense asking why. He'd answer one if he answered the other.

He looked at me, eyes guarded, making me wonder about the indecision I so plainly saw. Finally, he said, "I thought we might go on up to the South Axial Port, you know? Watch the, um . . . goings-on."

Like we used to do when I was a little boy. I remember those outings plain as day, Dad and I floating in one of the big obdecks, back behind the stemshine mounting bracket, looking toward the industrial complex with all its fancy stevedoring cranes, toward the big, fantastic ring of starship docking platforms. Sometimes, if we were lucky, there'd even be a ship in port.

He said, "I checked the schedules when I got up. There's a ship in dock now, *Sans Peur,* property of Les Citoyennes Occidentales. About ready to undock, heading out for Telemachus Major, then on down the Jet to Proxima." He looked at me with the oddest shine of fear in his eyes, then swallowed softly. "I thought we could . . . watch her go."

The elevator came to a stop, big doors sliding open, and all the people struggled to get out, families floundering in unfamiliar low G, up here at the 0.05 level, others, accustomed, loping away with long, easy strides. I expected us to go up the footstrap escalator to the obdeck, but instead we began following the crowd.

"Dad?"

He looked away, avoiding my gaze, then said, "Let's go down to the boarding ramp. We can—"

"You can stop lying to me now."

He stopped dead, some people behind us, carried forward by inertia, barely avoiding a collision, fumbling with bobbing bits of luggage and swearing at us in a language I'd never heard before, something full of velar gutturals and glottal stops. He sighed, a hard, gusty rasp. "Ah, Orb. I'm not lying, son. I just can't *decide.* I . . ."

"So where are we really going?"

One long, hard stare, tainted with an agony of indecision, then he reached into his pocket and pulled out a slim blue markerchit. Held it out to me. Swallowed again. Said, "I keep some of my accounts on the Timeline Segment, instead of down in the Audumlan bankertracks. The whole business is secured behind the firewall at Telemachus Major. Your mother doesn't know."

I looked at the thing in his hand, not knowing what I was supposed to do, but suddenly realizing . . .

He said, "I bought you a ticket on *Sans Peur*."

Ticket. Moment of stupid misunderstanding, then a bizarre thrill of hope. "We're running away?" Running away from home, like Tom and Huck and every other lost boy you ever dreamed of? My head filled with fantasies then, impossible dreams, Goshtasp and Darrayush, faring together among the stars and . . .

There was no diminishment of the agony in his dark eyes, now alight with something that looked horribly like impending tears. He said, "By enforceable legal contract, I'm your mother's chattel, Darius. If I leave . . . Well. There are laws. Laws everywhere."

"But . . ." But *I'm* her chattel too, not just her son, I . . .

He proffered the chit. "You take this, Darius. The ship leaves in three hours. I'll . . . go home and lie 'til you're safely away."

Home. I said, "But . . . Mother and . . . well, what about Ludmilla and her mother? I mean . . ."

He said, "If you leave, the banns are broken. You're still free, but another ship won't come by for months, not 'til after the wedding."

By which time . . .

He said, "The Telemachan government will enforce my written contract, but may not agree with her putative progenitive rights over you. I've arranged for some people to meet you at Telemachus Major, son. Timeliners. Old friends of mine. They'll hide you for a while. Help you find a job. Help you . . . figure out what you want to do."

"But . . . Dad, if you stay here . . ."

Agony in his eyes. And full knowledge of what would happen to him when Mother found out what he'd done. He said, "Take it, Darius. Take it for *me*. Please."

I held the chit in my hand, staring at it, thinking about all the things he'd wanted and hadn't gotten out of his life. Thought about all the things I might want, if I could learn how to want. Thought about if for maybe all of a hundred seconds.

Then I hugged my father, hugged him hard, the way I hadn't hugged him since I was a little boy. Hugged him and turned away, turned and ran down the great docking tunnel that led to the starship *Sans Peur*.

CHAPTER THREE

No one who hasn't lived such a moment for himself can imagine the bizarre exhilaration I felt as I ran down the corridor, ran from Audumla and the Mother's Children, ran from everything I'd been, through the crowded docking tunnel, through the ticketing gate, and on into the bowels of *Sans Peur*. I could never have imagined it myself, though I'd dreamed this dream a thousand times, as a woman in bondage dreams the Amazon dream.

Reality was that fabled bolt from the blue, burning my life clean away.

Burning it away, though it was a long, long time before it dawned on me what that truly meant.

The ship itself was immense, more than a kem in diameter, several kems long, a dirigible world. Unlike Audumla, it was a solid rock world, a three-dimensional space of tunnels and warrens and machinery, most of all a world solid with people. People of every sort, all the kinds of people I'd ever heard of, people the like of whom I'd never imagined.

Naked woman. Fantastically tall, impossibly thin, with

huge, burning emerald eyes, pale blue skin, and hair the color of oxygen-rich blood.

Where could she have come from?

One day, when I've got the time, I'll sit at a freeze-frame once again and look her up. Maybe I'll go there myself.

My stateroom, when I found it, proved to be a hole in the wall, a little plastic door set in a vast panel of such doors, much like a bank of gymnasium lockers where you'd store your street things before taking to the floor. I slid inside and closed the hatch, lay there in .05 G listening to myself breathe, looking at the little racks where I was supposed to stow my carry-on luggage.

Orb knows I haven't got a thing.

Is that what it means to be free?

One long, horrid twist of fear inside me, making me feel like I had to go to the bathroom.

I'm just a boy. I shouldn't be here alone.

Then go back, Mother's Son. Go back, while there's still time.

Go back home to Mother and Dad, Rannvi and Lenahr, and all your little friends. Go back to Ludmilla Nellisdottir, who loves you so. Go back and fall right through her beckoning gate to that . . . that . . .

I slid quietly from my hole in the wall, crept along the corridors, following the signs until I came to a forward ob-deck. Stood by a curving wall of transparent metal. Watched quietly, gripping the rail with white-knuckled hands while teams of spacewalkers uncoupled *Sans Peur* from Audumla. Felt a soft vibration under my feet as field moduli counter-latched the substance of spacetime. Watched Audumla recede, a smooth stone cylinder turning on its axis, falling away, slowly at first, then faster.

Audumla. Ygg and its ruddy moons, become specks, then

nothing. Nothing but the void and the faraway stars as *Sans Peur* accelerated on her way to Telemachus Major, four days' travel time . . . twelve billion kems from home. Meaningless number. Meaningless word.

Another nightmare pang.

Orb telling me, down deep where it counts, that I have no home.

When I turned away from the star-spangled darkness, fantastically hollow inside, the obdeck was thronged with people. Some of them looking out at the stars, faces full of, I don't know, longing, fear, exhilaration, peace, most looking away, at each other, at . . . whatever.

Not far from me a group of young men—boys my own age, really—were hunkered down by the wall, making a little circle, intent. When I came up and looked, I could see they were shooting craps, a variant involving three eight-sided red dice. After I'd stood and watched for a while, they motioned me into play, speaking languages I didn't know, obviously more than one language among them.

So I crouched and played for a long time, offering my chit for wagers, making my rolls, until I was so tired I could hardly see the spots on the dice. Came out a little bit ahead in the game too. Just enough. Not too much. Crept back to my little cubbyhole, where I thought about my new life, my new friends, my new everything, and finally went to sleep, where I dreamed about everything lost.

Four days later, I got one good view of Telemachus Major from space, standing in the obdeck with my new friend Hórhe as *Sans Peur* swept in from the interstellar deep, decelerating furiously, blue glow of the exhaust baffle wrapping around the hull like sheets of aurora at the poles of Ygg. It was a huge, blue-frosted sphere of a world, almost a thousand kems in diameter, I remembered from the atlas, air-contained at its surface, contained and conditioned by a vast eutropic shield absurdly expensive to maintain. Artificial world with artificial mountains, artificial seas, artificial clouds . . .

I spied a much smaller world, a little sphere of bright green, apparently in orbit around Telemachus Major, maybe only a hundred kems across, maybe less. I'd learned a little Sinyól from Hórhe these past few days, just as he'd learned a little Norn from me, so I said, *"Ke es la verdád?"*

He snickered and said, "What is truth?"

Um. How many words of a language can you learn in four days, even when it's obviously related to your own? Not many. I pointed at the little world and said, "The green thing."

"Green? *La vérde?"*

"I guess so."

"Telemachus Minor. *Es la párke."*

While we were talking—trying to talk, anyway—Telemachus and its moon swelled in the window, becoming so huge it was impossible to believe it *wasn't* a real world, that we weren't bearing down on manhome Earth itself. How would I know? I've never really seen a real world, other than Ygg. What's it like to come in for a landing on an object eight thousand kems across, with a natural atmosphere deep enough to swallow Audumla?

But we passed close to the little green worldlet on our way in, and you could see, see with your naked eyes, that it was a world of trees. I had one long moment of memory, remembering my last hunting trip, walking through the abandoned woods of Audumla, imagining myself on Earth. How much easier that dream would be on a place like this.

So we landed, *Sans Peur* settling down in a vast, oval depression atop a grassy mountain somewhere on Telemachus Major, and I stood frozen by the obdeck rail, looking out at my new world. Grassy mountain slopes, then . . . horizon line in all directions, and buildings, cityscape everywhere I looked, buildings leaning away from me, leaning giddily, letting me know I was on the *outside* of a sphere. Overhead, blue sky, fluffy white clouds, clouds floating on the wind.

How can this *not* be the doing of Uncreated Time? How can mere men have made such beauty?

No answer.

Hórhe poked me in the shoulder, made me look down at his smiling, flat tan face and beady black eyes. He held out his hand to me and said, "I got to go, Murph. Was nice meeting you."

I took his warm hand in mine, suddenly fearful. What was it he'd taught me to say? "*Asta la vísta, Hórhe.*"

He looked at me, shrugged, and said, "Maybe so, Murph." Then he let go of my hand, turned, and walked away into the crowd, and of course I never did see him again, went walking away on my own, missing him already, it seemed, in just the same way I missed Styrbjörn and the others.

All the others.

They'd filled my time, filled my life, kept me from . . . whatever it is friends keep you from.

Maybe just keep you from thinking about the meaning of the words you say.

Time turned kaleidoscope on me after that. With nothing to retrieve from my room, owning nothing but the casual clothes I'd put on when I came down to breakfast, that and my father's chit, I walked as slowly as I could down through the bowels of the ship, down to the axial corridor, then forward to the docking port and on out into Telemachan daylight. Stood standing under that blue and white sky, motionless, in the dwindling crowd of travelers, finally became aware of three men standing before me, tall, dark men, just like me.

One of them said, "Mr. Murphy?"

I started, jerked from a contentless reverie, and looked at them, switching from face to face. "Yes." More afraid than I ought to be. Too much. Too soon.

The man said, "We're friends of your father. My name's Cyraxidon." Speaking Norn rather slowly, with a pronounced accent of some kind.

I said. "I can speak Parthava."

A smile. "Usually we don't. Just at home, in the Firehall, in private. You know any classical languages?"

"English and Chinese. I'm, uh, not very good with languages."

He said, "You'll do fine, Murphy. English is popular with the big companies. Chinese'll come in handy as hell if you wind up working for one of the tongs."

Tongs. I didn't have a clue to what he was talking about. I let them lead me away, down into a city made of tall, very old-fashioned buildings, down through something they called a *ginza,* beyond into something else called a barrio, where the buildings were not so tall and definitely . . . inelegant.

Finally led me to something they called a flophouse and put me in a dirty little room, a room without windows, making sure, though, that I noticed there was a lock on the door, that I knew how to use it. There was an antique freeze-frame in the corner, next to the bed, freeze-frame with a little slot in its base where I'd have to put my chit if I wanted to use it. A little box of a side room with a toilet and shower, each with a chitslot as well.

Then the man who called himself Cyraxidon said, "We've arranged for you to take some tests, Murphy. We'll help as much as we can, but . . ." He looked at the others, all their eyes hooded and secret. "Well, you get some rest now. We'll see you again in a day or two."

Then they left, leaving me there all alone.

A day or two?

And what the hell am I supposed to do in the meantime?

After a while of staring at nothing, I put my chit in the freeze-frame's slot and watched this old clunker light up. Put my hands through the interface and felt the datatracks begin to stream. Made a connection to HytaspesMurphy. Helgashall.Audumla and . . .

Address rescinded.

Felt a little crackle of anger.

Made another connection to Goshtasp.HelgaBiz. Audumla and . . .

Address rescinded.

HytaspesMurphy.Audumla.TimeLine.Universal . . .

Audumla.TimeLine link severed.

An impossible gulf seemed to open. One runaway boy and . . .

I connected to RannviHegasdottir.Helgashall.Audumla.

The freeze-frame filled with light, then a ghostvoice said, *This address has been sequestered against certain external links in accordance with DataWarren Policy Issue 400.1. Further connection attempts will result in a fine levied at account Murphy.TelemachusMajor.TimeLine.Universal.*

I switched to anonymous mode and got the standard message about the address not accepting anonymous calls.

Then the light went out.

Numb, I withdrew my hands from the freeze-frame, pulled my chit, and watched the interface die.

*   *   *

What I did, with my little snippet of time on Telemachus Major, on those days and days between meetings with Cyraxidon, between trips to various entities called Human Resources and Personnel and Employment Security, between shadow trips to rich, fat Timeliners with something called *contacts,* was explore. Picture a rube from the provinces, rustic with bits of straw protruding from his clothes, rubbernecking the skyscrapers, ogling the crowds, wondering where the hell all these people, all these buildings, all of *this* had come from.

At some point, regenerated or remembered, I considered the datum that five billion human beings lived here on this little world. Little. Hell. I could pick any direction. Any direction at all. Walk for 3,141.59 kems, and here I'd be, right back where I started. But, all the while, the crowds made me realize what five billion people meant.

It was a beautiful world, with its endless cityscape of marble and granite, classical buildings with tall, fluted columns, domes of alabaster, silver and gold . . . faraway mountains, blue in twilight, though there wasn't a trace of either stemshine or natural sun in the sky, stars washed away but for the barely perceptible twinkle of Alpha Cee, A and B, one almost bright, the other quite dim. Broad white beaches, beaches of shallow tide and gentle surf, thronged with naked men and women, at once familiar and strange.

I saw a man like an elephant.

A woman who looked like some kind of huge, upright black spider.

One day, not long after I'd taken the entrance examination battery for employment with Standard ARM, I found a complex of beautiful old buildings, red brick, white trim, plain cylindrical columns like pillars of iron, something called the Museum of Natural History, maintained by the Telemachus Major Chamber of Commerce.

Went inside. Wandered for a while, as if lost. Saw a real elephant, real but stuffed, dead since the days, a thousand years gone, when there were no spaceships and humans lived only on manhome Earth. Saw a model of a something called a blue whale, leviathan from the terrestrial deeps hanging like a vast ghost from the ceiling, thirty ems long if it was a cem, extinct.

After a while, I found a pretty blond girl named Cindy, an average model human dressed in white shorts and halter top, barefoot, toes so straight and flat, so unprehensile, I wondered how she could walk. She smiled and chatted me up, found out who I was and where I was from, told me she was a museum docent and took me on the tour.

For some reason, I felt very comfortable with her. Maybe just the fact that she talked to me, smiled at me, sought me out, instead of wait for me to act in her stead.

That felt familiar, among all the strange new things of this strange new world.

Comfortable.

She showed me a burned little ball with a puppet man inside, *Vostok 1* and Yuri Gagarin. Made me imagine his awe as he looked out his tiny porthole at rolling Earth below. Showed me a spidery, gold-foil spaceship so fragile it made my heart rise in my throat, two clumsily spacesuited men on simulated Luna before it, Buzz and Neil, coming in peace for all mankind.

Let me look through a dramatized sampler of the popular fiction of those long-gone days. Could they really have expected to go from *Apollo* on the Moon to *Discovery* at Saturn in only thirty-two short years?

The movie seemed so agreeably stupid.

Naive in an unfamiliar way.

Showed me the statue of Lydia Brentano, Ph.D., standing on red-rock desert before the debarking ramp of *Hope*'s lander, a lifetime late, and made me wonder again at the long gap between Luna and Mars. Showed me the tall, elegant statue of Gem Dragovich, who, one fine day not quite five hundred years ago, hijacked Standard ARM Cargo Engine #164, dumped its payload and accelerated in the direction of Alpha Centauri. Accelerated until he was out of fuel.

Historians agree that, without him, we might have stayed home forever.

And still argue about whether that might not have been a Good Thing.

The statue looped out Gem's final message, masered back from a distance of almost sixteen light-years, reporting on a few new objects he'd spied as he drifted away from Sol and humanity's little sphere, noting that his medprobes could do no more, that they were letting him die, and now it was up to the rest of us, now that he'd shown the way. After he was dead, they renamed his ship *Forerunner,* and the exhibit has a live radio link, so you can listen to its faithful telemetry song, whispering back across the gulf between the stars, 120 light-years and counting.

That same day, I went to a public freeze-frame and pushed in my chit, made the link to Standard ARM Human Resources Division, feeling a slight, warm prickle of alarm as my test scores slid up. Stood for a long, hollow second looking at the contract they offered. Flight engineer. All right, I know what that is, know why I'm qualified. But what can a Deep Space Rescue Vehicle be?

I took a deep breath, then eased my hand down into the

frame, pressed my fingers into the contract's data record, and gave my assent.

Tomorrow morning. 0830.

I pulled my chit and watched the freeze-frame wink out.

In quicktime, I went through Standard ARM Aerospace Paramilitia basic training, earning a couple of badges for my nice new powder-blue uniform while the drill instructors made damned sure I knew my shit, made sure not only could I do the job I'd been hired for, but *would* do it as well.

The work we did was hard, the learning forced and swift, but not beyond the fathoming of anyone properly prepared. The tests, I suppose, made sure no one who couldn't pass would begin the course.

Academics made me grateful I'd spent so much time with the freeze-frame, studying things I knew I'd never need to know, indulging first my father's whims, then my own.

Gauge-control theory proved important after all.

Physical training was harder still, and here I was no more than lucky, having walked through the forests and rowed my father's small boat, when we went places unsuited to the electric. I did the calisthenics and went through the obstacle course, glad I wasn't one of the softer men and women who labored by my side.

Strange people.

All of them strange.

Not so much physical strangeness, the *what* of them, as the *who*. Men who stood snarling in your face. Women who seemed like nothing so much as shadows in the background.

I could see those women looking at me. See them wanting me, but . . . This is a different place, I kept telling myself. Different customs. I'll get used to it, by and by.

Or else move on.

One day, they made us climb a nearly sheer granite face, sleek stone that must surely have been imported from a geothermally active terrestrial world deep in the gravity well of a large star. Certainly there was no such stone out here.

They partnered me with a chunky, scowling, spiky-haired man named Zamba whom I'd known from the barracks. Known, perhaps, no less shallowly than any of the others. We placed our lines, rigged our hardware, and started up the rock, doing things just the way we'd been shown.

Not so hard, really, if you do it right. If you accept that what you've been told *is* right. Zamba kept trying to do things some other way, from something he said he'd seen in a text on mountaineering, though he, like me, was from the purlieus of the Centauri Jet and had never been within a thousand AUs of a natural mountain.

He kept slipping, kept falling, scraping himself on the rock face, getting angrier and angrier. Madder still when I made a suggestion or two. I found myself wishing I could detach the safety line between us and go off on my own. But they'd told us not to, and I imagined that was part of the test, part of the training.

Finally, he fell hard, slapping chest-first into the rock face, bleeding from a cut over one eyebrow, blood trickling prettily down the side of his head, curling under his chin, like the work of a dramatics makeup expert.

When I reached out to help, smiling, he slapped my hand away. "Goddamn it, I don't need no help from the likes of *you*!" Then he detached the safety line and climbed away.

Tempting to just go on up to the top then, forget about this asshole, but I stayed close, climbing just behind and below him all the way to the top. If he slipped and started to slide, maybe I could grab the tag end of his line. Though, if he toppled and dropped, all I'd be able to do would be duck to one side and hope not to be swept along with him.

When we got to the top, the instructor penalized Zamba for being a fool, then added points to my score for keeping with my partner, despite our "personal problem." All the while, the instructor kept glancing at me with some odd shadow in his eyes, even after Zamba stalked away, furious, not looking back.

Some of the others seemed to avoid me as well.

That was the way it seemed to go for me during those few short weeks. Unable to make anything like a friend among the men whose lives I now shared, though I'd had no shortage of friends back in Audumla, the memory of whom made me ache inside and . . . maybe regret what I'd done.

On the other hand, the women seemed to like me well enough, some of them bothering to sneak to my bed in the night, sneaking of course not unnoticed by the other men, making them scowl at me all the more.

And a few of the men were homosexuals, who seemed to like coming around to my bunk in the evenings for a chat. Nothing more than that.

Basic training was soon over, and I was glad for that brevity.

On a fine morning under a brilliant, cloudless blue sky, emanation from the eutropic shield prickling antiseptic UV on the exposed skin of my face, I found myself walking across the blond plastic landing slab of Standard ARM Cosmodrome 227™, order packet in my breast pocket, exhilarated and more than a little scared.

There before me, all around me, dwarfing the crowds of little men and little women, all of us dressed in that same powder blue, were rows and columns of spacecraft, like so many burnished bugs of chrome steel and brilliant brass, eyes of crystal and bright red glass, squatting on their landing legs, all turrets and thruster nozzles, field modulus antennae, exhaust manifolds . . . snappy little fighters, with their guns and beamer grids; attack vehicles covered with missile racks and rotary cannon; bulbous buddypack tankers; boxy mechanized assault force troop transports . . .

Somewhere back here among the hexes—hectares, they told us to say in military jargon school—somewhere among all the hexes of spaceships great and small, I'd find the DSRV squadron; somewhere among those, Deep Space Rescue Vehicle *Athena 7.*

There. *Athena* squatted on eight widespread legs, low and flat, a glitter of fresh-looking silver and gold, longer than she was wide, short and squat, with a sphere-shaped universal docking adaptor on one end, service pod with folded arms and grapples and torches on the other, medevac bay in the middle. Up on top, I could see the pilot's turret, down on the bottom, the engineering pod, my own bailiwick from now until . . . whenever.

"This your ship, pal?"

Soft, male voice, the voice of a mature man, a kind man, speaking the English they told us we had to use when on duty.

"Um. Yeah." I walked closer to the thing standing—no, more like sitting—between two of *Athena's* landing legs, at the foot of the embarkation ladder.

It said, "You must be Darius Murphy, then."

Interesting that it pronounced my name right. Dar-eye-us. "Yeah."

Hard to describe what I was talking to, no real sense of gestalt. A seven-foot-long antique beer barrel lying on its side, with tarnished bronze hoops, staves made of old oak, golden brown, streaked with black. Six fat, scaly green tortoise legs, barely able to hold it off the pavement. Complex clusters of arms at the barrel ends, sensors, manipulators, things I'd never seen before. No face. No eyes, no nose, no mouth.

It extended a skinny arm from one end, the end nearest me, arm with a hand like some kind of anorexic metal bug, and said, "I'm the ship's cyberdoc. Name's Dûmnahn."

I hesitated, boggling a bit, then took the warm hand in my own, and said, "Uh. Pleased to meet you. Darius Murphy, flight engineer."

It said, "I read your file, Murph. They say you're real good with robots."

"Oh. Are you a robot?"

Dûmnahn laughed, a really nice, friendly laugh, ironic and self-deprecating, that made me feel unexpectedly warm inside. "Less of a robot than the things you're used to, I guess. I'm an old-style cyborg, part of a manufacturing cycle initiated in the Piazzi Belt back in the late twenty-first century."

A long time ago. "Human?"

"No. My nervous system was genengineered from preserved DNA stock, from several lines of extinct pongidae." It wiggled one leg, making itself rock back and forth gently. "Muscle structure's from reverse-engineered reptiloavian stock. Very tough."

"How old are you, Dûmnahn?"

"Me? Don't know. I guess this carapace might be about forty standard, but . . ."

I remembered then that these sorts of cyborgs were cloned rather than bred like modern robots, realized that Dûmnahn would have been budded from some earlier version of itself, going all the way back to some original laboratory stock, all those long centuries ago.

It said, "I've got some fragmentary memories of the Piazzi, of working on the original Thetis structure. That's all."

A woman's voice, contralto, said, "*Athena 7.*"

I turned. Gaped.

Picture a naked woman.

Well, no. Not a naked woman. Picture a woman dressed up in a tight fur costume. Fluffy, red-violet fur. Picture a woman with a fox's face. Slanting, foxy yellow eyes. Pointed ears midway between terrier and pixy. Picture a naked furry woman with a long, bushy tail, powder-blue bag slung over one shoulder by a long sash spangled with campaign badges.

She said, "Hullo, Dûmnahn. Told you I'd get us the same ship again." Then the eyes looked me up and down, very slowly. "You must be Murphy, then."

"Um. I guess I'm the only one *hasn't* read someone else's file."

She grinned, showing fine white teeth not at all human. "Newbies don't know how. You'll learn."

Newbie.

She stuck out her hand, a human hand for all the fur, and said, "My name's Violet . . ."

"No shit."

I heard Dûmnahn cough behind me.

She cocked her head to one side and looked me in the eye. "Violet. Standard ARM Optimod 4044-XVII. Command Pilot."

"Optimod . . . ?" I tried to swallow the word before it came out, but failed, seeing a little sizzle start up in those yellow eyes. Orb knows what she may have been made of— human genes for sure, but what else? Dog, squirrel, bits of extinct wolf, fox, fragments of apes and whatnot . . . Off-hand, I couldn't recall ever seeing an animal that color, though, not in any bestiary on any damned datatrack.

Seeming exasperated, she said *"Ruricolae."*

"Uh. Sorry. I just . . . hell, I guess you must be my boss."

"Correct."

She swept past me, past Dûmnahn, went on up the ladder with swift efficiency while I watched, half-mesmerized by her sleek form and wonderfully fluid movements.

Dûmnahn said, "Well. Let's go."

"I guess I've gotten off to a bad start, huh?"

He laughed that nice warm laugh again, and said, "Maybe not. We'll see."

And so we flew, cyborg Dûmnahn, optimod Violet, backward, human little me, *Athena 7* lifting in a splash of blue fury, lifting with her DSRV squadron, lifting sedately through the eutropic atmosphere shield, then making formation, tearing away from Telemachus Major and its little green moon, down into the starry deep.

Somehow, when I lay my hands on the machines, felt the subtle pulse of their cybernetic hearts, felt the energies gather at my fingertips, I felt all my fears subside, fade away as if they'd never been. Violet flying the ship with her hands and mind, Dûmnahn lurking in his medical lair, monitoring us now, seeing that we were up to our task, and I . . . down in my own dark hole, making sure all the pieces worked together, as one.

I *knew* it. I knew it all along.

All those years of pointless study, of learning all those things a robot technician on Audumla wouldn't need to know. All the things a husband wouldn't need to know. I knew, someday, somehow . . .

Memory of my father, looking over my shoulder as I went

through the school catalog, pointing out this course and that one, suggesting, Hey, let's learn *this* stuff. Just for fun, you know? And so I did, just to please him, just for fun.

I'll come back for you, I thought then. I'll come back for you. I swear I will.

In no more than a few days' time, I began to feel like an old-timer myself, bantering with my fellows, playing billiards, swimming in the great, shimmering globule of the zero-G pool Standard maintained in orbit around the park, going to the park itself, a stunning experience, so much more *real* than anything I'd ever done with Styrbjörn inside Audumla.

You never know how much your heart can pound until you come on a big wild animal minding its own business.

Mostly, though, we worked and worked, getting to know *Athena,* getting to know each other, getting to know ourselves, understanding how important it is not only to know you can count on your mates, on your hardware, but also that you can count on yourself. Get to know at what point you'll turn tail and run. Make sure the others know it too.

There's always a moment of transition for you, that one moment when you turn from outsider to in, when you leave your past behind and suddenly mesh with the new life you've joined. Mine came one morning at breakfast, while I sat eating with Dûmnahn, whose biologic components lived off food, same as mine, the two of us chatting about nothing in particular, while, all around us, the room filled with the bustling fliers of Standard ARM.

As I sat looking into the middle distance, thinking about the day to come, Violet came in through the big double doors at the far end of the cafeteria, doors opening on a corridor leading to the optimod barracks. Watching her walk, I remember thinking that if you looked closely, you could see she *was* a woman, that you could so easily imagine her without all that lustrous fur, just the same way you imagine a *real* woman without her clothes. Yes, there'd be breasts here, nipped waist there, just above flaring hips, long, muscular thighs.

I could imagine the place between her legs without any difficulty at all, imagine myself lying with a girl who had a generous helping of stark violet pubic hair as stage dressing for Goddess' Altar and Child's Gate.

Not far from there to imagining myself worshiping at the altar, opening the gate.

And then I felt that same stark tingle of anticipation I felt every time I settled on a new girl, told myself, With a little care and dedication she'd . . .

Dûmnahn whispered in my ear, "It's not out of the question, you know. Just behave yourself for a little while longer."

Violet got her tray, movements so fluid I could see they attracted other men's eyes, optimods, humans, cyborgs with enough male mammal in them for it to matter—only the pure robots among us seemed immune—came and sat with us, eyes staying away from me as she settled down to eat, flickering my way every once in a while, with something I imagined might be a smile.

After a while, Dûmnahn said to me, "Sometimes, I regret the rigor of my own functional design."

Violet looked up and said, "What?"

Dûmnahn folded his arms up tight to his sides, a habit I'd started thinking of as his poker face, and said, "Never mind. Just the end of a conversation we were having."

Violet glanced at me, then made a tight grin back at Dûmnahn: "Stay out of my business, you old fart."

*　　*　　*

Snapshot of a moment frozen in time.

Violet and I got away alone together, during one of our weekends off from the endless round of training, went for a long walk together in some vast park, up by Telemachus Major's north pole, a huge, round valley where the North Axis Docking Structure had once been, or so she told me, in the days when this was a more conventional habitat.

I'd fallen behind her a little bit as we walked across a broad, windswept field of dark blue grass, wind rippling the sheaves, stalks reaching up to midthigh. Fallen behind so I could watch her walk.

"How long ago was that?" I asked.

I always liked to walk a little behind women, admiring the sleek lines of their backs, the way their hips would tilt gently back and forth with the shifting of their weight, step by step. Audumlan girls seemed to like this, but Violet kept twisting her supple neck so she could glance at me over her shoulder.

She said, "Oh, maybe two centuries back. I recall there was a lot of talk about it then, because it was the first big terraforming of a major extrasolar body, though eutropic shields had been in place for Mars and Luna for more than five hundred years."

From behind, Violet looked less like a human woman than from the front, tail erasing the central contour of her backside, fur camouflaging the narrowness of her waist. Fascinating, though, to see the way her tail moved seemingly on its own, flexing slightly, bobbing in time to her footsteps.

She suddenly stopped, turned around, and said, "You're driving me crazy, walking behind me like that."

I didn't know what to say.

She reached out and grabbed me by the arm, dragging me forward to walk beside her. "Why the hell do you keep dropping back?"

I thought about it. No reason to, uh . . . "I just wanted to watch you walk."

She stopped again, giving me an odd look. "You some kind of pervert, wanting to look at something as weird-looking as me?"

I said, "I don't think you're weird-looking, Violet. I think you're beautiful."

Her eyes became startlingly bright.

Because we had small private rooms rather than a group barracks, I got used to spending time alone, once again, though the DSRV crews were a friendlier lot than most of the people in basic had been. A lot of the trainees there had been bucking for fighter pilot, affecting a swagger I couldn't manage and didn't like.

If I'm going to work up a sizzle of testosterone, I'd just as soon reserve it for something better than bluffing other men.

I said that to the burly lesbian who'd had the bunk above mine in basic and thoroughly enjoyed her bellow of laughter. She told it to some of the other women, friends of hers, I guess, and they all thought it was funny, but it didn't seem to make me any more popular with the men.

I was alone in my room, standing at the dresser, staring at myself in the mirror, when Dûmnahn chimed and came through the door, still more machine than anything else in my eyes, two manipulators extended, each holding a two-liter bottle of beer.

He plunked them down on my little desk and said, "You'll like this, boyo. Hardesty's Black Ale, all the way from the

Laagerhavn Stream." When he popped the cap, a sharp, bitter odor wafted out.

I took one last look in the mirror, then came and sat down, picked up a bottle, took a sip. There seemed to be some kind of floating debris in the ale, sediment unsettled by his jostling, the flavor at once incredibly creamy and bitter.

Dûmnahn said, "Why're you doing that?"

I looked at him blankly.

He gestured at the mirror.

I shrugged. "I guess . . . I keep wondering what people see when they look at me."

I found myself wishing he had recognizable eyes. There was nothing about him that could make a facial expression anyone could read. He said, "I see a boy lonelier than he ought to be."

"You're not . . ."

He laughed, a too-human sound. "Not a person? Perceptive of you to notice."

"I'm sorry. I didn't mean . . ."

He said, "I've read up some on your background, Murph."

Murph. I'd been letting people call me Darius lately, but . . . "That make you see me as a lonely boy?"

"History's a funny thing," he said, "and we all see it through a variety of distorting lenses."

Sure. "Personal history or just . . . all of it?"

He said, "Back in the Classical Era of occidental Antiquity, when the Western world was divided between the romantic Hellenes and the practical Romans, a Greek woman would marry for love, would have sex for her own pleasure, while a Roman woman would find herself in an arranged marriage, sometimes premenarcheal, no more than twelve years of age. And then would find herself, on her wedding night, nothing more than a raped child."

I nodded, having read that in many a history track. "Must've been tough on the little girls."

Dûmnahn said, "After marriage, a Greek woman became her husband's slave, barred from public life in a society where only a whore could be free. A Roman matron, on the other hand, retained her full economic and social rights, almost unheard-of in the human society of the time."

"So?" The Mothersbairn had their own historical theories, which determines the content of what they teach.

"For some reason, we despise the pragmatic Romans, and yet we love the romantic Greeks."

I said, "Mothersbairn believe the Greeks stole their culture from the Pelasgian aborigines, who were . . . not of European origin."

He seemed to sigh. "Human society begins with what nature makes male and female mammals want from each other."

Great. "You got any other brilliant observations?"

I had to imagine what his facial expression might have become. He said, "Men work hard to enslave women, because it seems to be the only way they can preserve their own freedom. In most normal human societies, women are raised to be narcissistic."

Ah, the mirror. I started to feel just a little resentful at this bullshit psychobabble.

He said, "Narcissistic people, by their very nature, look to others for validation, rather than looking within."

"Why would men want narcissistic women?" Someone completely self-involved wouldn't make a very good lover, you'd think.

He said, "People who look for external validation become

passive-aggressive. And once you understand that essential nature, which the individual is unlikely to transcend, she is easily manipulated. A slave must have a collar, after all."

"So is that why you think I'm just a lonely boy? Mothersbairn made me into a narcissistic, passive-aggressive little girl?"

He said, "In the end, the only ones a powerless being can really trust are other, equally powerless beings. Everyone else can exploit you at will."

Angry, I said, "It's pretty transparent what *you* think."

He said, "No, it isn't. The Mothersbairn could not make you wholly into a woman and still keep you as a male mammal."

I had to think about it, unsure whether I believed him. "I suppose not."

I was back in my dorm room the night after we'd run our first full-scale simulated operational cycle, the entire DSRV squadron mixing with the combat ships as they played their own simulated war game, weaving about in the silence of empty space, stars infinitely far away in all directions, moving in on a field of little icemoons a couple of light-hours from Telemachus Major.

You couldn't see the moons more than one at a time as they floated millions of kems apart, tenuously orbiting a common center of gravity, but it gave a feeling of real rather than simulated danger, knowing what would happen if you ran into something while you were still decelerating, traveling three or four thousand kems per second or more.

People get killed in training, blown to tiny, irretrievable bits, burnt up into dissociated atoms, earning deaths from which there can be no return.

I sat in my room, too keyed up to sleep, fooling with the

freeze-frame, tapping Standard ARM internal news, running it in parallel with a feed from JetNet, with its pretense of impartiality.

Who's to say whether the political goings-on in the Centauri Jet have any meaning at all? Elections on democratic habitats, "office politics" on open corporate worlds, mysterious rumors from closed ones. Interservice rivalries from the military aristocracies. War between this tong and that.

Soldats de l'Organization des Citoyennes Occidentales. SOCO. Soldiers for the Organization of the Citizens of the West. JetNet was particularly interested in the movement of SOCO mercenary troops toward Proxima, where there'd been some sort of colonial trouble among the Glow-Ice Worlds. Curiously, nothing about it on the Standard ARM feed, though we had large holdings there, numerous mining concerns tethered to our parent holding company by cords of power and money.

I wonder when I started thinking of Standard ARM as *we*?

Restless, I keyed out of the news and dialed my father's number for the thousandth time. Dialed Rannvi. Dialed Styrbjörn. In desperation, dialed my mother.

The transition link is unable to grant access to those addresses. Either they have ceased to exist or the Audumla server has been instructed to deny access from your callback ID.

Checked my secret datatrack queue at the Telemachan Firehall node. Nothing.

Who was it said you can't go home again? Some old time guy who never got farther than the next big city on a closed world sparsely inhabited by no more than a billion or two . . .

The freeze-frame chimed and showed Dûmnahn at my door.

I shut the fucking thing off and let him in.

Despite the lack of any visible eyes, I could feel him looking at my face, could feel his concern. Empathy's something they build into a cyberdoc, I guess. Stock in trade. He said, "Still no luck?"

I shook my head, laying back in my bunk, folding my arms tight across my chest, staring at nothing.

"They'll forgive you someday."

Great. "What if they don't?"

"Then, one day, when you go home again, you'll find him there waiting for you, unchanged, I'm sure."

Lovely dream. "I wish I could believe that."

Dûmnahn slid over to sit on the floor beside me, green legs splayed across a powder-blue carpet displaying the parallel double-lightning bolt of the Standard ARM logo. "What if it never happens, hm? What if you never go home again? Is that what you're so afraid of?"

I felt myself bristle at the word *afraid*. Felt an urge to retort that I wasn't . . . shit. "I guess so."

"Murphy, my friend, everything in your life seems so big, so important now, because it's a newborn life you have. Time will pass, and your life will grow large, the past a very deep place. Then the things that happen now will come to seem . . . smaller."

Cold comfort when you're feeling you've betrayed the only people who ever loved you. I pictured my father, working alone, pictured Rannvi forced from school, forced into a marriage she wanted no more than I . . . "Why did you come here tonight? I really . . ." Hell, stop picking fights. This thing is trying to be your friend.

And you're a lonely little boy, remember?

Dûmnahn reached out and put a thin, warm hand on my shoulder. "I had a reason, after all: One of the comtechs intercepted a command gatepacket. In just a few hours it will be announced that the Committees of Public Safety of the Glow-Ice Worlds at Proxima Centauri have issued a formal declaration of independence from all outside influences."

I think I stared at the wall for just another second, then slowly sat up, turning to stare at Dûmnahn's featureless shell. "I . . . guess that means us."

Us.

Dûmnahn said, "And it appears the Glow-Icers have hired l'Armée du SOCO XXIII to defend them against counterclaims."

A full SOCO army. "That must've cost them."

"Yes. There's a lot of money at stake."

"So . . ."

"It means business, Murphy."

The business of war. Which is, after all, why I'm here.

I felt an awful cold thrill run through me then.

CHAPTER FOUR

On our way from Telemachus Major to Proxima Centauri, a long six weeks' voyage down the length of the Centauri Jet, we stopped once, at Standard ARM Refueling Station #67, no more than twenty light-hours from Proxima, where we could gas up, charge our weapons, make sure everything was in proper working order, then . . .

I don't know. I don't think I'd imagined yet what was coming. Until it happens to you, you really can't imagine.

From space, RS67 looked like a piece of old black slag, eaten through and through by holes that let in starlight, shiny surfaces lit up dull red by Proxima, a dim, sullen jewel in the sky, white light tinged with some faint, ruddy intimation of color. As it grew in our screens, I could see bits and fragments on the surface, technical installations, landing pads, movement of some kind here and there, or maybe just shadows cast by the reflected light of two little moons made from orbiting junk.

From the medical bay, Dûmnahn, voice oh-so-soft, said, "I've been here before." Just that, like a whisper.

Violet: "You?" A gentle inquiry. As though she knew that he . . .

"Not me, no. Some other me. Long ago. I think I may have died here."

Violet: "Do you remember?"

Long silence, then: "No."

I wondered how hard it was, remembering bits of past lives. Comforting to know, really *know* that you'd lived before? Or just the horror of knowing bits and pieces of what you'd lost?

Dûmnahn said, "This place is somehow tied to one of my oldest memories. Some . . . bit of code inside me . . . I remember being in a factory somewhere. Not all of me, just one arm, tied through a processor node to an index table. Mortise A in tenon B. Fastener C in orifice D. Mortise A in tenon B. Fastener C . . ."

"*Bastards,*" whispered Violet.

I had no idea then what she was talking about.

After landing, we turned our ship over to the base maintenance crew, walked across a darkling field covered with shadows, the shadows of a hundred moving, insensate robot arms and legs, got into the rec center, where we ate mess hall food, walked around and stretched and kidded with the other crews, took our seats in the briefing room and waited for Squadron Leader Chamônix to come and tell us what was what.

Rumors flying this way and that.

One guy heard SOCO XXIII was bribed, that the war was already over. That, tomorrow, we'd gas up and go on home.

Another heard that the first-in recon fleet was massacred, that the colonists and their SOCO hirelings'd gotten high-energy military weapons from somewhere . . .

Violet snickered. "Nothing like that this side of Sol."

... that we'd be thrown into the fray, stopgap, and be massacred as well, while Standard and her allies gathered strength, spent their accumulated wealth, got ready for a second strike.

Chamônix, a tall, thin woman like a walking white skeleton with long black hair, swept into the room with a short fat man in civilian mufti.

"Ah," muttered Dûmnahn. "Mr. ben Fars. Senior vice president for the Glow-Ice Mining venture. You'd think he'd be out of a job and standing in some headhunter line by now."

Well, that happens in fairy tales, doesn't it? In real life, when a manager fucks up and ruins a million working people's lives, when he bungles so badly the company loses a decade's profits, his Christmas bonus turns up a little short. That's all.

Chamônix and Mr. ben Fars had some things to tell us. Armaments for the warships. Some modernization for the medevac teams. And oh, by the way, said Squadron Leader Chamônix, beaming at us all, Standard ARM has decided not to use Internal Security ground troops for this operation.

No?

No. Too big an action for the police. They've hired l'Armée du SOCO IX for the job. They'll be here in a week. We'll wait for them. Then we'll head out.

She left the room, leaving silence behind.

RS67 turned out to have pretty good social facilities compared to what you might expect from a refueling station, probably because it was on the periphery of a major star system, right in the flow of heavy industrial traffic bound out for the Centauri Jet and points Solward.

Once it transpired we wouldn't have much to do other

than makework training, crews began taking liberty in the squatter town that'd grown up around the main base, buildings made of fused regolith and junk from the station's boneyard, as interesting an architecture as I'd ever imagined. Dûmnahn, Violet, and I joined in without waiting, heading out under a red-tinted black sky, the sure sign of a thin, old-fashioned eutropic shield that couldn't even color the sky blue, making it look like perpetual night, black sky spangled with familiar bright stars, the bright spark of Proxima, those two dull, irregular red moons, moving slowly but visibly across the heavens.

The first bar we made was a smoky place full of base technicians, overcrowded now with an influx of Security fliers, wait-things scurrying through the crowd dispensing whatever the hell you wanted, a brace of naked drumwiggle dancers up on the stage gyrating to tunes so old I'm sure my grandfather would've recognized them.

"You'd think, by now, creech would've made it here. I mean, the DataWarren . . ." Human Space is decades—hell, *centuries*—across, realtime travel, but it's only scant years across for the information flow. Some hot new popcraze arises among the densely populated moons of Jupiter, the news'll get to the shock-crystal miners at Sirius, way the hell out on the frontier, in under nine years.

I thought about what it'd be like, flying all the way out to Sirius in only one go. Fifty years? You'd be somebody else by then.

Violet: "Fucking Proxima's always been backward."

Then Dûmnahn: "Colonials tend to be conservative. Drumwiggle lasted a long time, even back on Earth."

Up on the stage, the dancers appeared to do no more than bounce, making their breasts seem to dance. Every last one of those women up on the stage a real human woman with a subtle thatch between her legs, dancing shadow of gate and altar that I . . .

Suddenly Violet said, "Let's get the fuck out of here. Must be something, somewhere . . ."

Dûmnahn said, "Hang on a minute . . ." Put one of his sensor probes in a tankard of frothy green beer, his fifth full liter, counting by the empties on the table, and made the level go down fast.

"How the fuck can you drink so much?"

Dûmnahn, flicking foam, said, "Ahhh! A manly man among manly men!"

Violet: "No reason a cyberdoc *shouldn't* be able to detox his own blood."

Outside, Dûmnahn lifted his leg against what looked like the broken-off stub of a lamppost and pissed for a full three minutes, foamy puddle glistening and steaming in Proximal light. I needed to go myself, started to reach for my fly . . . abruptly grew conscious of Violet standing there, watching Dûmnahn, shaking her head in mock amazement.

"Well," I said. "Where to?"

Long silence. Then Dûmnahn said, "Ahem. Um. Well, I've got some stuff I need to do. Cyberdoc stuff. You two'll have to toddle on without me."

"Dûmnahn? You sure you don't want us to . . ." A sharp feeling of loss at the prospect of having the evening's camaraderie diminished.

Violet clapped me on the shoulder and said, "Come on, Murph. Let's let this old sod go sleep it off. The night is young and so are we!"

Are we? Hell, I'm not even seventeen yet. No idea how old Violet might be. Until this very second, it never occurred to me to wonder. Just a state of mind, they say. "Sure."

The next bar was a much quieter place, a café, really, with

tables scattered around the floor, in dark corners, all nooks and crannies. The thing on the stage was a robot of some kind, android in nature but quite obviously not a real person. Plasticky. But it could sing very well, smooth, light baritone crooning slow, soft tunes in a language I'd never heard before.

When I asked, Violet told me the robot was extremely old, as old as Dûmnahn, maybe, a style of machine long abandoned, a newton synthesizer, she said, and that the language was probably Swahili.

After a while, sitting quietly, listing to the songs, drinking by her side, I began to notice that many of the other customers were optimods of various sorts. The waiter, who brought us drinks when we asked, just like a machine, was an optimod too, a big purple humanoid with a flat gorilla-face, who gave Violet a long look that seemed to make her angry.

After that, we left again, went on a walk in the darkness.

Beyond the edge of the squatter town, we climbed a rutted gravel road up a long, low hill that seemed to be covered with shadowy, broken ruins. Things like . . . I don't know. Fallen pillars. Collapsed stone walls whose pieces, when I touched them, seemed hand-hewn. "What is this place?"

Violet said, "I'm not sure. I've been here before, but . . . well, it's never daylight on RS67 and there's nothing about it on the local datatrack."

Like the collapsed remnants of some ancient Hellenistic city, some Seleucid Empire town decaying away to nothing on the Anatolian seacoast . . . impossible. Impossible for them even to be ancient, as human beings have been poking about Proxima for less than five hundred years.

And, of course, there *is* no one else.

At the top of the hill we sat on a precipice overlooking nothingness, sat on a low wall looking out at a dark, starry sky that went down and down, down below where a real world's horizon would be, down almost to the cliff edge just beyond our feet. RS67, then, an irregular mess of a world, chewed through and through with machine-bitten holes.

Nothing.

On a real world there'd be meteors in the sky. Here, they glance silently off the eutropic shield, are sent silently, lightlessly on their way.

Still. Here is the bright jewel of Proxima. Over there, stark and cold from a full 25,000 AUs are the Alphas, brilliant white A, dimmer, slightly orangish B. And over there, first-magnitude Sol. There Sirius. Vega. Fomalahaut . . .

"Hell of a lot easier to see them, see how they *really* look, from a world that's got an outside."

Violet said, "You're from Audumla, hm? What's that like?"

I glanced over, took in her angular, inhuman profile, silhouetted against black sky and stars, hardly more than a shadow. "Nothing much. Just an old decantorium-style habitat, used up, sold, repurposed." Nothing much. But then I could have told her, I suppose, about the Mothers' Children and the Timeliners, about Rannvi and Lenahr, Styrbjörn and Ludmilla Nellisdottir, about Beebee and Mrs. Trinket's lovely little kits.

Could've told her about my father, I guess.

She said, "I know what you mean. I was . . . born in one of those."

Notice the little hesitation. Is she ashamed she was born in a clean steel tank, like every other optimod who ever lived?

I turned to look at her again, was startled at how close she was, her face only a hand's-breadth of cems from mine. Maybe I jumped. Maybe not. Felt her breath in my face, sweet with a scent like lavender, a smell not so different from her name.

She reached out and touched my arm, ran her hand up to my elbow, seeming to trace the outline of the muscles through my shirt. Touched my chest, then my face, and said, in something of a throaty whisper, rough and raw, very different from her usual voice, "Your skin's so smooth."

The fingers on my face were anything but smooth, covered with short, dense fur, something like velvet. I could feel my heart pounding like mad in my chest, feel some kind of emotion coursing through my breast, but nothing that told me what to do.

She said, "Have you ever . . . been with a nonhuman before?"

There are moments when you want to ask the Orb for help, but he's never there when you need him. "Yeah. Allomorphs, a few times . . ."

She made a little sigh, almost like laughter. "Allomorphs. Hardly the same thing at all."

"No."

Then she took my face between her palms, soft, velvet palms, leaned in close and, I think, tried to kiss me, but our faces seemed the wrong shape for each other, so it was more like being licked by a dog. Puppy kisses, I remember thinking. Involuntarily, I turned my face away, lifting my sleeve and wiping away the wet.

Violet let me go then, let her hands trail oh-so-reluctantly down my chest, let them fall back into her own lap. Silence. Then. "Sorry. You . . . want me to stop?"

I stuttered, trying to formulate . . . something. "Oh, Violet. I, um . . ." Useless. Too confused.

She leaned in again, hands on my thighs, let them slide up to my hips. Then one hand crept around to the inside of my thigh, palpating the place between my legs, maybe trying to gauge whether I was interested or not, I don't know. I sat there, paralyzed, and let her do what she wanted. Sat still, hardly breathing, while she unbuttoned my shirt, while she ran her hands over my chest. Plenty of hair there, I remember thinking, but nothing compared to . . .

Sat still while she pulled my shirt off my shoulders, while she leaned in close, nuzzling the side of my neck, while I felt her long, dense, silky fur on my naked skin. Stood up, no more of my own accord than a robot on a preprogrammed subroutine, stood still while she unbuckled my belt, opened my trousers, and slid them down.

She seemed to purr, finding definite evidence that I was interested after all.

Whispered, "Say something, Murph. Say something."

All I could do was shiver a little. Shiver at the cool breeze on my skin, I guess, reach out tentative hands, run my fingers through the long hair running down her spine. She seemed to like that, stood up, put her arms around me. Pressed me close, and I could feel the woman of her through the fur, feel warm, doughy breasts against my chest, feel erect human nipples pressing through the fur.

Just a minute, I remember thinking. Just a minute and she'll change. Change like an allomorph. The fur will be gone and she'll be . . .

She took one of my hands in hers and made me touch her, pressed it to my breast so I could feel her underlying humanness, slid it down her side until it rested on her hip. Bone structure in there. Familiar bone structure. Tried to kiss me again, not much more successfully than the first time, merely getting my face wet.

We lay together on a smooth hillside of stone, stone warm as blood, and I did with Violet what you always do with a woman. Turned out she wasn't so different after all. Maybe I wanted to ask her, between one time and the next, if she'd ever been with a human male before, but I couldn't.

Maybe it would've broken the spell, made us human male and optimod female again, and that would've been too bad. What we'd become, for just a little while, is the thing you always go looking for: lovers.

An idyll lasts a day, two days, three, then the real world comes and sweeps it all away, as if it's a moment that takes forever to pass. Whichever one it was that I had with Violet, the day came when we mounted our ships and flew on down Proxima's gravity well to the Glow-Ice Worlds, Proxima growing to a fantastic disk in the sky, an impossible thing, ruddy pale, densely flecked with starspots, like bits of metal shining within a fire, mineral-rich debris ring glittering in our sensor screens, otherwise invisible.

A real star, I remember thinking, looking out through the one little porthole my engineering space possessed, looking ever so much like pictures of manhome's Sun, original giver of life.

Another conversation, far in the background. "I envy you having been there, seeing the real thing."

Dûmnahn's reply: "It's not so different, really. Bigger, brighter, hotter, but then you see it from so much farther away."

I suddenly realized Dûmnahn might actually have memories source-coded on the surface of Earth itself. That'd be . . . a wonderful thing. I wanted to ask, I really did, when I talked to him alone, when the two of us seemed like no more than . . . men together: How much of you began as a man? Just an idea, in the mind of a man?

I wish I had, but it seemed so rude.

And what if all he remembers of Earth is the inside of some construction node, deep in bowels of rock, occluded from the Sun? You don't want to carry a friend back to bitter memories, do you? Not when there are so many happy memories to . . .

Glow-Ice 9 was no more than a faraway twinkle in the sky when it began, a long streak of red here, then another one there. Two. Three. Ten. A hundred. Chatter of voices on the fleet's secure datatrack.

Tally-ho.

Hard blue stars suddenly winking on all around us as the fleet's battlecraft lit off their moduli in unison, drives so much more technically advanced than the cheap insystem fusion rockets that were all the colonists had to work with.

Where are the SOCO troopers? I remember wondering. They'll have real ships, real weapons, real . . .

Flash.

Orange globe, momentarily blinding, then a dull, small sphere of pale fire fading, fading. Gone.

Flash. Flash. Flash.

More pale, fading orange fire. People and machines turned so suddenly to vapor, souls gone Orb knows where. Reabsorbed by Uncreated Time.

There was a sudden rattle on the hull. Enemy fire? Violet's quiet voice: "No. I flew through a debris field. Harmless bits that used to be . . . something."

I checked my sensors anxiously, did my job, making sure everything was as it should be.

Hard flare of brilliant yellow light gouting in space not so far away, shockwave rocking our ship just a little bit, then more debris, like a cheap drum inches from my ears. Enemy fire? I looked in the datatrack. Yes, a hit on one of the troop transports, a big SOCO ship bringing the soldiers of IX down to mix it up with their friends from XXIII.

No damage at all. Missile deflected. Exploded. Little dings and cracks on our hull healing themselves as bits of missile hardware ricocheted and were gone.

Hard voice from nowhere: "Athena 7, *flyer down! Sector 823-five-Alpha. Your baby.*"

The ship tipped hard under my back, inertial force tickling right through the shields as Violet sent us plunging through the battlesky, lights flaring and popping all around us now. My job. My job. Orb. I held on, adjusting this field, poking at that one, working my control systems, making the modulus do what Violet wanted. Sure. Sure. Easy as hell.

I could imagine her complimenting my work later.

Felt a sharp little sexual thrill.

And, outside my window, Glow-Ice 9 grew from faraway glitter to circular world, to a flat, red ice landscape, flying by below.

"*There! There!*" shouted Dûmnahn. "Go down! *Down!*"

As the ship heeled over, stooping out of the sky, something went *wang* on the hull—groundfire, smallarms projectile, suggested the hull computer—then we were down, skimming behind a long, low ridge of pale, crystalline hills, coming up fast on a dull blue glow, hovering above some kind of mess from which long plumes of vapor jetted like so many frantic old ghosts.

Down.

The ship fell, landing legs extended, rattled on the ground, and was still. Silence for a long, empty moment, then the world groaned softly in my ears as Dûmnahn opened the medbay ramp. There was a machine-gun rattle, the sound of his feet as he ran down the ramp and . . .

Go. Get up. Do your fucking job!

I unharnessed, slid out of my hole into the medevac bay, brilliant red light pouring in through the open door. There was Violet, meshed in her pilot's nest, doing her own job and . . . yes, looking up briefly, seeing me as I ran out the hatch. I imagined warmth in her bright yellow eyes and . . .

Orb.

Ice 9 was a crystalline mirror under a hard pink sky, ringed by hills and mountains of metal and glass. The most beautiful thing I'd ever seen, this fantastic Glow-Ice World. Dûmnahn was already beside the crashed and burning warship, not waiting for me, arms extended, extended right through a plume that must be burning his sensors terribly, cutting. Cutting.

Somewhere inside, I realized, grabbing the antifire gun from its socket on *Athena*'s hull, somewhere inside that tangled mess, there are living men, men like me, women like Violet. Broken, torn men and women, men and women praying for salvation, praying otherwise for immediate death, praying as they burned.

I clicked on the sensors, let the gun figure out what was actually burning, opened fire. Flames winked out, like that and that, the jetting plumes fell away, and Dûmnahn's voice burbled in my ear, "Christ! Thanks! So fucking *hot* . . ."

Twin spears of brilliant blue fire suddenly jetted from the side of his carapace and described a quick square on one reasonable intact face of the warship's hull. Metal and plastic fell away with a faint, tinny *clatterclang* to the red ice ground, sounds propagated through knife-thin alien air, barely transmitted through my skinshield.

And there they were.

Soft voice, a man's voice, from somewhere in the tangled ruin, "Oh. Oh, my God." Soft liquid coughing. Then silence.

Dûmnahn sighed. "Well. Let's see if we can get them out of here."

I can't remember the rest of it.

Sorry.

A little while later, survivors and dead and all the bits and scraps of the warship's crew we could find in our fragment of allotted time safe in Dûmnahn's medevac lockers, I hung in my harness down in the engineering pod, worked my controls and watched my sensors, and tried to think of nothing but the welfare of my machines as *Athena* scurried low over the landscape, heading for the battlefield.

Impossible not to think about . . . oh, not the horrible things I'd seen, so unexpectedly stark, so different from the homely little horrors of my father's practice. Thought about the men and women stowed away above me. Some of them whole, merely asleep, awaiting repair. Others quite dead, awaiting hope of resurrection.

I remember suddenly picking up a hand, a little hand, as though from a child, turning it over and over, looking at long fingernails, painted powder blue. A woman's hand. I remember a woman from the barracks we shared, a small, pretty, slim woman with small hands, a woman with long red hair and powder-blue nails.

Dûmnahn's voice: "Get aboard, Murph. We're all done here."

I gave him the hand without a word, got back down in my space, and *Athena* flew on.

Fire outside now.

Habitat 155, iridium extraction facility, crew of seven hundred, under assault by SOCO IX.

Brilliant blue fire; something like a pink mushroom cloud.

Crisp, terrible sound, Dûmnahn whispering, "Like lightning. Like being struck by lightning . . ." Then we were down, down and out on the surface, doing what we could, filling *Athena*'s lockers with the meat of the fallen, fallen and slain.

This one a SOCO soldier, ours or theirs no way to tell, sprawled dead in his armor, surrounded by a hard-frozen puddle of bodily fluids, red ice hardly distinguishable from the substance on the ground beneath him. Dead. Helmet and head nowhere to be found.

Dûmnahn: "Save him for parts, I guess. Maybe his head'll turn up someplace else."

"Save him for parts? But Dûmnahn, this is a *man* . . ."

No reply.

Just pick up the pieces.

Pick up the pieces and go.

Later, down inside the habitat among smashed furniture, melted walls, ruins blackened by fire, the command circuit opened and we heard Squadron Leader Chamônix: "We're falling behind the timeline, people, get a move on! Command directive: Pick up anything that looks like it might be part of a Standard employee. Pick up SOCO troops from either side. Leave the colonists."

I was looking at a boy when I heard that, boy sprawled in one corner of a habitat room, holding something that might once have been a toy spaceship. How old? Nine? Ten? His eyes opened suddenly, little slits showing pale brown irises, eyes looking at me for just a second, then closing again.

Dûmnahn's voice whispered in my ear, "We've got to go, Murph. Work to be done."

Outside in the hallway lay a SOCO soldier in cracked

armor who sighed when I appeared, sighed and said, "Millie Bolduc, SOCO XXIII, yielding parole. Glad to see you, medic . . ."

By the time I got her back to the ship, she was unconscious. I peeled her out of the ruined armor, a pretty girl with a hundred broken bones, arms and legs bending in places and ways so unexpected I kept recoiling from her touch. Laid her tenderly down in a meat locker, took a good look before closing the hatch.

Pretty, pretty girl. Nice little pink-nippled breasts. Lovely blond gate that looked like it'd last you all through a long, happy night. I closed the hatch and, when I looked around, Violet was watching me from her pilot's nest.

She said, "You're doing just fine, Murph. Just fine."

Dûmnahn came back, bearing the last of them, closed the hatch behind himself, and then we flew away, taking our bloody cargo home.

Final interludes, the usual scenes of war.

Running toward RS67 with a cargo of dead souls, I lay with Violet in her pilot's nest, bright stars swirling all around us as we flew, Dûmnahn below, quiet, working in his medevac hold. I know, down there, he is saving lives, but we're up here, together among the stars, where no lives but our own seem to matter.

Violet has finished now with telling me tales of other battles, in other wars, is lying half on top of me, leaning out of her harness, holding my face between her hands, the way she always does, something she learned, I think, from an old datatrack romance, struggling with the aberrant shapes of our faces, so we can learn how to kiss, like proper lovers.

It does work, too, I think, feeling the strange form of her

face on mine, the line of her teeth where no woman's teeth have ever fallen before.

They're human teeth. This is not how I imagine kissing a fox might be.

There are real humans with faces this shape, dark black women from history tracks about New Guinea, about Ethiopia; women with that fabled hayrick head of hair, as different from my own as Violet's silky fur.

Violet backed away from me with a girl's sigh, looking at me, at my human face, with her lovely yellow eyes. What does *she* see? Something as alien as me?

No. Her world's been full of humans, human men, since the day she was . . . No, I remind myself. Not born. Violet, like all optimods, was decanted.

Less human in that regard than Beebee and Mrs. Trinket's kits.

Then why, I wonder, did they give her this?

My hand was between her legs, feeling wet fur, all too human female genital structures, rubbing that familiar swollen knob forward of the gate itself, up on the rounded prominence of her altar-bone.

Let my finger slip inside, feeling the albuminous ridges of a birth canal no baby would ever transit.

No way to ask why. No one to ask.

Maybe it never occurred to her engineers to leave these inessential parts off.

Violet purred in my face like a contented kitten, straddled my hips, lowered herself onto me, and, down below, I could hear Dûmnahn humming softly to himself as he went about his work.

One night, subsumed in the eternal night of RS67, a transport-load of SOCO mercenaries came in, freighterlike starship looming in our sky, black hulk glowing with fire here and there, and it grew larger, then larger still, blue fire from her exhaust baffles, red fire in patches, places on her hull blasted by Glow-Ice weaponry. Soldiers of SOCO IX coming in for a spot of rest.

And, someone said, picking through our wards for survivors of defeated SOCO XXIII, looking to enroll them.

Good fight, lads. Come with us and we'll do you one better.

Stalwart men, men my brothers, all that historical tommyrot.

Glorious tommyrot, they say.

So far, *I'd* seen only blood and death.

Blood and death in the service of rich men's money.

The bars filled up with SOCO soldiers, big, muscular, tough-looking men and women. We got into fights with them, barroom brawls just like in all the old wartime dramas, until I felt like I'd fallen right into the datatracks, was living back in the days of World War Ten, when Earth was so badly damaged humanity was finally forced to reach for the worlds beyond the sky, reach out or die sitting home.

Found myself trying to defend Violet against poachers, silly when she could defend herself so well. Had an interesting few minutes watching Violet tear the living shit out of a lanky SOCO blonde who'd taken a shine to me.

"Interesting woman you've got there."

I turned to face the voice, a beefy blond man with a lantern jaw and brilliant mulberry eyes, hair neatly combed, dressed in immaculate SOCO fatigues, corporal's chevrons on his arm, six campaign badges on his breast.

He held out a big hand and said, "Meyer Sonn-Atem IX." A nod over his shoulder. "My friend, Finn mac Eye."

The other man . . . oh, nothing special, I . . . Well.

Shorter, slimmer, much darker, mustache on upper lip, unkempt hair, uniform just a little bit shabby. Then he looked at me with eyes as empty as . . . I don't know, just empty, and I felt a pang shoot through me.

Meyer snickered softly.

And Finn said, "We'll put an end to this someday."

I looked back at the floor, where Violet was sitting astride the SOCO woman's middle, holding her by all that long blond hair, telling her what was what. Put an end to . . .

Finn put his little hand on my forearm and said, "They think they're the ones who count, but they aren't. It's us." Fire in his eyes now, filling the emptiness with passion.

And, somehow, without any more being said, I knew just what the hell he was talking about. They. All the men and women, holding the reins of power and wealth, believing themselves to be like so many self-made Atlases, supporting the world, maintaining the existence of the universe, and so deserving its rewards.

Foolish stuff.

Primitive stuff.

Unbelievably primitive stuff, the stuff a children's dreams that I . . .

One day, he said, we'll all be free. Free to have . . . capitalism, yes, just like now, only it'll be capitalism with a human face . . . Freedom.

Freedom from companies, from corporations.

Freedom from unions, from all these little bands of so-called brethren.

Freedom from all our tongs of power, from phalangist, mafii, from . . . organizations of *any* sort, I tell you, which exist independent of the popular will.

Popular will?

Imagine that.

Meyer said, "When he speaks, I believe."

What an odd pair, I thought, then bought them bottles of beer while Violet finished up with her opponent, got off the floor to polite applause, and came stalking back to me. Stood still for a long moment, looking back and forth between Meyer and Finn.

So we sat and talked to them for a long time. Well. Didn't really talk—mostly listened while Finn mac Eye talked, told us how he felt about the world and everyone in it. After a while, I noticed other people gathering round, listening as well, eyes wide. Fascinating. Beyond my experience. In the background, there was his big friend, Meyer Sonn-Atem, silent, smiling slightly. Something odd there. Some kind of . . . calculation.

Meyer understands something I remember thinking. Understands something the rest of us do not.

It got late and we left, all of us, going on home to sleep.

On the datatracks, in all the old romances, all the old melodramas, war is hell, or it's glorious; but war is even dull in scripts focusing on the "long stretches of deadly boredom separated by moments of sheer terror." What they never tell you is, even the moments of sheer terror are always the same.

Starships swinging through space, driven by the modulus' blue glow.

Streaks of the tracking missiles.

Lovely fireflower of exoatmospheric thermonuclear explosions.

Crackle of debris on your hull, evoking those brief moments of terror.

On the netlink, you hear the fighter jocks breathing hard, screaming out their rage and terror.

Missile away. Missile away.

And somebody dies, now and again ours, more often theirs.

And we in the rescue ships go down and down, cut their burning bodies from the crushed hulls of burning ships, put out their flames, extinguish their agony, packing them away for salvation or disposal.

Crystalline, set-piece memories.

No whole to grasp in my thoughts.

Habitats afire. Glow-Ice colonists abandoned to die. Begging us. Begging for their lives. Begging for their children's lives.

Plenty more where these came from.

Worthless meat.

Then the call for help. SOCO IX transport *Hephaestus,* troops lined up at the drop shafts ready to go, blasted from the sky over some little world, blasted by desperate colonists using a souped-up core-cracker, one of those things miners use to break open an icemoon's shell, get at the mineral meat inside.

Save us.

Save our souls.

Violet's the one who recognizes the raw, horrid voice on a static-shaded radio link. Isn't that your friend, Corporal Sonn-Atem?

Maybe so.

Please, he calls out, save us. Save my friend Finn.

We go down.

Down to the world below.

Then, only this:

Skimming low over red ice, I felt the ship, our precious little *Athena 7,* surge, felt my comlinks sever, saw my emergency boards light up, all amber and gold, not much green, very little blue.

Orb in Unformed Heaven . . .

Restitutor Orbis, Savior of the World . . .

World tilting so erratically outside my one little portal.

Violet screaming something. Something about . . .

Yes. Me.

I remember reaching out, taking hold of the system breakdown lever. Pull. Twist. Out cabins breaking free, solid fuel rockets driving us spaceward . . .

Too late.

I felt the inertial fields go down, whirling force grab my arms and legs, slamming them hard, helpless against the walls.

Felt my head bounce and crack on the end of my neck, felt my pelvis twist hard around, legs suddenly going numb.

The crash net snapped open, surrounding me, inflating.

Thought I heard Violet call my name as I watched the red ground come up.

Sound of a door slamming hard, then darkness.

Long, long hovering in pain.

Everything gone but me.

Even the pain so very far away.

Opened my eyes on fire, feeling so stupid, so tired . . . Oh, the crash net's deflated somehow, let me go. Let me fall on the floor. I'm just lying here, all tangled up with myself. Everything tingling, tingling all at once.

I lifted one hand so I could wipe simmering sweat from my eyes.

Look at my hand. Ring finger. Thumb. Something's bitten the rest of it away, leaving what looks like a half-eaten ortolan behind. Where's my other hand? Can't figure it out.

Seems to have disappeared. No feeling at all. Not even a phantom left behind.

I twisted, pushed. Screamed when feeling suddenly came alive in my back.

From the mouth of the connecting tunnel, I could see into the medevac module. Something big moving there, Something big, dancing in bright orange fire. It's Dûmnahn dancing, dancing in a little circle, six green legs, black now, drumming on the deck, drumming out a little rhythm as he dances.

I can't tell whether that high-pitched sound he makes is an endless scream, or just the boil of his juices, steam jetting from cracks in his shell, like a crab at a feast . . .

Twist. Push. Scream.

Then I could see up toward the pilot's nest.

There was Violet, hanging in her harness, arms reaching out, eyes open, staring at me so oddly.

No.

Not staring at all.

Below her on the deck was a long, brilliant smear of lilac blood.

Those things hanging from her. Not limbs. Internal organs, dangling from a long rip in her fur.

I looked away. Saw a curled-up length of bedraggled fur, possibly her tail.

I'd gotten to like that tail, liked the way it curled round my body, the way it stroked my back as we made love.

Vivid blue sparks crackled from the hull, then a square of metal and plastic curled away and familiar faces looked in. "Christ. Look at that . . ." A familiar voice. Gray smoke jetted, blowing out the flames. People came in and gathered me up.

And that was that.

CHAPTER FIVE

I awoke with a hard start, afraid to open my eyes, feeling various pieces of myself come alive, as if I were some old machine experiencing a cold boot after long-term storage. Twinges here and there, like power surges flooding limbs that'd been too long still.

Memories. Childhood me over there, school, playing gatesie with the girls, sharp memory of looking down at myself in half-light after that first time, looking down at my glistening skin, half-repelled, half-full of joy, remembered boarding *Sans Peur*. Never did get through on the link.

On and on. Friends, war, love, death. All the usual things of life.

Something important happened to me. Something terrible. Can't remember, quite. Then I opened my eyes.

The room was pale green, and here I was, floating naked between two field-plates, wires reaching out to me from terminal posts nearby, a young woman, brown hair, brown eyes, pale brown skin, looking in at me, smiling.

Why is she smiling?

I moved feebly, looking around, saw myself whole, hale,

and hearty, stiff little erection poking up out of my middle, waving in the air. Well. That probably explains the smile. I've known more than one girl thinks an erection's the funniest thing about a man.

Especially one not aimed at her.

I had a brief fantasy of pulling off my wires, getting out from between the plates, and grabbing the pretty brown girl, getting her down on the deck, pulling up her green skirt, getting at the meat of her, and . . .

I heard her chuckle softly, saw the little smirk on her face, looking not at me but at a tiny freeze-frame panel by my bedside. "Glad you're feeling better, Mr. Murphy," she said. "Here, let's get some of this mess cleared away."

Mr. Murphy.

She did something to the interface and wires started sucking out of my flesh, sliding away into their terminals. When they were gone, the field pushed me to one side, dumping me toward the floor, tilting me upright. I staggered, fantastically dizzy, while the green-clad, brown-eyed girl touched me with a warm hand, helping me stay on my feet, standing close enough my erection poked her in the side, just above one nice, round hip.

She looked up at me, bright-eyed and bushy . . .

Something inside my head shied violently away.

She said, "There's a bathroom over there, and scrub suits in the closet. When you're ready, come on out to the nurses' station and we'll get you assigned to a dorm." Then she left.

I stood still for a little while, not at all at home in my body, looking around the room. Rows and stacks of suspension plates, men, women, things, floating asleep in between them. Nearest to me, a man with no arms, no legs, not much of a head.

But still alive, I guess.

Over there, a woman. I can tell it's a woman from the face and the little flat breasts. Nothing else. The rest of her snipped away, at the waist and elbows. She'll sleep a long time, growing her bottom half back.

Felt my erection stir, firming up a bit, and wondered how the half-woman would feel when she awoke to discover herself a virgin again.

I went into the bathroom, intending to masturbate, just so I could be rid of this thing, found myself staring, crystallized with astonishment, at the face in the mirror. Nothing at all like the boy who'd . . . gone to sleep? Is that what I . . .

Man in the mirror with a hard and empty face. Maybe a little bit like my father. Not much. I leaned close, looking into the hard man's eyes, empty eyes staring back at me. Remembered staring into other eyes, eyes staring back into mine, and, just like that, I remembered Violet. Remembered her and started to cry, watching tears trickle down the hard man's cheeks and drip off his chin into the sink.

He cried for a long time, but no one ever came to comfort him.

So. Scrubsuit. Nurses' station. Dorm room. Dark and quiet, dim blue light and me all alone. I think I sat there for a long time, waiting for something, anything, waiting for other feelings to come, but nothing ever did. Or maybe those feelings came and went while I wasn't paying attention.

After a while, I thought, You know what this is, old Murph. You're just like all the burnt-up, torn-to-bits warriors you gathered from the frozen, bloody plains on all the war worlds of Proxima. You'll get over it—numbness'll go away, the world'll come closer and closer . . . might as well start getting over it now.

Yeah. But.

Easier dead than son.

Then that commonest of brainfarts made me smile, just a bit, at myself, and got me rolling again. I sat up, just like that, put on the freeze-frame by my bed, and started.

Three years packed on ice, while the Glow-Ice War went on without me until it came to an end. Why? Screens scrolled and shifted, answers coming my way: Because it was simply easier for the corporate armies to ship in new troops than hurriedly repair the old ones. New troops, because we could afford new troops, against the Glow-Ice Worlds' expending all they had, until there were no more.

I watched that part for a long time.

SOCO mercenaries capturing a Glow-Ice habitat, marching its people out onto the ice, buck-naked men, women, children, screaming their lungs out in the razor-cold air, walking on bare feet that froze, cracked, bled, broke right off.

Quite a memorable scene: Pretty young girl staggering on white bone stumps, falling on her face, pretty girl shrieking as a SOCO soldier pulled her to her feet—well, to the stub ends of her legs, anyway—parts of her face, face and tits, ripping off because they'd stuck fast to the ice.

SOCO soldiers marching Glow-Ice rebels into pits gouged in the ground; corporate maintenance men bulldozing ice chips over the whole wriggling mass, and that was that.

That segment ended on an advert, Standard ARM logo boasting jobs, jobs, jobs. Thousands and thousands of vacant, well-paid positions out here on the Glow-Ice Worlds, just waiting for you techies to come fill them. I wondered why a free technician, having seen this whole business from afar, would come work for Standard ARM now. Then I remembered who I was, where I was, and why.

Risk meaningless death at the hands of a soulless corporate entity?

Hmmm. How much are they paying?

Little prickle in the back of my neck.

I'm alive, against all odds.

So I ran the search engines, deeper and deeper still, looking for all my friends. Sure. People still alive. People I hardly knew, from barroom and bunkroom and ... finally stumbled over my own military maintenance records, was startled at the extent of the damage they'd had to repair. Lucky thing Standard is loyal to its own. Some companies would've left me behind, buried in one little ice pit or another.

Lucky, all right.

Links from there directly to Incident 5153, Glow-Ice War, Week Sixteen, Day 3: Downing of DSRV *Athena 7* due to friendly fire.

Saw the face of the Standard ARM fighter pilot who'd mistaken my ass for a hole in the ground.

Read a brief synopsis of the radiation flare that'd wiped *Athena*'s computer systems. Lots of shielding in the engineering pod. Not much up in the pilot's nest.

Medical report on Darius Murphy, contract employee. Salvage report on biocybernetic unit Dûmnahn. No links at all for optimod Violet, wholly owned chattel of the Standard ARM corporation, just a note to the effect that she'd been removed from the vessel's shell pending final hardware salvage.

Removed and taken away.

I briefly pictured her torn-off, curled-up tail lying at the bottom of some ice pit, lying atop a shuddering, shivering mass of Glow-Ice rebels, just before the bulldozers covered them up for good.

Would they do that to a loyal company optimod? Fucking Orb they would. This is business.

I shut the freeze-frame interface, forgetting for a while that I wanted to call my father, try to, anyway. Maybe later. Right now . . . I got up and got out of there, going nowhere, anywhere.

Outside the main hospital building there's a balcony and a garden, garden full of trees under a wide blue sky, sky full of pale white clouds, outlining faraway mountains. Sometimes, Telemachus Major's green garden moon hangs like an irregular, mossy boulder over the mountains, moving ponderously through the sky, sometimes drifting parallel to the mountains, barely skimming their tops, other times traversing the sky, climbing toward zenith, falling to one horizon or another, depending on which way the world is turned.

Down in the garden you can see soldiers being rehabilitated, mostly learning how to walk again, walk and run, not because they're so physically damaged, that stuff's easy to repair, but because they've forgotten how. Or why.

I went for a lot of walks out there, under rehab myself, I guess, and sometimes the little brown nurse who'd been by my bedside when I awoke from that long, deep sleep came with me. She seemed to like my company, though I couldn't really imagine why . . . Well, maybe I can. She kept walking too close to me, bumping me with her hip sometimes. Talking to me when I was silent, listening intently when I managed to say anything at all, laughing softly at things I hadn't realized were jokes.

Gatesie, isn't that what we called our game?

Found myself wanting little brown nursie badly enough that it was her I pictured as I masturbated alone in my dorm room.

After a while, she started walking with me less and less, until finally I wound up walking all alone, which, I guess, was what I'd wanted in the first place.

Dûmnahn.

I didn't stumble on the room where they kept him, here in the hospital with all the other meat animals because he was more org than cyb, just followed the historical links hitherward, terminating on a little flash of surprise. Surprise they weren't done with him yet.

Surprise at my little flash of hope.

By then they'd let me have a Standard ARM uniform, powder blue, with service and rank insignia, that one lone campaign badge right next to the little purple pin telling everyone I'd been wounded in combat. My engineer's blazon meant I got to walk right on through the cyborg wing, hospital staff assuming I must be here on company business, come to work some machine part or another back into its rightful place.

I found him easily; stood in the open doorway to his room, speechless.

Finally, that warm old voice said, "Hullo, Murph. It's good to see you again." That was what . . . one of him said.

Then another one said, "Hell. Thought I never would."

A hundred of him in here, row on row, column on column, tarnished beer barrels on six hundred green legs, standing together, tethered to the ceiling by a swaying mass of cables, power, data, telemetry stuff . . .

The Dûmnahn closest to me said, "Wasn't enough left of me to repair in one piece, Murph. Put me though the shredder, they did."

Some bizarre sorrow in that voice, evoking a feeling I couldn't identify. "Which . . . which . . ." Shit. I can't say it.

Someone back in the mass of beer barrels said, "None of us. Sorry."

None of you? Or all of you?

Softly, "A complete shredding bud-out leaves the end product without a sense of continuity, Murph."

A faraway voice, from somewhere in the back row, said. "But we remember you, Murph. You and Violet."

"Do you . . . know anything?" *About her,* something I was afraid to say out loud.

"No. Sorry."

Both of them dead, then?

I started to turn away, run back into the hallway, run away and . . .

Stopped myself. Turned back to look at the silent, swaying mass of Dûmnahns, every one of which was, apparently, genuinely glad to see me. Sighed. Rubbed a hand on my face, which had such an odd, greasy feel to it. Then I dragged a chair forward from one corner of the room and sat down with all my old friends. Sat and talked with them while the hours slid by.

"We remember so many things," one of him said.

"So many damned things," said another.

"Remember them as if they happened to someone else," said a third.

Silence.

Then a voice far back in the mass chuckled, rueful, self-deprecating: "Remember things just the way you'd remember something in a drama you once saw, read, heard. Nothing you actually . . ."

"I remember being something else," said one.

Another: "Me too."

Soft whispers from here and there in the room. Comparing notes. What did *you* used to be, my brother?

Can't remember, bro. Something, somewhere, some-time . . .

The Dûmnahn nearest me said, "I could swear I was once a man. I think I remember making love to a woman once, lying slim, sleek, sweaty between her legs, feel that . . . sensation you feel as you plunge all the way in, that . . . moment of utter contact."

I wanted to run screaming from the room. Didn't. This is your friend. Maybe the only friend you ever had. Maybe he just wants you to listen.

"Fat chance," said the Dûmnahn nearest the first. "That was just a dream."

"Just a dream . . ." it sighed. "Yes. Of course. Do you still remember being nothing more than a robot arm?"

Flat: "Yes."

Maybe they were still angry about that.

Bastards, Violet had said.

My stomach clenched as I struggled not to remember lying between *her* legs, struggled to get clear of that same moment of utter contact. Everyman's moment. Maybe so.

One of the Dûmnahns said, "I remember being a disembodied eye, floating in geosynchronous orbit, Earth's weather far, far below. Anybody else?"

A chorus of *ayes.*

What the hell are they remembering? And *why*?

Trying to . . . convince themselves?

Maybe.

It's all real, you see.

All real after all.

It said, "It seems I loved being a weather satellite. Can't remember when I ever had a nicer dream. The blue world, day and night coming and going, round and round the motionless continents, continents by day, blaze of human light when darkness falls . . ."

Another: "Remember the clouds, the storms, hurricanes sweeping across the face of those eternal seas."

Remember these things.

Make them your *own* again.

From back in the crowd, a being swaying in its repair wires said, "Part of us must once have been a deep-space comsat. Remember? Humans talking, always talking. Politicians plotting war. Businessmen plotting theft . . ."

The Dûmnahn nearest me said, "I remember the lovers, telling their secrets, whispers on the void . . ."

They were silent for a while after that.

I waited.

It's what you do for a friend in need.

If you're a friend.

Maybe someday . . .

Time passed, and one day I stood at the forward obdeck rail of commercial liner *Hélàs,* watching Audumla swim out of the interstellar deep, first the ruddy, banded ball of Ygg, slightly squashed, rotational flattening, then the not-quite-smooth silver-gray cylinder of the Motherworld itself, navigation lights flashing red, white, green, portals gaping, flooded with warm yellow worklight.

When we got close enough, I could see the little tugs moving out to greet us, thrusters twinkling, little flecks of white stuttering here and there. Closer still, and there were the spacesuited longshoremen, waiting at their stations.

In due course, Audumla grew huge, filling the sky, *Hélàs* shuddered softly and was still, and they opened all the doors, announcing our destination like the robot brain of an automatic elevator car in one of those immense self-serve stores they have on Telemachus Major.

I kept standing by the rail, feeling frozen, inside and out, wondering over and over again why the hell I'd come. Well. Because Standard ARM put me on a year's full-salary furlough as a reward for service well done . . .

Orb. Getting your ass killed and put on ice is a job well done?

Beyond that, the specter of a half-pay reservist's position if I wanted it. The company has plenty of pilots and flight engineers just now, flooded with new hires from the war. We'll keep anybody who wants to stay, of course, that's what they said. You work for Standard ARM, you've got a job for life, no matter how long that life may be.

But there won't be deeds for everyone to do. Not all at once, you see. And, of course, there were all those Dûmnahns, every damned one of whom knew me better than I'd ever know myself. Times change, they said. We all change. Go home now. Go see your father. Go see if . . .

When the Dûmnahns were finished, disconnected from the healing engines, when they were packed into crates and shipped away to new jobs where Standard might need a freshly cloned cyberdoc, I packed myself up and went away too.

Finally, I let go of the rail, went down through the ship and out into the world, reversing that last voyage I made with my father at my side, striding up the loading ramp where I'd hugged him, told him good-bye, turned my back, and left him behind. Flashed my Standard ID at the customs station, nothing to declare, no baggage at all, no reason for them to know me as a Mother's Son gone wrong, just some stolid company man, come here on a company mission, or maybe just come to see the sights.

I stood for a long time at the elevator station, while cars came and went, taking people away, delivering new, looking out over Audumla's vastness, orange stemshine, habitat panels, dusky sky, feeling old memories well up, spill back into the topmost layers of my life.

This is where you *lived*. The rest of it's . . . just a dream.

Funny how it seemed just the opposite, not so long ago.

So. Down the cliff-wall elevator, through the town, down across red hills, riding the monorail line, everything so Orbdamned familiar it made me wonder about the reality of Uncreated Time. As if this place exists someplace, somewhen, outside of time.

Inside my head, maybe. Nowhere else.

Then I stood in my mother's gateway, looking through the torii at Helgashall. There. The window to my old room, the little balcony where I sat so often, freeze-frame on the rail, doing my useless homework, studying subjects just because my father thought they might be interesting. Rannvi's room over there, at the edge of *kemenatë*. Broad red sandstone stairs leading up to the atrium, double doors behind, leading to the ballroom . . .

One of my mother's silvergirl servants appeared, cool-eyed, so patently, manifestly artificial, and said, "Welcome home, Dagmar Helgasson. I've alerted the mistress to your arrival. She'll be so happy to see you again at last."

Felt my fists clench, my bowels twist at the sound of my own name.

Happy to see me?

Well. It was one of the Dûmnahns reminded me I belonged to Standard ARM now, far beyond the power of the Mother's Children, beyond the reach of any mother, no matter how bold. As I walked up the stairs, I felt like a man going to the gallows.

And felt ridiculous as well.

Coming here's turning you back into a child, that's all. You'll do what you've come to do, then you'll go away, and the hard man will come back, ready to guide you through the rest of your life. It's a yawning void, right now, but . . . something will come of it, you'll see.

Stepped through the door, down the long atrium carpet, past the spiral staircase, feeling almost myself again, ready to smile and greet them all, prodigal son, proud man, free man, come home again at last.

And there they were.

Mother, lovely and ageless, almost like a silvergirl herself.

Lenahr, grown fantastically into a handsome young man, face sleek and dark, looking more like Father than I ever did, black hair combed back, shiny, eyes bright, smiling at me as though genuinely glad . . .

Mother said, "Dagmar."

I gave her a little hug, just enough, not too much, pulled back, and looked around. "Is Rannvi home?" Something peculiar here. I've been gone for a *very* long time and . . .

My mother said, "Married. I've put in a call to her, invited her for dinner. Maybe an hour . . ."

And . . . "Father?"

Just a bare hint of a shadow in her eyes. Then she said, "Your father has passed away."

Just like that.

Then Lenahr smiled and said, "Killed himself, Daggy. About three weeks after you left."

It'd been dark for hours by the time I got to the Timeliner Firehall down beyond the bayou country, back by the abandoned city of empty apartment buildings. Long hours, standing outside on my old balcony, watching the night form while Mother fumed inside, while the others ate dinner, while Lenahr sniped because I'd had to go through his room to get to the balcony, his balcony, his . . .

Rannvi telling her silent, pale husband—Vadim, I think she called him—to make his own way home, that she'd be needing the flitter for a while, then driving through the night, down the path I hadn't even known she knew about, parking the flitter, its landing legs going crunch on the parking lot's old, dusty gravel. Then just sitting there, looking at me. As if waiting.

Finally: "I'm sorry Murph. He was . . . my father too." As if she felt I was accusing her of something.

"Why didn't you call?"

"Mother."

"Even after you were married?" A married Mother is among the freest of the free.

"By that time, he'd been gone a long time. I guess I thought the Timeliners told you. I guess . . ." A bit of silence. "And then, Vadim thought we should . . . stay on good terms with her. You know."

Yes, I did know. I wondered, mind wandering, if Vadim was a decent husband, wondered . . . even had a momentary flash of picturing them in bed together, colorless man on my goldengirl sister. Useless. I said, "You coming in?"

She looked up at me briefly, then down again into the shadows under the dashboard, where her feet lay hidden. "I'm not a Timeliner."

Sudden shock of realization: He's in the Firehall only because the Goddess can't abide a suicide. Hideous fantasies then, of my father . . . doing it. I don't have the courage to ask how . . . Images of him in a nice, warm bathtub, slitting his wrists with a desplining scalpel, expiring quietly in a scarlet pool, sighing with relief, maybe thinking of me right near the end.

Well, no. Pretty picture but . . . they can bring you back from that easily enough.

I pictured him with the high-powered airgun I knew he hadn't used since he was a boy, taking it apart so lovingly, oiling all the parts, making sure it worked just right. Kneeling in his room, cocking the chamber, *ka-ching*, putting the barrel in his mouth . . . No. No, that's too obscene, image of my father fellating the gun. No, I see him putting the barrel on the bridge of his big nose, right between the eyes, just below his brow-ridge, where the dark hair of his brows met. Putting his thumb in the trigger guard. A slight tug. *Pap*.

Top of his skull bouncing off the ceiling, falling, landing in the doorway, Mother coming to see what the hell all the noise was, finding it there, empty but for a spatter of blood, rocking gently back and forth . . .

I got out of the car then and went inside, knelt at the altar, and said a prayer for Orb, to help him in his eternal battle, said another prayer to Uncreated Time, which is all the hope any of us ever had. Lit a candle in my father's name, a little gleam to help him find his way through the cavern of the night.

Went to the Hall of the Dead, walked down long rows of crystal vases, gleaming by firelight, until I came to him. Just a teacup full of soft gray ash, a little bit of bone. Silver nameplate that said, HYTASPES MURPHY. Nothing more. Nothing more needed. Restitutor Orbis knows who he really was. Uncreated Time has taken him back.

I felt the tears well up in my eyes then, but they couldn't spill over.

*　　*　　*

I spent the next few days wandering around my old haunts, checking up on all my old comrades, boys I'd known and hung with for all those years that'd once seemed to mean something. Found most of them hale, hearty, settled to a fare-thee-well. What the hell do they call it? "Comforts of the marriage bed"? Yeah.

Stopped by Styrbjörn's house so I could tell his mother how sorry I'd been to hear about her husband—damned if I could remember his fucking name, Gladulf was what it said in the freeze-frame directory—sorry as hell to hear how he'd been killed, he and his whole crew, by a freak accident on a routine cloudskimming run through Ygg's helium-laden cloud decks. Something, anything, threw them out of control, plunging deeper and deeper, and *gunch*.

Well, they said, at least it was quick.

I had a fantasy of being there myself, of being Gladulf, sitting there, struggling with the controls, listening to the hideous whine from without, listening to the creak and crackle of the hull as it shrank under the pressure, listening to his men, crying out, sobbing away their final prayers . . .

Or maybe they just sat in stolid silence, brave men all, waiting for it. Just waiting. You know.

I imagined sweat gathering, thick and oily, perhaps a little cold despite the growing heat, on Gladulf's brow. Then the machine-gun popping of the hullvalves as they failed, as they imploded, then the shriek of ripping metal, the soft crackle of dying plastic.

Then a wall of deadly, solid air.

Well at least that part would have been quick.

But the long fall . . . that would have been . . . interesting.

Her new husband, a much younger man, never did say anything to me the whole time I was there; seemed glad when I rose to go.

Then Styrbjörn himself, greeting me in the open door of Sieglindëshall, throwing his arms around me like a long-lost brother, leading me in to their small but well-appointed parlor. "Oh, Goddess, Murphy! We all *missed* you!"

Sieglindë Smillasdottir stood in the entryway to the rest of the house, demure, smiling, waiting for me to notice her. Tall, slim, blond like her husband, dressed in clingy white shorts that showed the outline of her vulva, a sheer haltertop that let you see the shadow of her nipples.

Okay, Styrbjörn. Got what you wanted.

When she came forward to give me a hug of her own, I wondered just how the hell I'd missed her, way back when. Orb, inhabiting my balls right now, was letting me know I'd been remiss and . . . shit. More gates like this one hanging around school then you could ever have opened in a million years, even if you'd had nothing else to do.

Missed her because the other ones were already queued up, turn and turn about.

Is that really the way it was? I can't know. These are only memories, after all. And I slept for a long, cold time.

Later, in a quiet time, after they'd shown me their little daughter Ylva, after they'd let me know that Sieglindë was pregnant with their second, this one to be a son, a son who'd be named Gladulf, we talked. Old times, new times. Dead fathers whose souls we mourned. I told him a little bit about the things that'd happened to me, about the places I'd been, the terrible things I'd seen, and he clucked his tongue and shook his head, stole glances at a concerned-looking Sieglindë.

And I asked, "How'd you like to go hunting again sometime? You know."

He gave me a look like somebody trying to swallow his

tongue, looked fearfully at Sieglindë, and said, "Well, ah, you know, Murph. Gee, I'd, ah, like to . . . um."

Sieglindë Smillasdottir smiled and said, "We've got a lot to do, Murph. It's . . . not like the old days for us." She jiggled the child in her lap. "Being a grown-up's harder than we all imagined."

Styrbjörn said, "Sorry, Murph. You know."

Yeah. Sure.

Some other time, Murph.

Some other time.

You're nothing if you don't have courage, so, after only a little dithering, I went to see Ludmilla Nellisdottir. Not at her mother's, of course, I didn't have that much courage. Imagined myself standing in the open door of Nellishall and . . . well, no.

I walked through the town for a long time, walked through dusty streets flooded with stemshine, passing by the walls and neatly manicured lawns of the Mothers' mansions, smelling familiar old smells under a familiar, dusky sky. Something wrong. Just my being here after all this time? Being here, while my father lies dead?

No. Something more. Maybe no more than that I'd really liked the blue skies and puffy white clouds of Telemachus Major, liked the brisk feel of that outside-in world so much better.

Thought about Dûmnahn for a little while, faceless thing of a thousand doppelgängers. Nothing new to him, merely to me, for the Dûmnahn I'd known as a comrade already had thousands of going doubles scattered across all human-inhabited space.

Then I thought about Violet.

Memories. You know?

Bits and pieces of her inside me.

Found myself on the walkway in front of Ludmillashall.

Red sandstone stucco, neat white trim, green lawn, dark windows, pale, lacy curtains dimly visible. No movement. No sound. I suppose I could turn and go away, but . . . right. You owe her this, don't you?

I think I stood for a long while, maybe waiting for someone, something, to give me an answer. What did I owe the people of this world, mother, father, brother, sister, the children I'd known and played with, pretended to be one of, the girls whose gates I'd opened? "Taken for a test drive." Did we really say that? Who the hell did we think we were?

Then the door opened and there was Ludmilla, unchanged, standing there, staring, face . . . expressionless. That's it. No smile, no frown, no anger, no sorrow. She said, "Come inside, Murph. I'm tired of waiting."

The freeze-frame told me she'd married about a year after I left, to a boy from some other school district, Sandow Francessson, three esses making me smile, making me think of the way I would have laughed, would have teased him way back when. A Mother should think of that when she names a daughter. "Frances? Why, then my grandsons will all have three esses in their name!"

I went up the walkway, and she stood aside to let me in, closed the door, and left us standing, facing each other in the silence of her parlor, in the deeper silence of her house. Freeze-frame said she had two children, daughters, Oddny and Nelli, no sons. For no reason at all, I imagined Nelli Ludmillasdottir was her grandmother's favorite.

She said, "The children are in school. When I saw you standing out front, I told Sandy to leave by the back way."

I felt a peculiar little pang, found myself remembering the way she'd . . . proposed. Imagined her throwing her husband out, then slipping off her panties before opening the door to invite me in. If I look behind the couch, will I find some crumpled little scrap of colored cloth?

"Doesn't he work?"

"Of course he does. Night shift."

Meaning he won't be home 'til tomorrow morning. This is going to be a hard night for you, isn't it, Sandow Francessson? Doing whatever you do. I pictured him at midnight, doing a robotic job, the same task over and over again, involving so little there was nothing to stand in the way of him picturing me, face down in his wife's altar.

She stood looking at me, beady-eyed, waiting for something, I guess.

Not really the same woman. If you look closely, you can see a hardness around her eyes, in the set of her mouth. This is Ludmilla Nellisdottir, Mother of Children, with a man to call her own, whose love she commands in just the same way she commands a silvergirl's obedience.

She said, "Damn you, Murph."

I think I expected her to cry then, but she didn't

Finally, I said, "I guess I came over to apologize, Luddy." Did I? Or did I just come over to say that because you're supposed to?

She turned away, walking toward the couch, and I could see the way her buttocks, curved, smooth, were neatly outlined under her short skirt. Not hard at all to imagine that colored scrap of cloth behind the couch.

It's neat as a pin in here, Murph. She'll have put them in the hamper before coming to the door and summoning you inside.

She turned to face me again, hands raised slightly, not quite tucked into the waistband of her skirt, making me imagine that she would, in the next second, put them there, would whip the skirt away and stand exposed before me.

She said, "There's no reason for you to be sorry, Murph. I backed you into a corner. I shouldn't have." A brief, mournful look on her face, quickly displaced with some wry, humorless smile. "I thought I was so damned smart, you know? I thought I could figure you out, plan a strategic campaign, outwit all the other girls, with all their silly, test-driving, gatesie-playing ways." A somber look at my face, smoothing the front of her skirt against her belly, hands not quite on her crotch. "Then I figured I could do it the Mothers' way."

All those words. I felt . . . breathless.

The somber look deepened. "I'm sorry about your dad. No one expected . . ."

Brief reimagining of my mother, finding the top of his damned head rocking empty in the doorway. "Why did you think you wanted me?"

A little shrug. "I don't know. Maybe just because all the other girls did." She sat down on the couch, played with the hem of her skirt oh-so-prettily, pulled it up slightly, showing me a few more cems of thigh. Any second now, the skirt'll come up, her legs will spread, and there'll be Goddess' Altar, Child's Gate, ready, willing, able, and wet.

She tucked the material between her legs and pressed her knees together. "I'm really sorry, Murph. I've always felt responsible for . . . what happened."

And then she started to cry.

Not long afterward, by the time we'd finished talking things out, her children came home, lovely little girls with long chestnut hair who seemed pleased to have company and didn't ask where the hell Daddy'd gone. Supper. A long evening chat, playing with two little girls who could've been mine and . . .

When the shadows were long outside, the stemshine growing dim, I took my leave, and Ludmilla made no effort to have me stay.

The next day, stemshine so bright it seemed almost yellow, I went out to the garden shed, where Lenahr told me he'd once seen the last of my father's effects. *My* father, as though he were the son of some other man. Hell, maybe he is. Who's to say a woman who'll marry a hooknose tinker won't then cheat on him later?

I tried to imagine that. Tried to imagine my mother sucking a lover's prick. Tried to imagine her groaning under him, conceiving Lenahr . . . No. Not her style. Not at all. Lenahr? Well, make that Lenahr Helgasson. Forget about all this Murphy bullshit.

Out in the shed, among barrels of potting soil, bales of peat moss, all the tools the family's silvergirl servants used to keep our lawns lustrous and green, our gardens fresh with ageless flowers, I looked for his things. Nothing. Tools. Diagnostics. Repair kits. Reference markers . . . over in one corner, leaning against the wall, stood our old plastic skiff, two oars stacked beside it. When I took it down, the inside was dirty, as though someone had used it as a tub for mixing soils. No sign of the old motor.

Eyes on me.

I looked up and found one of the silvergirls standing in the shed's open doorway, watching me. Nicely shaped, this silver one. Slim arms, strong legs, narrow, rounded hips . . . nothing between her legs, of course. They make them that way. "Where are Dr. Goshtasp's things?"

The silvergirl, voice light soprano, said, "Sold."

"And who repairs you all now?"

Long silence, silver eyes on me. Finally: "No one. When a unit fails, Mother sells it to the scrapman and buys a replacement."

Orb. "Think the scrapman fixes them up and sells them as secondhand?"

Another long silence, then the silvergirl said, "We hope so."

I stood looking into the robot's eyes, wondering what it really meant. Does this thing really feel enough to know hope, or is it just using the word in a preprogrammed way? No way to know. But I imagined it thinking about the alternative, imagining its own precious parts sold off, one by one, as components of some cheap repair kit.

Get your silvergirls working again for half the price.

I'd seen that ad a thousand times as a boy, never once wondered what it cost in . . . Hell. I almost said "human suffering," didn't I?

I had the silvergirl get out one of the utility flitters for me, one of the ones they used for hauling plants and dirt around, running errands, going to the grocery, and whatnot; had it tie the boat on top and drive me down to the foot of the endhills, then down the long road that led to my father's favorite stream.

Once the boat was in the water and I in the boat, I told it to come for me again just before darkness. Maybe I'll be here and maybe I won't. You just wait. Then I started to row, silvergirl standing on the bank, watching me grow smaller and smaller until I disappeared around the first bend in the river.

By midday I'd been rowing for a couple of hours, stemshine bright on my skin, prickling as though the UV threatened sunburn. Nonsense. Not enough UV here for that—even though we never think of it, Audumla's quite the artificial world.

Glow-Ice. Those were real worlds, red and cold, small, sullen sun in the sky. Deadly.

I rowed past one last familiar bend, brushing past feral vegetation, rowed toward a clear embankment I knew would be there, let the skiff crunch on the shore, tossing my oars in the bottom with a clatter as I jumped out, bending, pulling my skiff well up onto the muddy beach.

When I turned to look up the hill, nostrils well filled with the scent of organic rot, Beebee was there, looking down at me, motionless. Then, "Master Darrayush?"

Me. The name under which I might have done business. Darrayush and Goshtasp, Son and Father, partners. I took a deep breath, putting all that out of my head, and said, "Hello, Beebee. How you been?"

He began to shout, calling out all those familiar old names. Then the packing crates opened and the trampled-down, trash-filled yard around me filled with boxes and kits, machines and whatnot, bright-eyed, curious, reaching out to touch me, whispering my name.

They remember me.

And remember him as well.

So I played with Mrs. Trinket's kits all afternoon, chattered with her husbands, twenty in number now, teasing her about having the fortitude to handle them all. Asked after their health, asked who was caring for them . . .

Watched the stemshine begin to wane, knowing it was time for me to go.

What if I stayed here?

There's plenty of room for one more Timeliner tinker in this little world, isn't there?

Sure there is.

I could stay, sell my services, fixing up silvergirls, visiting Mrs. Trinket and all her kits on the weekend . . .

Sudden memory of my last "hunting" trip with Styrbjörn. Allomorph whores. Field of butterflies. Violet smirking, saying, "Well, it's not quite the same thing now, is it?"

I could visit Ludmilla, play with her children, get to know her husband . . . Orb stirred in my loins, letting me know what would happen if I spent much time at Ludmillashall. She hasn't forgotten. Nor have you.

After a while I said my good-byes, little ones clustering around my legs. Beebee helped me get the skiff back in the water, then shook my hand like a man and told me he hoped he's see me again one day. Stood and watched as I rowed away in waning purple stemlight, growing smaller and smaller until I went around the bend.

The next morning, before anyone else was up, I checked the freeze-frame, looking over freighter schedules. Then I went on up the elevator to the axial port, got aboard some nameless little ship, a tanker loading helium 3, bound for someplace I never heard of, and in only hours I was gone.

It was days before I realized I could've stopped by the Firehall and taken Dad away.

CHAPTER SIX

A couple of months after leaving Ygg and Audumla, the helium 3 freighter dropped me at its terminus, a deep-space transport nexus called Pasargadae 3. I shook hands with the crew, gave Commander Arunachal a hug for being so nice to me—mostly just for letting me be—then turned and walked away through a maze of frosty plumbing that defined the refueling depot, down into the belly of yet another beast.

It'd been a long, quiet time—not a healing time, I suppose, but at least a time for me to get used to myself again, as I floated in my bare little room, staring silently out a tiny porthole of dense, metallized glass at motionless, familiar bright stars, pointless flecks of light floating against the empty backdrop of the sky. Nothing much happens when you're flying at one-eighth cee. Every now and again a big rock will go by, but it's always too far away to see with the naked eye—passing that close to a macro-object would get the commander who permitted it cashiered.

If you turn out the cabin light, press your nose to the glass, every now and again you can just barely catch the glimmer of the deflector field turning away swarms of charged particles, shoving the dust aside. Just once, while I was looking, I saw the pathfinder laser flash, deep purple, vaporizing a speck in our path.

Toward the end, tiring of the sky at last, I came out of my cocoon, hung around with the crew until they started letting me help out in the engineering spaces. Had dinner with Arunachal in her quarters and saw her looking at me that way, was glad when we got to Pasargadae at last. Much longer and it would've been rude not to notice her desire.

Seen from space, Pasargadae 3 is a vast, irregular black clinker three hundred kems across that'd be invisible against black space but for the twinkle of her civilizing lights. Once upon a time, it'd been a fat ball of ice and carbonaceous rock, one of a number of such bodies that'd accumulated in the temporary trailing trojan point Proxima formed during her long, slow hyperbolic swing around the Alpha Centauri barycenter, more or less spherical, symmetrical, mottled. But people came, back in the same era that made Audumla, back when the Jet was first being settled, and pretty soon all the ice was gone, leaving black rock behind. Black rock that'd be black, stinking mud if it weren't so cold out here.

Pasargadae 3 and her sisters were convenient for the trade routes that formed back then, remain so for the trade routes that persist, huge, full of people and machines, starships clustering around, putting in for repair, refueling, refit, trading cargo, and passengers, coming and going through the infinite night.

I found myself standing one day, after a good night's sleep in a cheap transients' hostel, down at a place called Portal 771, watching the stevedores transship material from a longliner called *Sky Blue Eyes*. Nice, big ship, ten kems long, maybe, resting in her berth, front end gaping open like the mouth of a baleen whale, rear end sticking right on out into the starry sky beyond.

Soft, steady breeze blowing that way, out of Pasargadae 3, toward the open docking portal. I stood and watched men and machines labor, thinking about the captive air technologies of a big port like this. Mingy fields that let the air seep away, because air is cheaper to make than the power to keep it.

Armed guards here and there. Not enough of them, though. From my vantage point up on a grassy knoll, leaning back against the cool trunk of a gnarly old olive tree, looking down into the valley of the portal, I could see people sneaking through the woods, keeping as far as they could from the armed men, from the rumbling machines.

Smugglers? *Sky Blue Eyes'* yawning cargo hatch, all complex doors and shields, shifting cranes, patches of shadow and light, is fifteen hundred ems across, maybe more. Not much a few dozen security sloggers can do with that.

Pap.

Shipyard bull firing his airgun at something in the woods, lightweight charge bursting among the trees, bringing down a few leaves. I saw a group of men hurry away from the ship toward a dark tunnel mouth, staggering under a burden of fat, lumpy rucksacks.

There were more men at the tunnel, motioning them onward, one of them holding a long, slim rifle of his own.

I took a minute to imagine pitched battles, yardbulls pinned down, hiding behind this forklift and that, defending their turf, dying like good soldiers in defense of the cash, then I stood, picked up my own little backpack, all my worldly goods and chattels coming to fifteen kays, maybe a little less, dusted off my backside, and started on down the hill.

Armed men and women turning to watch as I approached.

When I got to the dockmaster's station and got her attention, she took my credentials and looked them over, identifying me as a half-pay reservist on furlough from Standard ARM. Handsome red-eyed woman with long silver hair, red eyes holding something that seemed like a glint of jealousy. Maybe just my imagination.

"So?"

"I'd like to deadhead on whatever Standard pallets are aboard."

"Hmh." Something like disgust in those eyes now, but she turned and pushed into her freeze-frame. "Well, you're in luck, bucko. There's a six-pallet rack of macrotome repair kits on deck 67, radial 5. Plenty of room for you to doss out. Here." She put a boarding chit in my hand, then said, "Make sure you stay in the Standard ARM hold space; don't mess with anyone else's cargo—there's a brig on this ship with a per-kilogram storage fee won't make your bosses too happy. You can go in the axial corridor if you want; there's a crew cafeteria at the hub where you can eat."

"Corporate charge?"

"If it's on your ID. We button up in six hours."

I turned away, holding up my pass so the guards could see, took a step toward the mouth of the whale, then turned back. "Ma'am?"

"What the fuck you want? I'm busy."

"Where's she going?"

"Wolf 359. Nonstop."

"Thanks."

I walked toward the ship, feeling my insides crawl a bit. Six hours and they button things up, then your decision's made, bucko. Wolf 359's more than a parsec away . . . Ludmilla's girls'll be grown women with babes of their own before you ever come home again.

But I kept on walking, threading a deadly path among the rumbling machines, kem after kem up the axial corridor to deck 67, then on down radial 5 to where Standard ARM's ship was waiting, my home for . . . sharp bolt of terror inside me then: Quite possibly home for more years to come than I've already been alive.

Bits of me wanted to turn tail and run, but . . . I found a nice, spacious engineering station, neatly buttoned up until some worker out on Wolf would be needing it. Opened it up with my company ID. Threw my stuff in a corner, kicked off my shoes, lay down on a brown leather couch where workers would one day break from their labor, fell asleep waiting.

By the time I awoke, we were on our way.

I spent the first few weeks sticking to my expected routine, walking up and down the radial corridor, paced fore and aft along the axial from the sealed loading doors to the locked engineering access hatches and back, down to the hull where I could look out a big crystal window at motionless white stars. Back up to the hub cafeteria, where I took sparse, tasteless meals with the crew, some of whom were disposed to socialize; with other deadhead passengers, most of whom were not.

Spent a lot of time sitting alone in almost darkness on my island of pallets, alone with my thoughts. Thoughts which turned out to be a lot less interesting than I'd hoped.

Couldn't really think much about Violet, receding to a dream, then less than a dream despite the persistent intensity of my feelings of loss. Began to realize the magnitude of the mistake I may have made as I sat there in the silence, alone on my nice brown couch, trying to reconstruct the vulval details of a girl whose name I couldn't remember, trying to bring her alive in memory so I could . . .

Well. Female crew. Female passengers. And you'll have damn-all *years* to . . .

I began to notice things out in the darkness, distant lights and small humanoid shapes moving through the endless landscape of cargo pallets, vast, sealed containers . . . Everything out there. Far away, well beyond my reach, restricted as I was to these two long corridors, I could see what looked like a fleet of halftrack trucks, shapes of men moving among them, flashlights glinting.

Other deadheads, I thought, but I never met them at the cafeteria.

Once, nearby, I saw a small group, two men and a woman, just a few tiers back in the mass, men working with crowbars at a container hatch while the woman, a tall, gracile blonde, kept watch. Looking at me, from time to time. What's going on there? They got inside, came out with some small packages, pulled the door shut so it looked unopened, vanished into the darkness.

Somewhere on *Sky Blue Eyes* there's a cargomaster and small security force. Somewhere a brig, the portmaster said.

One . . . *day,* I guess is as good a word as any, I was sitting on a corner of one of my silent machines, staring at nothing, wondering what the hell, if anything, would come next, when a slim figure clad in black patent leather melted out of the darkness and stood looking up at me.

Small, barely up to my shoulder, thin and soft-looking, with a pale, pixyish face, heart-shaped under short black hair not quite cropped to the point of being a black velvet skullcap. Finally . . . he? she? said, "Reese."

I said, "What?" Voice a little rusty, thick with phlegm.

"My name's Reese."

"Oh. Call me Murph."

"You a company guard?"

"Deadhead."

Reese grinned, a friendly flash of white teeth that made my heart jump unexpectedly, stepped up on the pallet, and swung beside me, folding his/her legs up into tailor's seat. "You kinda new at this game, ain'tcha?"

"You a boy or a girl?"

Reese smirked and said, "Asshole."

Meaning boy? Maybe not. I tried to steal a quick glance at the tight crotch of those black leatherette pants, but the shadows were too deep to give a clue. Still, something about this creature . . . And something like life inside me, stirring, very far away.

Reese pulled a small packet from inside his/her jacket and held it out. "Want a bite?"

I took the thing, opened the wrapper, snapped off a crispy hunk. Chocolate sponge, foaming luxuriously around my teeth, flowing lavalike over my tongue, seeming to evaporate as it avalanched down my throat. "Orb. That's good."

He/she took it back, took a little bite, put the rest away.

Long silence, Reese just looking at me, smiling. Why the hell can't I think of anything to say? Tell me you're a girl, Reese? Pull down your pants and prove it, please? Finally, I said, "Getting kind of hungry. You, ah, want to come to the cafeteria? I mean . . ." Hell. I wasn't this inarticulate with my first girl, much less . . .

Reese said, "Um. I don't—"

"My treat."

He/she grinned. "I'm a bum, Murph."

"What?"

"Christ! You really are a newbie! I'm a fucking stow-away!"

"Oh." Brilliant, Murph. "Well."

"Yeah. Right." Reese shrugged, unfolded his/her legs, and hopped to the deck. "Be seein' ya, Murph." Turned and walked away, not up the corridor but toward the gap between two racks of industrial pallets, already dissolving into the darkness.

Something—Uncreated Time, maybe—put a bolt through my head, making me feel a sudden, awful yawning loneliness. I scrambled to my feet, feet thumping on the deck, and ran into the darkness in the same direction, only to find that Reese had stopped just out of sight, was waiting for me, grinning.

I can't say why Reese picked me up. There're people who do that sort of thing, just as there're people who invite its being done. I never thought of myself as being one of the latter before. He/she led me through the narrow lanes between sealed cargoes, leading me on deeper into trespass-space, qualifying me for that brig.

Reese laughed when I asked. "Boy, those cargojacks are assholes. I suppose there's a brig someplace, probably stuffed full of the crew's own little smuggling ventures."

"So . . . where the hell's ship's security?"

"Here and there. You have to keep a sharp eye sometimes."

Reese, it seems, had been traveling the starways for free all his/her life, bum, child of bums, had been aboard *Sky Blue Eyes* for almost thirty years, come from someplace on the periphery of the Solar Oort, where those parents had finally decided to settle down.

"Oh, I stayed at Caledon XXVIII for a while. Nice place, but . . ." A shrug, a gesture at the darkness.

"So. Where do you think . . . uh, where're you going?"

"Everywhere, man."

"After Wolf?"

"I don't know for sure. I heard you could hop from Wolf 359 directly to GJ-1111."

I thought about that. "Yeah, you could. Standard ARM has a big depot at GJ and . . . well, you could reach the minus-fifteen frontier from there."

Reese stood still, looking up at me, eyes aglint in the darkness. "You know the Standard ARM routes?"

"Well. Sort of. I mean, I had a comp key to the flight log archives." Saw the look on his/her face. "I was a flight engineer. DSRV."

Long silence. "Oh. Were you at Glow-Ice?"

For some reason, I thought that little war was already forgotten. Maybe just wishful thinking for myself. "Yeah."

"Oh." After a while, we walked on.

Eventually, we came to a big, dark moonbus, six track-trucks, fully independent suspension and propulsion on each truck, articulated at two points—the kind of thing you'd use on a large, geologically active body, something with volcanoes, mountains, live glaciers. I tried to think about Wolf 359, about what I knew of its planetary system. Couldn't remember much. Someplace like Mars, maybe? Or the Glow-Ice Worlds?

Wolf 359 is a lot smaller, dimmer, and older than Proxima Centauri.

Reese rapped softly on the maintenance access hatch, a quick, antichaotic pattern. Something familiar there. The backbeat from an old song.

The door slid open, round, obviously female face freezing

in a half-grin as she saw me. "What the fuck, Reese." A throaty voice, classically sexy.

"New chum, Hibi. Let's get inside."

The face receded and we crawled through, sliding the hatch shut behind us, snuffing what little light there was. I could hear more than one person breathing. Reese's voice said, "Trell?"

A man's voice, thin and reedy, but definitely male: "Sure. Hang on." Then the light came up, rising slowly as a dimmer was twisted. It was a battery-powered camp lantern, the sort of thing my father and I used down in the bayou, just now plugged into the truck's charger tap, running off the engine's storage plates.

The man, who was a head taller than me and half as wide, face as pale as pink pastel chalk, sparse hair silver-gray, said, "So. What stray cat is this?" The woman, Hibi, half his height and twice my width, her own dark hair shining bronze in the lamplight, came and stood by his side.

Reese smiled and said, "Murph? My friends Trellis and Hibi."

There was a long silence while the two of them looked me up and down, taking in the cut of my clothes, the newness of my boots. Then Trellis said, "Welcome to our humble abode, Mr. Murph." He gestured at a campstove nearby, also plugged into the charger tap. "We were about to take our evening repast. Won't you join us?"

Something inside me melted on the spot. "I'd be pleased to, Mr. Trellis. Ms., um, Hibi?" I slid the little pack off my shoulder, zipped it open, and pulled out a two-liter coolbottle of fortified kvass I'd brought back from the cafeteria, intending to drink myself to sleep later on.

Trellis seemed to jump when he saw what I was holding,

gave me a broad grin, and said, "Well. You can pick 'em, Reesie!"

The supper wasn't much, some of the better components of emries they'd pilfered from the bus's larder, not much different from the things we'd eaten aboard *Athena,* but well-washed-down by sharp, narky-tasting kvass. Afterward, I sat and listened while Trellis talked, Hibi curled up, almost asleep in his arms, zoned out by unaccustomed liquor.

Improbable adventures of a man who'd run away from his robotic job a half-century ago, running away to nowhere at all, never looking back, Hibi awakening to giggle when he told about his sexual conquests, Trellis growing somber as he mentioned men and women, dead now, long ago done in by this yardbull squadron or that.

A long tale about the six years he'd spent working for GalactoFed Mining, out by Lalande 21185, having fallen afoul of a press-gang during a stopover at the Tralgiansk Nexus Habitat Cluster.

Don't know whether any of it was true or not, but it brought back any number of childhood dreams: all about a life out among the stars.

Is *that* what I've done to myself?

Later, as Trellis and Hibi snored on the floor, I followed Reese down the truck's maintenance corridor to the rear access space, a little room right under the battery, a space quite warm and comfortably dry. He/she had a bed made up here, quite a lot off stuff beside a rather big rucksack, pillow, blankets . . .

He/she turned and looked at me, face expressionless. Finally: "You got a blanket and stuff in that little thing?" Nodding at my backpack.

I nodded.

"Okay, you can sleep here if you want." A softening look, for just a moment, then: "Provided you don't snore."

When I zipped open the pack and pulled out the cammo, shaking it apart into a full-sized mummybag, Reese said, "Christ. That must've set you back some."

I shrugged, unable to remember whether it had or not. Money's meaningless, when you've got it.

Reese shrugged out of the leather jacket, then quickly pulled a pale gray, silky-looking shirt off over ... Well. Flat, smooth chest with little dark nipples. No indication one way or another. He/she stood bare-chested, seeing my stare, motionless, hands on an ornate silver belt buckle.

"Christ, you *are* kind of an asshole, you know, pal?"

I nodded, waiting.

A soft sigh. "Okay, you win, Murph. I *am* a, um, female I guess you'd want to say ..." She undid the belt, unzipped her pants, toed off her boots, slid everything to the floor, and stood there in scant, pale green underwear. Saw me still looking at her, looked away for a moment, frowning, then looked back.

I really can't imagine what the expression on my face must have been. Something troubling, perhaps.

"I'm sorry, Murph. I'm ... not interested in that stuff. You can look if you want."

Slipped out of the underpants, crawled into her blankets, and turned away from me, muttering a soft something to the bulkhead.

I said, "What?"

"Turn out the light when you're done."

One day, maybe a week after I started hanging with Reese and her friends, Trellis came home from a scavenging trip, breathless, eyes bright, dumping a frosty load of flash-frozen steaks on the truck workbench, and said, "Something you've just *got* to see! Put aboard at Pasargadae 3, I guess. Marvelous!"

Nothing any of us could say would pry it out of him, so into the darkness we went, winding our way aft and outward, dodging corridors when we could, transiting bulkheads through emergency hatches that should've been sealed and codelocked, but weren't. If this'd been a Standard ship, they would've been. And there've been no bums, company deadheads riding in steerage at worst, instead of down in holdspace.

Just as well.

Imagine a decade flying in the dark, keeping my little penlight pocketed except when I needed it to read a label or pick a lock. That impressed Reese no end, her eyes widening with delight when she saw I could open a two-layer slidegate by reprogramming the button panel.

"No shit!" she'd said, watching the first such gate pop open, both layers at once. "Now, why doesn't anyone *else* know that?"

Well. Manufacturers of the locking system don't publicize it. Not many people have a Timeliner daddy making them take techie courses seemingly at random. I remembered the look on his face the last time I saw it and wondered, for the thousandth time, if this *had* been his dream.

And Reese's innocent, childlike delight kept me hoping she'd change her tune, slip out of her clothes one night with something other than sleep in mind.

Keep impressing her, boy. That's how it's done, remember?

She was getting careless and comfortable around me too, parading around bare-ass as we prepared to bed down, ignoring my obvious physical reaction. I'd lay in the darkness afterward, wondering what the hell. Pure innocence, "not interested in that stuff"? Not bloody likely. Your typical, mean-spirited, man-hating cocktease? Maybe. And yet, a delight to be with. Though I knew she had to be at least fifty years old, she was every cem the image of your classic happy young girl, sparkle in her eye, cooing with pleasure over the least little thing.

Or, hell, like the nine-year-old boy I'd once been.

It made me remember standing in that open field, far down in the backcountry of Audumla. Made me remember an allomorph whore's simple joy, watching the butterflies float in bright stemshine.

Maybe she'd continued to watch them fly, continued to feel that joy, looking over my shoulder as I fucked her.

It took hours to get where we were going, the better part of what would have been our evening, before we finally slid through a bulkhead hatch and into the space beyond.

Reese, stock-still, said, "Christ." Unmistakable awe.

We were standing at the edge of a double hold, practically a full-sized wedge, and in distant shadows we could see the gleaming stubs of cut stanchions, where a permanent bulkhead had been removed. Look there. You can see the internal bracing frames of the hull. Two windows. Stars outside.

And much of this open space was occupied by a big, soft-looking sphere, baggy material of its integument glowing gently in pale pastel lavender.

Trellis crowed, "Wait 'til you see!"

As we walked toward the thing's flattened base, I said, "I've heard of these. Never saw one before."

Reese, impressed again: "What is it?"

"It's a portable ecologarium."

"And . . . ?"

Why spoil Trellis's fun? And hers. "Wait 'til you see."

Down by the bottom of the dome, on the side facing the hull, was the opening of an airlock, zippered shut with a sturdy plastic slider that worked with the barest whisper of sound, moving easily on silicone-greased rails. We crowded into a space so small we were touching one another and I found it difficult to shut the zipper, finally stretching up so Reese could slide between my legs and do the job crouching.

Brief, humid silence, then Hibi snickered. "All together, now: Fart."

Trellis said, "Jeez. Think that might inflate the place and give us more room?"

Reese: "Where the hell's the inner door?"

Hibi said, "Um. Here. I've got it." She peeled the thing open, pink light spilling in on us, and, "Oh, my God . . ."

Trellis said, "Told you you'd like it."

When my turn came to crawl out through the airlock flap, I stood, looking around in disbelief. Gently rolling hills under a soft pink sky, sky patched with a few pale lavender clouds, hills covered with yellow-green grass, pink and gray heather, stretching as far as the eye could see.

No, not quite. Horizon line, several kems away . . . I tried to do simple spherical geometry in my head, finally just guessed. "It's like we're standing on a world maybe ten, twelve thousand kilometers in diameter."

Trellis muttered, "You notice the gravity?"

I flexed my knees gently. "Point-eight G?"

Standing by my side, voice hushed, Reese said, "Where the hell is this supposed to be?"

I watched the clouds drifting slowly overhead, coming over the trees behind us, floating toward a faraway horizon. "I'm not sure. Maybe the Illimitor World.

Hibi said, "Where?"

Reese: "Never heard of it."

I said, "Nowhere. It's from a story I downloaded once. Preinterstellar, more than a thousand years old, I think." In the distance, far beyond the horizon, I thought I could make out the faint blue outlines of a mountain, things gleaming at its peak, as if it were topped by buildings rather than snow and clouds.

We started walking, going nowhere, and I filled with pleasure realizing this place had butterflies, little blue ones like tiny flowers, drifting ever so slowly over the heather, light here, there, everywhere, then flying again, like so many gentle, colored bees.

We could see the plume of pale smoke rising straight up, almost disappearing against the pink sky, from about a kem off, maybe a little more, after we'd been walking for a couple of hours, wondering how the hell they'd managed the illusion of space, Trellis fussing about it, "Goddamn, we saw this thing from *outside*! What, maybe twelve hundred meters? Don't give me any shit about it being done with fucking *mirrors* for Christ's sake!"

I'd heard about this technology, run across mention of it in trade journals, but it was something Dad and I just . . . never got around to. Mirrors? As good a word as any. Dioramae. Focused projection techniques. Some aspects of old-fashioned vr, I suppose. Just guessing. What it really felt like was simply that we'd stepped through a gate between dimensions, out onto the surface of another world.

A world where you really *could* see that plume of smoke over there, rising just beyond those trees.

We hurried a little bit, curious, went up a rise and through some little bit of forest, trees with waxy leaves so perfectly real . . . stood on the hilltop, looking down at a silver bright stream, and a group of men and women gathered round their campfire. Someone pointed, then a big man stood, hands on hips looking our way.

Trellis cupped his hands and yelled, "Shelly!"

The figure waved one long, thick arm, and called, "Hiya, Trell! Come on down!"

We went down the hill, stumbling a bit as our feet caught in the long grass, disturbing squadrons of little blue butterflies, stopping by the campfire, by the stream, where Trellis and Shelly threw their arms around each other, slapping each other's backs, Shelly lifting Trellis right off his feet while Hibi stood and smiled.

"Shell, my God it's good to see you! Did you come aboard at Pasargadae 3?"

Shelly was a tall, strapping woman, it turned out, but so broad-shouldered and muscular that, from a distance, I'd mistaken her solid, compact breasts for the pectorals of a strongman. She wrung his hand, squeezed Hibi half to death, and said, "Sure did! Me and my *bund* here . . ." Waving her arms at the others, a mixed bag of men and women, all sizes, shapes, colors, and cultures.

Count quickly, now. Yes. An extra woman or two . . .

Shelly said, "You know Españalta, don't you?"

"Sure! Been fuck-all *years*!" Hibi hugging a plump, blue-haired woman, whose name seemed vaguely familiar, possibly from one of Trellis' fanciful sex stories.

"And, of course, Mr. Jimberjaw and his wife Sally, and did you ever meet Bartolomeu? He's . . ."

Trellis gasped, "Why, it's Mr. *Zed*!"

Sitting cross-legged on the ground, quietly spooning up a hot emrie, the old man seemed to flinch. Old. Like something from an ancient drama. Sparse white hair. Washed-out yellow eyes. Spindly arms and legs. Mottled skin hanging in folds. Face almost . . . nonhuman. Like a badly made android, some antique model that should've been discarded as a factory reject.

Now he looked up at Trellis and said, "Oh, dear. Do I know you?"

Trellis knelt, taking the man's hand, grasping it gently, as if he were afraid it might shatter. "Oh, no, sir. It's an honor to meet you!"

I glanced at Reese, puzzled, but she didn't look back, was instead focused on the old man, eyes alight with interest. I nudged her and said, "Who . . ."

Trellis looked up at me and smiled. "Mr. Zed, this is our newbie friend, Murph." Then, to me: "Mr. Zed is the most famous bum who ever lived."

Mr. Zed seemed disgusted.

Gradually, the ecologarium's day waned, sky drifting from pink to lavender, purple, indigo, then black, colored stars spangling the sky like so much metallic glitter. Impossible, like the false-color mesh headers that adorn most astronomical studytracks. If you looked carefully, you could see it all up there. Stars colored in spectral order, oh, be a fine . . . swatches of nebula, blue, red, green, black coal sacks thrown in for good measure, golden stardust of the Milky Way, blotchy glow of the Nebeculae, the dim, wide oval of Andromeda. And, everywhere, in the dark between the stars, distant blue spirals, ragged white irregulars, the mother-of-pearl glow of dying ellipticals . . .

Shelly and her friends stoked their fire, cooked a meal made of fish freshly caught from the ecologarium's stream and, as the smoke thickened, I felt a lovely breeze spring up, not quite enough to bring on gooseflesh, the bubble's air-conditioning system working on high.

We ate the fish together, laughed, talked, told who we were in fits and snatches. I swigged sour liquor from a bottle Shelly passed around, strange, milky-looking stuff one of Shelly's *bund* made from the raw potatoes you found in a certain kind of emrie. Proud of it. Proud as hell.

I sat looking into the fire, sitting between Reese and the old man, who apparently had nothing to say, whatever the basis of his fame every now and again . . . yes, that woman over there, looking like a girl, lanky and lean, long black hair and eyes like holes into nothing, looking over at me, gaze lingering.

Mr. Zed turned to me in the flickering shadowlight, put his bony fingers on my forearm, and stroked softly. "So very young . . ." Long pause, then he said, "You *are* young, aren't you? I mean, *really* young."

I shrugged. "Yeah. I guess so."

"How old?"

"Well . . . I was in hospital stasis for a long time, I . . ."

Mr. Zed muttered. "Shit. I know what *that's* like."

I'm sure you do. All this damage . . . poor maintenance? Or . . . hell, nothing lasts forever, and Mr. Zed looks . . . what? Old as the hills? Older than any hills I'd ever seen. Certainly older than Audumla's hills. I said, "I've had about twenty years of consciousness, I guess. And you?" Seemed like a polite enough question, but I saw Reese flinch out of the corner of my eye.

Mr. Zed shook his head sadly. "I don't know." Then he smiled. "Wish I did, Murph." Another long silence, Mr. Zed's eyes far away, slitted, almost as if he were falling asleep, then: "I used to know a guy named Murphy once . . ."

All the other conversations around the campfire were stopped, bringing out the soft wheezing of the wind, the popping of wood in the fire.

"He was my best friend, I think." He peered at me, leaning close, inspecting the lines of my face. "Maybe an ancestor of yours, a long time ago."

Long, long silence, Mr. Zed dreaming again. I asked, "How long? Can you guess?"

The silence from the others hardened at my rudeness, but Mr. Zed smiled. "That's a nice, polite way to put it, Murph. I still know my history, still remember it all, I think. I just can't put it in order anymore."

The mythology of Old Age, left over from the Dark Ages. Old people reminiscing over a campfire, while young bucks and children listen, amazed. No one really gets old anymore. After a long, long time, a variable time, impossible to predict, wear out. Go to the hospital. Die. Sooner or later. I guess in Mr. Zed's case, it turned out to be later.

Much later.

"Murph and me left Earth together, oh, I don't know, right around the time when it first got to be possible to really leave on your own. Back when the big companies were first opening up the Belt and all. Took me twenty years of hard work to save up the application fee. More years to buy all the stuff you were supposed to need . . ." Soft laugh. "All bullshit. Companies feeding off a mythology they helped create. Company store and all that buttfuck."

This is just a fairy story, I told myself. It's unlikely he's really that old.

He said, "Murphy was a lot younger than me, of course. Never knew any different. Couldn't remember a time when it seemed things might come out different."

Silence. Wind. Fire. A soft splashing from the creek. Finally, I said, "Different how?"

Mr. Zed looked at me, almost surprised, as if he'd forgotten anyone was here listening to his tale. Just an old man, dreaming his dreams. He said, "I remember how I felt, sitting with all my friends in a dive down on Fifty-second Street, uncertain and afraid, watching Armstrong's ghost walk out on the Moon."

Reese whispered, "Armstrong? What moon?"

Mr. Zed turned to look at her. Then he said, "All forgotten. It shouldn't be a surprise. He wasn't Columbus, after all, nor even Bjarni Herjolfsson."

I remembered the museum on Telemachus Major. These people might not visit such a museum, visit such a world, surely wouldn't have wasted so much time freeze-framing the DataWarren.

He said, "Who remembers the names of the Chinese sailors who left their rock carvings on the stones of New Zealand, before even the Maori came?"

Maoris and New Zealand. Ancient history with a wealth of detail all its own. I saw a nice drama once about the first Maoris, so much like spacefarers themselves, stepping ashore on uninhabited New Zealand, maybe fifteen centuries ago. There was a really horrific scene, impressed me as a kid, six guys standing in awe, watching the moas graze. Then this huge, ugly thing called a harpy eagle stoops out of the sky, not knowing a six-foot man from a six-foot bird . . .

Mr. Zed said, "Me and Murphy went out to Callisto, worked for fifteen years at the fuel volatiles plant Case-Western was building there." Then, faraway again, "I used to love working out on the surface, Jupiter a fat, featureless orange ball in the sky, like a dying sun. Murph used to tease me, laugh like hell when I'd pretend it was Proxima, Wolf 359, one of those places."

Reese said, "Is this your first time going to Wolf, Mr. Zed?"

He laughed. "Oh, no. I made my way out to Wolf as soon

as it was possible . . ." He made an old-man sigh, high and sharp. "Disappointed at first. But . . . hell. I always loved reality more than my dreams. Worth it, every time."

Colonists got to Wolf 359 more than four centuries back. Wonder if it's changed any since then?

Mr. Zed said, "Murphy and me finally got better jobs, jobs for your more experienced sort of worker, went on out to the oil refineries Royal Nihon was building in the Fore Trojans . . . That's where old Murphy got killed, of course. Pressure blowout when we tried to tap a fracture zone . . . stupid. I don't know what the hell he was doing down at the wellhead that day. Don't know why the work site AI didn't track him and stop the operation . . ." He turned away, toward the fire, seemed to rub his chin on his arm for a while. "By the time we got to him, he was frozen solid in a hunk of black asphalt ice. Docs thawed him out, but there wasn't anything left but mush. Nothing left to resuscitate."

That made me shy away from my own memories, quickly dumping fragmentary images of Violet, of Glow-Ice Worlders, SOCO soldiers . . . people. Just people.

These are the kind of memories Orb makes you keep.

He said, "I married his wife the day after that, just so she could stay on and work. Adopted his kids and took care of 'em 'til they grew up. By that time they were opening up the Kuiper Belt, so I moved on when I could."

A whole life in a few words. Maybe not a fairy story after all. Orb knows. Who are we to judge?

He sighed again. "That Melissa. Christ, she sure was hot in bed . . ." A slow shake of the head, eyes a distant glimmer, looking pastward. "I thought she was being disrespectful to poor old Murphy at first, me his best friend and all, but . . . hell. He was dead and we weren't. That's the way it goes."

Then he turned and looked at me. "You look just like her youngest, Jenny. Jenny Murphy, that was her name."

"Did you have any kids with her?"

"Oh, no. I was . . . too old. And too young. You . . . don't know?"

"No."

"I was a hundred years old before I ever got off earth. What they called a geezer in those days. I was working out in the Oort, working for Standard when they . . . made me young again. Funny. Looking in the mirror after waking up in the rehab center, it made me think about my own kids. Made me wonder what'd become of them."

Reese whispered, "Where are they now, Mr. Zed?"

"Dead, I guess. Everyone dies, sooner or later."

Some time later, when the fire had died down and most of the others were asleep, Reese and I wandered away from the group, going for a little walk by the stream. It'd gotten warmer, the wind dying down, the world growing quiet and . . . Hmh. Funny to call this thing a world. Still, it's as much a world as Audumla ever was. As much a world as anyplace I'd ever been save Glow-Ice. Real worlds there. Inhospitable as hell.

After a while, we came to a nice little pool, glittering by starlight. Flat surface, still like a mirror, shattering to ripples as Reese knelt and touched it with her fingers.

"Warm," she said. "Almost like a bath."

Surprising? Too damned easy to forget this was a plaything, not a place. Even in little Audumla, we were used to thinking the water of feral streams would be cool.

Standing in front of me, Reese started to get undressed, watching me watch her, eyes invisible in the darkness, no more unfathomable. When she was done, a pale wood-nymph in the ersatz night, she turned and waded into the pool, turned back and watched as I undressed, alone on the bank, then waded out to join her.

The water was wonderfully warm and soft, the product of some conditioning machine or another. When my face got down near the surface, I could smell a faint scent, similar to the smell of the heather, not quite the same. Reese rocked back in the water, bringing her legs to the surface, floating, head thrown back, looking up at the artificial sky, sky flooded with what seemed like ten thousand fake stars.

I suppose I should have looked at the stars too, appreciating the artifice of the ecologarium's builder, but, just now, all I had eyes for was the little black island of Reese's pubic hair, floating not far away.

There's a purpose behind all this, you know that. Voice of experience, me talking to myself. Some women are aggressive, let you know what they want and when they want it. Others are . . . not *shy*, that's not the right word. Some women want to feel as though you've decided for them, even though the decision is theirs alone. Women who guide you with hints, glances, nudges, and looks . . .

Is that what's going on now?

I drifted closer to Reese, watching her face, etched in shadow made by bright starlight. Peaceful, as if dreaming. But she knows I'm here. I put my hand on her thigh, just barely touching her, and waited for a sign. Nothing, Reese just looking at the sky.

Well. That's sign enough.

Ran my hand underneath her, feeling slim buttocks floating weightless, as though I held her in the palm of my hand. Reese drifting gently, floating with her legs slightly apart. Just the position she requires in order to float like this, or another sign?

Certainly a shift in her awareness now. You can feel that. Reese is aware of me—she has to be. Ran my hand up the inside of her thigh, skin so soft it was softer than the water, would have been like velvet suede if it were dry. Reese's eyes turning toward me now, a half-smile visible on her lips.

Let my hand drift oh-so-slowly over to her vulva, let my fingers comb through crisp, wet human hair. Felt for the groove of her pubic symphysis. Yes. Here. And I can feel Reese changing her position to accommodate what I'm doing.

There's your answer.

Listened to a soft sigh as I found the little bump of her clitoris, apparently already starting to swell, felt her muscles clench as I palpated it gently, back arching slightly, making her sink a little deeper into the water, surface rising around the sides of her face.

Okay. All she wanted was a little coaxing . . .

I left off soft rubbing, letting my hand drift downward, feeling for the opening of her introitus. There. Right where you expected it. Put my index finger inside, feeling ridges of muscle, the slick albumin of arousal, and . . .

Reese squeezed my finger gently, where it lay in her vagina. "You know, I'm pretty good at sorting out relationships in a group dynamic, Murph. You're . . . not."

A little confusion, startled at her words. At this point, when you've got your hands on a woman, if she talks about anything it all, it's usually a confession of love. I said, "Uh . . ."

She laughed. "Oh, I know you don't have any trouble getting laid, Murph, but that's just a consequence of your being so goddamned pretty! Come on, admit it: Women come to you, not the other way around."

"Well . . ." No one likes being pegged, but . . . "Yeah. Right."

She grinned. "There's at least two women in this group who're being . . . well, shared."

"So?"

"So let's make a little deal, you and I."

"A deal."

"Come on, Murphy! You're not too dumb to figure this out!"

I pulled my finger out of her and said, "No, I, uh, guess not."

I suppose we would've finished what we were doing, Reese and I, deal or no deal, shared women or not. She floated upright in the water, arms around me, and we kissed for a while, tasting each other, testing each other. I liked the way she felt against me, the way she rested her mons against one pelvic blade, grinding softly, like an earnest of intent. Liked the smallness of her, the way I could hold her just so . . .

I seemed to forget her words, head filled with visions cast futureward, images of us together in a thousand places, mostly variations on a theme. Images of myself holding her off the ground, her slim legs wrapped around my waist as I thrust into her, she light as a feather and—

Sudden loud voice, no voice I knew, breaking us apart, making us splash in the warm water as we floundered, confused.

"What the hell . . ."

Then the sky lit up dull yellow, no stars, no drifting clouds. Looking upward, I could see the surface of the dome, striated with delicate white lines, electronics that supported a world of illusion.

Another shout, clearly the voice of Shelly, followed by a panicky gabble, several voices at once.

Reese looked at me, dark eyes wide with alarm, then said, "Shit."

We started wading toward shore, toward where we'd left our clothes. Before we could get in, someone came running over the crest of the nearest hill. Hibi, short legs pumping for all they were worth. She saw us, screamed something at us, "*Run!*" I think it was. A ball of crawling blue fire came over the hill and hit her with a soft *pop,* bursting into a cage of electric blue snakes that writhed around her like so much blue lighting, then she fell, rolling to a stop by the side of the stream.

More voices, loud, full of electronic distortion, someone shouting through a broken intercom.

We got out of the water, running for our clothes, but it was too late, there were other people on the hilltop now, dressed all alike in crew uniforms, the pretty sky blue of *Sky Blue Eyes,* each breast bearing the red badge of Ship's Security.

Reese said, "Shit," again, and started to run.

One of the men raised his wand and fired, wriggling ball of fire shooting across open space like Saint Elmo's fire, streaking for Reese's back. Not a thought in my head. No idea, no will, nothing for me to . . .

When the ball was about to pass me I stepped into its path and that was that. Not even time to hope Reese would get away.

Or to know exactly why I'd done it.

I awoke with a start, looking up at a pale green ceiling, at an embedded light fixture, muscles knotted all over my body, shivering and shuddering, joints creaking painfully. I'd never been shot by a stungun before and, as I lay there listening to my teeth chatter, I decided I might try to avoid this in the future . . . After a while, things quieted down, my skin crawling, as though I were being trampled by ants, fingers, and toes prickling and tingling . . . When I tried to sit up, pain stabbed through my head, starting at the back and shooting out the middle of my forehead.

When I finally did manage to sit up, Orb knows how many uncounted minutes later, I found myself in a standard medical examining room, walls racked with unfamiliar hardware, sitting on a hard leatherette bench, folded gynecological stirrups at the foot.

I used to have fantasies about these things when I was a boy, imagining girls I knew from school stripped and strapped down, downy gates at my tender mercy . . .

Reese.

I got to my feet, wobbling a bit, and staggered to the door, which slid open to my touch.

"Ah, Mr. Murphy!"

There was an office outside the examining room. Not quite an office, I guess. Desks here and there. Modern freeze-frame equipment making me remember, with just a flash of longing, how long I'd been isolated from the DataWarren. But there was a gun rack over by one wall, long rifles neatly locked up beside a stack of stun wands.

The man behind the desk, short, fat, clad in sky blue with that malevolent red badge, said, "Glad to see you're awake again."

"Uh. What's . . . um." I stood there, flat-footed, staring at him.

He said, "Sit down, son." Motioning to a chair beside the desk. "Sorry you got shot, kid, but you shouldna been trespassing. Hanging around with bums is never a good idea." He glanced at the freeze-frame in front of him. "Company beaners're gonna be pissed when they see the size of the fine we'll have to levy. Hope it doesn't land you in the shit."

I sat, splinters of pain fading throughout my head. "What about . . . my friends?"

"Y'mean the bums?"

My friends. "Yeah. Any of them get away?"

"Nope."

"Well . . ."

He shrugged. "Look, who gives a shit?"

"I'd like to know."

"Well, hell. The usual thing. We'll keep 'em on ice from now on. At each stop we make, we'll try to sell 'em off as indentured servants until we're rid of the last one. Won't take long, kid. Brig'll be empty long before *Sky Blue Eyes* ever makes its way Solward again."

Sell them off. The casual way he said it made me feel numb, made me realize how little I really knew about the universe in which I lived. Audumla and Ygg. Telemachus Major. In the service of Standard ARM. Little more than that. I said, "Is there . . . anything I can do for them?"

He looked at me strangely. "What d'you mean?"

"Any way I can get them off?"

"Christ! You ain't through shittin' yellow yet, are ya, boy?"

I found myself getting very tired of the faux-tough way he liked to talk, a slack-bellied crewbull who'd probably spent most of his life sitting right here at this desk while his ship flew between the worlds. "Still . . ."

He sat back in his chair, looking at me. "You can buy them all lounge-standby tickets. Then I guess we'd let 'em go."

"How much?"

He fished in the freeze-frame, then motioned for me to

lean in and take a look. I poked at the converter and let it match things up with my private account figures, crossloaded from the Telemachus link when I came aboard. It said I had enough for 1.73 tickets.

"Sorry."

I said, "I'll pay for Reese."

"The scrawny bitch? Sonny boy, you could pay for a *much* better cunt than that!"

Silence.

Finally, he said, "Okay. Your money. You go wait in the security access lounge while I thaw her out. It'll be ten, fifteen minutes."

I got up and started to go, stopped abruptly, and turned back. "What about Mr. Zed?"

"The geezer? Oh, hell. He's already gone."

I pictured him dead and run through the ship's recycler. "What do you mean, gone?"

"Son of a bitch has held an all-worlds travel pass for the last three hundred years. We logged a trespass fine and let him go."

There's a saying I hear every so often, *Time passes, and we are passed within it.* Time has to pass, in your life, around your life, before you can understand what it means, but eventually I did.

Sitting in the waiting room, waiting for Reese, I sat visualizing what our life together could be like—now all I remember is the hard pang of astonishment I felt when they brought her to me, still naked, short hair wet and plastered to her skull like so much matted black velvet, yellow bruises on her face, blue fingerprints on her thighs.

She let me put my arms around her, seeming confused, silent, let me lead her away, getting her out of there as quickly as I could. I'm not even sure I thanked the angry-looking crew-woman who gave me a torn old blanket to wrap around her just before we went out through a hatch that led back into cargospace, back down the axial corridor to passengerland.

I took her to my Standard ARM pallets, locked her into one of the control pods, then cut through the darkness to our old bus, where I picked up our gear, hers, mine, Trellis and Hibi's, that fat armload of steaks we should've stayed to eat, brought it all back to the pod and . . .

Found her hiding in the footwell of a control station, where a system engineer's legs would one day rest, eyes shut, ratty blanket pulled tight around her, shivering. I tried to get her to talk, but she wouldn't say a word, wouldn't come out, get dressed, eat . . . nothing. Finally I shoved a pillow in to her and turned my attention to the meat, which was thawed, but still sealed up and fresh.

Even the sweet smell of microwaving steak didn't bring her around.

Maybe nothing ever did.

But time passes, one way or another.

The next day she awoke, seeming her old self again, though the shadow never left her eyes. She ate, we talked, days passing, turning into weeks and months of their own accord. After a while she got willing to go bumming again, protected by the ticket of legitimacy I'd bought her. We made new friends, and never talked about Trellis, about Hibi.

Maybe we thought of them. I know I did.

Mr. Zed turned up, ate dinner with us, told us stories about olden times as bad as anything you could imagine, while the months went on to become years. Long before then, Reese had crawled into my bedroll and let me make love to her, maybe too gently at first, a bit too tentatively, but it wasn't long before the past seemed remote and times were good again.

Until one day *Sky Blue Eyes* docked at an exostation of the Wolf 359 system and I got off, while Reese did not. I hung around the dockyard while they put a few old bums up for sale like so much frozen sausage, but no one bought any after all. Watched while they unloaded all the Wolf-bound cargo, including my pallet of Standard ARM construction gizmos, loaded up new shit bound for Ross 128, her next destination.

Hers. Theirs. *Sky Blue Eyes.* My friend Reese.

A chapter in a book closes, a new one opens. A book comes to an end and maybe there's a sequel, maybe not. You can always find another book. Sometimes that's best.

CHAPTER SEVEN

So.

Was I in love with Reese? Was she in love with me? We never had the time to find out. Real life intervened in our story, shut down the splendid potential of that particular alternative plot line, and sent us will-nilly on our way.

I hung around the exostation dockyard for a few days, waiting out the transfers, waiting, I guess, for her to change her mind, but they buttoned up *Sky Blue Eyes,* finished with her, closed the airseal, a much better grade of hardware than you ever saw back in the vicinity of the Centauri Jet, let loose the grapples . . .

I stood watching out a cold, grimy old window, face pressed to frosty glass, breath waxing and waning like so much ephemeral fog, as the ship backed away, thrusters twinkling, a huge, near-featureless stone log at first, then smaller and smaller, turning, engulfed by darkness.

Finally, the drive modulus' exhaust lit up blue-white, washing away the dimmer stars, blue glow growing pale and ghostly before I turned away. If you live long enough, I told myself, you'll see them all again, someday. Some fine day.

I tried to picture that reunion, but could not.

Another day and a night found me bobbing in low G as I walked across the surface of an external platform, slow breeze ruffling my hair, walking toward a waiting insystem transport. We're not far from a *star* here. Why can't I pick it out of the sky?

The flat surface of the exoplatform came to an abrupt edge, dark sky beyond, sky cluttered with stars, all white, untwinkling hard points of light. All around the edge were workcraft, transports, people and things doing the business of Wolf 359. My transport—the crude paper boarding pass said Psillum Skytrails Flight 227—crouched on its tripod beside the abyss, her barrel-shaped fuselage lined with a hundred tiny windows, bracketed by two fat engines. Old-fashioned engines, I saw, thermonuclear resistojets, and those two other pods, spherical, one for, one aft, would be condensed hydrogen sponge matrices for the working fluid.

Funny how we can't stop being interested in the world's petty details, even when the rest of life has gone grainy and gray.

I got aboard and found the inside nothing but row on row of seats, most of them already taken by men and women, tired-looking men and women dressed in a variety of gray and brown uniforms, none of them interested in me. Men. Women. A soft rumble of voices. I found a window seat down near the bottom of the cabin, in what was apparently the most unpopular section.

It took another hour for the thing to fill up completely, more men and women, all the same, a few families with squirmy, whiny children. Once, a coupled dressed in flame-colored finery, flowing, silky stuff, came through the hatch and stood blocking the entrance, looking down at us, man poker-faced, woman with a look like she smelled something unusual. A crewman in teal green came through the forward hatch and led them away to somewhere else.

Finally, a big fat guy who smelled a bit like fresh Brie threw himself wheezing down beside me, grumbling under his breath. He gave me one long, suspicious look, then turned away, busying himself with the contents of a dusty tan duffel he carried in his lap.

Outside, ground crew bustled about, mostly human beings in leatherette work clothes, a big turquoise robot that seemed to handle all the refueling tasks covered with frosty condensation, shrouded in fog. The fat guy said, "You better stop looking out the window, pal."

Something pulsed hard through the structure of the ship, then blue-violet light blossomed outside, making me close my eyes and flinch away. Beside me, I heard the fat guy snicker and mutter, "Fuckhead," as gentle acceleration pushed me into the seat.

After the engines stopped firing, after I'd blinked the pale yellow shadows out of my eyes, the view outside was . . . shifting. White stars turning this way and that, exo-station swiftly growing tiny, vanishing into the nothingness. Every now and again the engines would burp, fire raging beyond my window, ullage pulse warning me just in time.

People all around me talking—I could hear seven or eight different languages. With a ship like this, it will be a voyage of no more than a few hours . . .

Looking out the window as the minutes slid by, I watched the star system of Wolf 359 grow. All of it. A star system whose ecliptic diameter, edge to edge across the orbit of its most distant "major object," was seventy million kems, hardly more than the width of Sinope's orbit around Jupiter. No planets to speak of here. Ransacking dusty school memories, I could recall something called Hardraade, an irregular ice mass some four hundred kems across.

There: Wolf 359 itself, already showing a disk through brilliant pinkish glare. Not so brilliant you couldn't look right at it for a good long while, Wolf more like a luminous world than a star, off-white light shining from the surface of the disk, a system of silver rings more glorious by far than Saturn's, platter of rings around a sun only sixty-three thousand kems in diameter, a little larger than Uranus, about half the size of Saturn.

The fat guy beside me said, "Hey. You a fuckin' tourist or something?"

I glanced over at him and shrugged. "I guess so."

"Man, you gotta be fuckin' *stupid* to come here."

I looked back out the window and saw that Wolf had grown gigantic in no time at all, our transport orbiting obliquely in toward the edge of the rings. You could make them out now as a whirlwind of orbiting masses, large, small, in between, shimmering like metallic glitter, whipped around and around by the star's mass, a little more than four percent that of the Sun.

Call it forty Jupiters, crushed into a thing so small, crushed until its fusion phoenix lit, flooding the sky with pearlescent fire.

A day, a night, another day, wandering around nearly weightless in the deep tunnels of a solid body called Holger's Heaven, hanging out at a crummy worker's hostel while I tried to find the authorities, any authorities at all, finally stumbling on a hole-in-the-wall office where a gray-bearded man with shiny yellow eyes scratched his whiskers and tried to figure out what regulation applied.

Okay, young fellow. Go ahead and . . . do whatever you want, I guess.

A few days after that, after renting an antique freeze-frame at some kind of public library deep within the rock and ice, I found a place to go, found a way to get there, and I was off.

Call them the Sunrise Mountains.

Everyone else does.

Everyone who comes to Wolf 359.

Comes and visits a place called the Sea of Green.

Cold here. Vistas like Antarctica, distant white hills, shadowy black crags knife-edge sharp under a deep, starless mauve sky, Wolf 359 huge in that sky, brilliant red-gold light making your eyes ache, making them leak tears that threaten to freeze on your cheeks.

When you stand on the edge of the world like this, bundled up against the cold, you can look back away from the sun, look down the runnel of your shadow toward darkness . . . there, beyond the mountains, the dim, twinkling stars, feeble, barely able to force their way through the cold mist.

Or you can look the other way, down across the Sea of Green itself, toward this little body's substellar point, where the meltwater comes to a boil, column of water vapor rising up into an almost-transparent mushroom cloud that does nothing to hide a too-big, too-bright, too-close star.

Something *skritch*ed near my feet, seemed to duck away when I looked. There, over by that little black rock, bit of meteoritic flotsam undamaged by its slow fall through Green's epeiric atmosphere, something. I knelt, feeling cold through the kneepads of my rented hotsuit, pulled the rock gently out of the way . . . It was a little pink thing, like a bit of molten putty, cowering in the snow, seeming to shiver.

I reached out, thinking to pick it up, cradle it in my gloved hands, maybe warm it some to stop that unseemly shiver . . . stopped myself just in time as the stuff shrank from my touch, starting to flow slowly away.

It stopped when I did, seeming to wait. A little pseudopod grew from the upper surface, paused for a second, then blinked open a tiny green eye, faceted, like a flake of emerald fresh from the jeweler's wheel.

I said, "Hi, there." Nothing. Little green eye staring at me, motionless. After a while, a second pseudopod grew, off to one side, blinked open a blue sapphire eye that stretched away, bobbing and weaving.

I started to reach out again, not intending to touch it, knowing its fragile substance would splash and burn if I did, but the thing flattened abruptly, seemed to sink into the snow, and was gone, not even a stain left behind.

Not even a fare-thee-well.

I straightened up and started to walk, UVless rays from Wolf 359 without substance on my face, walking down a long, icy hill toward the sea. Wet ice here. Careful not to slip. Harmless in the low G that makes you bob and sway like this, but still . . .

When I accidentally stepped on a little green crust, it popped and snapped like frying bacon, smoking and curling as it burned away to black flakes. Sorry. Whoever you were.

I remember reading once how surprised the first expedition to Wolf was when they found life here, the most complex life found anywhere up to that time. No planets? How could you have life around a dim little M8e like that, a cold red star whose only activity was an occasional deadly burp of starfire, prominences licking up in periodic fury every time the magnetic field lines reversed.

And yet, over the long, long eons . . . well, the inner ring system, you see, lies within Wolf 359's ecosphere, a million whirling little worlds made of wet ice and carbonaceous chondrules.

Down by the edge of the steaming sea, the air actually begins to seem warm, water vapor swirling about in little puffs, like ragged, miniature clouds, wreathing suddenly about your head, appearing and disappearing like magic.

By the time I got close, could hear the sharp slopping sounds of little wavelets bouncing off the ice shelf, I was walking ankle deep in what I imagined was freezing water, glad for my nice waterproof rental boots. Up ahead was a broad crescent of something that looked like shiny black mud, parked on it a lozenge-shaped vehicle finished in bright red enamel, forward end bracketed with windows, interior dark.

A flitter, perhaps, fancier model than the one we'd had back home.

The sudden surge of remembering myself in Audumla came like a tiny electric shock, quickly suppressed.

The black stuff was indeed mud, sticking to my boots like soft shit, every footfall liberating a puff of ripe organic stench, making me remember an unpleasant night when I'd helped my father repair the failing digestive system of a decrepit CHON processor, poor old thing living all by itself, trapped in a clearing of its own design, deep in the feral forests of Audumla.

Nobody in the car. A trail of footprints, full of muddy water now, like a chain of little lakes, making a trail to the sea. I followed them down to the water and, shading my eyes from Wolflight, scanned the choppy green surface.

There. A few hundred ems out, a little black dot, the head of a swimmer. Every now and again, you could see the flail of an arm as it rose above the surface.

I remembered a thousand old dramas, stories of people deciding to end it all by swimming out to sea until they drowned. Every now and again, one of those would provoke a suicide in Audumla, where we had lakes if not seas.

I remembered a girl from school who pulled that one, was dead for hours before someone missed her and went looking for the carcass, was in the hospital for weeks afterward, because some scavenger'd eaten away part of her guts.

No one said much about it after she came back to school; she still had few friends, fewer still after that. Watching the swimmer, I wondered briefly if I should make an effort to . . . what, swim on out after this one now? I pictured myself drowning in an icy Sea of Green and wondered what the medical facilities were like here.

The black dot began moving closer to the muddy beach, leaving a little white vee behind it in the water. I guess this gravity would facilitate swimming, and, as it got closer, I could see the shape of a human form, outlined in pale flesh and green shadow, stretched out, more or less on the surface of the water.

Finally, close to shore, she stood, the two of us looking at one another, and I marveled that Uncreated Time would bring me all the way to Wolf 359, only to be confronted by yet another naked woman, when all I really wanted, here and now, was to find a wilderness in which to be alone.

"Who the hell are you?" she said, standard English, in a voice hard with the habits of command, harder than any voice I remember Violet using. Harder even than my mother's voice.

She was a bizarre sight, even after all I'd gotten used to, pasty white skin netted with blue veins, splotched with pink here and there, skin covering up a banding of stark musculature, long, ropy black hair hanging about her shoulders, runneling icewater. Flat face, almost featureless but for the pale blue eyes of a fantasy ghost.

"Speak up, boy!" She put her hands on her hips, showing big tufts of black axial hair, matching a bigger swatch spread at the base of her belly. When she walked out of the water, squelching up into the sticky mud, I saw she had broad, spatulate feet ending in stubby little toes, the feet of a human bred for high G.

I'd never studied adaptive physiology, but guessed her features added up to somewhere between nine and ten ems per square second.

I held out my hand and said, "Hello. My name's, um, Murph."

A flash of anger in her pale blue eyes, eyes looking at my hand like I was offering her a fistful of mud. "So? What the fuck're you doing *here*?"

I'd not given much thought to the social structure of Wolf 359, but was beginning to guess a few details. So: "I'm a, uh, tourist. From near the Centauri Jet."

Anger fading suddenly, replaced by interest. She scratched herself under one heavy breast and said, "Traveling in style?"

I shook my head, then, seeing my body language meant little to her, said, "Company deadhead. Standard ARM."

She shrugged. "We don't get many of either out here."

I remembered the smelly fat guy on the transport.

She turned away, facing back out to sea, arching her back, taking a deep breath of dank, shit-scented air, startling me with the way the muscles shifted and flexed under the skin of her back. She said, "You swim?"

I pictured myself in the green sea, bumping up against little ice floes. "Well. I, um . . . I guess I'm not used to the weather here."

She looked back at me, face crinkled with amusement. "Idiot. Wade out a little and feel the water with your hand."

I sloshed out until it was up to midcalf, thankful for the waterproof suit, bent down and ... Hmh. Warm as a tub.

She said, "Water's boiling a few hundred meters out, you know. It stays warm on the surface because fresh meltwater sinks to the bottom and flows out under the substell."

Which made perfect sense, now that I thought about it.

She grinned, fingering red nipples puckered into stiff little raspberries, and said, "Warmer than the fuckin' air, anyway!" Held out her hand to me and said, "My name's Porphyry. Porphyry Campobello, of Melina's Nest."

Her hand, when I took it, was hard and strong.

We swam for a while in the bath-warm waters of the Sea of Green, then Porphyry led me, shivering and naked, to her flitter, pulling me inside, dripping icewater, reeking of metallic salts, to sit on the car's furry upholstery, throwing my hotsuit in the back with her own.

"There now," she said, "let's get some heat cranked up and ..." Something in the flitter controlbox must have been listening, for little lights came on and dry, warm air started blowing around my ankles. After a while, I stopped shivering.

"Well, let's get the hell out of here." I felt a soft vibration start up somewhere in the car, then she put her hands on the steering pads and we lifted off.

For some reason it didn't surprise me when the thing turned out to be a little more than just a flitter, angling sharply upward across the Sea of Green, cutting straight through the vapor jet, craft shuddering softly as it punched through turbulence, mauve sky turning deep purple, then black, spackled with a few bright stars, the rest of it washed away by Wolf's bright light.

Below us, stretching away in all directions, the ring plane was like an ocean of molten metal, Sea of Green hanging suspended above it like a flattened eyeball, quickly growing smaller.

"Where're we going?"

She looked over at me and said, "Home. You *do* want to come with me, don't you?"

Home. Just a word.

I said, "Sure."

Soon, there came a moment when I was lying beside Porphyry in her huge, magically soft bed, bed made from aerogel and silk and who knows what, deep in the folds of Melina's Nest. Waiting, I guess, for her to say something.

This is that terribly familiar time, when the squirmy getting-to-know-you preliminaries are over with, when the heart-pounding excitement of new-partner sex has come and gone, when you wait to see just whose depths you've plumbed.

Easy preliminaries, sturdy Porphyry in command of her emotions and body, doing something so obviously a familiar part of her life. Good sex, after a quick, muscular fashion, Porphyry greasily lubricious, targeting her pleasure like some gamepark quarry.

And plenty of adaptive skill in there so I could find what I wanted, as well.

Now she stretched, making a sound that was almost a purr, arching her back, nuzzling silk pillowslips full of spongy gel, then curled on one side, looking at me, face set in something that was not quite a smile. Should I say something? No. This is just a moment in time. Tomorrow you'll be somewhere else.

She edged closer, reached out one hard, blunt-fingered

hand, ran it across the damp surface of my chest, down onto my belly, ran her fingers through wet-matted pubic hair, curled them round the flaccid, shrunken mass of my prick.

Somewhere inside, I felt a pang of renewed desire, as though from a ghost not part of me at all. And with it, a desire to be elsewhere. Something about this woman. Something very different from Reese . . . and I thought of Violet.

Porphyry said, "You look so funny, so . . . I don't know." She was massaging me now, blood-sponge tissues struggling to reengorge. "Sort of . . . halfway between a contract worker, a bondservant, and . . . one of us."

Plenty of people bustling about Melina's Nest, doing things, busy, busy. People, real people, men and women, but behaving, maybe, just a bit like my mother's silvergirls.

She snickered at my renewed erection. "A real man wouldn't want this. He'd get up and leave, go do something . . . manly."

I didn't have the slightest idea what she was talking about.

She said, "Damn. Look at those little round feet of yours. Long toes. Long, skinny arms. You look like a fucking chimpanzee."

I sorted through remembered images of various extinct apes, trying to remember which ones had been chimpanzees. The middle-sized ones, I thought, not the big gray critters or the funny-looking redheads.

She said, "You're not a runaway optimod, are you?"

Stupid. There must not be very many optimods out here or she'd know the difference. I said, "Racial adaptation. This is what we look like around Centauri Jet, these days."

She grinned, then rolled away, sprawling onto her back, flexing her knees so they pointed in opposite directions, feet pressed together, cocking her pelvis back so her vulva opened like a black petaled flower. "Come on, Superman," she said. "Let's get that big old thing inside me some more. Let's see what you can do."

Orb knows what a man can do. He doesn't tell us what women really want, realizing we don't need to know.

For a moment, I remembered the things Dûmnahn had tried to tell me, once upon a time, time that seemed long ago now.

I climbed in her saddle as directed, wondering at the cultural referent in her remark. Superman? English term translated from a keyword, *übermensch,* in some centuries-old racialistic doctrine. To what master race does she think I belong?

Certainly not hers.

Afterward, she led me to a shower stall the size of any decent human's bedroom, larger than whole apartments you see in the slumcrawl dramas of the DataWarren, washed me with her own hands, dried me off with impossibly soft, ridiculously fluffy white towels.

Hard to know what to think, standing there with this bizarre woman kneeling on the wet tile before me, nuzzling my genitals with her face.

She grinned up at me and said, "Kind of fun, doing it without servants or anything . . ."

I couldn't even guess. Somewhere on some datatrack or another, I could have found stories about this world and all its people, but I never had. In the volume of space inhabited by humans, a couple of dozen cubic parsecs, there are a handful of stars, a few hundred planets . . . millions of comets, hundreds of millions of planetoids, billions of lesser bodies, trillions of people in uncounted habitats.

She led me, still naked, out of the bedroom, whose door

we'd never closed, out into the byways of Melina's Nest, where men and women bustled about, part of the background, not quite invisible.

Not quite.

The sun deck, when she led me through broad, folding glass doors, was so improbable as to be unexpected, a wide expanse of lacquered red wood, a rough-hewn railing; beyond, a sheer drop, hundreds of ems to crashing surf below, sparkling blue ocean under a wide blue sky, striated by just a hint of wispy white cloud.

Porphyry said, "You like?"

I nodded.

She said, "It's California. My grandparents used to live here!"

Here on this deck or . . . California? Now, where . . . I tipped my head back, staring up at that tiny, absurdly bright white sun until my eyes started to ache and tear, feeling a flood of hard UV prickling on my skin. In a little while, long-unused melanin pumps would start to work, and soon I'd be tan.

When I glanced at Porphyry, I could see she'd already started to darken, skin equipped with much newer, much more expensive pumps than my own.

Over on the far horizon, far out to sea, there was something, some kind of surface vessel, with a low, dark body and great white wings, heeling over before the wind. Ships. They called them ships. In the sea off the coast of California. California. America. Earth.

You have to be rich indeed to live on Earth, whose general population was forcibly evacuated to Piazzi, Kuiper, and Oort more than eight hundred years ago.

"Why'd they leave?"

Sprawling in a soft chaise longue, Porphyry said, "Taxes."

I sat down gingerly in another chair, across a little wooden table from her, carefully leaning back until it caught me in its embrace, looking at her body anew. Realizing how it'd gotten like that, why it was so different from my own.

Chimpanzee? I felt a little fuse of anger light, sputter, and go out again.

She said, "They went back after a while and took my parents with them. No taste for frontier life, I guess."

Now a couple of servants came out, a slim blond girl and a slim blond man, each dressed in a short white linen robe, barefoot, each bearing a loaded silver tray. They knelt, beginning to put out what I supposed was breakfast food, uncovering hot dishes that wafted steam, liberating strong smells. Coffee I recognized. Glasses of thick red juice. A selection of raw vegetables with little bowls of varicolored dip. A plate that smelled of cooked meat. Little link sausages. Flat strips that seemed to consist mostly of wrinkled, burnt fat.

Odor a little bit like what you smell when a careless technician burns off his fingers in an electrical accident.

Finished with their task, the man and woman stood back, waiting, eyes downcast, side by side.

Porphyry leaned forward, breasts dangling so that her nipples brushed across the surface of the table, picked up one of the strips of burnt fat, bit, chewed, smacking her lips as she crunched. "Ah, the bacon is *excellent*, Sheelah."

Bacon. I remembered the stuff we called bacon in Audumla, thick strips of rich red meat sizzling and popping in the fryer. Odd. The woman, Sheelah, dipped in a curtsy that made her robe ride up, almost to the top of her thighs.

Porphyry's eyes were on me, amused. "You like Sheelah, do you, Murph?"

Embarrassed, I shrugged and said, "Well. Things are . . . very different here."

She said, "What d'*you* think of my new toy, Sheelah?"

The woman raised her eyes to my face, staring, expressionless. "Very nice, ma'am." The man beside her, still nameless, continued to look at the wooden surface of the deck.

"Pull up your skirt, Sheelah. Show Murph what you've got."

She turned, handed the tray to the man, who clasped it to his own, posed just so, and lifted the hem of her robe, one leg extended forward and to the side. Light blond pubic hair, hardly there at all. Pink-skinned vulva, small and flat, lips parted to show a hint of structure.

"Very nice." She glanced at me. "Isn't that so, Murph?"

I nodded, wondering if there was any way I could just get up and run away. Not bloody likely. You're down the rabbit hole now, Mr. Murphy.

Porphyry said, "Let's see you get wet for him now, Sheelah."

To my astonishment, beads of clear moisture started to form back where I knew the introitus of her vagina must lie hidden. Beads that grew, collected into larger droplets, started, one by one, to run down the insides of her thighs, leaving shiny trails behind.

She said, "Ah, operant conditioning's a many-splendored thing . . ."

I looked at Porphyry, aghast.

She laughed, reaching over to ruffle my hair. "God, it's so much *fun* having you here, Murph! You're a babe in the fucking woods!"

*   *   *

A woman's laughter can charm a man out of his senses. And Porphyry's laughter seemed, I don't know, keyed to my moods, perhaps, lifting me out of those moods like some kind of psychiatric drug, as if she could sense the depths of my despair and knew just what to do. Add to that the fact that Melina's Nest, whoever Melina may have been, was a playland of considerable sophistication, also just right to counter what ailed me.

Perhaps I came to the worlds of this dim sun hoping for ice and darkness, hoping for soul-numbing cold to match how I felt, had felt for so long.

What I found in Porphyry's artificial paradise was a landscape of sunshine and splendor, blue skies, skies without clouds other than those decorative few, high and white against a manhome-friendly sun, a land of mountains, mountain streams, fields of green grass dotted with myriad gay flowers, drifting honeybees, butterflies, colorful songbirds, beaches by a sea warm enough to welcome, cool enough to refresh . . .

And all of it peopled by lovely folk with downcast eyes whose only purpose was to please, real human beings, as human as me, more human than many I'd called friend, all trained to serve and only serve, as if without needs of their own, as if . . .

Maybe I would have abused them cruelly, flying from whim to selfish whim, again I don't know. Porphyry never afforded me the opportunity, monopolizing my time, intercepting my desire. I made love to her by the sea, in sundappled forest glades, in her bed of aerogel foam, in public streets walked only by her servants, in the dining room, rolling about on our dinner.

Time passes, as they say, and now it passed in a haze of requited want.

One day, she dressed me up in a fine brocade robe studded with jewels she swore were real, rubies and emeralds, diamonds and sapphires, bundled me into her spacegoing flitter and took me to a place called Norman's Hole. A party, she said. We're going to a party.

And so, in a ballroom thronged with people, flat-footed men and women dressed in extravagant costumes, vast room a riot of color, threaded through with white-robed servants, people with downcast eyes who did as they were bid, carrying trays of viands, trays of drinks, lighting smokes for master and mistress and . . .

I'd already been introduced to dozens, so many people I'd forgotten their names already, flat feet rendered all the same by their overblown garb, when Porphyry, towing me by the hand, called out, "Ah, *there* you are!"

A tall, round man, artificial sunlight glinting from a bald head so polished I suspected furniture wax, whose broad back hid people clustered beyond him, turned and held his arms out. "Porphyry! Where the fuck've you *been*? We were starting without you!"

I wondered how the hell they'd gotten his teeth like that, teeth like irregular bits of rock crystal—implants, perhaps, but looking razor-edged, making me think about the safety of his tongue.

Porphyry said, "Silly Gorgo! What good is it without the pièce de résistance?"

Gorgo smirked and said, "Well. *You* know."

She sighed. "I guess so. I sure know how stupid *you* can be, dear Gorgo. Come on, let's see what we've got here."

He moved and Porphyry pushed through a mixed group of flat-footed men and women, some of them dressed in their nonsensical finery, others prancing around buck naked, as if they'd been up to Orb knows what. Me? Dazed, just the way I'd been for days and days. Then Porphyry said, "Ah. Sheelah. They *have* got you started, haven't they?"

They had her on a thigh-high table, flat on her back and naked, the same serving girl who'd made herself wet for me on command, slid to just the right position, buttocks even with the table's edge, legs held apart by two other servants, a man and a woman still in their white robes, eyes downcast, holding her legs as far apart, I imagined, as they could go without breaking.

I imagined the crackle-pop of breaking gristle.

Sheelah's eyes were open but slitted, glassy with something I imagined must be pain, lips set in a flat line. Thin, watery blood was seeping from her vulva, trickling down across her buttocks, and it was spattered on the floor below her, soaking into the fine white carpet.

I felt my daze lift, haze carried away by horror, and looked up from Sheelah's battered crotch, looking around at Porphyry's grinning, expectant friends. Opened my mouth to speak . . .

Pop.

A prickle of pain in the back of my right shoulder, a spreading numbness, tingling down my right arm, diffusing through my back, emerging in my chest, descending swiftly across my belly. There was a sharp, bitter smell in my nose, odor making me think of the color purple, then just a hint of some odd taste on the back of my tongue.

And there I stood, mouth hanging open, looking at people who smiled and waited.

There was something I wanted to do here. Something I wanted to say. What was it?

I can hardly seem to catch my breath.

Something happening down below. Bizarre, faraway sensation of heaviness at the bottom of my belly, erection flexing upward, lifting the weight of my brocade robe.

Porphyry's voice, sweet with amusement, said, "Well, turn around, Mr. Murphy."

My feet made all the movements necessary for me to turn, slowly, swaying just a bit, until I was facing her, looking down at her, seeing her smile. She was holding up a military-grade injector, waving it in my face like a glassy finger.

"So. What d'you think, boy?"

My mouth opened, tongue flexing articulately, and it said, "I think you gave me a drug."

She grinned. "Smart boy!" Then she held the injector up, close to her face, squinting at the little words I knew these autoampules always had printed on the barrel. There'd be some milspec stuff, then . . . she read, "ParteeTyme Brand Yohimbine-Rohypnol Injection."

Gorgo's voice said, "Ah, what *would* we do without it?" I felt his hands on my shoulders, pulling gently as Porphyry tossed the injector aside and started undoing my fasteners. The robe slid to the floor suddenly, as if I were a statue being unveiled.

"My, my. Look at that!" A woman's voice, which went on, "Give him another shot. Let's see how big it *can* get!"

Porphyry, frowning, looked up into my eyes. "No. I think he's just right."

Someone said, "Come on! Let's get saddled up! This'll be *cool*!"

They turned me around, got me lined up with Sheelah, still laid out on her table, got my prick aimed, and pushed me forward, so I slid right in. The pain in Sheelah's eyes seemed to deepen, but I thought I saw forgiveness there as well. Knowledge. Resignation. I saw she was biting her lip now, denting it deeply with strong white teeth.

Porphyry said, "Okay. Start fucking her, Murph."

My hips started to pulse. In. Out. In again.

Orb, this feels good, Sheelah strongly ridged inside, a sign of deep arousal and . . . Something still alive within me remembered my own startling erection, come from nowhere at all.

Porphyry said, "Longer strokes, Murph. And slower."

That other woman said, "Yeah! And lean a little, so we can *see* better!"

Like this? Am I doing it right, my friends?

Porphyry: "Okay, who's first?"

Silence, save for the soft liquid sounds my prick was making as it slipped in and out of Sheelah's bleeding cunt. Then Gorgo said, "Well, it was *my* idea . . ."

"Be my guest."

I thought, for just a second, that it was my voice that'd spoken.

Then I felt his hands on my shoulders again, felt that big belly billowing against my back.

He felt like a medical probe going in, erratic at first, then matching his thrust to mine. When he was done, another man took his place. After a while, a quiet voice, hardly my voice at all, something far down beyond the reach of the drug, began to pray, first to Orb, then to the larger vessel of Uncreated Time, humbly asking only that I be permitted to survive.

CHAPTER EIGHT

Sirius is far away.

I remember that song, with its eerie, echoed chorus, from some datatrack I loved as a child. Something about an athletic contest, about honor and decency, about first contact with some fanciful extraterrestrial intelligence.

We've journeyed to the Milky Way.

I can't remember any more.

Now, from the forward obdeck of the little tramp starship *Sign of the Labrys,* Sirius A was a white hole in the sky, fantastically bright even from a hundred AUs out. Two-point-three Solar masses, one-point-eight Solar radii. Twenty-three times Solar luminosity. Meaningless numbers, given definition by this thing that erased all the stars from half the sky.

All but the tiny fleck of Sirius B over there, climbing steeply toward aphelion, a glimmer of hard white light in the washed-out black sky. Just shy of one Solar mass. Just over thirty-five thousand kems in diameter. No more than half the size of Wolf 359.

And yet, five hundred times as bright.

I couldn't remember how I came aboard this little ship, cobbled together from leftovers of larger, older ships, cavernous holds, yes, but only that, not entire worlds in darkness. I couldn't remember for the longest time, though Captain Lee told me, more than once, how she found me lying naked, frozen, still breathing, by the muddy shores of the Sea of Green, not far from the foothills of the Sunrise Mountains.

Can't remember how I got there. Why'd they let me go? Common decency? Some legalism I never heard of?

I never knew who they were.

Never knew who they thought they were, what they stood for, by their own lights.

All a dream?

I thought so.

Wished it so.

I still don't know what made her bring me back to her ship, with its crew of women in gray.

But I remember her telling me, amused now that all this time has gone by, how she and her crewwomen argued about bringing me aboard, about what was the right thing to do.

The innocent are innocent, she told me. An innocent man is just as innocent as an innocent woman.

I remember trying to tell her about my lack of innocence. Remember her laughter.

And, of course, she told me how their own innocence came to be called into question, how they almost decided to put me ashore, alone, bewildered, lost, at their next port of call, a little almost-deserted refueling depot on the long line between Wolf 359 and Sirius.

Some of us, Captain Lee said grimly, were not so committed to their vows as they thought.

And then she'd laughed again.

Not your fault, bright angel, she'd said. Not your fault at all.

Alone among the stars with each other, all we had to control was our desire *for* each other. In port, all we had to control were those little spasms of desire, soon over, for anything else we . . . wanted.

Keeping you with us . . .

A long, sorrowing frown.

Some wanted to . . . sin with you. Others, imagining themselves pure, merely wanted . . . someone to care for.

Maybe that's a sin too.

In time, I understood. A man wants a submissive woman, granting joy only he can know. A woman wants a submissive child, granting joy only she can know. Where's the sin there?

Ask those who submit.

In those days, donning *Labrys* gray, working among the crewwomen as though I were one of them, I thought often of my father. Time passed, starship stopping at one place and then another, habitat worlds hanging between the stars, as varied as anything the old fabulists dreamed. We'd stay for a day or a week, sometimes more, doing what was needed to support the ship.

I'd go ashore, sometimes with crewwomen, sometimes alone, an anomaly either way. In time, memory coalesced, and with it forgetfulness. I found myself accepting whatever submissions were offered, unthinking, unafraid, and so found myself growing away from the refuge that'd found me.

Until, one day, in the stellar deep off Sirius, I watched the infrastar Wernickë grow in our sky, a flattened, ruddy ball so very much like Ygg, just now making a slow hyperbolic pass through the outer reaches of Sirius A's ecosphere, her moons fuzzy white balls shrouded in water vapor, out-gassing wealth.

Captain Lee watched with me, admiring the way the blue light of our modulus exhaust reflected, flickering, off the clouds of one nearby moon, Suzdal Habitat a gleaming scin-tilla of green and gold, orbiting nearby.

She said, "Another century and all this will be gone, back out into the cold and dark again."

Silence, while we turned about the moon's center of mass, while our ship bore down on the mottled sheen of Suzdal.

She said, "I wish you'd reconsider, Murph. There's so much trouble here. Rebellion. Change. The Mobilitzyn fleets are well on their way, coming to reclaim what's theirs."

I remembered the Glow-Ice Worlds, not quite against my will.

She sighed. "We'll miss you."

I looked at her and smiled. "No, you won't. You'll be glad to get rid of me at last." And I must go, if I'm . . . ever to be myself again. You know that, for I've told you so.

She looked hurt for a moment, but then grinned herself, shook her head ruefully. "We'll be lucky if some of the crew don't get off with you. Poor Nettie."

Childless mothers. A loveless yearning for home and hearth, husband and family. I don't know whether it's true, this genetic determinant, or just the trap they wove for them-selves when they invented a celibate sisterhood that would go roving the stars.

And I suppose it doesn't matter.

Time changes everything.

And nothing.

*　　*　　*

Suzdal was a beautiful world, as different from the others as they'd been from each other. People living on the outside, beneath the sheltering wings of a eutropic shield, on the model of Telemachus Major, rather than within a scooped-out shell, as in Audumla, a warren of tunnels like . . . Well. No sense remembering that one.

Call it a little bit of Telemachus Major. Telemachus Major without the unending cityscape.

Sitting in a little rooftop café, sipping sweet red Altopashtûn coffee, rented freeze-frame on the table before me, I could look out over the red-tile rooftops of a little village called Sereniál, out over the sharp curve of Suzdal's horizon, nearer trees already leaning away, rolling, grassy hills, dotted with grazing cattle, oddly twisted, sense of perspective failing. Half a nearby forest was sunk below the horizon like a fleet of faraway ships . . .

Faint, ancient, grainy fear. Those images, images of a terrestrial sea. The diorama sea I admired from Porphyry's sun deck.

. . . only the crowns of the forest giants were visible, and only the nearest of those.

In the distance, against the cloudless backdrop of a cornflower sky, the flat vee-shape of a buzzard circled. Familiar. We had them in Audumla, didn't we?

The attempt to remember made a faint, barely perceptible constriction of fear, deep in my chest, back by my spine.

Beyond the sky, eerily, I could see the half-faded crescent of reddish brown Wernickë, and, there, the sparkle of Sirius B. No sense looking at A, blinding even through the shield. I suppose, if I looked away, down by the far horizon, I might even make out a few bright stars.

When I looked, I was startled to see the tiny shape of a starship, *Sign of the Labrys* rising in her orbit, which I knew was, technically, west to east. Just now, Captain Lee will be on her bridge, making sure Goddess is in her heaven and all's right with the machinery. And, down in the engineering spaces, Nettie will be looking at the post I made my own, occupied by one of her sisters just now.

I looked away, down into the freeze-frame.

Well. Here are my accounts, transferred from *Labrys'* node, just as they were when Captain Lee uploaded them from the master datatrack at Wolf 359. Sometimes I wonder why Porphyry troubled herself to put money against my name.

Hell, maybe that made it a business deal, rather than a crime. Only Orb knows, and he's not telling.

Material at the Sirius node belied the peaceful world around me, waiters quietly bringing me what I asked for, all too human men and women passing quietly about their business in the bucolic streets of Sereniál.

There. The data placard of the Wernickan People's Independence Party. Tall, dark, handsome man explaining the reasons he and his comrades had for separating themselves from the service of Mobilitzyn Associates, world, habitats, and all.

Some nonsense about lives, fortunes, and sacred honor.

When I looked up, away from the depths of the freeze-frame, *Labrys* was halfway up the vault of the sky, thrusters twinkling now, turning the mass of the ship, positioning her just so. I wonder if Captain Lee is looking down on Suzdal, thinking of me.

Probably not. Too busy with her job.

Back in the freeze-frame, I called up fresh news from the heartland of humanity, news only a few years old, the business of *plus ça change*. Something called the Historical Humanity Movement big in the Solar Oort right now. Standard

ARM advertising its big new mining venture out by the twin red suns of Krüger 60, ten million corporate colonist positions opening today, come one, come all. Bring your skills. Pay is great. Opportunities boundless.

Down in the Centauri Jet there'd been some kind of political trouble, a mass movement sweeping the democratic habitats, just now deep in the grip of icy economic failure. Something called the Ultima Thule Society had induced a few of the more important habitats to band together—the Progressive Union, they called it—and begin regulating the interhabitat activities of the smaller corporations.

Smaller. I like that. Pick on someone your own size, hm?

But the big sharks take notice after all.

The government of the Progressive Union had been overthrown, *status quo ante* soon restored, then the officers of Ultima Thule had been arrested and put on trial for crimes. That's all the datatrack said. Officers put on trial, rank and file dispersed.

I found myself looking at the proud face of Mr. Finn mac Eye, executive director of the Ultima Thule Society, as they led him away to prison. There in the background, head cast down, his associate Mr. Sonn-Atem.

What do I . . . yes: Freedom, from any organization that does not reflect the popular will.

Turned out, I guess, to be unpopular after all.

Sidebar: mac Eye in suspensor imprisonment, cold as ice for an unspecified time, Sonn-Atem and his lovely wife Karinn escaped, fleeing to the safety of her father's extraplanetary estate, an independent habitat deep in the Alpha Centauri B system.

Interesting. But no more than that.

And no news from Audumla, of course.

The landscape around me was suddenly flooded with pale

blue light, and when I looked up, *Sign of the Labrys* was firing her engines, modulus exhaust flaring like the corona of a variable star, leaving me here, all alone, shrinking away to nothing in no time at all.

I went back to the data placard of the People's Independence Party. Listened to the dark man's speech again. After a while, I dialed up their contact point and told them who I was, told them what I knew.

I am, you see, a man who knows spaceships, knows weapons, knows all about war. That's not stretching the truth too far, is it? I had been, after all, at the Glow-Ice Worlds . . .

Maybe I just wanted somebody to admire me, want me, for something . . . practical.

Just this once.

You know?

When I saw Jade Qasawhár for the first time, I felt a certain atavistic dread, a certain "here we go again" crawling at the bottom of my belly.

I was standing in the big conference room at WePIP headquarters, the big, glassed-in room atop the old Civitan center that was the major landmark of downtown Clydesbûrh, talking things over with operations director McNelly Broadbent beside the brand-new 3vrD tank that turned up among the Mobilitzyn property they'd confiscated during the Wernickë takeover. It was a beautiful thing, a little tripod the size of a hibachi you could stick on any handy desktop or even drop on the floor, snap your fingers, and the universe would blossom, expanding like a spreading flower of magic indigo paint 'til you raised your hand whoa.

We were discussing the job I'd taken on, and Mac was pointing out various obscure features of the Sirian system, including the places around the Pup, white dwarf Sirius B, where gravitational resonances made "phantom planets" a smart pilot could use to his advantage.

I said, "Be a damn good thing if whoever they send our way doesn't think of this."

He looked at me, flat-faced, tired-eyed. "You think we should count on that?"

"No."

I'd given them all the advice I could, remembering more than I expected from the Glow-Ice Rebellion. At the time, all I thought of was the excitement of youth, combat, and Violet's odd, exciting body, of my sense of friendship with Dûmnahn and the others, but . . . Something, somewhere inside, took note of what was going on, the tactical mistakes made on both sides, and of how the smarter side, *our* side, had exploited the mistakes of the other.

Had they not been clueless, the Glow-Ice Worlders might have fought clear of Standard ARM, might have beaten the rental warriors of SOCO. Maybe just the way the Continental Army fought off the British Empire, what? Twelve hundred years ago? Something like that.

I rubbed my chin, staring at the moving lights inside the vr stereo, and said, "Mobilitzyn's a much smaller company than Standard. Maybe . . ."

Maybe a lot of things. And the job *I'd* taken on, arming and training a little fleet of warcraft WePIP had made up from insystem freighters and whatnot, mining craft, and a small interstellar vessel they were pleased to call their *battleship* . . .

The door dilated and she came through, walking through my peripheral vision, passing behind my back, just as I wondered, for the thousandth time, if I was really up to the job.

What if you fail them, Murph? What if there's someone else hanging around who'd've taken the job and done it well if only you hadn't come here with all your silly tales of combat experience among the Glow-Ice Worlds?

Fucking ambulance mechanic.

I turned because of the red dress she had on, and because of the scent of jasmine that suddenly filled the room, overpowering even Broadbent's excessive wintergreen cologne. I'd gotten used to the Wernickan's perfume habits quickly, but the constant interplay of scents was a distraction.

So I turned, and caught her best possible view, standing before the sideboard coffee service, smooth, long back in clingy red dress, sweeping from broad shoulders shrouded in silky black hair down to a breadth of hip that perfectly matched her form, not too much, not too little. And heels. The women here wear those peculiar high-heeled shoes that make them stand just the least bit swayback, making an outthrust of hip and bosom that . . .

I heard Broadbent snicker, then he murmured, "Some things never change, eh, Murph?"

I guess not.

Jade looked over her shoulder, showing a delicate profile, somewhere midway between a flat-faced Old Earth Caucasian and some generalized more modern type, smiling. She said, "Hi, Mac." Finished making her coffee and turned to walk toward us.

Gravity here, like that on Telemachus Major, is maintained by a generator. Somewhere around a half-standard G. Remarkable that she could walk in those shoes at all, much less be so alluringly graceful. I kept expecting her to teeter, stumble and fall. Instead . . .

She came to stand beside us, sipping delicately from her demitasse of *mit schlag,* little pink tonguetip retrieving a dab of white cream from upper lip as she looked thoughtfully into the 3vrD display, then, finally, up at Mac, up at me.

Broadbent said, "Jade, this is Darius Murphy. I told you about him last night." She held out a small, slim-fingered hand, hand surprisingly warm, making me wonder if my own had turned suddenly cold. "Jade Qasawhár was a mining engineer for Mobilityzn, Murph. She heads the team that's building the fighters you and your group will fly."

And she had jade-green eyes.

Looking at me . . . that way.

I realized with a start that, finally, I had no urge to run and hide.

That famous bit about time healing all wounds.

What, you didn't believe it?

When you're down and out, seems like that can only go on forever.

Sunshine's for other people.

People not so stupid and useless as you.

In the end, Jade and I had little time for one another, though we worked together every day of the frantic weeks that went by, getting ready for the Mobilitzyn fleet we knew must soon arrive. She proved to be a superb engineer, with a knowledge base deeper than anything I'd ever pretended to, solving problems with a quick decisiveness that sometimes took my breath away.

And, for my part, it turned out that I knew more about military matters than I'd thought, taking my team of battle-craft aloft day after day, learning to deal with all the peculiarities of the Sirius System. Guerrilla warfare, I thought, attacking from ambush in the sky.

Watch for the Hun in the Sun, all that rot.

Surprising how many important memories we carry, deep implants from this drama and that, every bit as important, every bit as real as anything that ever actually happened.

Then came a lull, ships honed and armed, fliers and fighters trained to a pitch of perfection, and still the fleet didn't come. Out there somewhere, monitoring the datatracks, waiting for just the right moment. I tried to help them with that, too, knowing Mobilitzyn would have to be bringing its ships in from a cluster of infrastars about five thousand astronomical units away, off in the direction of Procyon.

Nothing. Not a peep. Corporate security perfect.

One night, Jade invited me to have dinner at her apartment, just the two of us, and, as I got dressed to go, I felt a sharp tingle of "this is it" excitement. I could picture the way it would go, from a thousand scripts run over and over again back when I was in school, back when I was an innocent boy caught among Audumla's women.

She'd invite me in. We'd have drinks, give each other intriguing looks. There'd be witty chitchat, then dinner. Candlelight, maybe? They seemed to go in for things like that, hereabouts.

So the room would be half in darkness, making our pupils grow large, accentuating the interest we would, I dare say, really be feeling, eyes highlit by reflections of candle flame. We'd drink our wine and eat whatever she'd made, food and alcohol lulling us, making us feel comfortable and relaxed.

Seduction's so easy when its target has the same object in mind.

Maybe we'd go out on her balcony and stand side by side, looking up at the nighttime stars, Sirius A's corona brightening the western sky in Suzdal's long green sunset, red Wernickë hanging in the heavens like a romantic half-moon.

We'd touch by accident, more than once, would look at each other. Maybe Jade would look away, face slightly flushed, half-reticent, half-aroused. If she was well versed in these matters, she'd turn toward me, would lean forward, putting her head almost on my shoulder, then turn her face up to be kissed.

And that was, almost, the way it turned out. We were on the balcony, kissing under the stars, and I could feel the firmness of her rubbing gently against me, letting me know, in no uncertain terms, that there'd be no girlish reluctance tonight, when her freeze-frame chimed in the background.

She broke our embrace, looking up into my face, lips parted still, breathing a little raggedly, half-smiling, eyes bright, and said, "I'd better answer."

I nodded, and watched her walk away. Interruptions are only a problem when you think they might give your quarry a chance to think twice, then run away. Here, I was as much the game as the hunter, the best of all possible worlds.

I stretched, putting my hands behind my back, turning away from the candlelit room, looking up into the night sky, looking in the direction of Procyon, brightest star in Sirius' firmament.

One blue light flickered on, then burned steadily. A second. A third. Ten. Twenty. Fifty. More.

I felt a hard bitterness spring up in my heart, a deep resentment at whatever cruel being was spooling out my life's script. Is it you, Orb, always playing with me? Or, as the Timeliners believe, just the random havoc wrought by Uncreated Time?

Jade came back from the freeze-frame, filling the night with her jasmine perfume, put a softly trembling hand on my shoulder, and said, "They're here."

Silent. I put my arm around her and gestured up into the night sky, at a burning constellation of terrible blue stars, surrounding Procyon like so many staring blue eyes.

*　　*　　*

We rode into the heavens, my comrades and I, in our jerry-built warships, soaring up and away from the little worlds we'd made our own, just like real warriors, real historical men and women out to do battle with the forces of evil that confronted us. They'd wanted me to carry my flag aboard the star-battleship *Bakunin,* formerly the interstellar light freighter *Maurice Sendak,* but I demurred, making my place at the comm console of one of the ordinary missile boats, a five-man job without a name, just *MS-655,* which had once been a rock tug.

Commodore. Commodore Murphy.

I still flinch when I remember that.

Remember Jade laughing at the comic opera uniform they'd found for me in some costume shop, taking snaps "for the history tracks." Somewhere in the DataWarren I guess you can still find Commodore Darius Murphy even now, in brush epaulets and a cocked hat.

They found something even sillier for newly minted Vice President Broadbent, who seemed to like it.

We relish this business, don't we?

Maybe it's why these things happen.

Now, though, in the realtime of my then-life, I put my face down in the boat's astrogation frame and looked around. *Bakunin* over there, accelerating hard, missile launchers gaping, particle beam turrets twisting this way and that, going through their setting-up exercises. My little fleet divided into ten squadrons.

The pilot of *655,* voice anxious, said, "Commodore . . . ?"

I looked up at him and smiled, trying hard to remember his name, failing. "Hang on."

There. Dark shapes approaching, no more than thirty ships, big ships, fanning out into a flat disk, stretched all the fuck over the place, millions of kems between them, like a net sent to engulf us. Just the first wave, sent to deal with our puny little attack, wipe the way clear for the rest of the fleet, hanging back almost five AUs now, a half-day's travel time, at least.

Our little ships, their big ones. I imagined myself Drake facing the Armada. Imagined myself a statue, standing in pompous grace upon a pillar high . . . Hell. That's Nelson I'm thinking of, isn't it?

The pilot said, "Please, Commodore. *Bakunin*'s got to start her turn if we're going to—"

"Patience." I almost said *trust me*, buttoned my lip just in time.

While I watched, the black ships' thrusters twinkled, rolling them about their long axes. Something about these ships . . . I leaned deep in the frame and barked, "Operation Nine, startpoint theta."

Heard the pilot sigh with relief, felt 655 surge beneath me, surge through her barely adequate shields. They never meant this ship for violent maneuvering, ship whose life should've been dedicated to hauling great big boulders around the sky.

Squadrons Three and Seven swirled like so many swarms of red hornets, twisting along the projected path of blue-streaming *Bakunin*, making for one edge of the oncoming saucer of the Mobilitzyn fleet. I watched, and remembered walking with Styrbjörn and some friends one bright, stemshiny day, deep in the woods of Audumla. This was in the days before we were ready for the allomorph whores, though no boy is ever really innocent of such desires, and we stumbled on a nest of bald-faced hornets hanging from the thin branch of a peeling old birch tree, stood mesmerized, watching the insects come and go.

These are the things you see in all the old cartoon dramas.

Some talking bear gets one stuck over his head and runs howling to the horizon, furious hornets stinging him on the ass while his betters laugh.

It was Styrbjörn, I think, who made a joke that day about getting up a game of touch football with the thing. The rest of us laughed at his wit, remembering our cartoons.

Big, dark portals on the Mobilitzyn ships gaped open suddenly and swarms of blue fireflies came pouring out, some swinging toward Squadrons Three and Seven, some making for *Bakunin,* some . . . well, streaming toward the rest of us.

"Commodore . . . ?"

Getting tired of that.

I called in the other squadrons, directing them this way and that, watching as portals opened on each and every one of the Mobilitzyn ships, portals belching out streams of blue bees, bees coming straight for us. Which ship does Jade command? I forgot which squadron she joined.

"Commodore . . . ?"

I said, "Well. If I'd been the Mobilitzyn commander, I'd've sent at least half-frigates to guard the carriers. This guy . . ." Every last one of the ships a carrier, filled to the scuppers, as they say, with fast little fighters, closing in on us now, outnumbering my fleet three to one.

The pilot said, "So what do we do now?"

I smiled at him and shrugged. "Nothing left now but to fight. That's what it's all about anyway."

Blue light suddenly flared up from the astrogation frame, flickering around our little chamber, and, when I looked, I saw *Bakunin* had exploded, a great, mottled ball of nuclear fire, taking out Three and Seven, taking out an entire squadron of Mobilitzyn fighters as well, doing nothing at all to square the odds.

The pilot stared down at me from his nest for the better

part of a minute, and I saw by his eyes that he was deathly afraid. Should've thought about this while you had the chance, hm? I said, "Let's go." He turned away then, put white-knuckled hands to his controls, while our three gunners turned to their weaponry and the ship began shuddering around us.

Time.

I shoved the astrogation frame out of the way, grabbed the controls of my own gun, and put my head down in the nerve induction box. There. Blue lights rolling up all around. I normalized the sighting system, told the gun what I wanted it to do, and . . .

There.

Particle beam sizzling, a line of hard yellow pixydust, swinging, swinging . . . one of the blue lights flared and burst, shards tumbling away, disappearing in night.

That's one.

The ship shuddered hard, twisting under me, and someone shouted *yahoo,* maybe the pilot, courage emerging in all this action, maybe only one of the gunners, taking out his quarry.

There.

Aim. Tracking, tracking . . . sizzle of yellow, another blue light exploding in flame, a brief helter-skelter of debris, and that's two . . .

Something hit me in the back of the head and bounced away as I tried to track a third. Definitely the pilot's voice now, a panicky babble of swear words.

Tracking, tracking . . . *bam.* That's three.

"Commodore . . . ?"

Tracking, tracking . . .

Something slammed hard into my back, making me break contact with the gun controls, and I found myself in a cockpit full of blue smoke and coughing men, snakes of fire crawling here and there on the inside of the hull armor.

"Shit."

I started to lean back into the gun, but the pilot said, "Commodore, I'm getting us out of here while we've still got plasma pressure. Maybe I can make Suzdal. Maybe not."

I pulled the astrogation frame back into my lap and looked inside. We were already behind the principal scrimmage plane of the Mobilitzyn fleet, and there weren't many red hornets flaring anymore, just swarms of blue bees making for their home ships. I let the frame count for me and shook my head slowly. Not one single carrier destroyed.

I sat back in my crash couch and relaxed, feeling 655 shiver underneath me as the pilot tried to save our lives. Be a hard death, suffocating out here rather than dying in flame with our brethren, hm? Tried to think about all this "ours is not to reason why" business, but . . .

You knew. You knew this would happen, didn't you? And yet . . .

And yet you went right ahead and did it anyway.

Fool?

Or hero?

No answer, as usual.

I remember standing on a landing stage near the north pole of Suzdal, the one we'd left only a day or two ago, standing beside the smoking ruin of *MS-655*, smoking ruin long ago abandoned by its crew, standing under an eerie sky of green and gold, red Wernickë turned rusty mud brown seen through a eutropic shield hardened by burst after burst of intense gamma radiation and a swarming neutron surf.

Far away beyond the sky, in the direction of the Pup, you could see blue lights flaring, mingled with lovely fleurettes of scarlet as Broadbent's fleet did its best against Mobilitzyn, playing tag, catch as catch can among the gravitational and magnetic anomalies around Sirius B.

Days away.

No one will come back from that one.

Just as well.

Wish it was me?

Maybe. Maybe not.

I watched another little fighter—one of ours, of course—dip down through the eutropic shield and begin straggling in over the field, trailing pale blue smoke. Maybe this one will be Jade's little ship.

It hit the edge of the apron with way too much lateral momentum, belly scraping along, flaring sparks. Good job, that pilot, working with mangled hardware . . . her nose dug in and the little ship tumbled end over end, gouting smoky orange flame, shedding bits of this and that.

Good job.

The field's fire-suppression automata went into action, vomiting foam while the ambulance sirens wailed. Medical equipment here's not as good as what Standard had, back in the Glow-Ice Rebellion. Most of *these* people will die.

Unless Mobilitzyn Associates wants them saved, for some reason or another.

So much for Act One.

I remember standing once again on the balcony of my apartment, looking out at the burning city, struggling to remember its name, failing, my mind seeming as hazy as the smoke that hung beneath Suzdal's eutropic shield.

Tiredly: *Clydesbûrh.*

Capital of what would have been the People's Republic of Sirius.

Would have been.

There were fires everywhere, but localized, mainly—perhaps entirely—set by fallen bits of military debris. Our own munitions, failing, falling back on the people who fired them. Even pieces of crashed Mobilitzyn fighters, exploded beyond the sky, continuing along their inertial track and . . .

I heard the glass door slide open behind me and marveled briefly that it was still unbroken, despite the concussive events it must have suffered already. Jade came up behind me, leaned against my back, looking over my shoulder at incipient devastation.

"It still looks beautiful," she whispered, breath blowing on the short hair over my ear.

The city was burning, yes, here and there, everywhere soon, but, beyond the skyline, you could see the trees and mountains, the forests and plains of Suzdal, crescent Wernickë hanging in the sky, reflecting bright Siriuslight, Sirius flaring just on the horizon, subdued by the shield's optics.

I could feel her breasts flattening against my back, the gentle nudge of one pelvic blade. Maybe that other brief bump, the mere promise of a contact, was her pubis bone, below that, one knee touching the back of mine.

She said, "The others are waiting. We've got to go now."

I felt an urge to make some bitter response, along the lines of, *Why bother?* Nothing ever changes, you see, and now? Well.

It's all over now, isn't it?

There was a flicker-flash, just above the sky, no more than a few kems away.

Disturbance in the eutropic shield.

Sharp, high squeal, making splinters in my ears.

Then the incoming missile burst through and slammed down on one of our missile sites, bloomed into an impossible ball of violet light that made my eyes squeeze shut, tears leaking under the lids.

The pressure wave slammed me in my face, carrying with it a hard thump of technological thunder. *Bam.* Then a long echo.

When I opened my eyes, the fire was dark red, rising from the crater it'd melted in Suzdal's ersatz ground, rising like a little mushroom cloud, death's-head rising back through the skyhole it'd made, up into outer space and gone.

The eutropic shield tried to heal behind it, rings forming, squeezing the hole shut, leaving a brown bull's-eye scar on the sky.

I staggered back, banging into Jade, almost making her fall, turned and looked at her.

She reached forward, eyes wide, taking me by both arms. "We've got to get *out* of here, Murph! Come on. The others are *waiting.* Broadbent's *dead,* for God's sake! *You're* in charge now!"

I nodded slowly, looked over my shoulder at the yellow-white hole where the missile site and its crew had been. Right. In charge. Responsible. I said, "Of . . . course. We'd . . . better get busy."

Something kindled in her eyes then. She smiled, leaned forward, kissed me lightly on the lips, and, as she turned away, said, "That's the spirit."

Never say die, hm?

Which story is that?

Crouching in the dry brush lining Plumbago Ridge, near the crest of the Yellow Mountains, rounded peaks by the western shores of the Saddleback Sea, I froze under a hard teal sky, sky banded with streaks of deep vermilion, listening to the soft grumble of fighter moduli running at minimum power.

I raised my head cautiously, flipping my flash goggles down, and looked out over the flat black waters of the sea. There. Two narrow gray lines, slowly lengthening, beyond them, beyond the gently curving horizon, a column of brown smoke rising in a fat wedge, staining the heavens above. I remember how the ground shook, how the whole world shook, when the missile hit.

Try as I might, I can't remember what the target was.

Doesn't matter.

Not anymore.

Jade's hand was on my calf then, warm through the leg of my pants.

Funny. It seems like it should be cold up here, like we should be crawling through snow. But Suzdal's become a steam bath from all the fire, explosions, destruction. As if the seas are boiling now.

I flipped up the goggles and looked back along the length of my own body. Jade, with her goggles still down, half-lying on the flitgun resting beside me; beyond her, beyond the gently curving horizon of her backside, six more men and women, waiting.

Soon, now.

In the distance, I could hear another soft rumbling. All right, our information's correct. Here they come. I crept forward through the bushes again, dragging my gun along, slid around the bole of a thick old maple tree, crawling across hard, lumpy roots, slid to the edge of the bluff.

Down below, a road. On the road, some trucks.

Suzdal is like a world from the past, filling my life now with so many datatrack dramas I can't separate reality from fiction from history from . . .

Orb knows they could have brought flitters and flier-gunships. Nothing. All they brought were carriers full of space-fighters, troop transports full of ground pounders. So they've had to use whatever local transport they could impound, which was most of it, and Suzdal is an antique world, almost, not quite, left behind by history.

Jade crept up beside me, flipping up her goggles so she could look down at the Mobilitzyn truck convoy sliding between the hills, and I could smell a faint touch of jasmine, some last concession to the memory of her old life.

"Well," she said. "Glad to see them out here at last." Bitter, angry grin on her face, a smile of real pleasure.

In the months since they'd so quickly wiped out our space fleets, since they'd taken over the principal habitats around Wernickë, since they'd occupied the cities of big artificial worlds like Suzdal, they'd tried to sit us out.

But that never works. Sängershaven. Mars. Afghanistan. Vietnam. America. The Song Empire. Achaemenid Persia. To name just a few, the lessons of history.

Now they have to come out here and find us. Find and kill us all.

And, sometimes, with her perfume in my head, I think about the fun Jade and I would have, if we weren't so busy with the business of killing and dying.

I flipped my goggles back down, made sure they were tuned to just the right frequency, checked the settings on my flitgun, and said, "*Now*."

A long collective moment, eight men and women steeling themselves, scraping together the scraps of courage, then we rose from concealment, standing like little gods on the brow of the hill, outlined against the sky, and opened fire.

Down on the road, little red flowers began twinkling all over the trucks as we hit them with our explosive rounds.

Down on the road, as the trucks turned and spilled, you could hear men and women starting to scream. Shouts of anger and agony, dismay, confusion, noncoms bellowing commands. Down on the road, you could see the soldiers scrambling from the trap made of wrecked trucks, running this way and that, scrambling for the safety of the trees.

When they started to return fire, little missiles snapping around us, exploding into the trunks of trees, ripping up the bushes atop Plumbago Ridge, we ducked down, ducked down and dispersed.

Alone now, well separated from Jade, wherever she'd gone, I got myself one good view of the road after another, crawled around 'til I could see the ravine beyond. Forget the fucking trucks, they're on fire anyway. Go for the soldiers. Flitgun rattling, shaking in my hands. Six men near the end of the ravine, six men who thought they were safely hidden, sprawling suddenly as my fire twinkled over them, six men dying not quite suddenly enough.

Though it was too far, I imagined I could hear them screaming, hear the liquid sounds they made as blood flooded their lungs, hear the soft *splat* of bursting flesh.

Lovely, hm? Every boy's dream.

After a while, they stopped returning fire. Maybe we killed them all, maybe some got away, fleeing by ones and twos through the forest, back down the rivers and streams of the Yellow Mountains, back to the safety of civilization.

What difference does it make?

Days later, a hundred kems to the south, Jade and I sat with our backs to the pebbly trunk of a big old oak tree, cleaning our weapons under a sunny sky. Things seemed almost back to normal now, omnipresent haze fading away, sky slowly losing its green tinge as Wernickë's magnetosphere bled out excess radiation, as combustion by-products were absorbed by Suzdal's ersatz ecology.

Now Sirius A was a bright flare, high in the sky, the Pup a little sparkle not far away, close to aphelion herself, but almost line of sight with the other star from our perspective. Wernickë itself was nowhere to be seen, back on the other side of the world.

Our world.

Can this go on forever?

What will we become?

I started reassembling the flitgun, hands working by rote, full of automated skill. Is this what it's like to be a robot? Lots of old friends I could've asked; I remember them all, one after another.

Beside me, Jade was working her own weapon, and I was startlingly conscious of her, form, figure, and presence. We've both grown thin, hiding in the hills, eating what we can, when we can. No sign of jasmine perfume anymore, all of that behind us now, part of former lives, half-forgotten.

She had the pieces of her gun on the back of a shed jacket, taken apart, resting between her spread legs, beads of sweat on her forehead, brought on by bright sunlight, lips compressed in concentration, listening to the clink and clack, the soft metallic music of her task.

Conscious now of the spread of her thighs, the creased cloth covering the flat place where her legs come together. If I turned my head and leaned forward, leaned a little closer, I could make out some hint of altar and gate . . . strange, I haven't thought of it that way in so long.

Part of another life, all right.

I felt a tingle of arousal somewhere deep inside.

Well. It'll come in good time. You know it will. She knows. Not hard to tell. All the killing and dying, that's just the life we lead, a life that seems like it's gone on forever already, stretching infinitely deep into our past. Life has other parts, parts that won't go away. Our bodies see to that, just as they see to it that we grow hungry every day, that we go on eating, no matter that the killing beckons, no matter that death looms.

I grinned, struck by the silly poetry of my thoughts.

Jade looked up at me briefly, briefly smiled, then went back to the task of her gun.

In a nondark night, full Wernickë blazing overhead, backlighting the clouds, adding its light to the light of red fires blooming beyond every horizon, Jade and I sat and ate our light meal, bits of this, scraps of that, in some bombed-out ruin.

We had a roof over our heads, and walls, but the windows were gone, scorched furniture collapsed . . . no people here. Not bodies. Not remains. Hope they got safely away.

I imagined them living in some Mobilitzyn reeducation camp. Mama. Papa. Kiddies and all. Maybe they'll even get their old jobs back, someday, sometime. *They* didn't make the revolution, after all, just us, we few, knowing the masses would go along with it, just the way they go along with everything.

Mobilitzyn won't waste good workers, surely.

Cost money to import all new.

Explosions flashed far away, strobing our faces pale white.

I could feel the ground surge under me, very faintly.

Sometimes you can feel it jolt like that, even when there's no distant explosion to see or hear. Some trick of Suzdal's internal architecture.

There was a faraway rumble, not at all like thunder.

Jade knelt in front of me now, meal done and forgotten. Knelt before me, eyes oh-so-serious, and slowly unzipped the front of her dirty coverall, breasts popping out, still full and sleek, though her ribs were striations under the skin, though her belly had grown quite concave.

When the zipper reached the bottom of its track, you could see the tuft of her pubic hair, mounted on a pubic bone that'd grown deliciously prominent.

When I knelt to face her, she said, "I love you, Murph. You've made it . . . all worthwhile."

I kissed her then, trying not to think.

Weeks later, a thousand kems away, down near the Suzdalian south pole, I stood in chains by the side of an open field, waiting with a half-dozen other prisoners. Jade, standing a few ems away, similarly chained, kept looking at me. Trying to smile, I think. Encouragement, perhaps, or maybe just working through her own fears.

Over in the middle of the field, next to a landed gunship, one of the new ones they'd just brought in, six bodies lay dead, tattered, spattered with blood, four of them Mobilitzyn troopers, two of them our friends.

More Mobilitzyn troopers hiding around the edges of the clearing, gripping their guns, wide-eyed with fear, nervously alert. No way for them to know they got us all. For all they know, a hundred more guerrillas are creeping nearby, about to attempt our rescue.

The noncom I'd spoken to last came back across the field from the gunship, an officer of some kind at his side. Look at the badges. This is Mobilitzyn Corporate Security, not some temp-agency hireling.

The officer said, "This the one?"

The noncom lifted his face shield and looked at me. Nodded. "Yes, sir. Standard ARM."

"Okay. Checks out just fine. Put him on ice and let's get this business over with." He turned, started to walk away.

"Um, sir?" My voice was a little high, betraying me.

He looked back. "Murphy, your fucking contract checks out. You're covered by Standard ARM's general indemnity policy and you were perfectly within your rights as a half-pay reservist to hire yourself out to these people. I'm sorry you did, but you'll get your repatriation anyway. Next freighter back toward the Jet, I guess." He looked at the noncom. "Let's go."

The soldier tapped me on the shoulder. "Come on, pal."

I looked back to where Jade and the others waited, watching the corporate officer approach. She was looking at me, eyes wide, not knowing what was going on. I felt my guts tighten suddenly. Restitutor Orbis, I want you to tell me now, in the name of Uncreated Time, that things will be all right, that she'll survive prison, survive reeducation, that I'll see her again some sunny day.

As usual, Orb didn't answer.

The noncom whispered in my ear, "Maybe someday our positions will be reversed. So remember my face, Murphy. Remember the name Benny Wallace. Remember who just fuckin' saved your ass today. All right?"

Ching.

The officer was standing beside my friends, had taken out his sidearm, had slid out the clip, checking his load. As I watched, he slid it back in, *snap.*

Like echoes in the forest, hard and empty.

Jade, voice dreadful with panic, cried out, "*Murph?*"

Then the gun went *bang,* her head exploded, and what was left of her fell down in the cool green grass.

CHAPTER NINE

Telemachus Major.

I sat on the balcony outside the resthome room where I was supposed to be recovering from decades of cold sleep, looking out over cityscape and landforms, wondering how it could be a hundred years since the last time I was here.

Telemachus Minor, green forest moon, hung not so far overhead, close enough I could make out its landscapes, make out the distinct shapes of tall green trees, giant red-woods and the like, make out the twisting silver gleam of her wonderful trout streams, lakes where I'd swum with my flier friends . . . only yesterday? That's what it seems like.

Telemachus Minor hung beyond the sky, beyond the eu-tropic shield's glimmering ersatz blue, beyond the clouds, far, far away, in just the same way she was close by.

I wanted to think of her as I thought about my previous life: so close I could see every detail. And yet so remote. Forever out of reach.

Better to pretend I'd died out on Wernickë's little Suzdal moon. Died and been reborn as someone else. Someone with a whole new life to live. That other man's bones would be lying back there, far away, lying in the grass with . . .

I got up and went inside, turning my back on a long, shimmering vista composed mainly of tall, ornate human architecture, architecture superimposed before a horizon of snow-topped artificial mountains, blue sky, green sea, went and got dressed in the plain street clothes the resthome left for us in the closets of every room, trying not to see myself in the mirror.

I'd grown thin while I slept. Thin and pale.

Down the stairs and across the foyer, waving to the smiling receptionist who already knew me well, I went out into bright, sourceless sunshine, sunshine without the power to brighten me. Waited on the corner with other thin, pale, silent men and women. Got aboard the tram and went on down to the cityscape world below.

Walking all alone through the dense crowd filling the bottom of a canyonlike avenue in a part of Telemachus Major's world-city known as the Blue Hole made me realize my problem quite fully. I could tip my head back and back, look up at the facades of the buildings, see windows of glass, bright and dark, balconies empty or full of people.

Who are they, so tiny, so far above? A man and a woman, maybe, holding hands.

Hundreds of ems overhead, the sky was like a long, thin, square-edged river of dark blue, my eyes imagining stars beyond, just on the edge of perception.

Then again, I could see the people all around me, walking, walking. A bustle of voices, constant murmuring, though I couldn't see anyone actually talking to anyone else. Mostly, it looked as though they were all alone, just like me.

I stopped and stood in front of a restaurant window, looking in at the diners, eating who knows what meal. Since I came out of sleep, time seems to have lost its familiar meaning. Day, night. These are things we manufacture for ourselves, manufacture for all the little worlds we made and hung against the sky, inside gimcrack shields that keep away the real darkness outside.

Darkness and stars. That's what's real. The rest of it . . .

Inside, at the table nearest the window, a tall, blocky-looking man with short silver hair was spooning up a soup that seemed composed of spaghetti and beans. Not talking to the thinner man across from him, skinny boy with long yellow hair who toyed with an unlit smoke of some sort, silently watching his friend eat.

After a while, the silver-haired man stopped eating, put down his spoon, and turned to look at me, staring through the glass.

Sullen. Go away, asshole.

I went.

There's a life story inside the restaurant, two men sitting at a table, two life stories, each one as complex as my own. What about all these other people, thronging all around? In the time I've been gone, the population of Telemachus Major had grown from five billion to six.

I picked a random corner and leaned against the grainy, gray, featureless stone wall of a building, watched the crowd spilling past, trying to see if they had lives as well. Nothing. Nothing but the details of my own life suggesting themselves. Look at that pretty girl, all too human girl, pale pink dress, white buttons, white patent-leather shoes, pink headband confining hair like golden wool. You'd like to fuck her, wouldn't you?

I imagined myself getting her down, right here in the

street, pulling her out of those pink clothes, prying her legs apart as she struggled and screamed.

Why do I imagine she'd struggle and scream?

Maybe for the same reason I imagine people stepping over us as I pin her to the sidewalk and rape myself senseless.

I watched her walk away, striding purposefully, hands clenched at her sides. a woman alone in a dense crowd, presumably going somewhere. But I didn't imagine her life. All I did was imagine it intersecting with my own. After a while, I walked on too.

Down in the Blue Hole, there's a store somewhere that sells anything you could possibly imagine. I wonder who buys life-size, semianimated statues of extinct hominids? There was no one in the store, other than a motionless human clerk, who sat behind his counter, staring at the store's centerpiece, a male *Australopithecus robustus,* standing in the middle of a fountain structure and pissing for all he was worth. Garden art?

I wondered, for just a second, how much intelligence they'd built into the art objects.

Not hard to imagine who buys the wares advertised on the front of the pornography shop. And the place across the street, Sex Toys 'n' Erotica . . . this one had a window so you could look in and see a fair number of women, picking over an assortment of doodads and doohickeys. Smirking, nudging each other.

Interesting. Women together in groups, laughing at what they saw. A few women alone, eyes so terribly serious. A few women with embarrassed-looking men in tow. What's that all about? More life stories for me not to know.

Farther down the street was a live sex show, one of those places where the performers take suggestions from the audience. Lick this. Suck that. Okay, now stick this in there and . . . Great. Wonderful. A couple of blocks later, I passed by a place where you could get live sex for yourself, advertised by 3D posters of men and women whose main selling point seemed to be their exposed, shining wet genitalia.

Makes sense, I guess.

I was tempted to go in, of course, but I kept on walking, heading on down the street, deeper and deeper into the Blue Hole, unable to imagine where I was going, or why.

One day—the same day, in fact, that the resthome judged me sufficiently rested—I was summoned down to the Standard ARM corporate headquarters, way the hell on the other side of the world. Summoned to the personnel office, where I sat for three hours in a waiting room with a number of other men and women, all of them tired-looking, most of them nervous. One by one, we were called to another room.

One by one, 'til they got to me.

The guy in the room, fiddling intently with a freeze-frame embedded in the top of his desk, dressed in a variant of the powder-blue Standard active duty uniform, though without any badges of rank or insignia, motioned me to a chair.

Finally, after I'd been sitting, watching him fiddle for about fifteen minutes, he said, "All right, I guess that's it."

Great. Now what?

He sat back, looking at me expressionlessly. "Well. You know why you're here, don't you, Murphy?"

I crossed my legs and said, "Since you're a personnel auditor, I assume I'm in trouble over what happened out on Wernickë."

He smiled. "Not exactly."

"Exactly what, then?"

"Mobilitzyn Associates went bankrupt partly as a result of

your actions. Standard ARM picked up all their Sirian properties for a song, including some extremely valuable mineral rights involving the Wernickë infrastar and associated bodies."

I sat and waited.

"On the other hand, Standard ARM can't be seen as encouraging independent action against the interests of other corporate entities. These are . . . not the best of times for us to be seen in an unflattering light."

"So?"

He said, "Well, if you read your contract, you'll find that the insurance policies covering you as a Standard ARM retainee have a restitution rider." He poked inside the freeze-frame again. "Historically, of course, those riders have never been activated. But these are . . . difficult times."

"So what're you saying . . . restitution? I mean . . ."

He smiled. "No way anyone could pay back the amount of the judgment against Standard, of course, not to mention the cost of your freeze-down and transport. And, of course, we had to pay more for the Sirian properties that we might have had there been no . . . questionable involvements."

"Of course."

He shrugged. "So. You go get yourself a little apartment and we'll come up with a modest lifestyle budget for you, Mr. Murphy. Then the rest of your reserve pay will be docked as restitution."

Um. "For how long?"

He smiled. "Forever, I guess."

I imagined myself stuck in some slummy section of Telemachus Major for . . . how long *is* forever? I said, "So what if I just quit? Go work for someone else?"

He said, "Then we'll send you a bill for the full amount, Mr. Murphy. You don't want to know how much."

Nor, I guess, was I supposed to imagine how or from whom they might collect.

Then he said, "Of course, you *could* re-up, Mr. Murphy. Active agents of Standard ARM are not subject to the restitution clauses of the reservist insurance policies, even on an *ex post facto* basis. And there are *lots* more openings these days, Mr. Murphy." A very broad smile. "There's a great deal of work to be done."

These days . . . I kept trying to remind myself just how long I'd been gone, how long I'd been asleep. "So you're saying if I go back on active duty, my restitution is . . ."

"Suspended. For so long as you *are* on active duty."

"And . . . if I went back on reserve status later on? Maybe retired someday?"

Still smiling, he shook his head.

I sat back in my chair and said, "Oh." And thought for just a second about the pension fund contribution every active-duty Standard ARM employee must make, five percent of every duty pay cycle.

"Look at it this way," he said. "At least you'll have something to do."

I didn't go back to the resthome that day, though I suppose they'd've let me hang around. No reason to go there. No friends. No possessions. It's an odd way to feel, almost like feeling nothing at all, my head not really spinning, not really empty as I wandered away from Standard HQ in a business district of Telemachus Major whose name I hadn't bothered to look up.

Sky just as blue overhead, striated with those same remote, diaphanous clouds, though the green forest moon was elsewhere I suppose, somewhere below the horizon. Tall buildings, in much better shape, architecturally more profound than those of the Blue Hole, but . . .

I stopped on the sidewalk in front of a gizmo store, same faceless crowd sliding around me, not noticing me at all, it seemed, and stood looking in through the window at a display of brand-new freeze-frames. The one nearest the window had its isogloss tuned to an unnatural height, so passersby could look through into wonderland and see what was what. Maybe they have a lot of walk-in business, businessfolk who just can't wait to pick up the new-model freeze-frame so they can use this pointless feature or that one . . .

There was a random trackslider going, threading its way through the data intelligently, picking up nodes the latest demographic surveys indicated would catch and hold the interest of any random citizen who . . .

The election results from Tant'Athool, one of the more populous bodies deep inside the Centauri Jet, tall fat man with a flat, pasty-white face, wearing a woolen cap and a bizarrely plain military-style uniform, waving his hands overhead.

When I pressed my hands and face close to the glass, I was close enough to the field surface I could catch the sound of his words, speaking in some fluid language that had a lot of words in common with the various dialects of Spanish I knew, but not enough for me to catch their drift.

Go inside, get close enough so the translator can reach inside your head.

I stayed pasted to the glass instead, watching the trackslider do its job, wondering if I was close enough to influence its choices. Well. More politics. Another world, another politician giving a speech, waving his arms in victory, barking out his triumph. Other men on the platform with him, arms folded behind their backs, faces impassive, eyes gleaming.

I recognized Meyer Sonn-Atem first, then realized who the speaker was, and wondered just when and how Finn mac Eye had managed to get himself out of stasis-prison.

After a while, I got tired of watching the slider blink through various politicians, politics of the Centauri Jet a long-dead issue for me, as dead as anything I could imagine. I walked away, walked on down the street to a tram station where I waited patiently for a train, heading for the other side of the world.

Maybe I'll go on back to the Blue Hole. Maybe I'll find that sex-for-hire store I passed by, go on in, pick out one of those fine, wet, athletic-looking women, pay my fee, and take it all out on . . .

Take it out on what? Or who?

Well.

A man would understand.

Any man.

Any male.

I got on the next tram instead, which turned out to be headed for the seashore. There was a fine vista, as we passed from pole to pole, hanging more than a kem above the varied skylines of Telemachus Major, mountains and forests here and there, some far away, others embedded in unending town.

Once, we passed over the middle of an immense green park that was hazed with a thin layer of pale blue smoke. Looking straight down, I could make out huge crowds of milling people, thousands, maybe millions of dots, like little black ants.

Flash. Flash. Twinkles of firelight from the edges of the crowd. Men firing guns? Police? No way to know from all the way up here. The twinkling, dots of red going on and off, seemed to give definition to the swarms of milling antmen.

In the seat behind me, a man riding with a woman, both of them dressed in beachwear, carrying armloads of towels and umbrellas, a hamper that smelled like fresh food of some kind, very spicy, with a strong odor of grease, whispered, "Look. Thulian rioters."

The woman craned her neck to see, and said, "Bastards. Why the hell can't they stay back in the Jet and leave us the hell alone? We've got work to do."

Work to do.

At the beach, where the sourceless sunshine was brighter than ever, the sky clear blue, sea reflecting it like flat, waveless, tideless blue steel, I stood on the platform for a while, watching the man and woman walk down across white sand to the edge of the sea, disappearing into a mass of a hundred thousand other people, every one of them just the same as his neighbor. And when the next tram came I got on it, heading right on back to the business center and Standard ARM HQ.

You damned well *knew* this could happen, Darius Murphy. People that get in a fix like this are called sixteen-tonners by their mates. Like it was a joke. Like it was their own fault.

So why the hell don't you *care*?

Maybe because it doesn't make any difference at all.

I found the aerospace service guild hall hard beside the Standard ARM Human Resources departmental office tower, and was walking across the broad, black marble floor thronged with employees, both active and reserve, headed for the Assignments Bureau, when a hand tapped me on the shoulder.

I turned and beheld a tall, slim female optimod, foxlike

woman covered with long, glossy, well-brushed lavender fur.

She stared at me for a long moment, foxy eyes wide, almost frightened-looking, then she said, "Don't you remember me, Murph?" Voice unnerved, as if fearing that I might not.

All I could do was stand, speechless, mouth hanging open, until she laughed a wonderful laugh, threw her arms around me, and hugged me like a long-lost friend.

Life holds miracles. It really does.

Standing there in the middle of a crowded concourse with my arms around Violet, reemerged from the substance of Uncreated Time, dragged bodily from beneath the pall of Orb's long shadow. I wondered who to thank for my fortune, if fortune it was.

No one.

No one at all.

Finally, finding words: "I thought you were dead."

Violet held my face between her hands, just the way she used to, eyes softening fast as they looked into mine. "Dead . . ." A wan, familiar smile. Familiar despite the passage of years. "Well, I went the rest of the war without a tail, carried around a set of scars instead of belly fur, but . . ."

"I saw you," I said. "Saw you dead. Looked for you later."

Deepening shadow in her eyes. A slow nod. "I didn't lose any important parts. Wasn't burned. Didn't take much to patch me up."

Still, that memory, Violet hanging torn and lifeless in her pilot's nest, while Dûmnahn, sundered into thousands by now, danced in the flames, while I crawled broken across the deck.

She said, "They let me look in on you just once. I talked a tech into opening your capsule for me and saw . . ." Her eyes closed for just a moment. "They took you away, sent you back home, and . . ." A little shrug. Life goes on.

And why couldn't I find you, Miss Violet?

Demure look, not quite brooding.

Because I'm . . . not a . . .

Not a person. Right. If I'd been looking for a particular monkey wrench, I wouldn't have found *its* personnel file either.

Stupid.

My expression made her laugh.

Her laugh made me smile.

A little while later and we'd walked, holding hands, out of the concourse, down some long street in that same nameless, lifeless business district, Violet leading me to a favorite restaurant, high on the side of an ivory tower, building reaching high above the Telemachan cityscape, reaching almost to the clouds, so high the eutropic sky itself seemed flat, a flat surface not so far overhead.

We took a table near the railing, placed our orders, and I looked away from her, frightened now, so uncertain I felt weak, looking out over the spires of the city, farther ones tilting subtly, then dramatically away, as they marched over the near horizon. Look at those mountains. From here, you can see the dark undersides of the white clouds that shroud their peaks.

And the sea. The surface of the sea looks round.

Softly, Violet said, "Murph?"

Some part of me didn't want to look. So much safer just to keep my eyes out on the world beyond the railing. So much easier to hold myself close inside, to . . .

I felt her hand, gentle on mine, and looked, despite myself.

There was absolute terror in her eyes.

Just holding my hand and looking at me, so afraid.

Tension inside my chest. Like something straining in there, threatening to explode.

She said, "Murphy, I . . ."

Look at her. You've got to speak. Say something, before . . . The words popped out, not even close to the words I was trying to plan: "I never stopped missing you, Violet."

Her hand tightened on mine for a moment, making me afraid for just a second . . . She looked away, letting her head fall, gazing down at the table, exhaled a long breath, and when she looked up at me again, whatever was in her had dissolved, dissolved utterly, eyes beginning to shine.

I'd slept for a hundred years.

Violet had . . . worked for that same hundred years.

A hundred years of no tomorrows.

Now this.

The beach at sunset, if *sunset*'s the word to use.

No sun here on Telemachus Major, but the light goes dim, fading to black overhead, colors banding outward in subtle concentric rings, as though there were a nearby G-class star just gone down below every horizon.

When the dimming's about halfway done, you can see that famous flash of green out over the sea, no matter what direction you look. You can even run backward up the dune face and prolong the effect, just as if this were a real world.

Neat trick.

I wonder why they bothered.

I found myself running with Violet, following her along the sunset sand, while soft breakers rolled in with a gentle crush and hiss, water fizzing like seltzer as it slid up the beach.

You could stand still with the water quieting around your

ankles, look down at your feet as the water retreated back out to sea, and watch the mole crabs emerge from the sand like so many bubbles, like so much turbulence.

Standing beside me, Violet said, "The first time I saw that, I couldn't believe it was animals. Silty sand, I thought. Like dust in the water." She laughed. "Then I thought about sitting naked in that same sand, about these things finding their way into various . . ." She laughed again.

Gentle, self-deprecating laughter. If the fur were swept away, would I see her blush?

Would I like that?

We stood still, looking at each other, the water gradually deepening, rising about our legs, then surging away, back down to our ankles.

She reached out and took my hand, lifting it away from my body, barely holding on to my fingertips. "I couldn't forget, no matter how hard I tried."

I could only nod, wishing I knew the right words to say. Maybe there are no right words.

She said, "It was like . . . losing your first lover. You know what I mean."

I realized with an electric shock that I did. My first lover. Not any of those gatesie girls. Nor Reese. Nor Jade.

She leaned forward, kissing me on the lips, our skin barely contacting, leaned away, then in again, renewing the touch, strengthening the touch, entering me in a way that . . . made it seem as though the last hundred years, hers and mine alike, had never happened.

Time gone.

Just like that.

Taking with it all those empty tomorrows.

* * *

We went to our little beach house, rented beach house straddling the crest of an ersatz dune, and in due course I stood in a furry tan room, looking out at the twilit seascape with my furry lover, watching the night sky evolve.

Waiting, perhaps.

The green forest moon began to rise, bright against the black and starry sky.

Then her hands were on me, breaking the barrier of a century that was mostly sleep, sleep and dreams, hard nightmares that couldn't possibly have been real, one hand on my shoulder, the other trailing slowly down my side, coming to rest on one hip, waiting again, while I hardly breathed at all, bathing in her lavender scent.

Felt her chin rest on my shoulder, mouth close beside my ear, as she whispered, "Time's supposed to heal, supposed to make us forget. But I dreamed about you over and over again."

I tried to imagine that, imagine my fearless warrior woman, caught between wars, tossing and turning, unable to sleep, thinking of me. Tried to imagine myself worthy of such a thing, while I remembered, all too briefly, Reese and Porphyry, Captain Lee and Jade, and all the nameless ones in between.

Nonsense. Only a dream. That's all.

Both her hands were on my hips now, resting still for just a moment, then they stole around until they could clasp in front of me, crushing her breasts flat against my back so I could feel the hard-ridged muscles of her belly. Hard, and yet . . . so soft, gently curving, downward, around and in . . . blades of hipbones there and there, down here the definite bump of pubis.

I turned in the circle of her arms and forgot about the green moon, turning my back on the whole world. World enough for me, just now, in here, in these slanting yellow eyes. I took her head between my hands, leaned in and kissed her, closed my eyes and could not remember a time when our faces hadn't fit together as perfectly as they did now.

Maybe those times were part of a dream as well, and this is the only real thing that ever happened to me.

Then we lay together, tousled, matted, wet with each other, snuggled under blanket and sheet at last, looking out our window at an empty, flat blue sky, cityscape and mountains invisible below the sill, green moon gone obliviously on its way while we free-fell a million years, back to our former lives.

Nothing to say.

Not even a thought to think.

Stillness.

But Violet whispered, "I used to think if I lived long enough these things wouldn't matter anymore. I guess I haven't lived that long yet."

I thought how silly it was to be made whole by something so crude as this. Then thought how silly it was to think I'd been made whole, that anything could make me whole again. But here was Violet, nestled beneath my arm. And here was my heart, beating quietly in my chest once again.

So we talked the way lovers will talk, lying in each other's arms. I told her all about Reese and Mr. Zed, all about the worlds of Wolf 359, about Porphyry and her marvelous friends. Told her all about Wernickë, Jade, and Suzdal, and . . . and listened to all her stories about life in the service of Standard ARM, stories of war and peace, life, love, what have you.

Stories with names that didn't seem to matter anymore.

As she dried, her fur grew fluffy and lustrous once again.

And, inevitably, I talked about what we might do, now that we'd found each other once again, almost forgetting all the problems I'd made for myself, the deals I'd made, been forced to make, with various devils. We can go away, you see, you and I, beloved Violet. We can run from the scenes of our separate pasts, run far, far away, until we find some little frontier world, someplace where we can . . .

She sat staring at me silently, something hard and terrible in her eyes.

I suddenly remembered who she was: Violet the optimod, wholly-owned chattel of the Standard ARM Corporation, Violet who would never marry, who would never have children of her own, who would serve at the pleasure of her masters until the day she died, however remote that day might be.

The rest of it?

Just a dream.

I folded her in my arms again, and wondered what we'd have to do.

CHAPTER TEN

There are moments when you'd swear the sun shines indoors, even on worlds where there's no sun at all.

That's the way it felt as Violet and I walked hand in hand across the broad concourse floor of the Standard ARM guildhall, moving obliviously through a crowd of utter strangers. Did people turn, stop, and stare, nondescript human man and naked optimod woman striding together, cocooned? Maybe they did, probably not. People are so wrapped up in themselves, wrapped up in their own lives, their own happinesses and miseries, what other people feel doesn't seem to matter.

Maybe just one person noticed us. Maybe that one person saw us, envied us, smiled at our happiness, went on his or her way knowing that, every now and again, life can seem to work out, at least for the moment.

No shadows.

No shadows at all.

None that we *wanted* to see, at any rate.

Ultimately, we sat in a little cubbyhole of a room, somewhere deep in the bowels of ARM HQ, across a freeze-frame-equipped desk from a short, thick-waisted woman, who did indeed smile at us out of pale green eyes, eyes in a face with coffee colored skin under feathery white hair and sharp, slanting white eyebrows.

The woman said, "Good to see you again, Commander Violet. Hope you had a, um . . . nice vacation." Eying me then, smirking. "And Mr. Murphy, back from his little, ah, *adventure*."

Violet gave my hand a squeeze, somehow conveying private amusement.

The woman fished in her freeze-frame, tut-tutting like a movie grandma under her breath, trying to see if she could give us what we wanted. "Ah, me, so much work to be done . . ."

Standard ARM doesn't really *care* that we want to serve together, but, as Grandma noted, it doesn't really *mind,* either. No regulation, you see, stopping two people from serving together, so long as there are slots for both.

She said, "I see, Violet, that you've taken a combat-vehicle certification on your pilot's license."

An optimod in Violet's form can't really nod, shape of the head and neck all wrong for it. Still, with her ears pricked up and her head cocked to one side, you got the message.

Grandma said, "Nice long string of commendations you won during the Mezzandrée Police Action . . ."

Not even a hint of that, whatever it was, from Violet, though she'd filled our between times with an endless string of tales.

Grandma looked at me, frowning, disapproving look buried somewhere in the green. "And you, Mr. Murphy, have been remiss. Your technical education ought to be woefully out of date. Still . . ." Fishing in the freeze-frame

a little more, rubbing her double chin, going, *hmmm.*
"You're lucky technical progress is so slow these days."

These days? Technical progress has been slow for centuries, my dear. It's not so much that we're up against the
frontiers of physical knowledge, as that we long ago hit the
barrier of what's physically practical. Oh, sure, we could
build starships that'd go 0.99 cee. But at what cost?

And what difference would it make?

Historians remind us that humanity went from a motor-
ized box kite to supersonic jet aircraft in forty-five years.
And what we fly now, more than a thousand years later, are
starships recognizably derived from those same early jets.

Grandma said, "I'll sign you up for a series of
hypnopaedic updates. Should take about a week."

I myself could nod without any trouble.

She turned to Violet, obviously the only one who mattered here. "Harbinger Squadron 33, flying out of Nulliterrae, has openings for several flight crews. All right?"

Another bright-eyed head cock.

"Fine. I'll ship you out for the Harbinger mk. VI training
center at Saad al'Zuhr in fifteen days. That'll give him time
to absorb the updata and start some integration." She
looked from Violet to me and back again, smiled slyly, then
shook her head, as if amazed at something. "Ah, me. Well.
Put your right hands in the freeze-frame . . ."

I found Violet's hand within the interface, felt the
datareader's soft tingle.

Grandma said, "There you go. Have fun."

That evening, as the sunless sky turned scarlet and vermilion, light from nowhere flooding the undersides of a
flat, decorative cloud deck, Violet and I took a cab into a
section of Telemachus I'd never heard of before, a barrio

called the Pixsea. The first transport company we called refused to send a car.

The second did so, cabby giving us an unpleasant look when he saw us step to the curb, holding hands, before saying, "Where to?"

When Violet gave him a, to me, meaningless set of street coordinates, he sat twisted around in the pilot's seat for a long moment, looking as if he were going to throw us out. Finally, he said, "That's Au Pair, isn't it?"

A narrow grin showed her teeth, making her look even less human. "Ain't Bal Musette, pal."

"Jesus. Hmh." He looked at me with something between amusement and disgust, then revved up and slid away down the street.

Pixsea was like the Blue Hole, only bluer. Streets that, for a modern, well-maintained artificial world, seemed impossibly dirty. Buildings with broken-out windows, as if they'd been made from an inferior grade of industrial glass.

At one point, as we slid along, I saw a man, definitely a man, almost naked, in tatters, on his knees, vomiting convulsively.

The cabby muttered, "Nice place to visit, huh, kid?"

I suppose he meant me, though . . . how old *am* I? Do the sleep years count? How about the time I spent *getting* to Sirius, one day like the next like the next, safe in the Sisters' starship haven?

Finally, we got to a warehouse district, where the cabby charged our fares and sped off as soon as we were out the hatchway, raising a cloud of dust as he vanished back the way we'd come.

It was cool here, a slight breeze ruffling my hair as I stretched. The sky was full black overhead, the clouds vanished on cue, the heavens black velvet spangled with metallic glitter. Milky way. Pleiades, Hyades recognizable as discrete clusters. Omega Centauri perceptibly fuzzy, belying its false identification as a star. M-31 like a ghost behind the constellations . . .

Au Pair was a big windowless building, long and low-slung, with only a single lamplit door, the rest of it dark, centered in an immense parking lot that was almost but not quite devoid of cars. Not all that many private vehicles on Telemachus Major, of course, what with the ubiquity of public transport.

I wonder who the parking lot was originally for.

Ancient history, lost in time.

There was a naked optimod standing by the door, a short, squat, black-furred being, male-looking, though you couldn't really tell since his fur was rather long. Cradled in his thick, stubby arms . . . I started, took a shortened step that almost made me stumble.

Violet nudged me and said, "Sh. He knows it's an illegal military weapon."

The black optimod was staring at me with dark, beady little eyes. There was a little liquid reflection of starlight and . . . when I caught them at just the right angle, the eyes seemed to have a faint yellow-green glow.

Violet stepped close to him, leaned in, almost as if for a kiss, whispered something in his ear. The optimod grunted, not quite a word, and gestured us toward the door, gesture hardly qualifying as movement.

There were two doors, one right after another, like an airlock, sound baffle, light shield. Inside . . .

Huge, open room, dimly lit, small round tables around the periphery, people sitting crouched over them. Large open area, floor of smoothly polished faux wood, like carefully sanded yellow pine. A rocky altar in the center of the room, bearing a small red fire, flames licking lazily upward, occasionally tinged with a bit of blue, a brief flicker of green.

Violet was standing there, facing me, looking expectantly into my face.

I looked around the room.

Let out a gusty breath.

These people aren't all people, are they?

No.

Look closely.

Most of the couples are . . . mixed. Man and optimod. Woman and optimod. A few human couples. Even a few optimod couples.

At the far end of the room was a little stage, with a group of . . . beings on it, men, women, various sorts of optimods, fiddling with musical instruments, mostly percussion and metalwinds, one or two reeds.

Violet said, "I told you we'd have fun." She reached out and took my hand, started leading me through the sea of tables.

Up on the stage, the drummer, a thick-waisted human with arms bulked up like an extinct gorilla, started drumming, a quick, heavy beat, staccato bass throbs that suggested a particular sort of dance rhythm.

Before us on the dance floor was another couple, a tall, heavy, bearlike optimod, a slim brown woman with close-cropped hair, dressed in a short, clingy, fringed, charcoal-gray dress with a square neckline that emphasized the relative flatness of her chest, the clean line of her waist and hips.

The horns blared, squealing into the body of the number, and the black woman began to shimmy, arms held down by her sides. The bear-man didn't really dance, but . . . the way he watched. Performance enough.

Violet grabbed my hand again and spun me around to face her. Grinning. So happy. She said, "You know how this goes?"

I didn't, but . . . with a rush, I felt the old skills flooding back into me. Audumla. Gatesie. Parties and friends. Yes, I can imagine how it goes.

I started to dance, and it turned out I did know.

In short order, Violet was laughing, real world fading away, and then I was laughing too.

Hours later, she and I and a group of friends who'd turned up at the club walked under the vaulting sky of the Telemachan night, going from Au Pair to another club a short distance away, a different sort of club called Iles d'Essenses.

Violet and I walked hand in hand, and I felt a thousand ems tall, vibrant, blood flushed with the oxygen of vigorous dancing, head expanded almost to infinity by the liquor I'd drunk.

What a wonderful night, this little bit of fun.

Hardly anything at all, just dancing, music, newfound friends who, for now, seemed just like me, but . . .

For some reason, as we walked, I found myself remembering Reese and her curiously circumscribed life in the dark between the suns. Reese who was always looking for things to do, locked in the black bowels of a starship's hold, ways to fill the empty days, to lighten the . . . darkness.

Reese, always looking for fun.

I wonder where she is now.

Still with Mr. Zed, I hope, looking after him while he

looks after her. When I asked, Violet had never heard of Mr. Zed, though he was the most famous bum who ever lived.

Iles d'Essenses was nothing like Au Pair, built up from an old café, looking a lot like the dinner theaters of Audumla favored by my mother and her friends. The floor was full of little round tables, audience more human than optimod, but still well mixed, and there was a stage, really just a platform raised from the floor, at the one well-lit end of the room.

We found a table, where we ordered cocktails and beer, and, at the time we arrived, there was a cyborg up on the stage, something that looked like a cross between crocodile and a drilling machine, telling jokes based on cultural referents that I didn't get. The human component of the audience seemed to find it very amusing indeed.

When he finished, the sleek blond human emcee led a round of applause, then introduced the next act.

There was a handsome, muscular, swarthily virile-looking Caucasian human male who slowly undressed while a slim, very small optimod female, covered with short gray fur, watched every movement. When he was naked, the woman carefully shaved off every bit of his relatively dense black body hair, then they made love.

The optimods around us, the ones at our table, watched this in rapt silence.

When it was over, Violet reached out to stroke my forearm, very softly, with the velvet-furred pads of her fingertips.

A week went by, and then we were lying together on a white sand beach by the shores of a still blue lake, lake ringed with tall, dark green trees under an empty pale blue sky.

I was exhausted, enervated, and bewildered by a quick series of hypnopaedic updates, from days and nights strapped into a learning chair while miniature freeze-frames force-fed me new knowledge, all of it now whirling, useless, round and round in my head.

Why the hell would anyone have wanted to change the indexing language through which control structures are programmed? Tactical Dissonance Type Sixteen had been good enough for generations before I came along—and programmers had been decades waiting skeptically for the promised land of Type Seventeen. Now all of that had been swept away by something called the Motor Cortex Imaging Toolkit.

Better? Faster? Apparently not, but here it was.

So I lay there, stunned to silence, while the light of a nonexistent sun prickled on my skin, while Violet the optimod made love to me, equally silent, soft-furred hands like velvet gloves wandering over me, here and there for a while, then merely there.

Over the distant trees beyond the lake, a rim of clear deep blue began to show, the edge of a world, Telemachus Major rising. First the edge of the atmosphere, bound in by its eutropic shield, then the horizon, a bit of curved azure sea, then land, a wriggle of beachscape. Then city, seen from above, looking a little like a map, a little more like a model miniature, little buildings, little streets, the flecks of tiny aircraft dodging about among tiny white clouds.

Violet moved down my body, patient with me, knowing my needs, knowing how I felt, knowing how the abuse of my nervous system by a not-quite-insensate machine had . . . laid me low.

All those little differences between us, some mental, most merely physical, some inconvenient, others convenient indeed. Her mouth so warm, so much deeper than a human woman's would be, tongue longer, thinner, so much more supple.

Someone sighed. Must have been me.

Silly, but . . .

Well, you know how these things are. How they seem . . . magical when they're happening to *you*, rather than merely vulgar.

Telemachus Major broke free of the horizon's trees, became a vast blue-green-brown-white dish floating up in the sky. City. Sea. Mountains. Clouds. There: I could make out Spyridion Cosmodrome, foreshortened by the limb. Just as I looked, a bright blue spark rose and disappeared behind the sky, the blue flare of a modulus exhaust, some little starship getting under way.

The sky seemed to brighten and I gasped, Violet holding her mouth still, one hand grasping my thigh, the other sliding under the small of my back.

There. There, now.

She let me go, warm, gentle breeze seeming cool where I was wet, put one hand on my chest, rested her head on my shoulder, and began waiting again. Knowing full well, I suppose, that, in time, I'd snap out of this prolonged updaze, would give as good as I got, and . . . I held her close, watching Telemachus Major pass overhead, unable to fathom my own good fortune.

Wishing like hell I could articulate it now.

Violet knows. Knows how you feel.

And you're damned lucky to have that, Mr. Murphy.

And, finally, the fifteenth day.

We were in the little apartment, the one Violet had rented for her furlough, where we'd lived the last few weeks . . .

Strange. Seems like an eternity since we stumbled upon each other, crossing the concourse at Standard HQ.

Endless days and nights of Violet, like a haze covering my world, wrapping me in a delicate mist of happiness.

Violet was packing her kit bag and duffel, making sure she had those few possessions accumulated over decades . . . centuries? Orb tells me it's so, though I can't really feel the weight of years. That's what Uncreated Time is all about. It comes from nowhere . . . goes to . . . ? No one knows. And so, I've lived for more than a century, fifty years and more of that in cold, unhealing sleep.

Violet? I never ask. The years, decades, centuries, seem to mean little to her. We live our lives, she says. Nothing ever changes. And yet, I see the light in her eyes when she looks at me.

Is that change?

Maybe not.

Maybe it's just the living of life.

I sat at the foot of the bed with nothing to pack, knowing I'd just pick up an active-duty kit on the way to the transport, watching our rented freeze-frame autosurf one last time, interface cranked tall so we could see it, interact with it, even while lying in bed. We didn't use it much, absorbed as we were in each other, though Violet startled me with a liking for the crudest sort of pornography, watching median-format men and women doing things to each other, the seeing of it exciting her.

A certain charm to that, pushing aside the long-held lies of the old Occidental culture that had, willy-nilly, pushed all of humanity spaceward.

I had a stark memory of Violet and I making love, oh-so-sweetly, while perfect strangers fucked, growling, in the background.

And I wondered, briefly, uneasily, if Porphyry and her friends had recorded their last little . . . party, with me.

The freeze-frame caught my attention and halted its cruise, seeing my interest. "Shit."

Violet looked up from her careful folding and packing, getting as much as she could into as little space as possible. "Something?"

I gestured at the interface, which double-shifted so she could see it straight on as well. The Centauri Jet elections, over and done with. Riots. People marching in the streets. Ultima Thule victorious on a thousand little worlds. Finn mac Eye, First Counselor-elect of the incoming CrossJet Althing, tall, handsome Meyer Sonn-Atem smiling silently behind him.

There was a pale, strikingly pretty blond woman there too, Princess Karinn, the freeze-frame marked her, Sonn-Atem's wife of many years. Something so ethereal about her. So strange.

Like a being from another universe, grown here by mistake.

The freeze-frame showed us riots on some worlds, suppressed by local police, told us how the Intercorporate Board had met on Telemachus Major and set aside its local elections, decreeing that it was external to the Jet and would not participate in any interworld politicking.

Meanwhile, Fin mac Eye told us all that he'd see to it, now, that justice would be done. Justice for all, not just the few. Billions cheered, I suppose. That's the way it always goes.

Violet sat down beside me, watching quietly, one hand resting on the small of my back. Finally, she whispered, "Nothing good can come of this."

I said, "You remember meeting him?"

She rested her head on my shoulder and said, "Something about him, even then."

I could still remember the things he'd said that night in the barroom, things coming to fruition now. And then I remembered rescuing him, remembered the call from an anguished Meyer Sonn-Atem: Save our souls. Save my friend Finn mac Eye.

Because of them, Violet and I lost each other for a hundred years.

She said, "Well. It's none of our affair. We've got work to do."

So we gathered our few things, shut down the freeze-frame, and were on our way.

The big training center at Saad al'Zuhr lies one hundred fifty AUs from Telemachus Major, a mere week's travel time as the starship flies.

Violet and I spent some of that time, as much of it as we could stand, holed up in our tiny stateroom, continuing to suffocate one another like newlyweds, but the ship was full of beings, our comrades in arms, men and women, human, optimod, machinelike robot, faux-life android, ultimately drawing us out, pulling us from each other's clutches before we could do any real harm.

And so, bantering in the dining hall, a turn or two at the poker table, time spent sweating and panting in the transport's pathetic little gymnasium. Exploring, I recognized the ship as a converted insystem ferry, probably flown out from the Solar System hundreds of years ago, hardly suitable for the transport of so many living souls, doing it nonetheless. Nowhere to go, nothing to do, but then, not much time to do it in.

One day, the last day, we stood in the forward obdeck of

the transport, watching Saad Al'Zuhr grow from nothingness in the company of a couple whose society we'd fallen into, fellow Harbinger mk. VI trainees headed for our base. They were an odd couple, though Violet laughed when I called them that in private. Santry a tall, severely thin, voluble human woman of Old Caucasoid format, with black hair and flashing black eyes, who tended to run around the transport barefoot, clad only in her white linen underwear, material so thin you could see the shadow of pubic hair and nipples right through it. She seemed utterly incongruous in the company of her sidekick Regis Gosseyn, a short, rather broad man with beetling brows and a flat, chinless head.

Seeing him for the first time, walking across the messhall with his characteristic rolling waddle, Violet whispered to me about old preoptimod genetic experiments that had been aimed at resurrecting certain characteristics of Archaic *Homo sapiens,* people who would, with their sturdier bones, be a dozen times stronger than unmod humans.

I guess, she said, they thought they'd make better soldiers.

Foolishness.

Experiments given up, moving on to the ones that gave rise to the optimod strains, but the lines survived, continued of their own accord.

Now Santry said, "There. Right there." Pointing at a spot in the black sky forward, at an indistinct wad of pale yellow light. That would be Saad al'Zuhr, and the transport's modulus exhaust was flaring around us, staining the sky dim blue, right on schedule, dropping us from 0.125 cee to zero in as few hours as it could manage.

Most of it was canceled by the ship's fields, but you could still feel the deck surge and shift, ever so slightly, underfoot. Regis looked down, scuffled his boot softly on the rubber flooring, and muttered, "Old junk."

In only a little while, as we watched, Violet and I holding hands, Saad al'Zuhr grew to an irregular yellow mass, like an iron-heavy rock glittering with pyrite flakes, superimposed against the starry sky, somehow shining, as though in sunlight, all alone in the heavens.

Out of the corner of my eye, I could see Santry standing with her back against Regis, squat man barely able to see over her shoulder, watching the world grow huge as we swept in for a landing. He had his arms around her, black hair on his arms making him look more like an animal or an optimod than a human man, clasped near the bottom of her belly, holding her tight against him.

Like us, I thought. Just like us.

Soon, all too soon, we stood on the ground of Saad al'Zuhr, sky blazing pale yellow overhead, flooding us with classic butter-yellow skyshine, standing flat-footed in better than one-half G, not quite standing at attention on the glassy surface of Landing Domain Ax3, while an immense fat man in Standard ARM blue, Bustamonte Palafox his improbable name, bade us welcome.

I'm here, he said, hands clasped behind his back, thrusting his big belly forward, jackbooted feet planted wide, to show you the ropes, get you used to your ships, move you on to Squadron 33 and the Nulliterrae Swarm.

Patience. No time for this. No will to listen. Behind the fat man, a dozen sleek, spindle-shaped Harbinger mk. VI high-energy turretfighters were lined up in one long row, mechanics of various sorts still poking at them through open service-bay doors.

I could feel Violet's tension beside me, her desire to be

aboard, to begin . . . while Palafox droned on, telling us there was no time to waste, that the work was waiting for us.

I reached in my pocket and surreptitiously fingered my orders tab, tiny consciousness in that bit of crystal directing my eyes to . . . yes, *that* one. Harbinger mk. VI serial no. R1080.331, ventral service door open, two men who looked like yellow-limbed automatons poking away at something inside, pilot's canopy cranked open, sticking up like the beak of a bird, partially hiding the dorsal power turret behind it.

Count 'em. Dorsal and ventral turrets. Side sponson missile launchers. After-firing long-range particle beam device mounted between twin modulus exhausts. Imagine that. *Two* exhausts . . . little voice in my head, some not-quite-internalized bit of hypnopaedic update murmuring, *in case one should be damaged* . . .

In front of us, fat Palafox had fallen silent, was merely grinning at us. "Okay, boys and girls. I give up. You can go play with your toys now." Hell. Maybe they pick beings his size for the job just so they won't be trampled by the rush of eager trainees.

I ran between the legs of 331's landing tripod and slid through the belly hatch while Violet swarmed over the side, got the hatch secured, bringing up the interior lighting system as I listened to the whine of electromechanicals bringing down the canopy, high, then dropping, ending on a soft growl, filling my ears with just a second of overpressure.

Just a momentary pang of terror, looking around at a capsule barely large enough to accommodate me, feet in stirrups, butt in bucket, head resting on its little pad . . . The hypnopaedics kicked in, making me look, here and there, at control systems mostly based on freeze-frame technology, patches of mist that'd became whatever they needed to be, when I needed them, overhead and down by my sides, emergency panels of brute-force solid-state switching, circuit breaker resets, a rotational controller that I could switch from gun to gun, helping out A-semi-Eyes that . . .

Pale, soft shock, difficult to fathom. Still a flight engineer, yes, just like in the old days, those dimly remembered sweet days so long ago, but only during cruise mode, and only if . . . something goes wrong.

Combat Systems Officer.

CSO is the real reason this ship exists, Violet merely the taxi driver who carries you to your . . .

Pressure in my ears changed again as Violet opened the little connecting hatch between us, stuck her head through, grinning, and said, "This is better than *anything* we had at Mezzandrée!"

Better than anything. Behind her, through the mesh of the pilot's nest, I could see she already had her external panels lit up, showing a vista of the landing stage, the bright yellow dome of Saad al'Zuhr's ridiculously artificial-looking sky.

Dimly through the hull I could feel little jolts, like the slamming of tiny doors; then, through Violet's imaginary windows, I could see flight-line mechanics scurry away, going down little rabbit holes in the planetary integument, getting out of the way.

Over the command circuit, Palafox's voice: "Okay, boys and girls. Listen up."

I lay back on my couch while Violet sealed the connecting hatch. Yes. Crashfield fittings here and here. If and when. When and if. I remembered the Glow-Ice Worlds. Remembered Wernickë. And thought: *When.* That's all. Just when.

Put my hands into sidesaddle freeze-frames and brought my new world to life.

The little ships were everything we dreamed of, now, everything we lived for, Violet twisting and turning, keeping 331 in formation, living her role with the squadron, dodging imaginary debris, imaginary attackers' weapons, while I dry-fired my guns and launched imaginary missiles at imaginary foes.

Once, we accompanied a vic of mobile ASM launch platforms, headed out weeks to attack an imaginary habitat cluster, were suddenly, days from our goal, set upon by a flotilla of software-generated defenders whose only aim was to destroy the things coming to wreck their world, coming in from all angles, at speeds so high the interstellar dust was visibly eroding their hulls, leaving long contrails of sparkling plasma dissipating behind them.

And outgunning us ten to one.

People shouting over the intercom. Generated fear becoming real. Shouts of dismay, turning into rage at controls locked up and frontline, cutting-edge Harbinger mk. VI turretfighters began drifting helplessly.

They lost every one of their ships in seventy-nine seconds of combat. But they took out all three of the launchers and killed half the fighters as well, people pissing and moaning as their controls came back up and the simulated battle came to an end.

Where the *hell*, demanded Santry, aboard 976, are we going to run into an enemy who outguns us ten to fucking one? Hm? Tell me that.

Palafox's face floating disembodied in my little room: "And you, you fucking idiot. You put that last shot of yours right *through* one of the goddamn launch platforms!"

Oops.

And then on we went, pretending to be a *new* squadron, unattacked, undestroyed, simulating our bombing run against a simulated group of helpless little worlds, ASM launchers sweeping in from the dead black sky, laying down fire against targets visible only in our freeze-frames . . . Well. Just the way they'd be if this ever turned real.

If it ever did.

In my monitors, I watched simulated habitats explode, gouting nuclear fire. All of them were very old-fashioned habitats, inside-out worlds pretty much like Audumla had been.

Had been.

Is.

Not thinking much about Audumla and Ygg anymore. My mother and her robot silvergirls. Rannvi and Lenahr. Ludmilla Nellisdottir . . . Orb letting me know her kids must be grown and gone, maybe even gone on to new Mothersbairn colonies, with children and grandchildren of their own. I had a brief memory of my father, resting quietly in his urn all these years.

Then the long trip back, all the way back to Saad al'Zuhr, Violet and I talking through the open hatch, whiling away the empty hours, me crawling through to be with her, the two of us packed together in the pilot's nest, quiet together, looking out at the motionless stars, she crawling down to be with me, down in the gunner's hole, where we had a little room to squirm.

We were down there one evening, evening as the clock flies, not saying anything, not doing anything, quiet together in our private womb, when Violet, with uncharacteristic shyness in her manner, reached up through the hatch and retrieved a stiff little brush, something from her kit bag, hesitantly handed it to me, then, with almost an air of embarrassment, turned her back.

Something here I don't quite understand. Something . . . with meaning only to another optimod.

She'd waited a long time for this.

Not saying a word.

Just waiting.

I started brushing her long, lustrous fur, finding tangles, making them smooth, and heard her sigh, an oddly contented sound, not a human sound at all, felt her relax under the brush, under the gentle touch of my hands.

Graduation day was only a week off, marking the end of a period I knew we'd remember almost like a honeymoon. Whirlwind of training, punctuated by nights of . . . just us, that's all. Nights and days of us, spaces in between filled with people we were beginning to think of as friends.

Curious friendships forming. People and optimods, robots, and whatnot. Life here in this confined little world so different from what it was like elsewhere. I could think back. Think back all those years and remember fucking an allomorph whore, allomorph really just one more sort of robot, helpless before human will.

Remembering, I tried to imagine myself wanting to marry one.

Sure as hell would've made marital gatesie a breeze, hm?

My pecker's up, honey. Lie down over there. This'll only take a minute.

Tried to superimpose that fantasy over some other life I never had, life with Ludmilla, plenty of gatesie, sure. Plenty of worshipping at the Goddess' Altar.

Sitting in the messhall, Violet grabbed my chin with her soft velvet hand and turned my face so she could look into my eyes. Violet smiling a doggy smile as she said, "Where the fuck are you? You look like you're a million AUs away."

I shrugged, put my arm around her, and said, "I dunno. I get . . . a little lost sometimes. You know?"

Brief, somber look, that familiar head cock she used for a nod. "Sure."

The flightcrew messhall was brimming with trainees just now, people so much like us they'd never think to question closeness between a human man and an optimod woman, people milling around, eating, drinking, making noise, whole front wall of the room taken up by a multilayer freeze-frame that could serve a hundred minds at once. Not quite that many people in here now.

People.

Orb knows they're people.

I remember Violet and I, during our brief time on Telemachus Major, knew to avoid certain kinds of establishments. Remembered back further, back to Glow-Ice, to unpleasant looks we'd gotten one night in an optimod bar.

Remembered Violet putting her hand on my arm, restraining me, just weeks ago, when, in a tavern on TM, I'd turned to see just who might've whispered, ". . . takin' his bitch for a walk. Hope she doesn't squat on the carpet . . ."

Not worth it. Forget it. Let's get out of here.

Glad to.

Forgotten. All forgotten now.

Santry, looking overdressed in Standard blue, plopped down opposite us, followed by Regis, waddling up with fists sprouting bouquets of bottled beer, brown bottles held by their long, thin necks.

I looked at the label as I popped the lid. "Where the hell

is Mexico?" Thousands of AUs away, at least, if I didn't know its name. Nowhere near the Centauri Jet, anyway.

Santry said, "Earth."

I looked at the bottle again, then stuck the neck in my mouth and took a long pull, bittersweet stuff foaming in my throat as it went on down. "Hmh. Earth." Beer's free here, a perk of employment, but I couldn't imagine . . .

Regis finished his own bottle in one long swallow, thumped it down on the table, and burped. "Well. Not bad. I've had better."

Santry said, "You know Standard owns Mexico?"

"No." I tried to picture the map of Earth and discovered it was long gone. "Still don't know where it is either."

Violet said, "Just south of California."

"Oh." I sat back and put my arm around Violet's shoulders again, looking up at the freeze-frame, and remembered Porphyry's diorama deck. Remembered those two servants; remembered the girl who could make her cunt drip on command. Couldn't remember her name. Or if I'd even known it.

The freeze-frame suddenly clicked into hard focus, a hundred fuzzy layers falling together all at once, people all over the room suddenly seeming to sit forward, look up, beer forgotten, each other forgotten. Santry craned around in her seat, murmuring, "What th' fuck . . ." and I felt Violet stiffen under my arm.

Political news, that's all, but . . .

Scene from the Jet Althing, Finn mac Eye sitting on the dais, Meyer Sonn-Atem standing just behind him, as the delegates voted, one by one, transmitting instructions from their home habitats. We surrender our sovereignty. We abrogate our treaties and contracts. We join together in forming a new nation, nation of the Centauri Jet. One people, who will deal with outsiders as a group, and . . .

Again and again and again, Mr. mac Eye, Mr. Sonn-Atem.

Heroes.

Of the people. For the people. By the people.

Freedom and dignity.

Bratska i swoboda.

All that rot that kills us dead.

Rot from the . . . popular will.

Violet said, "Oh, hell. I guess the shit and the fan are in sight of each other now."

CHAPTER ELEVEN

The Nulliterrae Swarm floats within the physical confines, if you can call them that, of the diffuse distal end of the Centauri Jet, just over two hundred AUs from Saad al'Zuhr, not quite so far from Telemachus Major in the deep black sky.

"Actually," Violet said, as we watched the Swarm form up, from tiny freckles all but hidden among the dense background of Milky Way stars, to a fistful of pale beads that drew apart as they grew larger and the Swarm took on depth, "this area's inside the Jet's no-fly zone."

As if they could enforce that.

Santry's voice, chipper over the comlink, her face blinking on briefly in one of my freeze-frames: "And so appropriately named."

Nulliterrae. Italian? No, Latin. Not so different from various Hispanic dialects I'd known. No-man's worlds? Something like that. I said, "Think the Jetties'll come for 'em?"

Regis Gosseyn's voice said, "Hope so," while his face came and went between me and my imaginary controls.

Violet muttered. "Idiot . . ." Just to me, to herself, comlink suppressed. Regis doesn't mind being called names, but it'd make Santry mad.

I had a brief memory of glimpsing the two of them together in a little park somewhere near the training ground on Saad al'Zuhr, during the darktime, when Grounds Maintenance turned off the skyshine so the garden plants could have the nighttime they needed. Slim, classic human girl dwarfed by the raw, hairy bulk of Regis the Pseudo-Neanderthaler, the two of them with their faces pushed together, he with one paw groping between her legs.

Violet had giggled softly, nudged me in the ribs, then dragged me off to a private corner of the garden where we could bill and coo for ourselves alone.

All around us in the sky the planetesimal worlds of the Nulliterrae Swarm grew, first seeming huge, then smaller as they receded from one another, our little fleet, Squadron 33 Replacement Unit 5, bunched together, singling out one little white world, an angular bit that looked like it might be freshly broken quartz, maybe even ice.

Palafox: "Landing Stage 33. Welcome home, boys and girls."

We spiraled down into a haze of white light like so many silent, deadly hornets returning to their hive.

Life, perhaps, is made up mainly of those moments from which our memories are made. The rest of it really happens, I guess, but it goes away, slinks on back to the gray mist of Uncreated Time, becomes unmemory, waits in the quiet darkness for you to join it.

Maybe that's what the between times are like, after you die, before you're born, waiting in a welter of lost memories, an undifferentiated smear of unmemorable events, while you wait for Orb to call you forth, extrude you back into the Universe of the Living.

And the moments that make memories once again.

So Violet and I carried our duffel bags down a long blue corridor, carpet and walls alike clad in Standard ARM blue, until we found the door with our names on it. Our names. Darius Murphy. Violet . . . just Violet. Our names. Serial numbers. Beyond the door, our room.

When I put out my hand, the door slid open and the room lights came on, dark plastic furniture visible within. Dressers, desks, two little beds neatly made up with coverlets of Standard ARM blue . . .

Why are we hesitating?

When I looked at Violet she was grinning, and had dropped her duffel on the hallway floor.

Right.

I dropped mine beside it, picked her up, and carried her feather-light over the threshold, door sliding shut behind us. It was a while before we realized we'd left our luggage out in the hall.

Details. Details. You move into a new situation, you get to know the people, the places, the things. In some matters, we were lucky. Usual practice in the Standard ARM Aerospace Guard is to keep the new chums together for a season or two, keep them under the wing of archangel Palafox until you see whether they work out or not.

If you're smart, you poke around, see what's what, get to know the seasoned fliers, see what you can learn from them, get to know the admins and dog-robbers, who're the only people who can *really* get whatever it is you need at any given time. Most especially, get to know the mechanics.

Our unit's maintenance chief was a very small, roly-poly

woman with yellow-brown skin, slanty eyes, and black hair so tightly coiled it formed little island tufts all over her scalp. A roly-poly woman, name of Gordil, with incongruously thin arms, who eyed me up and down and said, "Hell, you Saggies are all alike. Every damn one of you wants special treatment . . ." She threw her arms up in mock alarm and, in a rather gruff voice, said, "My ship! My ship!"

Then she grinned as if she'd said something unusually clever, as if waiting for a reaction. Well, um . . . she said, "Course, if you got anything to *trade* . . ." Looking at me pointedly, an awfully familiar look, bringing back memories I thought were gone for good.

I did have a moment in which I tried picturing what she might look like under those baggy coveralls, but . . .

She laughed at me and said, "Naah. That fuckin' oppie you're with'd take fuckin' big bites outa my sorry fat ass . . ." Still, just talking to her was enough—she seemed to appreciate that I'd once been in training for a job like hers. And, who knows, maybe she secretly wanted to fly herself.

Mostly, in the days and weeks that followed, flying is what we did, going out on maneuvers just as we had back on Saad al'Zuhr, only now with the entire squadron all around us as we worked our way into the complex mesh of the command network, getting used to our . . . comrades in arms, I'd guess you say, learning our jobs better and better while the need of their doing grew stronger.

Out on maneuvers, back to base, then on out again.

And, of course, things back at base, back on our little Nulliterra worldlet, continued to evolve as well.

We were coming back from a pretend escort mission that had taken us days from the Swarm, skirting the edge of a space where Jet forces actually made a pretense of patrol, packet-destroyers they'd bought who-knows-where shadowing our operation at a distance. I was down in my module, reviewing my engineering checklists, when the hatch to the pilot's nest opened.

I craned my head back, looking at Violet, upside down in the hatch, and smiled. For some reason, she wasn't smiling back, just looking down at me, face very serious, rather odd look in her eyes. "Something wrong?"

She said, "Well. I, uh . . ." Uncharacteristically shy. And not the same kind of shyness as when she first handed me her brush, first turned her back for currying. "I've been meaning to talk to you, Murph."

Like we needed to make an appointment or something? I flipped over in the module's cramped space so I could see her more normally. "What is it?" An uneasy crawling in my stomach. What's going on that I should already have noticed? What've I done that I shouldn't have? Orb knows, but never tells.

She said, "Well. Santry came to me just before we left. She, uh, she said she'd like us to swap for a while."

"Swap?"

"Swap you for Regis."

"As flight crew? Why?"

That brought out a shadow of exasperated amusement. "Idiot. For a fuck!"

"Oh."

And then I sat there, staring at Violet while I pictured Santry. Since the day we met her, she'd been notoriously careless about herself and I'd seen her buck-naked more times than I could count, emerging from the mist of the shower room, seen dressing through the open door of her room.

And then I sat there imagining her in my bed, imagined her smooth, hairless human skin, sleek and slick against my own, very different from Violet's silkily tickling fur. Like in the olden days, playing gatesie with real human girls, shallow human mouths working hard to do their job, wiry human pubic hair in your face, tits you could *see* as well as feel . . .

"Murph? I'll do it if you want. I mean, it'll be all right if . . . for a while . . ." The alarm on her face was almost comical, the agony in her eyes like an endearing fist, clutching me deep in the chest.

I grinned; put out my hand to touch her. "Hey. Let's not accidentally talk ourselves into something neither of us wants, hm?"

Back in the Swarm, huddled in the darkness of our dorm room, squeezed together into one of the little beds, Violet and I lay, postcoital, quiet, curled up together, form matching form.

I had one hand on her breast, human shape beneath the fur, and could feel the beating of her heart. I imagined she could feel my heart, beating against her back.

What a strange interlude, as if it could go on forever . . .

I felt myself grow hazy, mind drifting far away, vaguely conscious of the way Violet's heart slowed under my hand, as her breathing grew shallow.

As if it's already gone on forever . . .

Sometimes, making love to my optimod girl, it seems like there's been no other, just she and I, since the dawn of time.

No Audumla, with its Mothersbairn and gatesie girls.

No Reese.

No . . . I still shied away from those brief days at Wolf 359.

Then . . . no Sirius?

Abruptly, right on the edge of a dream, I remembered

crouching in the ruins with Jade, Jade kneeling before me, shrugging out of her grimy coverall, clinging to me and . . .

All of a sudden, I remembered how she cried after we made love, clinging to me, shaking, so afraid . . .

I came back to consciousness, clutching Violet, Jade's terror ringing in my ears, then . . . *bang.*

Violet murmured, "Murph . . . ?"

I whispered, "Nothing. Bad dream. Sorry."

She reached back and patted me gently on the thigh. Snuggled closer against my chest, settling back toward sleep.

It was a while before I could relax again.

About a dozen kems from the SAAG base where Squadron 33 was billeted there was a little patch of woods, a swatch of field with a winding stream where some of us used to go during off-duty time. Not quite a park, overgrown, weedy, kept up mainly by the action of trampling feet—plainly artificial, like everything else.

Violet and I had our picnic blanket spread on yellow-green grass by the side of the stream, which bubbled softly in the background, a flow of pale, yellow-brown water, the reason the place was called Runnymead. Because of it, because someone once wondered about the name and had the commissary place a special order; we were drinking mead now, honey-scented stuff so different from beer and wine it was in a class of its own. Drinking mead, eating little sandwiches, fatty goose-liver pâté, almond butter with marshmallow, some sliced stuff they called dachshundsarsch synthesized in a habitat I'd never heard of before, nodding to Santry's portable freeze-frame while we watched her play in the water with Regis.

He looks silly with all that dense black hair pasted flat to his skin, fat pecker bouncing into view from time to time. Santry, though . . . I tried hard not to watch her too much, too closely, water streaming from her long, shiny black hair, making her skin glisten in the sunless light of the bright yellow sky.

All the same, Violet put out her hand, reclaiming me with a touch.

Political news on the freeze-frame. A lot of it, focused through the spin filters of Standard ARM, all about what was going on in the Jet. Negotiation. Endless negotiation. Standard and seven or eight other really big companies leading a legal challenge to the Althing's blizzard of new regulations, its horde of new regulatory agencies.

Governments have no *right,* the freeze-frame said . . .

I looked back at the stream. Santry and Regis were standing belly to belly in waist-deep water, faces pressed together. Violet had her head down on the blanket now, just touching my side, arm thrown over me in a protective curl. I wondered for just a moment what she was thinking; wondered if I was supposed to ask.

All around us, little blue flying things buzzed from flower to flower, little things Santry insisted were called hummingbirds, though I couldn't see them well enough to know if they were truly avian, or something else. Big blue bugs, maybe. Bees. Or just completely man-made doohickies, left over from when this place had been something else.

Special program coming up in the freeze-frame, transmitted broad-band across all local channels, straight from the Standard ARM news center. I felt Violet stir by my side, lifting her head slightly. Out in the stream, Regis and Santry were grinding gently against each other, and I realized they might actually be fucking under the water.

Beyond them, beyond the stream, beyond the far field and

a rim of woods made up of raggedy yellow trees from which thin plumes of pale blue smoke seemed to rise, a dome of glittery white ice stuck up straight through the yellow sky, poking through the habitat's eutropic shield into airless space.

While I watched, a vic of turretfighters rose from the base beyond the hill, friends of ours, I supposed, banked hard, sparkled blue exhaust, accelerated, and was gone.

Odd.

Not your usual sort of maneuver, this wasteful use of emergency thrust. More a livefire combat sort of thing . . .

Then the freeze-frame chimed, much louder than the volume setting should have allowed, the same noise it's supposed to make when they announce some sort of civil emergency in a populated habitat. You hear that chime, then somebody tells you to run for your life.

Out in the stream, Regis and Santry went suddenly still, holding each other close. Maybe Regis is having his orgasm now, pulsing softly away inside her. But then they pulled apart, with evident reluctance, heads turning to face the shore.

And then the freeze-frame told us, in so many words, that the government and Althing of the United Habitats of the Centauri Jet had withdrawn from all negotiations, had then nationalized corporate operations on all member worlds. Ours, and everyone else's.

And then the freeze-frame said, *All Standard ARM personnel will report to their duty stations immediately.*

Beyond the glitter-ice hill, another vic of fighters lifted off from the base, banked hard, sparkled blue, and was gone.

We got up, slowly, silently, while Regis and Santry waded to shore. Slowly folded our blanket, put away our food, slowly walked back to the flier we'd borrowed for the afternoon. And Violet held my hand more than usual.

War, they say, is just business conducted through other means.

No time flat and we were aboard the 331, Violet and I, out in the dark between the stars with the entire squadron, escorting three LSTs full of Standard ARM AstroMarines— Sammies, they're called—from the base complex at the Nulliterrae Swarm to a piece of Standard real estate called Morgan's Round. Standard's until just the other day.

I could look out through my biggest freeze-frame, see the boxy LSTs surrounded by a swarm of little turretfighters. And, off to one side, our unmanned companion, a bulbous, matte-black Smoky Rose Gun Platform.

Unmanned but for a laconic AI who knew it might be expended like so much ammunition.

Do your job, it seemed to say. I'll do mine.

The connecting hatch to the pilot's nest slid open and Violet popped her head and shoulders through, filling the module with her faint lavender scent. Looked around for a second, then slid on down, squirming in beside me.

Not supposed to do this. Technically we're in combat right now, but what the hell. Morgan's Round is still a hundred hours away.

We'd made love in this little vacuole from time to time, giggling away at our naughty little transgression, but not now. Violet just seemed to want to hold me close, snuggle beneath my arm, and look out at the stars. After a while, she whispered, "Just like it was before . . ."

Before?

Before a hundred years of solitude. A hundred years in which Violet the optimod went to a hundred little wars all by herself. A hundred years in which I wandered, loved and lost, fought and was defeated . . .

An abrupt memory of Jade surfaced.

Nothing left of her inside me now but a memory of a dead woman's body sprawled headless in some bloody grass. All the good parts went away, poisoned by that last.

Violet said, "Just like in the Glow-Ice days. You and me. Dûmnahn . . ."

You and me. Dûmnahn. The dead and the dying. Remember them too.

She said, "I wonder where he is now. Sometimes I still miss him, after all these years."

I held her close and said, "Maybe we'll see him again sometime. After all . . ." After all, he's still alive. We could easily run into . . . one of him. Run into a being somewhere that calls itself Dûmnahn and remembers both of us, just the way you remember characters in a book. Not *quite* like old friends, but . . .

Violet whispered, "Bastards."

That was like old times too, back when she still had the will to hate what'd been done to us all by . . . Hell. By the people who pay us, that's all. When did we lose the will to hate them? Maybe when they gave us these nice, cushy jobs. Maybe when they let us . . . be together.

All these weeks, so much like heaven. So much like . . .

And then, unanticipated, came the warning chime, loud in our ears.

Over the freeze-frame, Palafox's voice cried out, "Tally-*ho*!"

Bring your revolver, Watson. The game is afoot . . .

Little blue lights, sparkling against the sky.

Coming our way.

*　　*　　*

The little blue lights descended on us, but we'd seen them in time, several wings of Jettie fighter craft, spiraling in toward us, spiraling in for the kill, I suppose. As it happened, we had better ships than they did.

Violet oiled out from under my arm, slid back up to the pilot's nest, hatch snapping shut behind her. I felt my heart start to pound as I ignited the inertial harnesses, as I put my hands in the sidesaddle interface controls, looking at this freeze-frame and that, making sure all was right with my engines and subsystems and . . .

The ship bounced and tugged at me through the inertial compensator field as Violet made it twist and turn, our wingman, the ship holding Santry and Regis, turning hard alongside us, crossing the path of the three LSTs, whose Sammies, right now, must be holding on tight, hoping they weren't about to die, swooping low above Smoky Rose which, I noticed abstractedly, was rolling about its long axis.

Right. Right. Things you can do too . . .

I said, "Weapons systems up. Optical alignments to null. Pulse radar . . ." Damn it. Ah. There.

Something flashed outside, nowhere nearby.

I shoved my face into the multiplexer and had at them.

There. There.

Bright blue stars whirling all around.

That one. Now.

The star went nova, burst into a pale blue puffball, and was gone, like so many dandelion seeds blowing on the wind. Do I really remember that? Yes, I do. We had dandelions in Audumla, I think. Can't remember. Can't remember.

Not now, I . . .

There! There! That one!

Another blue fireflower, another Jettie gone off to Uncreated Time.

Twisting. Twisting. Multiplexer looking around. Looking for . . .

Cold sweat bathing my face.

All gone. Every last one of them.

Three LSTs cruising onward serenely, as though nothing ever happened. Over there, Smoky Rose was falling back into place, gunports sliding shut all over its hull. Wonder how many Jetties it killed, all by itself?

Orb.

I got two.

Good work. Good work, I . . .

All around us, Squadron 33's turretfighters were sliding back into place, slowing down, taking up their positions, and I . . .

I said, "Violet?"

Nothing.

"Violet? Where are Santry and Regis?" Not like them to be out of position.

There was a long, empty silence; then, ever so softly, she said, "They bought it, Murph."

I tried hard not to understand, but . . . I can't remember. Did I see it happen? Can't remember. Sometime, while I was making fireflowers out of those two Jettie ships, a Jettie gunner was looking through his own multiplexer, heart pounding, thoughts chaotic, as he made a fireflower out of them.

Nothing left of them but atoms.

Atoms and memories.

And whoever did it, they're gone too.

How many people did we kill today?

Don't know.

More to come.

So we flew on, flew on to Morgan's Round, dropped on it

out of a dead black sky, doing our job of killing, and Palafox, damn him, played "Hall of the Mountain King" over the intercom, while we flew and killed, and killed some more, until the job was done.

It seemed like no more than one long day, two quick pulses of battle separated by a few score hours of unnervingly empty travel, stars a motionless backdrop as we slid our deadly way toward Morgan's Round. Then we fought, twisting, turning, skidding from kill to kill, while Smoky Rose turned its guns on a garden-green world below, fires blooming in cityscape as we fought through the heavens.

Somewhere near the end of it all, long after the Sammies were down and doing *their* job, 331 was rammed by a dense ball of electrically charged plasma, the hot, gasified remnants of an enemy ship.

I remember how Violet screamed as fire danced and roared on the inside of our hull. Remember how sparks jumped from my fingertips as I pulled them from my sidesaddle interfaces. Maybe I screamed too, calling out Orb's name in vain. Not much time for screaming: I felt the ship surge and buck underneath me as Violet struggled to regain control, as I made a frenzied dance from frame to frame, trying to see if . . .

Palafox: "*Three-thirty-one!* Status, 331!"

"Uhhh . . ." Orb, get it together! "Gun systems down, Leader. We're out of it." No shit . . . "Uh. Engine power at four percent and falling." Falling fast.

"Can you make it?"

"Uh . . ."

Violet snapped, "We'll be all right, Leader. Pick us a spot."

Silence.

She said, "Goddamn it, Palafox!"

He said, "Uh. Okay, 331. Sammies've recaptured the Standard stage at Hobart 5 Intersection, just over the limb from your position. I'll let 'em know you're coming."

Very dry: "Thanks."

And what if she'd told him the same thing my instruments told me, that we stood a better than even chance of splattering ourselves all over Morgan's nice round landscape? Well, you know the drill. Try to come down on residential habitat. Not so goddamned expensive to replace.

The ship started to shudder and sway, stars, explosions, pseudoplanet on fire below, all of it tipping back and forth. I realized with a pang of horror that the inertial fields had come down. We run into anything now, anything at all, and I'll be jelly between the switches of my fucking circuit breaker panels in the twinkling of an eye.

"Violet?"

Moment of silence, then a tight, "Not now."

Okay. Understood. Do your job.

I found a control frame that was still working, put both my hands in, and starred to feel around. Restitutor Orbis, I . . . Well, shit. Lookee here. I mated two disconnected subsystems that seemed otherwise all right, felt the world suddenly stabilize as the compensators came back up. Watched, blinking, as the engine power histograms climbed toward green.

Violet's voice, gasping in my ear: "Oh, God, Murphy! Thank you."

And so down we went over the humped-up hills of Morgan's Round, me at least praying all the way, hoping like hell old Orb was out there somewhere, approving of the work I'd done, brave, brave little man-child, that he'd give us a little push, you see, and today wouldn't be *my* day to settle back for a nice long rest in Uncreated Time.

There!

Familiar-looking Standard ARM installation, buildings like broken teeth, fire and smoke still coming out of them, surrounded by neat green lawns, little lakes, and . . . yes. One nice landing stage, painted pale blue, Standard ARM logo with its blazing sun and double-thunderbolt, just off to one side of the Sammy LST . . .

Violet said, "Jesus. Hang on, Murph!"

I felt the shields sputter and start to fall. Reached inside the control frame again, but . . . fuck. Useless. The ground seemed to be coming up awfully fast now and . . . Fire sprayed outside as we poked through the eutropic shield, hull suddenly coming alive, rattling, banging, wind moaning just a few cems away.

Now. Now . . . I felt like shouting up to Violet, telling her we *really* ought to be slowing up now, getting ready to settle down on the stage, and . . . I took a quick look at the histogram, watched it fall through blue and amber to red. One percent. No more.

So.

I tried to imagine what it would be like when we hit the ground in just a few seconds. Would I see the walls explode apart, just before I died? Would I carry that memory with me into death, a seed on which my next life would have to form?

And just how many of those marines are going to die now, just because we were afraid to?

No answer.

The image of Restitutor Orbis and the promise of Uncreated Time suddenly faded, receding beyond my reach, leaving me with nothing.

Then Violet applied lateral thrust. I could hear her grunt, high and raw, through the intercom, as the world outside twisted and spun, going flat underneath us, racing by, racing . . . the ship screeching as she touched down, running not quite parallel to the surface.

Bang.

The emergency pyros went off by themselves and the ventral hatch blew, falling away. Down below my ass, a hands-breadth away, I could see the blue-painted surface of the landing stage rushing on by.

Look at those fucking sparks, will you?

The ship screeched to a halt, rocked once, and was still. I sat back, looking up at the ceiling, with all its dead instruments, smelling a tang of burned metal, feeling the sweat trickle out of my hair and run down the back of my neck like hot oil.

Then the connecting hatch to the pilot's nest, twisted and askew in its mount, creaked open, and there was Violet, blood coming from her nose, looking down at me, eyes so very wide.

She whispered, "Murph?"

I reached down comically and felt the seat of my pants. "Hey. Do farts have lumps in them?"

A bizarre, lopsided grin, then Violet started to sniffle as she slid through the hatch on top of me, getting blood on my nice clean uniform.

It took less than a minute for the rescue team to get over to what was left of 331 and get us out of there, though they said they were somewhat alarmed when they cranked open the upper hatch and found the pilot's nest empty. There's no provision for bailing out of a turretfighter. I mean, where the hell would you go?

They had an ambulance ready, but we didn't really need it. I had some burns on my hands that they fixed up with a quick spray; Violet's nosebleed had come, apparently, from the force of her sudden stop as she flew out of her crash net and went face-first into her dead viewscreens.

I was absolutely fucking *blind* up there, she told the medics. Just *hoping* the goddamned radar altimeter was right . . .

Back along our track, you could see a long white gouge where we took the paint off the landing stage. We missed running into the LST by about six ems, which would've made a fuck of a mess.

Scared the shit out of *me,* said the medic. We were parked right by the fucking *ramp* . . .

Good enough is good enough. I turned and looked in the direction we'd been going. Edge of the stage right there. Then a parking lot full of surface-effect cars, most of them still neatly in their spaces, the cars of the landing stage employees. Then a nice terminal building whose front glass wall had been blown out by some earlier event, shards sprinkled like diamonds all over the lawn.

Inside the blown-open building was a small crowd, couple of hundred people, I guess, under guard by a few armed Sammies. Waiting for something.

The Sammy officer who'd come out to see if he could help looked where I was looking. "Not sure I feel sorry for them."

I looked at him, then back at the people in the ruined terminal. "Who . . ."

"Employees . . . Well. former employees of Standard ARM."

Violet was standing beside me now, nosebleed over. And looking at something else, standing very still. A cargo shuttle was grounded to one side of the terminal, bay doors yawning open, and another group of people, people tied together by what looked like chains, were being led inside, being made to lie on the deck, also under guard.

Furry people of various sorts. Optimods.

The officer said, "Valuable property, I guess. We heard they were being taken away for . . . reprogramming." He glanced at Violet and said, "Sorry ma'm. I didn't mean . . ."

She just looked at him, then shrugged, a barely perceptible shift of her shoulders.

I gestured at the people, the human beings sitting inside the terminal. "What about them?"

I don't think he wanted to answer, looking at me owl-eyed for a second. "Well." He looked down at his feet, seeming to search for something, then up at the sky. Took a long, deep breath, then looked back at me. "We've been told to shoot them."

CHAPTER TWELVE

It's too easy to say, War is hell.

War is more like a poem.

My war's like a red, red rose . . .

Fucking idiot.

After those opening battles, it went on and on, all the same. That's all I remember, really. We fly around. I shoot the guns. The explosions are pretty. People die. What the hell are they fighting for? *Freedom?* What the hell is that?

You're born out of nothing. You live for a while. You die. You go back to nothing.

What kind of fool dies for a word?

A better class of fool than the one who dies for a paycheck?

Don't know.

I remember the pretty battles; I remember the between times, making love with my pretty purple fox. If I might die for a paycheck, what the hell am I living for? The wet between my purple fox's legs? Maybe the light in her eyes when she looks at me.

Don't know.

Other things changed, after those first battles. We never again talked about Regis and Santry, or any of the other lost ones we'd known so well. Made friends with our comrades, sure, went out and got drunk, raised hell, did what we were supposed to do. But you can't quite get hold of them, these ghostlike friends. Not anymore.

Someone said it's like they're already dead, but that's silly. Everyone dies, sooner or later. What difference does it make, if sooner's the one for you? Still, Violet and I stuck mainly with each other, you know? Because if we die, when we die, it'll be in a blinding flash of light, ending as a lovely flower of nuclear fire outlined against the deep black sky. And, of course, we'll be together when it happens.

So it went on, battles, landings among ruins, where we'd see those same scenes over and over, of people led away for reeducation of one sort or another or, valueless, shot and buried, later on, for efficiency's sake, buried alive, just like those remembered scenes from the Glow-Ice Rebellion, so long ago.

Furlough times too, as the war dragged on, Violet and I going away alone together, making love in some quiet garden spot or another, on mountaintops above rolling amber plains, by the shores of some nameless, ersatz blue sea, making believe we were on vacation, that we had some other life we could go back to, other than the one stark life we'd made.

After a while, I stopped trying to imagine what that life might be like. No images available, other than false ones from millennia-old stories, the white picket fence, the dog, the children, the flat blue skies of Earth.

Honey, I'm home.

There'd never been a world in which Violet and I could

have coexisted, could have known and loved each other, except this one real world, here and now.

The furloughs always ended, real world waiting.

Always more of the same, until one day, one fine, sunless, black-sky day, we backtracked, corporate fleets streaming homeward from the havoc they'd wrought in the heart of the Centauri Jet, back toward Telemachus Major, where the forces of Finn mac Eye, under the direct command of Sector Marshall Meyer Sonn-Atem, having snuck past us somehow, were attacking.

Attacking the corporations at their heart, on their headquarters world, hoping against hope . . .

Even from a distance, you could see it happening, Violet whispering to herself as she worked her controls, looking out through her viewscreens at black space, I with my head down in the gunnery interface, my best view, tuned to the forward-looking optical rangefinder.

Telemachus Major was no more than a distant glitter of blue light, tinted green off to one side, just as I'd first seen her so long ago, from the forward obdeck of *Sans Peur,* epeiric friend Hórhe by my side . . . and, I guess, imagining my father back on Audumla, imagining him imagining my new life with envy and pride.

I'll come back for you. Is that what I said?

I guess, by then, he was already in his urn.

Wish I could picture him now, ghostly spirit one with Uncreated Time, waiting among his dreams, waiting to be reborn.

Things were twinkling in the sky around Telemachus Major, things brighter than the background stars, things that flashed blue-white, grew to yellow sparks, grew red as they faded. I cocked my guns, took off the safeties, alerted my AIs, and watched Telemachus Major grow, scanning through the soft, frightened, frightening babble of voices on the fleet command circuit.

At some point, the connecting door to Violet hissed shut, pressure a momentary pulse in my ears, then the ship, the fourth turretfighter we'd flown together, this one a mk. XII, began to shudder and shift as she brought us down from interstellar flight status to the combat regime.

Ships appeared in the sky around us, enemy ships sweeping in, while voices howled in the freeze-frame universe, the same voices you hear in every old war story. I put my hands to the guns, latched my AIs, and started killing them.

Conformal time passes of its own accord.

When it does, I almost can't remember I once believed its passage was driven by the pressure of newly created time, time freshly emerged from the universal forge, fed by the infinitely deep reservoir of Uncreated Time, extruder of souls.

With the greater battle over, Thulian fleets destroyed or in ragtag remnants fleeing back toward the temporary safety of the inner Centauri Jet, we swept down on Telemachus Major itself, Violet and I in our brand-spanking-new mk. XII, surrounded by our comrades, those who survived, watching a familiar little world swell in the skies, familiar and yet strange.

Things were afire down on the surface, atmosphere englobed by the eutropic shield no longer blue, holding instead a sky full of haze and smoke, partly hiding what'd been done in freedom's name. There, beside a beach I may once have visited, a bowl of liquid fire, burning blue beside a steaming sea. And over there, a cityscape made of broken toys, plumes of gray smoke rising swiftly from a hundred places, swiftly flattening against the underside of the sky, lit from underneath, dull orange.

The world grew flat below us, changing from planet to landscape, and I felt a curious pulse of amazement, of disbelief, as we passed over what had once been a range of mountains, mountains stripped of their pretty green trees, of their snowcapped, ski-trail white peaks. Mountains reduced to low hills of mud, somehow crushed.

I remember seeing those mountains from a window once, remember thinking how nice it'd be to go there, for Violet and I to go there, ski on the trails, climb among the pine-scented green trees, sit drinking cocoa, snuggled together before an open fire in some woody chalet . . .

We punched through the eutropic shield, wind suddenly moaning outside, turretfighter swimming through haze, billows of smoke, clouds of steam.

Below us was a cityscape that'd been swept away by some godlike hand. You could see the roads, flat surfaces unchanged, and because of them, you could see where the city blocks had been, thousands of square kems of rectangular places, empty space, exposed basements, foundations full of rubble.

There. That must have been a little park. See the holes where the trees used to be?

Sharp voice in the freeze-frame now, calling out vectors.

Ground support role.

Mopping up.

I leaned into the gun interface once more and watched the world's surface slant and twist close below. Watched the sighting rings converge on a cluster of still-standing buildings. Flicker-flash of groundfire coming our way. The pale white trail of a single pathetic missile lifting off.

Now.

Seven or eight of us opened up together, not the entire squadron, just enough, and I watched the cluster of buildings burst, fire and smoke gouting, pieces flying off this way and that. When we passed on by, there was nothing much left.

I could hear Violet's soft breathing in my ears, transmitted through the open intercom. No words. Nothing for her to say.

More vectors from the freeze-frame, fleet command circuit sending us to the next target, ground twisting and turning below. Wonder why they don't surrender, these last, trapped Thulians?

No one's asked them.

One lone surface-effect vehicle rushing across the ground below, raising a cloud of dust as it flew low over the rubble. It turned its turret skyward and the rotary cannon began pelting us with armor-piercing rounds. Violet stooped on it out of the hazy sky, I picked a suitable weapon, fired just once, and the tank turned to a ball of red fire, spilling to a stop among the ruins, flattening out, made, all at once, into a pool of burning slag.

That's it.

Violet pulled up, skimming low over the fiery ruins that'd once been a whole world, aiming us toward the pale gray sky. Looking back through the freeze-frame, I couldn't remember how many billions had once lived here, only that one of them had once been me.

A whisper from Violet.

In front of us, Telemachus' green garden moon was rising out of the haze, clearing the horizon like a golden dream.

Not quite the same, I saw, patches stripped bare of forest, holes gouged in her integument, bits of scorch here and there . . . I sat back and watched it grow huge while I waited.

Violet brought the turretfighter in low over a forest of broken trees, empty gray toothpick trunks reaching for a pale gray sky, brought it to a stop, slowing over a brown oval lake, dropping us to the ground with a soft crunch, as of gravel, on our landing tripod. I sat still for a bit, listening to the pops and pings of the relaxing hull, feeling the tug of the moon's low gravity.

There was a faint mechanical grunt, followed by a soft, hissing whine, the sound of Violet's canopy rising. I popped the ventral hatch, looking between my legs as it dropped open. Disheveled sand, a lone, broken seashell. Sharp shadows, as of sunlight, warm breeze swirling in.

Faint, fishy smell, as of the seashore.

I pulled my feet out of their stirrups, unfastening the crash net, and slid through the hatch, dropping to a crouch, ducking under the curve of the hull and standing upright, staggering just slightly, looking around, squinting.

Violet was standing just beyond the turretfighter's nose, looking toward the muddy lake, arms folded tight to her chest, as if she were cold.

Is this the one? Is this the lake we came to, up on Telemachus' moon, that last real vacation? Is this the sand on which I lay, befuddled by software updates, while Violet sucked my dick 'til I came in her mouth?

She knows. She picked this spot on which to land. Why else?

There was a soft, dry rustling sound in the distance, coming from everywhere all at once, the sound of the warm wind blowing through the ruined trees. Violet unfolded her arms and straightened her back, began walking across the scuffed sand toward a pile of boulders at the water's edge.

I followed her, catching up.

There was nothing at all inviting about the muddy water,

unconnected in memory with the cool blue lake water where I'd swum not that long ago, cool water somehow easing my confusion.

Violet turned and looked at me, looked into my face, eyes darting nervously from one eye to the other and back again, maybe looking for some sign of the man with whom she'd come here once before.

I tried to smile for her; felt it turn into something like a shrug.

She turned away then, and we started to walk along the shore, skirting the pile of rocks. I looked down. Stopped abruptly, Violet turning back, coming to stand beside me.

In the shadow beneath one tawny broken rock was a small animal, something the size of a big mouse. I knelt, looking closely, and saw a brown tarantula spider, alive, black dot eyes oriented toward me, middle legs shifting slowly as it worked its book lungs. When I reached out, as if to touch it, the spider's two front legs lifted and its back arched, exposing black fangs.

Violet touched my shoulder gently. "Better let it be. No telling what it's been through."

I tried to imagine the spider cowering here, bewildered, as the world blew up all around it, roaring fire and smoke, hot wind and cascading debris.

I withdrew my hand, looking up at Violet, nodding, then stood, brushing sand from my knees. Why had I wanted to pet the spider? Tarantulas are covered with soft, brown velvet fur, have eight little cat feet with two little cat claws on each one . . . Maybe for the same reason I liked to pet Violet, on whose arm my hand rested now.

We walked on, not saying anything, headed along the shore toward what appeared to be the ruins of a small building, a collapsed, shapeless pile of wood and stone. I tried to remember what it might have been. The bath house, maybe.

I remembered getting Violet to come into the shower with me, her fur matting down in the steam, flat against her skin, making her look like a naked, purple-skinned woman. I remembered the two of us laughing as I braced her in the corner, legs up, as I fucked her with quick, jerky thrusts, hot water needling on my bare back.

Down in the water was a half-collapsed pier, gray wooden structure that'd almost survived whatever had happened here. Not far away, half-buried in sand at the base of a small, humped-up dune, was a dead naked woman. The dune, I realized, had been caused by her presence on the beach, warm wind piling up sand beside her as the sunless sunlight beat down, day after day.

Violet leaned down and, seizing one thin ankle, pulled her free of the sand, turning her over. The woman, covered in wrinkly brown skin, was stuck in an odd position, arms and legs poking out in peculiar ways, blond hair like a stiff old mop on her head, flattened and matted where it'd been lying on the ground.

The expression frozen on her face seemed one of mild, poignant regret, half-open eyes clouded over so you could barely make out the blue of the iris, teeth bright white between half-open lips. Between her partly spread legs, her vulva wasn't hidden at all by her short blond pubic hair. Looking at it, pads of flesh partly spread, shrinking as their moisture fled, inner folds protruding slightly, I could feel a slight stir of arousal.

Could feel Violet's eyes on me now.

When I didn't look up, look away from the dead woman's pretty crotch, she turned from me, walking slowly toward the ruined pier, head cast down, looking at the sand, as if deep in thought. I followed her then, and we took our seats on the surviving part of the dock, leaning back against wooden posts, facing each other, an em or two apart.

The way she was sitting . . . legs apart, arms resting on knees . . . I could look between her thighs, was forced by nature to look between her thighs rather than up at her face, at her level, questioning gaze. Her own vulva, swathed in purple fur, was popped open by the spread of her legs, gleam of delicate flesh beyond all that long, soft hair.

I could feel my splinter of arousal deepen.

Is that all it takes?

Yes.

Take away a male's power to be aroused by the mere *suggestion* of a woman, by a smell, an idle thought, a 2D photograph . . . take away that and you've taken away the male.

Is that all we are?

Violet said, "Do you miss naked women, Murph?"

That made me look at her face and, for a moment, my familiar Violet, whose expressions and moods I thought I knew so well, was swept away, replaced by a stranger, just one more dog-faced optimod.

The eyes, though. Demanding an answer.

Do I have one?

I thought about all of them then, all together, one by one.

Ludmilla Nellisdottir standing on the half-lit hillside under the red light of Ygg before the backdrop of the junkyard, junkyard full of dead, decayed robots, standing there with her skirt pulled up, showing me Goddess' Altar and Child's Gate, making her proposal of marriage. What was I looking at then? At her? At *it*? Maybe craning my head sideways just a little bit, so I could peer between her legs, try to make out the spot where my prick would slide in, spreading soft lips made wet by excitement, made . . . ready for my use?

In those days, despite everything, I'd've sworn to Orb it wasn't so.

What else?

That nameless allomorph whore who'd stuck in my memory so well, standing before me in a brightly lit field of butterflies somewhere deep in Audumla's belly. Standing there, stuck halfway through the transition from formless child to rounded woman, waiting for me to decide. Did I look down the length of her then, looking for that little curl of cunt?

I remember laying her down on the soft green grass, butterflies swirling in the air above us; remember sticking my prick in her ever-ready vagina, thrusting in soapy softness until I filled it with my own gelatinous goo.

I don't remember what I looked at when I was done. Don't remember if I knelt between her legs, looking down at a mechanical imitation of Goddess' Altar, of Child's Gate, soiled now with the artifacts of my . . . what? Artifacts of my happiness? Is that how I remember it?

I tried to remember Reese. Tried to remember her naked, splayed open for me. Shadowy images, maybe. Some from before, some from after. All I could remember was a faint tingle, an afterimage compounded mainly of shame at what I'd done.

I hope Reese is somewhere safe, that she's learned to feel good about herself once again.

Porphyry?

Stark, terrible images of naked Porphyry, sprawled in her bed of wealthy luxury, legs spread for me like an infinitely deep, dark well, liquid heat waiting for me to jump in. Legs spread for *me* . . . No. Legs spread for herself. Porphyry, naked, like the demonic answer to a stupid boy's prayer.

All the others, all the lesser ones, girls, women, things, burst out at me, nameless, like a bright explosion of autumnal leaves, falling groundward, floating in memory.

Sitting on the broken pier, between the dead woman's pile of sand and the flat, motionless brown waters of the mud-choked lake, I looked into Violet's eyes, seeing her fear, and felt my own dread start to build up. Some disaster will come and put an end to us. Surely it will.

Some disaster always comes.

Almost a pleading in her eyes, compelling me to answer, to tell her the truth, no matter how horrible.

Do I know the truth?

Just say it.

I said, "No. No, I don't miss them, Violet. You're . . . really all the things that they never were."

Seeing her eyes light up then, I wondered if I'd lied.

How will I ever know?

She shifted forward, leaning away from the pier post, coming to her knees, vulva suddenly closed and hidden, then crawled across the little space of splintery gray wood between us, crawling over to come between my legs— maybe I expected her to open my fly then and suck me dry. I don't know. I pulled her up into my arms and kissed her instead.

Long moments of silence, Violet lying against my chest.

Then she said, "We never *say* that we love each other."

No. We never do. I said, "Maybe we're afraid."

Another silence, then, "Maybe so."

We made love then, old friends, maybe something more, comfortable with each other.

In the middle of it all, doing what we always did, I could

always feel that comfortable certainty. Now. Now, Violet, we are more than the sum of our interlocking parts.

Can't you tell?

Of course you can.

The physical damage to Telemachus Major wasn't as bad as it'd looked from the sky. If it'd been a *real* world, maybe it could've been, but any significant release of energy *here* and her icy core would explode. You could look down from the sky and see scoured-away cityscape, see ranges of flattened mountains, sure, but those mountains were as much an artifact as the city had been.

Remember those grainy black and white films of that first man-made cataclysm, Hiroshima. Remember the great explosion, filling the sky with light in an instant, filling it from horizon to horizon, ground to zenith; remember the ominous black mushroom cloud boiling up out of nowhere. Then remember the empty, ashy ground, cityscape vanished, marked only by the gridlines of the streets.

A decade later, Hiroshima was a bustling metropolis, paper and wooden buildings replaced by stone and concrete skyscrapers. All that was left of the old city, all that was left of the devastation was a ruined hulk, the twisted girders and broken concrete of the telephone exchange.

Whose operators, safe in a concrete basement, had survived.

On Telemachus Major, the eutropic shield had lived through the battle, the atmosphere had stayed on the ground, and so it too would revive, would come to life again.

I suppose I was thinking about these things as I lay awake in the darkness, curled around Violet's furry form, feeling the soft rise and fall of her chest as she slept, lying in the darkness, cuddled in a bunk with me in our barrackroom down on Telemachus, bunkered under some recently liberated Standard ARM installation.

Darkness. Violet breathing beside me. The gleam of a little night light at ankle height, over by the door. The soft, far-away whisper of the freeze-frame, mandated to be left on, left on to carry the alarm, if it should come.

I moved my hand across Violet's abdomen, rubbing slowly back and forth, feeling her shift at my touch, not quite waking up, somnolent body aware of me. I could reach up to her breasts, down between her legs. She'd awaken, yawning, maybe ready for whatever I wanted, maybe too sleepy, merely turning in the circle of my arms, putting her head on my shoulder, nuzzling against me, falling, willy-nilly, back into some dreamy abyss.

Her breath caught for a moment and there was a little sound from her throat, nothing like words, then the slow breathing resumed. Maybe a dream. Maybe just a reaction to my touch. Maybe nothing at all.

I shifted my attention to the freeze-frame, making it start to wander the net, wondering when I'd fall asleep again myself. Don't know what awakened me. Maybe Violet moving in her sleep under my hand, the texture of her calling to my nerve endings.

The freeze-frame whispered something about Earth. Something important. I turned slightly, turning toward it, not quite looking over my shoulder. That was enough to make it fill my vision field with gentle blue radiance, though I knew if Violet were to awaken, she'd see nothing. Nothing but darkness.

News of the war, that's all.

The Centauri Jet War. Historians have a name for it already.

The Jet sparkled above me in schematic array, Thulian

holdings in sapphire, eaten away into many separate pockets and isolated globules by the ruby glitter of Corporate Alliance invasions. As I watched, two bright blue bands reached out toward one another, bridging the gap between two pockets of resistance, making them one.

We haven't won yet.

The Jet War will go on.

Far, far from Earth.

What has Earth to do with this, with all of us out here, so very far away?

Well. The government of the Earth and Solar Space, in conclave with the many societies and nations of the Kuiper Belt, with the far-flung habitats of the Oort, has put together some new mediatory body, the Human Defense League.

Politicians giving speeches, nothing more.

Politicians giving speeches, denouncing Ultima Thule, denouncing the corporations, calling for the cessation of hostilities, the arbitration of differences.

In my ear, Violet whispered, "I wonder if anyone who matters is listening."

I turned to face her, holding her in my arms, breathing in her scented breath. "I wonder if there *is* anyone who matters anymore."

And Earth is so very far away. The last thing I heard, before abandoning the freeze-frame, refocusing my attention fully on Violet, was an HDL politician suggesting it might be a good idea if something could be done.

Good idea. But Violet's with me here and now, human politicians far away, far away and safe. For us, tomorrow . . . I held my dog-woman close and wished tomorrow would stay where it was.

* * *

The morning of our internal clocks came, Violet and I awakening at last, looking forward to a little R&R, a few days off while our faithful turretfighter went through its maintenance cycle. We bathed together, playing in the shower, then I sat on the bunk and watched, mind empty, while she worked herself over with a blow dryer.

It's a magic transformation, Violet changing from naked purple woman, all breasts and belly and arms and legs, to lustrous, fluffy creature, a monochrome rainbow. I thought about her question, up on the moon; dismissed it once and for all.

No, Violet. I don't miss them.

We ate breakfast in the underground cantina, joking with people we'd been using for friends, noting a few unremarked absences, flier teams lost in the recent battle, already forgotten, then we went for a long walk aboveground, holding hands under a hazy, blue-gray sky.

Looking up at it, I knew the environmental control systems would have it cobalt again in no time. Soon the grass will start to grow, then the trees. Engineers will come and put the mountains back in place, and Telemachus Major will be a world again.

Seen from the ground, there was a lot more cityscape left than there'd seemed from the air. Buildings all smashed though, ground vehicles lying wrecked in the streets, rising from them an occasional wisp of smoke or steam.

And the dead. The dead are still here, though seldom anywhere in sight. We'd walk along, hand in hand, gaping at ruins, looking in through smashed storefronts at strewn merchandise. Every now and again we'd catch a whiff of decay.

That's all.

It felt like window-shopping, passing by the stumps of buildings, stopping to look inside, see what had once been sold here, there, everywhere. I stood by idly while Violet knelt in a pool of broken glass, picking over diamond bracelets.

"You think it'd be all right for me to take this one?"

Violet kneeling, looking up at me, holding a pretty confection of clear jewels and pale gold. I shrugged, thinking how natural it looked, draped over the short fur of her wrist.

She started to put it back, sighing, then stopped, looking down, looking at the thing in her hand. As she slipped it into her Standard-blue shoulder bag, I said, "No one will know."

And no one will care.

A little farther on were the ruins of one of those live sex show places. Nothing there for me to steal. The advertising poster out front had been torn off halfway up, broken off along with the wall behind it, leaving bare brown legs and curly black pussy for us to see.

I tried to imagine the woman's face, but what was left of her was all I could imagine. There was a faint flavor of rot about the place, making me wonder if she lay dead inside.

Beyond the shopping district was a little park, some of its trees still standing, though most of them lay on their sides in the dirt. Over by a clear-watered little lake, lake water reflecting the blue-gray sky so far overhead, there was a little cluster of people, maybe a couple of dozen, all human beings. From their midst, a man was babbling, pleading for something in run-together words.

Obviously pleading, though his words meant nothing. As we approached, he started to scream, short, high, choppy pulses of sound, separated by sharp gasps, lungs tearing air into his throat so he could scream again.

They had him tied to a tall, fractured stump, stripped naked, bleeding from a hundred cuts, little red rivers running over plump, blue-white flesh. Just now, a woman was kneeling before him, holding his little prick in one hand, trying with the other to slide a long, dark splinter of wood in the little hole, doing a pretty good job of getting it to go while the bound man wriggled and shrieked and begged her to stop.

I nudged a man near the back of the crowd. "What's going on?"

The man looked at me, taking in my blue Standard uniform, glanced at Violet, then said, "What d'you care?"

The screaming stopped and the woman stood, wiping bloody hands on her skirt while the man tied to the stump struggled in his ropes, panting for breath.

I said, "Just curious."

A tall, thin woman beside the man said, "His name's Derben. He was District Manager under the Occupation."

Violet: "So this is a captured Thulian? Ought to turn him in to the authorities."

The man snorted. "Ain't no Thulian. Derben used to be in charge of the local shopping mall."

Derben was screaming again, louder than before. There was another woman kneeling before him now, cutting open his scrotum with what looked like a steak knife. Someone in the crowd shouted, "Just one, Julie! You only get one!"

Another voice: "Yeah, Julie! The other one's *mine*!"

That made the crowd laugh merrily, but Derben, screaming and bucking, didn't seem to get the joke.

The woman by us said, "We're all taking turns. All the women he did, whether they wanted his money or not."

Oh.

Violet said, "Just the women?"

The other man said, "Naw. My wife's dead, so I get her turn." He held up a long, slim, silver pin. "I got dibs on his left eye."

After the steak knife woman had finished pulling off his right nut, Derben didn't seem to be able to talk anymore. Or maybe he'd figured out it was a waste of time. He did whimper, though, watching the next woman step forward, holding a garlic press up for him to see.

Violet and I turned and walked away, getting out of the park as quickly as we could, heading back toward the Standard ARM bunker. Pretty soon we couldn't hear his screams anymore.

A day later we were summoned to a special meeting of senior tactical combat teams, making me wonder just where the time had gone. Years. The war's been going on for years already, Violet and I cocooned together, wandering through the wilderness of nothing between the worlds.

We had no idea why they'd interrupted our little vacation, but it didn't matter. There was really no place to go on Telemachus Major, not anymore. No place where scenes like the one in the park weren't being played out, people doing what people always do, when they can.

Bitter moments when I envied Violet her status as a nonhuman. No way of knowing how optimods would behave, if they were free.

Better, I hope.

They sat us down in a big amphitheater, kems beneath the surface, down deep where the bombs had never reached. There were scars here, of course, footsoldiers had battled in these underground warrens, Thulians come to capture the corporate world, Corporate soldiers come to take it back.

So now a thousand of us sat murmuring in our chairs while two corporate security executives, one in Standard ARM blue, the other wearing the red and brown of General CHON, bracketed a freelance technarch in a colorful civilian toga. Little man with big green eyes and a piping voice, too valuable to be harassed by lawyers, too smart to sign a restrictive contract.

Must be wonderful, being free. Free as a *ronin* scientist, is how the saying goes.

The murmuring gradually faded, people and things turning in their seats, waiting while the execs made their introductions, then listening as the little man with the squeaky voice made his presentation, all about the new All-Purpose mark one Tactical Assault Craft, about how we, as senior combat teams, were being given the wonderful opportunity to volunteer for this new duty.

Retraining to be had.

Exciting new frontline duty in your future.

Opportunity for advancement, you see.

Advancement and promotion.

Promotion to what, I wondered, but by then he was telling us how much we pilots would enjoy flying this splendid new high-performance battle platform, how much we combat systems operators would enjoy its new weapons systems.

Particularly the firehaze projector.

I glanced at Violet, who cocked her head to one side, pretty as can be, and muttered, "What the hell."

They made us volunteer before taking us down to see the prototype. Very few teams stayed behind.

ATAC-1.0022, waiting in a row of identical vehicles on a landing stage inside a small corporate habitat, a dirigible world at the heart of something called a carrier task force, was externally identical to the partly mocked-up prototype we'd been shown on Telemachus Major. Same double-ended boat shape, same dull bronze hull with its two dark-gray, side-mounted field modulus pods, same four articulated landing legs ending in flat black saucers, same unobtrusive hatch mounted just under the matte-finish nose-cap.

Seeing her for the first time, Violet and I stood at a little distance, admiring the sleek, clean lines, not quite like the day we'd come to board our first Harbinger turretfighter. Still less like the day I'd walked up to *Athena 7* and found Dûmnahn waiting to greet me.

I tried to imagine this ship, in front of me now, roaring through the atmosphere of a large habitat, maybe streaking through the skies of a real world, plasma tail streaming behind.

There's beauty in these birds of war.

Maybe that's why we're all so easily fooled.

Violet went first, popping the hatch, which dropped open, unfurling a small, rigid ladder, and disappeared inside. I waited a second, then followed her in, looking around in the half-light. Much better than the prototype, which had had generic crash nets and pretend control panels. Violet was already sitting in the left-hand seat, a seat whose nets and harnesses were recessed, invisible, were supposed to appear like magic when needed, running her hands over the armrest controls, looking forward at the dead gleam of inactive freeze-frames.

I slipped into the right-hand seat, the CSO's workstation. Directly in front of me, slightly below face level, was a modern combat interface, retracted now, dark. Beyond it was a flat surface with a gleam like black marble.

Seeing me look, Violet said, "Stereotaxis hood."

I nodded, imagining what it would be like when all this stuff was live. We'd feel like we were riding our little seats, naked in space. Scary as hell, maybe. That's how it'd feel.

Violet thumbed the system master switch at her side.

There was a soft whine from somewhere, a faint vibration, a puff of warm air from a pair of vents down by our feet. A rapid scroll of data as freeze-frames erected themselves here and there, green and amber indicator lights cycling overhead as discrete emergency panels talked to themselves, to each other.

All's well.

Is that what they're saying?

Better be.

I twisted in my seat and looked over my shoulder. Behind the cockpit was a niche holding a single narrow bunk, set up for zero-G sleeping, off to one side an exposed zero-G toilet and a collapsible mistbath, to the other a tiny kitchen module, refrigerator and oven doors side by side.

Violet was looking at me, head cocked, not quite smiling.

I shrugged, trying not to grin, and said, "Feller could have a good time in a place like this with the girl of his choice."

Violet looked back at the little bunk. "Beast," she said.

Target number one for Carrier Task Force Alpha was a place called Ogygeia, not far from the proximal end of the Centauri Jet, many weeks' travel from Telemachus Major, off the distal end.

Even from far away, Ogygeia was lovely, a pale blue dot hanging in the megascope screens of the pilot's lounge aboard the carrier, where we waited with our little ships, slowly drawing closer, undetected, unsuspected. And that's just the way it looked once we'd launched into free space, Violet and I alone together in our little ship, like a pair of long-haul truckers, bound from world to world.

But our wing of two dozen ATACs drew closer, bearing down on Ogygeia, which grew in our secondaries from a blue dot to a mottled freckle to a lovely blue and white ball,

Violet watching and watching, watching from my arms over the backs of our combat seats, until she said it was just like Earth.

No Moon, of course, but you can't have everything.

I found myself wondering, briefly, just when she'd been to Earth, who'd been with her then.

Her long past sometimes hung over us, like the ghost of a shadow. And I just didn't want to imagine myself one of those horrid people who feel they must completely possess a lover, erasing any past that hasn't been shared.

One day, the last day, Ogygeia hanging immense before us like some child's fancy balloon, lost in space, the alarms came and the fleet drew together in full combat array, Violet and I disentangling ourselves at last, scrambling over the seats, netting ourselves in.

One. Two. Three.

The stereotaxis device came on and we were dustmote gods. Flying together, side by side through the dark sky, riding our witches' seats, waiting for the defenders to rise. Waiting, I called up the gunnery interface, which obligingly unfolded from its console, filling with the usual amber-green-blue array of combat data, dots and lines, objects and vectors, tensor numerics flickering beside them.

I said, "Not much. Not much here at all."

Violet took one hand off her armrest controls, reached out to stroke me briefly on the forearm.

Somewhere behind us, still plunging down from the infinite deep, the carrier task force was coming, empty carrier ready to take us in when our job was done, corvettes with their circling swarms of defensive fighters ready to disgorge their marines, finish the job that we would start.

I looked at peaceful Ogygeia one last time, thinking just

how really *pretty* the goddamned place was, then I put my head in the gunnery interface and got my ass to work.

Defenders rising.

Bright amber sparks, amber showing us unmanned vehicles, not even harboring so much life as a Dûmnahn might represent. AIs, lightspeed computer nets. What the hell. Call them missiles. We fired on them from as far out as we dared, directed energy weapons lingering on mirror-bright hulls, heating, heating . . .

I watched as the warheads cooked off one by one, red disks appearing briefly against the backdrop of the fake planet, reflecting red off man-made clouds, man-made seas, vector lines fading, tensor numerics gone like that.

Okay. Much closer now.

Careful, boys and girls. They'll have saved shorter-range surface-to-air missiles for later on. Right now . . .

Swarms of fighters suddenly appearing, like magic, hundreds of engines blinking on, so many blue pinpricks in the sky, much closer than we expected. Somebody, somebody in one of the other ships, whispered, "Fuck. Lying doggo, the bastards!"

Very clever, launching long before we'd arrived, putting themselves in remote orbits around Ogygeia while they waited for us to come, pilots powering down their little ships, sitting there all alone, silent.

While we'd come prowling on in, confident in our stealth, our surprise arrival, so far from the main battle lines.

But they'd known anyway.

And maybe our corporate masters had known too, merely hadn't bothered to tell us.

What difference can it make? they'd have asked themselves.

None at all.

Expendable is expendable.

Right?

That's what we pay you for.

Time to see if this fancy new targeting computer can do its job. I started picking out targets for myself, feeding navigational data to Violet, counterforce data to my counterparts in the other ships of our little fleet. No sense getting in each other's way.

Our two dozen ATAC boats flew apart, squadron blooming like an invisible flower. Imagine how it looks on the combat scopes of our worthy opponents. Imagine the vector lines, tensor numerics, revealing our few numbers.

We opened fire, I and my comrades, and the sky started to twinkle all around as enemy fighters were destroyed.

Hundreds dying right now.

No one will miss them.

Not when we've finished what we came to do.

I could hear my friends whooping and hollering through the command circuit. Look at that. Look at 'em go. Yee-hah.

It's a lucky soldier who has this experience, showing up for battle possessed of an invincible edge. Ogygeia. Remember it well, Mr. Murphy. Next time. Next world, they'll be ready.

I imagined myself part of a twinkling sky seen from some defender's cockpit. See that one over there, that nice silvery little twinkle? That's Murphy and Violet, gone to their reward.

Our fleet formed up into a flat line, bridging Ogygeia's circumference like a string of blue modulus pearls. By now, we'd be visible in Ogygeia's sky, people on the ground, innocent civilians, if there is such a thing, looking up at us, listening to the air-raid sirens moan.

I heard the flight commander's crisp voice: "*Alpha?* ATAC-1 Rainbow here. We're go for ground."

Some corporate admiral's voice in reply: "Roger, Rainbow Leader. We copy you go for ground."

Yee-hah.

The red dots of short-range SAMs began sparking off the ground as we approached, looking for all the world like so many fireworks, Roman candle balls puffing heavenward, heading our way. My defensive weapons, preset, began snuffing out our share as Violet fought her controls, killing our velocity, slowing us, slowing . . .

We slapped through Ogygeia's eutropic shield with a jolt, sky changing from starry black to cloudy blue just like that, air suddenly screaming round our hull. Behind us, I knew, a long yellow plasma trail would be forming, but I couldn't be bothered to look.

The command circuit said, "Oh-twenty-two? Rainbow. Primary target grid six-bravo. Secondary twelve-trillium. Then targets of opportunity to fifty percent load."

Violet said, "Roger, Rainbow. Six-bravo. Twelve-trillium. Ops to fifty."

As the ground flattened under us, I bent my face to the hood, tracking, assigning, managing my resources. Pulled it out again and took a quick look, realtime. There. Low green hills, covered with tall trees. A yellow grassland, encompassing the snaky twists of a small silver stream. Beyond it, backed by snowy gray and white mountains, a wide cityscape of slim tan buildings.

Violet said, "Six-bravo, Murph."

"Right."

Head in the hood again.

Hit the firehaze.

Watch it sparkle in my weaponscope, backscattering radar as we flew over the city. Wonder what they call it?

Called it.

Called it!

I . . . hit the detonator.

Hit the detonator and pulled my head out of the hood, twisting in my seat so I could look back through the stereo-taxis sim and see it happen.

Ah.

Just in time.

Curtains of purple haze hanging like a magic fantasy over the tan Ogygeian cityscape.

Not even time for a heartbeat.

The haze turned to pure white light, white light that slammed to the ground like a heavy foot, heavy foot under a million Gs acceleration.

The city disappeared, just like that, going out with the light, going away, gone.

Imagine.

Imagine.

Peal of thunder sweeping around the world, bowling over forests, sweeping everything from its path . . . I took a deep breath, unable to imagine.

Violet said, "Okay. Let's head for twelve-trillium."

Twelve-trillium. Then targets of opportunity, if any.

I took another deep breath, wondering why the hell I felt like I was suffocating right now, and croaked out: "Rog. Twelve-trillium. Go."

She put her hand on my forearm again, very briefly.

Then we went about our business.

CHAPTER THIRTEEN

Down on Ogygeia, when the battle was over, the skies were a beautiful, serene, clear blue. Cloudless. Utterly cloudless. Standing on the ground by the edge of a landing stage we'd made our own, you could look up into the sky and see nothing but blue, other than those times when the carrier would slowly rise, slowly transit the sky like an improbable moon, itself stained blue by the sky, ejector ports hanging open, defensive turrets motionless, modulus exhaust grids gleaming with a special blue light all their own.

Every now and then, you'd see a little ship come and go from the carrier.

Or see some smaller ship accelerating away from Ogygeia, heading back into the starry deep.

They'd set up a mobile garage here, bringing ships down from the carrier, emptying it of all but its own defensive squadrons. When that was done, the carrier task force would head back to reload, take on new ships, new men, new machines, and we, here, would marshal ourselves, would mount the next attack from Ogygeia, using it as a nonmobile carrier, striking deep into the heart of the Centauri Jet itself, striking at the heart of Ultima Thule.

When people under assault haven't got a chance, why don't they just give up? What's the point of going on, when you can't win?

If they give up now, we won't kill them all, just the leaders. The workforce of the Centauri Jet is too valuable a resource to be so utterly destroyed. That's just what the corporate heads have said.

Don't they believe us?

Walking with Violet, away from the landing stage, toward the pilots' cantina, toward the little row of huts we'd call home for the next few weeks, thinking these thoughts, I smiled to myself.

Not believe us? Not believe the proud, self-made men who enticed their ancestors out here with lies and more lies? Not believe their bosses, the men and women they dealt with day after day after day, long before the war ever came, long before Ultima Thule?

Violet said, "I like it when you smile, Murph. What's so funny?"

I shrugged. "I was thinking about the Thulians."

She gave me an odd look, didn't say anything else as we walked on.

Near the edge of our impromptu base, beside the force-fence that grounds maintenance had set up, there was a little footpath, made in the last day or two, being walked over and over again by heavy-footed AstroMarine guards. Walking along it, you can look out through the pale purple glimmer of the fence at the ruins of the city beyond.

This area hadn't been firehazed, so there was plenty left to see. Most of the buildings were intact, low buildings typical of the architecture used on Ogygeia, the faux-Greek cityscape so popular on your older sort of habitat, from back in the early days of the eutropic shields, around the time they stopped building inside-out worlds like Audumla.

Funny how I still think of Audumla as normal, how these places that mimic *real* worlds are the newfangled oddities.

Maybe they are. There's only *one* natural world, where people walk around under an open sky, sky that thins all the way up to open space, where there's no eutropic shield, a world where, if civilization fell, men and women could live on until the end of time.

Think of that.

Think of our technology failed, of all the people on all the colony worlds dying, one by one.

I wonder how many people are left living on Earth?

I wonder how many of us could get home again, if it came to that?

Enough?

Too many?

Meaningless words.

Maybe someday I'll ask Violet about Earth. Maybe she'll tell me something different from the things I learned about in Porphyry's diorama. Or maybe she'll just tell me Porphyry's world is the one true Earth. Maybe someday. Not today. Maybe never.

You hate to kill a dream on purpose, however faded it's become.

I thought about walking through the backcountry of Audumla, Styrbjörn at my side, pretending I was some old-time man in an old-time forest on Earth. Funny how that fantasy's no longer so comforting.

On the other side of the forcefence, we could see some people on the marble steps of a nearby building, standing in the shadows of its faux-marble colonnade, trying to pick the lock on its bright and dented brass door. They had the electronics access plate open and were fooling with the control structures, obviously having no luck.

It isn't possible to guess how something like that works. If I was over there, I could show them how to do it.

When they saw us walking along, saw me looking at them, they stopped, stood back in the shadows, and stared. Three grown men. A little boy, maybe five or six years old. A rather attractive young woman, so young she had something of the child about her.

Afraid we'll do something about them, call the . . . authorities?

I realized with slight surprise they were merely staring at Violet.

After all, what more can we do to them?

We walked on, went on into the pilots' cantina, where we sat with our friends, all of us so happy to be alive, to have survived another battle, marveling that not one single ATAC vessel had even been damaged, much less destroyed, either by accident or by enemy action.

And praying with all our might that our luck would hold.

I felt like praying, though there's nothing left to hear my prayer.

I miss old Orb.

He was all I had.

So we drank our beer and ate our pretzels, laughed with our temporary comrades, and watched a freeze-frame documentary sequence about ongoing negotiations between the leadership of the Human Defense League, the councils of Ultima Thule, and the chief executive officers of the Corporate Alliance.

Thulians now saying they'd be willing to take a look at outside binding arbitration.

The corporations let some spokesman from Standard ARM do their talking: Nonsense, he said. We can win the war with no help from you or anyone else. Win it no matter how many Thulians have to die. Three words, he said:

Surrender.

Restoration.

Reparations.

In that order.

Later, in our quarters, when we were holding each other close, Violet told me she thought there was something funny about this HDL business, about these negotiations. Like they're not really *trying* to stop the war, to resolve the parties' differences. Like they don't really *care* what happens next. Like something's . . . up.

But what *can* they do? I'd asked.

What can they *really* do?

Let's go on a picnic.

Just the two of us.

The sun-no-sun is shining, the sky is blue, the air is warm, the winds are soft.

I liked seeing the shine in Violet's eyes when I said those things to her as we lolled about in our room, week's work done, wondering what useless, dull thing we could do with our day off.

Her voice was very soft when she told me what a great idea she thought that was.

Just like in the olden days. Just like before . . .

Three more days.

Then we mount our steeds and ride hard for battle.

Maybe there'll never be another chance like this.

Maybe that's what made her eyes shine so, though I confess all I imagined was getting her out under a featureless blue sky, getting her down on the warm ground, sprawling myself naked on top of all her welcoming softness, and dreaming there was no tomorrow, only today.

It's okay to pretend isn't it?

Just for now?

We got our stuff together, pulling the blue blanket off our bed, going on down to the cantina and picking up a big bag of carryout food, sandwiches, drinks, little hotboxes of this and that. Headed on down to the motor pool, marshaling our arguments. It's not against the *rules,* is it? Of course not.

We imagined ourselves wheedling so well.

When we got there, the motor pool sergeant proved to be an old mechanic we'd known for years, a sturdy cyborg named Elcano, designed somewhat along the same lines as Dûmnahn, a gleaming, upright cylinder almost two ems tall, with eight sturdy black legs arranged around the bottom end, six long, spindly robot arms around the top, belt of extensible sensors and replaceable toolmounts girdling his waist.

Very pleasant baritone, the soft voice of an attractive man.

Well, no, it's *not* against the rules, and a picnic *does* seem like a great idea, but . . . Well, the Ogygeian eutropic shield is damaged, you see, leaking air—it'll all be gone in a month or two—could blow out unexpectedly, anytime now . . .

Violet rapped her furry knuckles on his bright chrome chest, bringing out a hollow, almost musical sound. "So what? Throw a couple of space kits in the back of that little ATV over there. We'll know what to do."

There were kits, compact, packaged vacuum emergency suits stacked in their familiar blue cartons, over by the back wall, next to a pile of old nuclear batteries.

A couple of his sensors extended, one looking at the boxed-up spacesuits, the other at the jeep. "Well, sure. I know that. But the truth is, there are still plenty of survivors out there, people who don't know about the leak."

People who imagine they'll somehow survive.

Violet: "So?"

"Marines're gonna stop you at the gate, Vi. Nobody's gets outside the perimeter without a full combat kit."

Violet, sounding exasperated now, said, "All right. Hand 'em over."

Elcano's voice, which seemed to come from nowhere, not even his insides, sounded mournful. "I'm sorry, Vi. I can't issue a positronic rifle to anyone who doesn't have a combat infantry badge. You know that."

And so much for picnic day. I started to bend down and pick up our blanket and bag of food, wondering if we could find some secluded corner somewhere . . . somewhere where we could just goddamned well *pretend* we . . .

"Hang on."

Violet started fishing around in her shoulder bag, obviously looking for something. "Goddamn it . . . Oh. Here." She pulled out a silvery wafer, a common ID disk, and handed it to Elcano.

"Hmh. You surprise me, Miss Violet."

He slipped the thing into a readerslot mounted on his toolbelt, was silent for a second, then said, "Well, well." He extruded the disk and gave it back. "You all take what you need. Marines'll make the final determination. Bring it back when you're done."

We turned away, starting to load up the ATV with junk Elcano was lugging over, and I said, "It's been a long time since Standard ARM was stupid enough to use expensive optimod devices for cannon fodder."

Nothing. Violet climbed into the ATV, sliding behind the driver's seat, while I got in the other.

Elcano put the combat kits in back, then clipped a couple of long, thin rifles to a gunmount behind the front seats. "Okay. Have a nice time, kids. I'll see you later."

As we drove out of the service bay, out into bright, sunless light, back out under that same leaky blue sky, I said, "When were you in the combat infantry, Violet?"

"When?" Very distant, troubled, reluctant look, deep shadows behind her eyes. "I don't know, Murph. It was a long time ago, in a galaxy far, far away."

I knew not to ask any more.

She'd tell me when, if she wanted me to know.

I wasted a few more seconds wondering about it as we bounced over rough ground, headed for the gate. If Violet was one of the very first optimods, she'd've experienced every sort of misuse, back in the days when the corporations wasted expensive machines and biotechnology in a misguided attempt to save the hides of useless human beings.

The guards at the gate gave us no trouble at all. Checked our kits, checked Violet's badge, saluted her, ignored me, sent us on our way. We drove down a ruined street, went round several corners, and . . .

Violet pulled up, slowing to a stop, and we sat staring, unable, at first, to understand what we were seeing. Damaged cityscape stopped here, level ground going on to the horizon. Level ground covered with square boulders, a regolith of dust, bright places where liquid rock had flowed, however briefly.

I wanted to have Orb's name to take in vain. All I could do was say, "I guess this is one of the areas we firehazed a few days ago."

Guess so.

Yup.

Finally, Violet whispered, "A billion people lived here."

After a while, we drove on. I punched up the local mapping system on the dashboard freeze-frame, and said, "It'll take us about ten minutes to get to that reservoir I saw."

Ten minutes. Hell, if it's still there, maybe we can go for a swim.

The air is so nice and warm here.

The reservoir was still there, though there was no telling what it'd originally looked like. Maybe the ravine'd been built up a little bit, for there were still signs, here and there, up near the top of the broken rock walls, of piers and yacht basins and . . . Hell. Everything here is artificial anyway, including the ravine. It looked the way they wanted it to look.

The bright white concrete dam bridging the opening at the bottom of the ravine had fallen, breaking off most of the way down, toppling to lie like a broken shield across the river below. I guess the water must have all rushed out at once, scouring away whatever lay below the dam, leaving mudscape behind, the sinuous trickle of a little creek winding away down in the riverbottom.

There was a boat of some kind stuck nose down in the mud a couple of kems away, shining bright yellow and white, looking like a lost toy, from this distance, though, it must've been fifty ems long.

I tried to imagine the interesting ride its crew and passengers would've had, once the dam gave way.

Funny how people'll go out on a pleasure cruise when there's a battle going on in the sky. Maybe they thought it'd be fun, watching the war from their boat.

Maybe they brought a picnic lunch.

We parked the ATV down in the bottom of the ravine, down where there was a fair-sized pool of clear, clean bright water left behind. It was tempting to imagine that this was a natural lake, the lake that would've been here had the dam never been built, but . . . Right. When was that?

We got out and Violet leaned against the fender of the jeep, watching me get undressed, dropping my clothes on the ground. I've seen optimods wear clothes from time to time, but not Violet. It's not common, anyway. Most of them don't want to be like us.

Her eyes brightened as I became more naked.

Something else I've never asked about.

Maybe someday.

So we went for a swim, laughing, fooling around, doing the things you usually do when you go swimming in private with a woman. I remember, from a long time ago, groping some girlfriend in a public pool, children frolicking all around. Interesting and titillating, feeling her crotch through the thin material of a polka-dot bikini bottom, feeling her shy hand on my prick, maybe imagining no one could see us, under the water.

She'd whispered in my ear, "I wish we were alone . . ."

At the time, I'd been remembering an earlier swim, myself as a child, swimming along underwater, seeing some guy with his hand down the front of a girl's swimsuit. Sure enough, when I looked around, there was a boy chin-deep in the pool, with dark hair streaming water down into his eyes, grinning at us from a few ems away.

Up in the now-world of realtime, Violet and I crawled out of the water, up onto the bare stone beside the remains of the lake, sprawled ourselves under the bright and featureless sky of lost Ogygeia, sat and talked about nothing at all, looking at each other. After a while, we moved closer together and started doing familiar things to one another. Not long after that, our empty talk faded away.

In time, good time, I found myself lying face down between her legs, doing what I knew I was supposed to do, listening to her breathe out those familiar, pleasure-scented sighs, sighs making a lovely tingle crawl right down my spine.

Even animals have this.

Dogs and cats. Mice.

Even goddamned bugs.

So what the hell does it mean to be a sentient being, a creature with a mind?

Nothing.

Nothing at all.

I want my purple fox lady to be happy.

Even if it's only for ten minutes.

Even if it's only this.

Time passes, even when nothing changes. We lay under the blue sky, unable to detect Ogygeia's fatal leak, ate our lunches, and made love again, this time slightly uncomfortable, our stomachs too full.

I remember how Violet put her arms around me, holding me close as I curled my hips under, pushing as far into her as I could, waiting while my orgasm finished itself off, then relaxing as I relaxed, as I let my weight settle fully on top of her, like a man relaxing atop a balled-up rug.

"Sometimes," she whispered in my ear, "this is the best part."

Sometimes it is. Nothing for me to say. No easy way for me to agree.

I could recall being with women who didn't understand that.

Told myself I'd have to figure out some way to tell Violet how much I appreciated the fact that she did.

After a while, we went swimming again, washing away

the mess of sex. Got out and dried ourselves under bright skylight, ate the desserts we'd packed, heating wedges of apple pie in the ATV's campstove, getting them hot enough to melt little wads of stark white ice cream.

When it was time to go, I started putting my clothes on, Violet watching me, eyes full of some pale, washed-out regret.

"Funny," I said, "how the sky's stayed bright for so long. Don't they have night here?"

Violet said, "Maybe the timer's broken."

Maybe so.

We got in the ATV then and let it climb back up to the rim of the ravine, following the same track by which we'd gotten in, driving up the almost-empty bed of the feeder-stream. Somewhere, the mountains that gave rise to the stream were gone, no way for them to skim out rain. Or maybe they never were. Maybe the pumps that fed the rivers of Ogygeia were broken.

Doesn't matter.

When the eutropic shield goes, the atmosphere will go. When the air's gone, the water will boil away to nothing. Ogygeia will be dead as the natural cometary source-core it must once have been, and that will be that.

We parked at the top of the ravine, standing by a collapsed building of some sort, standing at the foot of a broken-off pier, looking down across the ruined landscape for one last time. Someday, a long time from now, I'll be thinking of something entirely different. Something will remind me of this vista, and this one lost moment will live again. I'll remember standing here with Violet, will remember how it felt to have my arm around her furry shoulders, and remember how I felt when . . .

She said, "What's that?"

"Hm?"

She got out from under my arm, cocking her head, turning around, ears erect, obviously listening. "What—"

"Sh."

Then she reached into the back of the ATV and took one of the positronic rifles from the gunmount. "Take yours."

Um. "Violet, I don't know how to operate this."

She said, "Push the black button on the thumb side of your trigger guard. A bayonet'll pop out."

Great. I guess I can look menacing and scare the living shit out of whatever she hears.

I followed her around the side of the collapsed building, watching her tip her head this way and that, erect purple ears like dish antennae, trying not to make any noise, thinking how damned *alien* this made her look. Like the product of some other evolutionary scheme. She stopped at the back of the foundation, by what looked like a flight of concrete stairs, over which the lintel had collapsed, looking down into dusty darkness.

"Vi—"

"Sh."

Still listening.

And, suddenly, I began to hear something too. Faint. Distant. Muffled. Soft whimpering, like a crying child. Violet turned and looked at me with the most incredible alarm in her eyes and I nodded slowly. Yes. I hear it too.

So now what?

She said, "Well, we really ought to . . ." A longing look in the direction of our ATV. I nodded. Right. That's what we ought to do. This is no business of ours.

But.

Yeah.

I think Violet could read these thoughts, plain as you please in my eyes.

She turned away and knelt by the hole, then slowly crawled inside. Just before her feet disappeared, a light came on down there, flooding back past her body. I heard somebody say something too, not Violet, real words, though nothing I could understand.

I looked at my rifle, trying to figure out how to make it light up, gave up quickly for fear that I might make it explode somehow. I knelt to crawl after her, pausing to retract the bayonet so I wouldn't accidentally stick it up Violet's pretty ass and ruin my next few days.

She was lying at the bottom of the stairs, looking down over the edge of a broken ledge into a dark, dusty space below. I crawled beside her and looked myself. Maybe it was a basement or something, but the ceiling had fallen in, fallen under the whole weight of the collapsed building above. Probably just a storeroom, there seemed to be all sorts of crushed junk down here. Broken-open barrels with dark puddles around them. Other things solid enough they were probably all that was holding the space open.

In a weary voice, Violet said, "Oh, Murph . . ."

Down in the dusty shadows, as I lay staring, I could make out the half-naked form of a woman, obviously a woman, white skin, large, saggy breasts, a dark thatch of pubic hair between her spread legs . . . I flinched away from looking at where her left leg flattened, disappearing under a fallen beam. Her other leg was cocked up at a sharp angle, still covered with blue denim.

Probably the other one was too. Probably she'd ripped open her pants to see what she could do. Probably . . .

There was a long knife, some kind of cooking knife, lying beside her. There was what looked like a nice, straight cut on her thigh, not far from where it disappeared under the beam. Not a very deep cut.

And there was a little boy, covered with grime, kneeling beside her, one hand under her head, the other holding a cup from which we could see the reflected shine of some liquid.

Something moved in the shadows beyond, It crept forward, and seemed to be a little girl, naked from the waist up, clad from the waist down in what might have been the tattered remains of a sundress. Her left arm was gone halfway between shoulder and elbow, stump sealed with a tourniquet, skin above it nicely blackened by gangrene.

Artificial worlds are seeded with the regular microbial biome from natural worlds. From *the* natural world. And gangrene organisms also have their regular place in nature.

The woman on the floor, looking up at us, said something in an anguished voice, Ogygeian words no more than a babble of phonemes.

The little boy, fear in his face, stood up, putting down the cup, and took a step backward. When he did, he accidentally bumped against his sister's stump. The little girl grunted and began to cry. It was her voice we'd heard from above.

When I looked back at Violet, she was looking at me, eyes bright with . . . something.

"What'll we do?"

She tried to look back at the people in the hole, turned her head aside, turning to look back up at the little patch of blue sky at the top of the stairs. I wondered if they could see it down below, wondered how many times the boy might have climbed up here, climbed up the stairs, and waited for somebody to come.

"Well," she said, "I guess we could just head on back and . . . report this."

"Nobody'll come. Once the fleet leaves, Ogygeia will be

abandoned." Yes. The shield will fail and . . . long before then, these people . . . The woman was shouting up to us, desperate words, transcending language.

Violet said, "We can take them with us. We were in medevac. You can get her leg off easily enough."

True.

"And then?"

Violet bit her lip, looking back down in the hole again, obviously forcing herself to look. "Marines won't let us bring her through the gate, of course. I guess . . . those people we saw, maybe they would . . ."

I thought about the little band of looters. Sure, we could . . . "Violet, everyone left alive on Ogygeia's going to die shortly."

The woman below had fallen silent, was listening to us talk. Does she understand us? We're talking in one of the more widely known languages, so . . . so maybe she knows. Maybe that's why she's silent.

I said, "So we can put her through the agony of a field amputation done with a first-aid kit, take her and her kids back to the city, and abandon them to die."

Silence. Then Violet said, "Or we can leave them here to die in this hole."

Yeah.

Or we can do the right thing.

I sat looking at Violet, who sat looking at me.

Finally, without a word, she rolled onto her belly and lifted the rifle, pointing it over the ledge, down into the hole. When she thumbed something on the stock, the rifle's business end began to sparkle a lovely emerald green.

Below, the trapped woman suddenly screamed, voice vibrant with horror, full of renewed life.

We lay there for a long, long moment, listening to those

screams, which drowned out the crying of the children, then Violet thumbed the stock again and the tip of her rifle went dark. When she lowered the gun and looked back at me, I felt a pale, awful pang of horror, seeing the triangles of dark, matted fur that had formed so suddenly under her eyes.

I never saw you cry before, Violet.

Very softly, she whispered, "I feel like I'm killing my own puppies, Murph. Mine."

What does it take to make a man's heart stop beating?

Maybe listening to Violet talk about the children she could never have. Maybe that's enough.

She said, "I don't want to leave them here."

Looking into the bright shine of her eyes, I said, "There's no place we can take them. Nothing we can do."

When I looked down at my useless rifle, Violet said, "The red button over there, that's the safety. Press that, then all you have to do is aim it and pull the trigger."

Right.

I rolled onto my belly, looking down over the ledge at those three helpless people. I thumbed the red button, the tip of my rifle began its deadly green sparkle, and this time the woman didn't scream. Through the rangefinder, I could see her face, plain as day, dark eyes looking up at me hopelessly. Her lips seemed to be moving, though I could hear nothing.

No point in looking at the two kids. No point in seeing that.

I said, "I don't think I can do this."

Violet said, "Then we'd better just leave them here."

Yeah. Maybe someone else will come and do what we can't. Or maybe a miracle will happen. Maybe Orb will reach down from the foggy depths of Uncreated Time and lift them straight on up to Heaven.

Violet said, "Murph?"

I shut my eyes and pulled the trigger.

After a while, Violet took the gun out of my hands and locked the safety, then helped me crawl back up into bright blue daylight.

We had a long damned drive back to the base, much longer, it seemed to me, than the nice little drive we'd had coming out. We just rode along in silence, following the directions of the inertial guidance system, bumping over uneven ground under a flat blue sky, going from nowhere to nowhere.

Every now and again, Violet would reach out and pat me on the arm, touch my thigh, whatever.

It seemed to take forever for the leftover cityscape to reappear, but eventually it came over the close horizon, growing out of the ground like a shambles of off-white vegetation. Violet pulled to a stop near one edge, in something that looked like it might once have been a park. Dangerous to stop here, what with all the looters in what was left of the city. No reason to stop here.

Violet sat looking over at me, pathetically hollow-eyed. Finally, she said, "I'm sorry, Murph. You shouldn't have had to do that."

Did I have to? What *was* the right thing? I said, "I'm glad I could do it for you, Vi. I didn't know how you felt about . . ."

She looked away for a second. "I guess I didn't know either. Not 'til right then."

Brief flash of memory. I remembered Dûmnahn talking about what it'd been like, being the self-aware software of a strapped-down robot arm. What was it she'd said then? *Bastards.*

When I said it aloud, here and now, she looked over at me and said, "Who? Us or them?"

No answer.

We got out of the ATV and stretched, looking around at what was left of the Ogygeian park. It'd been right on the edge of the firehaze crunch and represented a damage cline, showing the precision of this new munitions technology, which some smily-faced Standard ARM boffin had probably dug out of the Solar System research archives. Standard probably paid a premium price to buy these patents from whatever rich man owned the rights.

On one side was the broken city, on the other the flat, half-melted, dusty white ground that'd been under the crunch. In between were scattered artifacts, trees, benches, fountains, flowerbeds, more or less destroyed depending on how far they'd been from the edge of the pressure zone.

I realized with a slight start that the odd, humped-up shapes on the ground were mummified human beings.

Maybe they'd gotten a nice view of the battle, sitting out here under the open sky.

Hell, maybe it was night on Ogygeia when the end came.

That would've been pretty, sitting out here in the darkness, looking up at the starry, starry night, watching the flicker-flash-flare of the war pass on by, seeing the purple firehaze curtains rise up and up, like some oh-so-lovely auroral blaze, and then . . .

Yes.

And then.

I flinched, seeing Violet bend low over one of the smaller forms, fearing it might be the remains of a child, but when I came close, I saw it was only a dead dog, looking like a stuffed toy left to bake and shrivel under the fires of a kiln.

Violet said, "Just a puppy."

And then the ATV's caller started to beep.

We went back to the jeep and punched up the dashboard freeze-frame, calling forth a demand-page document. Alert. Alert. Combat emergency recall. All crews to battle stations.

I felt a little flood of relief as we started the engine and drove on in. Stopped me from wondering about Violet's feelings. Stopped me from wondering if we'd been the ones who'd dropped this particular firehaze.

Back at the base, things were in an uproar, ships lined up on the landing stage, technicians rushing about, getting them ready. Our own 022 had been dragged from its hangar with its service panels still hanging open, trailed by techies and trucks while the sirens wailed and ships lifted for the sky.

Violet and I, useless, waited beside our ship, waited, watching the technicians hurry, aghast, knowing how dangerous it was to hurry a task like theirs.

I pictured us lifting for the sky. Pictured us exploding, taking the base with us, because someone had done his job badly, under duress.

Overhead, hanging like a phantasm in the pale blue sky, the carrier was full of shifting light, turrets going this way and that, projector ports opening and closing as it drank down its fleet of defensive fighters. Pretty soon, it would fly away too, flaring brilliant modulus light, growing smaller, then gone.

The crew chief, an odd-looking man with tufts of hair on his face, other tufts poking out of his ears, looking like someone somehow cross-bred from an optimod, came up to us, wiping his hands on his tunic. "Almost done, Commander," he said. "Yours was in good shape anyway. We were done with the rebuild; all we're really doing now is checking connections and reloading your guns."

I said, "What the hell's going on?"

He gave me a peculiar look, something in his face that made me feel like an idiot. "You don't *know*?" Incredulous. How could anybody not *know*?

Violet said, "We were . . . out of touch, Chief."

"Oh. Well." He shook his head slowly, turning away from us, looking up at all the activity in the sky. "Hope the hell we can get these ships finished in time. Hate like hell to get left behind to fend for ourselves."

Surprise. Standard ARM wouldn't leave its techies behind. They're its stock in trade, its most important . . .

Violet said, "Chief?"

He smiled at her. "Observatories started picking up hard radiation fronts from several points around the periphery of the Centauri Jet a few days ago. Weird stuff, like nothing they'd ever seen before. Yesterday, one of the corporation-controlled observatories on this end of the Jet resolved the wavefront system as the modulus exhaust from a large mass of spacecraft undergoing strong deceleration."

I said, "You'd think they might've noticed something like that right away." Modulus exhaust has a rather distinctive spectrum.

The chief said, "The exhaust cones were blueshifted by about one-half cee. Made them look like an incoming high-energy wavefront. Like a pocket supernova or something."

Violet said, "You telling me there's a fleet of ships out there running in on us at half the speed of light?"

"Yep."

Just about four times nominal interstellar transit velocity. "Who the hell . . ."

The chief snickered at me. "Who do you think? Space aliens? Hell, technology back in the Solar System's always been more advanced than what we've got out here. All we ever did was *buy* their fucking research."

Violet said, "You think . . ."

The chief said, "I heard there's already been some kind of fucking broadcast. I haven't seen the full text, though, so I don't know exactly. I guess this is just the first wave."

"First wave of *what*?"

"I heard they're calling it the Human Defense League Arbitration Force. I guess they've come to make us behave." The chief, hands on hips, looking up at the busy sky, seemed to grin. "Think they can?"

We got aloft with no trouble at all, orbiting away from Ogygeia, forming up with our squadron, following an ad hoc carrier task force back into that fabled starry deep. Looking back over my shoulder, I could watch a little blue and white globe recede, looking so much like a whole real world it was hard to believe it was anything else.

And so unchanged. So undamaged. You'd never know we'd done what we did.

Just like old times now, Violet riding in the pilot's seat, I in the CSO's, stereotaxis hood pulled open so it seemed like we rode our chairs, our little pod of control panels, naked to space, stars all around us, peaceful, far away.

Our orders came over the freeze-frame, and we moved in response to them, following the squadron forward, taking up our positions in front of the onrushing enemy fleet, fleet come to strike us all down, force a conclusion to our pathetic little war.

Make us all behave, that's what the chief said.

We won't know about it, though. Out here, without an edge, facing a vastly superior foe. We're just a tripwire force, here to delay the enemy, a little stumbling block that may delay the assault long enough for Standard ARM's main battle fleet to arrive and take them on.

We won't know how that turns out.

We'll all be dead.

So we took our positions and waited.

I turned off the stereotaxis hood and we were engulfed in the warm cocoon of our spaceship cabin, cut off from the universe, alone together in a little vacuole of soft, comforting light, Violet and I side by side, with nothing to say, nothing to do.

When I reached out and touched her arm, not saying anything, she looked at me and smiled a little smile so familiar I'd lost the ability to recall its actual details. Just a smile. Violet's smile. That's all.

She said, "You want to make love one last time, Murph?"

Ah. One *last* time.

But we *might* survive.

Isn't it okay to pretend?

I don't think I wanted to, not right then, and I don't think she wanted to either, but . . . hell. That's what it's all been about, hasn't it? So we'll make love one last time, and then we'll lie together in some quiet, sweet aftermath, and then they'll sound the battle cry, and then we'll go die.

Simple as that.

There weren't many more words for us to say. We crawled over the seats and got into the little bunk, made love one last time, just as we said, clumsy, mechanical, unbearably tender. And then I lay quietly on top of her, our passions cooled, feeling that familiar warmth and closeness evolve toward an inevitable aching void.

Violet said, "I always wondered how a real woman feels, lying here like this, when her man's spilled his seed inside her and she knows the babies will come."

Nothing to say.

No way for me to know . . . anything.

All I could do was hold her close for just a little while longer, then it was time for us to get up and do what had to be done, get back in our seats and watch blue flowers of light form in the sky, separating us from all those faraway stars.

Violet said, "All of this is for nothing, isn't it? No matter how things turn out, it's all for nothing."

I nodded, opening the gunnery interface, tuning up my weapons systems, getting ready.

Violet said, "I keep thinking about those kids we killed, back on Ogygeia."

We didn't kill them, Violet. I did. But thanks for . . . helping me carry the burden.

She said, "There were hundreds of millions of children killed on Ogygeia alone."

And, probably, an Ogygeia destroyed for every day of the war.

What am I supposed to say?

That's life?

She said, "I was ashamed I couldn't kill those children. Couldn't kill them because I had to see their faces. I was ashamed I made you do it."

Nobody made me do it, Violet. I'm a free man.

She said, "I'll be glad when this is over."

Glad when we're dead, Violet? Maybe I will be too, come to think of it. But our deaths won't bring those children back to life. Or any other children, however invisible, we killed just because we were supposed to.

I think I might have said something to her then, something about how glad I was to be here with her now, here to die by her side, about how my last thoughts . . . It seemed so damned stupid, so damned trivial, that I hesitated, wondering if there really *was* anything I ought to say, anything I needed to say, or if I should remain what I'd always been, mute, inglorious, loyal to a fault, and . . .

Then, of course, the freeze-frame began to blink, alerting us to the presence of an incoming demand page.

I started to call it up, hesitated again while I listened to a command circuit override message: *Switch all freeze-frame communications to secure coded channel six and . . .*

I smiled, wondering why the hell they hadn't thought of that before, as I pulled up the demand page circling in our storage ring.

Right.

HDL Arbitration Force demands your surrender.

Right.

Individual crews surrendering their ships will be spared.

Well, what did you expect?

Command circuit was breaking in, reminding us of the corporate Articles of War. No trial, even for those of you who have rights. Just death.

A footnote on the demand page said, Oh, by the way, Solar System Supreme Court has ruled ownership of sentient biotechnologies illegal. HDL has decided to apply this principle throughout human space.

I heard Violet gasp, but I don't think I quite understood what it meant. Not right away.

I said, "Fuck. Dead is dead. What difference do they think it's going to make?"

There was a silence in our ship, then Violet said, "ATACs are the best ships we've got right now. Our squadron mates might get us, but nobody else will."

I twisted in my seat to stare at her, was astounded by the light of hope in her eyes. "Are you saying you want . . ." I gestured at the blue lights of the HDL fleet, looming at us out of the sky.

She said, "It's been almost a thousand years, Murph, since I was made in a vat. Made in a vat and sent out to do my masters' work."

And what difference does it make if this is just another lie, hm? What if HDL turns out to be just another set of masters? What if there *is* no freedom for the likes of us?

I sat back in my chair and watched the lights of the HDL fleet grow larger, brighter, faster, spreading before us, blotting out the stars. It may be that they won't even win, you see, that, one day, Standard ARM and all the others will stand like giants astride the Earth, masters of all they survey.

And yet.

What do I want to say?

That I'll follow you, Violet?

That I'll follow you to the ends of the Earth?

I leaned forward and engaged my gunnery interface, tuning the scanners to maximum range, then I glanced at Violet and said, "Let's go."

Long moment of silence, then Violet brought our field modulus devices up to full power and opened the exhaust grids wide. A few seconds later, one of the other ships followed us, surging away from the line of battle, toward the oncoming enemy fleet. I think, for almost a minute, nobody could believe what we were doing, then the rest of our comrades opened fire.

The other ship, friends whose names we'd never know, was hit, exploding in a ball of golden fury, just before we got out of range.

CHAPTER FOURTEEN

The war went on for another thirty thousand days.

Here at the other end of history, time kills us statistically, not inevitably, but we die nonetheless.

Worlds destroyed, like so many popped soap bubbles. Endless billions dead, lives snuffed as though they never were, yet there were always more billions waiting in the wings, more worlds waiting to be destroyed. And the war, begun with a technology of profitable lassitude, ended with a technology driven by desperation to make up the lag of a thousand years and more.

Over.

Over and done with.

Violet and I rode homeward, threading the center of the starbow's eye, sitting side by side in naked black space, surrounded by the stereotaxis hood's descendant, heaven's glory crushed flat in the sky but for the pale blue dot of our destination.

Homeward.

No home for time's orphans, of course, but there's always

hope we can make a home for ourselves, somewhere, some-when. That kind of hope always dies hard.

Killing time, the same deadly time that'd formerly killed men, I worked with the freeze-frame, trying to extract information from the DataWarren's microwave squeal, but it was useless. We were moving too fast, crossing too many beam-lines at too sharp an angle. We have better computers nowadays, better able to process that red- and blue-shifted data, but the transceiver technology is old, reaching its endpoint long before humanity ever tried for the interstellar deep.

Maybe someday.

Violet looked over at me, face shadowed, half-lit by the layered coloring of the distorted sky. "Why bother? We'll be there soon enough."

I pushed the freeze-frame back into its mount, watching the swirl of static fade away to nothing, the gray carrier tracks shimmer and go dark. "They were about to put Finn mac Eye on trial when we left Mireille. I keep wondering what happened."

"What difference does it make?"

"I don't know. Maybe none." Finn mac Eye and Meyer Sonn-Atem weren't the bad guys here. What happens to them . . .

Violet said, "You think the corporations got what they deserved?"

I shrugged. Who knows? Not quite the same thing as *who cares,* but . . . Rules and regulations. Companies broken up into their component parts and turned over to minority stockholder consortia. Principal officers and boards of directors convicted of crimes against . . . not humanity.

Crimes against us all.

And sentenced. Stripped of their wealth, placed in suspended animation, and shoved into a museum exhibit on

Earth. Here lies the Chief Executive Officer of Standard ARM, name forgotten, who figured he owned everything he could steal.

Not quite a sentence of death.

They'll sleep until someone, somewhere, somewhen, wants them to live again.

I said, "Seems fair to me."

"Time."

Violet hit the brakes and our PBX-15 relativistic patrol bomber, destroyer of whole worlds, shuddered around us, starbow opening like an accordion, colors fading to monochrome, growing dim, reevolving to a black sky, full of stars. A hundred thousand AUs from Mireille to the near-empty space just off the Centauri Jet's distal end. Twenty months of threads pulled from Uncreated Time. Three hours for us.

What would the lost millennium have been like, had these things been available from the time Violet was decanted?

Different.

Wonderful?

Or more horrible than we can possibly imagine?

No use wondering.

History's what happened.

Ahead of us now, Ygg was a small, sullen globe, unchanged from when I'd seen it last. Try as I might, I couldn't remember it from my last visit home. Those few pathetic days are smothered under childhood memories of Ygg seen from various vantage points, assorted times. Mostly, I remember it peeking down from the sky, peering over the edges of the habitat panels.

Imagine seeing all that again, just as if my life hadn't happened.

There.

A pale diamond in the sky, reflecting starlight, Ygglight, the distant glow of the Alpha Centauri suns. It grew larger swiftly as Violet flew us down to the system ecliptic and swung us in toward rendezvous with Audumla.

She said, "I was born on such a world."

Maybe even the same one. I can't remember now if Standard ARM Decantorium XVII was built in situ or towed here from far away, long ago. I'll have to look it up sometime.

I extruded the freeze-frame again and started trying to rouse Audumla's traffic control center. Funny. It should come right up, should already *be* up, challenging us for having entered their vector space at such high velocity. Just who do you think you *are* . . .

Violet said, "Murph."

I knew what I was going to see, even before I looked up.

Audumla was hanging motionless between us and the backdrop of stars. Dark, motionless, looking like some discarded oxygen cylinder, cast off from the ruin of an exploded starship. One of the lightpanels between the habitats was blown out, huge triangular shards clinging to its frame, though the other one we could see seemed intact.

No light from within.

Nighttime?

Surely that's all it is.

The stemshine's been put out so the people and plants and animals and things can have a good rest.

Violet, voice quiet, said, "Maybe we should just leave. Go on to Earth."

Go on to Earth, where we'd be part of the new universe abuilding, the new future for humanity, for mankind and all its children. Children that now included everything we, in our arrogance, in our arrogant innocence, had made.

I said, "No. See if you can dock to the axial port. There are . . . standard manual emergency procedures we can follow."

From the hub, Audumla was an empty black cave, Violet and I standing side by side in a vacuole made from the faint glow of our skinshields, standing at the edge of the abyss. For just a moment, it was as if the universe itself had disappeared, leaving just the two of us, all the matter still in existence, as a seed for the new cycle of being to come.

I felt Violet put her hand in mine, appreciated her silence.

There it is. There's my whole world, darkness giving way before my senses. Now I can make out the dim shadow of the dead stemshine, stretching away to infinity. Below, I can make out the faint mass of the south endcap mountains, blackness blotting out the lesser darkness beyond.

Directly below where we stood was a lightless habitat panel, but to either side, and directly above, beyond the long, narrow bulk of the stemshine . . . that's it. Stars. Only stars. Pallid little dots barely able to pass through murky . . . This one over here. Brighter. Cleaner. That's the one from which the integument is gone.

We could jump that way, jump right out into the space between the stars.

As I watched, the dim leading edge of Ygg appeared, seeming to light the landscape around us with a pale imitation of sunlight.

Violet said, "You don't have to do this if you don't want to. We can just go on back to the ship and—"

I shook my head. "No. If I don't *see*, I'll always wonder."

She said, "I . . . guess I understand."

And maybe she did. Who knows?

On our way to the elevator portal, which turned out to be

dead as the rest of Audumla, we stumbled over a body lying quietly in the middle of the walkway, not decayed at all, of course, only withered from its long exposure to vacuum.

Natura abhoret a vacuo.

Not far from the body, which appeared to be that of a man—it was a little hard to tell—were others, grouped together, all sprawled on their faces in various grotesque postures. "As if," Violet said, "they were killed as they ran."

Ran. Running from the elevator toward the south axial docking port, where there may or may not have been a waiting ship. I suppose, if I wanted to, I could look up the records for the Battle of Ygg. Seized corporate archives. The internal histories of Ultima Thule. Even records from my own HDL. *My own.* Mine. Maybe they'd even mention somewhere the unfortunate destruction of the Audumla habitat.

The Mother's Children of Audumla are gone.

I can't quite make myself understand that.

Violet said, "It must have been a hell of a sight. Big explosion outside, not far from the broken lightpanel, maybe a starship getting it. The blast would have come in and flattened everything, then the backdraft—" She stopped suddenly, looking at me. "Sorry."

I patted her on the arm. "The exciting parts were always so tempting, weren't they?"

Tempting us to the excitement of participation. Exciting to be the destroyer of whole worlds. And all those pitiful billions of ants who lived down there? What difference does it make?

They were only ants.

When we got to the elevator stage, we found three elevator cars lifted off their tracks and flung up against the back wall of the platform, a fourth car hanging at an odd angle from its mount maybe a dozen ems below the platform rim. There were more bodies here, scattered like so many life-size black dolls, no longer worth our attention.

The other six tracks were empty.

Violet tried to talk me into going back to the ship one last time; then, when I was adamant, put her arm around my shoulders. Just one small, quiet squeeze, then we went on down the cliff face using our skinshield impellers, dropping silently downward, our globe of blue pastel light making a moving disk on the endcap mountain wall, as though we were being followed by a wan spotlight.

On stage.

Always on stage.

Performing for the invisible masses.

My mother's house looked like a giant fist had punched it in, collapsed to flinders and splinters and shards of walls, very little left of its interior volume. There was a corpse in the front yard, obviously human, but when I turned the thing over, light and stiff and waterless, the distorted face was un-recognizable, no one, I suppose, I'd ever known. A neighbor, perhaps.

The face had an expression of sorts, recognizable through all the leathery wrinkles, white teeth glimmering past down-turned lips.

Dismay.

We walked around the side and climbed over the rubble to where my room had been, to the balcony where I used to do my homework while looking out over the interior of Audumla, looking down on the bayou country, thinking about Himerans and allomorph whores when I should have been thinking about my future life, soon to come. It'd fallen an em or two, and the room behind, my old room, was collapsed.

Among the debris, we could pick out distinct artifacts, homely things. A man's faux-leather cordovan shoe. An athletic sock. Something that looked like it might once have been a portable freeze-frame.

This might be my brother's stuff. Lenahr always seemed like the sort of boy who'd stay home with his mother forever.

Maybe if I dug through the rubble long enough, I'd find them now, huddled together in the atrium, perhaps, cowering in fear, just as they died.

Violet touched my arm and, when I turned, looked into my eyes. "I keep expecting you to cry," she said, "but you don't."

No. I said, "It was a long time ago."

She looked away, out into the darkness. "I keep trying to imagine how I'd feel if it was me, but . . ."

Right. Violet, optimod, daughter of the vat.

We left the balcony, going around back, walking through the rubble-strewn yard. The grass was still neatly in place, all dead of course, like a dry carpet under our feet. Here and there, the antlerlike remains of rosebushes poked up, still surrounded by their neat circles of bare earth.

All the care that went into this place.

All the imitation love.

To my surprise, the storeroom outbuilding was still standing, its door gaping open, still attached to the hinges. Last stop, I thought, stepping inside.

How odd.

Some fluke of physics had kept the blast and reflux from reaching in here. Everything was still in its place, mostly potting tools, bags of soil, the organic fertilizers my mother lavished on her gardens. And there, over in the corner, just as I'd left it after my last visit, was my father's abandoned skiff.

Huddled beneath it, propped up in the room's corner, arms wrapped around her knees, head down, was one of my mother's silvergirl slaves. Stone cold.

Violet knelt beside the thing, making a quick inspection, then she said, "We really should take this back to the ship. If we can power her up again . . ."

Right. The newly promulgated code of ethics regarding the disposition of artificial life-forms . . . I said, "There would've been a pretty bad radiation pulse in here. I'm sure her programming's long erased."

Violet nodded slowly, slowly coming to her feet, still looking down at the silvergirl. A trillion dead, maybe? What difference can one more possibly make?

She said, "Can we go back to the ship now?"

As we came back out through the storeroom's door, I looked up at the sky, toward the blown-out lightpanel, filled now with round Ygg's red light. "No reason," I said, "why we couldn't fly the ship around and land it down on the bottomland of the bayou country."

Violet looked at me for a long time. Then she said, "Maybe I *do* understand."

Seen from above, lit by the waste light of an interstellar drive running at dead idle, the bayou country looked like nothing at all, like a dead lawn, flakes and stalks and swatches of dry forest, the sinuous rilles of empty riverbeds curling between the flat black knobs of the denuded hills . . . Nothingness. Just bits, reflecting back the guttering blue light of our exhaust, catching it for a moment, then gone.

It seemed almost as though we were drifting, or hanging motionless in space while the dark inner surface of Audumla turned underneath us. Going nowhere. Nowhere at all, but . . . there was silent Violet purposefully piloting, driving our ship toward the destination I'd specified, slowing, slowing . . . There.

The Timeliner Firehall still stood, though the old, abandoned apartment blocks beyond were leveled, nothing left of them but a field of stony rubble, no pile more than a few ems high. The Firehall had been made of solid granite, shipped in from elsewhere at some expense, at the whim of some religious dictate I couldn't remember.

Authentic, my father called it.

Just as if it were real.

Just as if we were real.

Real man. Real boy.

When Violet landed us in the parking lot, drivelight flickering and swirling, lighting up the facade for just a moment before winking out, I imagined I could hear the crunch of gravel under our landing skids. There weren't any cars here today. Maybe there *had* been when . . . I imagined them blowing away on quick winds of plasma fire, or being sucked back out through the broken lightpanel, out into the black of space, where they'd presently join Ygg's orbiting ring of debris.

We got out of the ship, walking down its shallow ramp and across the parking lot, surrounded by skinshield glow, like two sprites dancing in the corner of someone else's eye, like two young ghosts showing up for their job of househaunting.

Somehow, it was darker inside, starlight snuffed by the walls, alcoves and altars highlit by shieldlight, casting stark, impenetrable shadows beyond. I wanted to show things to Violet, tell her all about my boyhood dreams, illustrate the things I'd already told her during long nights between the stars, idle moments between terrifying battles.

Useless.

All of it useless.

I led her quickly down the long corridor, just as quickly found the niche.

My father's urn was on its side, lid missing, empty.

I picked it up in one glowing hand and peered down inside, looking at the shiny bottom, then put it back on its base in the niche and stood for a moment, staring, not knowing what to do.

There's dust all over the place in here.

Some of it must be him.

Violet said, "When we get to Earth, there are some places I want to go too."

I turned and held her in my arms for just a minute, or maybe she held me. Then we turned and walked away, walked away just as quickly as we'd come.

I turned back just once, looking over my shoulder just before we went through the crooked remains of the empty doorframe, looking back into the black, empty shadows of the Firehall, wondering what Orb himself might have made of it all.

Back aboard our deadly little ship, warship drifting over what little remained of the Audumlan landscape once again, I told Violet I wanted to make just one more stop, or maybe two. Then we can be on our way, on our way to Earth and the beginning of all those dreams we've waited so long to dream.

Violet took her eyes off the landscape, off the controls, knowing the ship could look after itself, as needed. The expression on her familiar face was serious, but . . . something of a smile there as well, faint, hardly visible at all.

"Take as long as you need," she said. "Close all the doors. Lock them. Walk away when you're ready."

Somewhere, sometime, she'd have doors that needed closing too. Then I'll be waiting, standing by to give whatever help I can.

That's all you ever ask of a friend, isn't it?

All you can ever ask of anyone.

I pulled out the freeze-frame, switched it over to radar light, and watched the underlying structure of the inside-out landscape map itself in front of me. Familiar hills. Rivers and valleys . . . I remembered motoring our little skiff up a river just like that one, my father, back toward me, head bent over his toolkit, working steadily away between the thwarts, whispering softly to himself, seldom speaking to me.

A composite memory, perhaps, standing in for the real events of my childhood.

Those years were so few in comparison to the ones I've had since, but they stand out in stark relief, fantastically detailed, as if they are the only real things that ever happened, as if everything since then has come out of a dream.

A dream that I'll soon forget.

Sometimes you meet people who say that, for them, it's just the other way round. I can't imagine what that would be like. I stole a quick glance at Violet, bent over her controls, looking from instrument to instrument and back again. Can't imagine what her sense of having lived is like either.

"There," I said, marking a certain hill, half-surrounded by the curve of a small, empty river, marking it with a brief pip of green light in the global display.

Violet brought the ship in low over the tall, bare sticks that were all that was left of the trees, brought it in toward the crest of the hill almost as if she were gliding in air, setting it down not far from what appeared to be a low pile of rubbish, a scattering of debris.

For just a moment, I thought I was going to be too afraid to go out, but . . . You're here to close doors, I told myself. So close them and move on.

There was a soft whir as Violet extruded the ship's ramp, blue light of the skinshields spilling softly as the life-support system put our environmental air back in storage. The world grew still then, no more sounds.

I got out of my seat, went down the ramp, and stood in the darkness outside. There was just enough light from the stars, combined with the localized, weaker light from my shield, I could make out the shadows of my surroundings. The remains of the old "house," made so lovingly from boxes and scraps, packing crates, whatever else they could find.

Here were the trees, bare sticks standing up, many more lying flat on the ground, all singed, short of the leaves. Here was the long, once-muddy slope of hill, leading down to a bare sand beach, leading down to the hollow curve of what had once been a river.

I imagined myself waiting on the shore, waiting for him to come, listening for the soft whir of the outboard motor.

No more.

Gone into the shadows, never to return.

Is that all I have left?

Shadows?

There were shadows on the ground around my feet, bits and pieces of things, unrecognizable. I turned one over with the softly glowing toe of my boot and saw that it was part of a small robot. A kit. This is one of Mrs. Trinket's kits.

I wonder where she is now? If I search the rubble, will I find her there, the battered, empty shell of a refrigerator, nothing left inside but fragments of gears and dry lengths of old plastic tubing? Worse still, I might find her intact, lying there, mind erased, fluids evaporated, no expression at all on her little doll face.

Violet had come out of the ship as well, was standing by my side, looking down into the darkness, silent, pensive. I wonder what she makes of all this nonsense.

She said, "There's something moving over there." A slight gesture, secretive. "Over there, by the edge of the forest."

I looked, careless, and saw quick movement, the movement of a greater shadow, occluding the lesser darkness beyond.

The shadow stood taller and began lurching unsteadily toward us. If there'd been air to carry the sound, I imagine I would have heard sound effects from some romance horror fantasy, something from the corroded depths of the net. The unsteady thump of the crippled monster's heavy boot.

It came into the circle of light cast by our skinshields, a tall, bent cylinder with two short legs positioned at two points of an equilateral tripod, walking with the aid of its one long arm. We waited.

Finally, a soft radio voice was in our ears: "Yes. Dr. Darrayush. Thank God you've come at last."

God.

I said, "Hello, Beebee. I'm, uh . . . glad . . . are there . . ." Words failing, as usual.

He staggered forward like a cripple on a crutch, coming close to me, and said, "Only a few, Darrayush. Only a very few indeed." Something like the tinge of pride in that radio voice. "I was an outside welder, you see. My makers thought I might need to survive an industrial accident of . . . considerable magnitude."

Violet said, "Radiation-hardened."

Beebee looked at her. "Yes, ma'am. Ah, I see you're a very fine optimod indeed. They used to make optimods here."

They.

He said, "But it was a long time ago."

"Trinket?"

He stood absolutely still. Then, "Nothing much that wasn't meant for hull work survived, Dr. Darrayush. We found a couple of baby incubators in cold storage, buried under the wreck of an old warehouse upcountry. Just unused leftovers from the good old days."

I remembered Mrs. Trinket's kit, what was her name? Maxine. That's it. I remember her watching Mrs. Trinket giving birth, big-eyed, to that baby welder, so long ago. She must have lived long enough to have kits of her own, for those kits to have kits, but . . .

Beebee said, "We've managed to put up a pressurized habitat down by what's left of the industrial monoblock, so when they get old enough . . ."

Beebee and the other hull machines can breed more hull machines, which will also be able to live without warmth, without air. And, of course, every once in a while, a new baby incubator will be born.

"Is there anything you need?" Stupid. Stupid words popping out of my mouth, unbidden, as always.

They need everything.

He tipped back to rest on the crooked base of his cylinder, balanced teetering as he lifted up that one remaining arm. "Spare parts would be nice."

I said, "All sorts of things laying around in the big dump on Mimir's Well."

"We know that. It'll take us a while to build a spaceship,

though. There aren't any left here. Except for bits and pieces."

I looked toward our attack bomber.

Well.

Hardly a cargo hull, but . . .

Violet put her hand on my shoulder and said, "We could put in a call to the Reconstruction Authority. There are several programs for helping damaged habitats get back on their feet. And, of course, you'd qualify for any number of low-interest loans from the Manumitted Intelligences Welfare Agency. I—"

The tattered sensor pack at Beebee's crumpled waist turned toward her, solid-state sensors gleaming in our light. "We'd . . . like to do it on our own, if we could." A silence; then, "An optimod should understand that."

Violet said, "Yes."

I said, "I'm not sure if there are any Audumlan Mother's Children left alive besides me. I'll do what I can to see a proper quitclaim's been filed. Audumla's yours now."

"Himera. We called it Himera before the Mother's Children came."

Himera, then.

On the way out, floating over the wan and shadowy bayou country, drifting toward the smashed lightpanel and the hard white stars beyond, I stopped us at a place I hadn't thought I wanted to visit, Violet swinging the ship up the course of a wide, flat riverbed, full of dry sandbars, banks well trenched by anomalous erosion.

I remember how seeing this, seeing it when the world was alive, made me realize how far Audumla had gone downhill over the years. I remember imagining that someday the ruin would be complete. Someday, the Mother's Children would evacuate Audumla, leave it to suffocate and die, too expensive, too complex for them to maintain.

Now it lies dead anyway, hard-frozen in time.

There. There's the little village I remember so well, little white houses smashed to splinters and scattered across the bristling, dead remnants of the green. Maybe Styrbjörn's dead down there as well, crushed flat atop one last mechanical whore.

Stupid.

I picture him dead like that because it pleases me to imagine his last moments, thrusting away, feeling his orgasm build, then the final white light, painless and swift.

But he probably died hunched over his desk, doing the job he was so proud to have, auditing one last account.

Still, the white light would have come.

I remember how I always imagined Violet and I would die in combat, facing the white light together.

Flash.

Then gone to some impalpably serene eternity.

Beyond the river, beyond the crushed town, beyond hills littered with the ruins of dead trees, Violet set our spacecraft down in a splash of blue haze at the top of an exposed slope, the remains of an open field.

We got out, and I stood still, stood quietly, looking across my grassy knoll at nothing. Not even shadows here. What the hell? Did I expect to find my long-lost allomorph whore lying here, waiting for me, empty eyes turned up toward the darkened heavens, legs spread just so?

Don't know what I expected.

Maybe only this.

Violet said, "Why are we here?"

She'd come to expect my relics, expect their physical reality.

So I told her about my field of butterflies. Told her about my formless, featureless, nameless allomorph whore, whore with eyes of glass who lay underneath me one day, a long time ago.

There was a silence. Then she said, "We remember funny things, don't we?"

Idle relics of the past. Things that let us imagine we've lived, when nothing else remains.

She said, "I have a memory too. I can't remember where it comes from, or when it happened. Can't be sure it really happened at all. I'm lying under a man. He's finished with me. The night is damp and still and quiet as I feel him recede. And I imagine that . . . just this once . . . somehow . . ."

It's the same memory as mine.

I knelt on the ground, deep in the shadows, trying to call up memory of my past, trying to see those ancient perspectives, imagine that *this* is the spot where . . . Something on the ground in front of me, a tiny, flat, dark shape on the dry dead grass.

Maybe it's a yellow butterfly, like a buttercup shining in the stemlight, preserved for me, the relic I seek.

When I tried to pick it up, it crumbled away to nothing like a flake of dry ash.

I stood. We turned away and walked back to the ship, walking slowly to the ramp, which rose up behind us.

The sun, the real Sun, grew before us in rectified stereotaxis as we flew onward, as we braked our speed, slaking the interstellar drive, dropping into the controlled flight patterns of old, established commercial lanes, passing among all the inhabited worlds.

The war never came here, though it ended here, in some very real sense.

And, as we passed among the worlds, Violet grew increasingly quiet, increasingly pensive, wrapped in herself, not quite closing me out.

My turn now to stand by, ready to hold on, ready simply to *be* as she went about the business of closing doors, of making room in her heart for all our tomorrows.

I found myself imagining us standing together, holding hands in a room full of stainless steel vats. This is where I was born, she'd say. From this tub right here. Patting it on a chipped white enamel rim, looking down into its shiny depths, like a child adoring its mother.

That would make us the same, wouldn't it?

The old habitat, when we finally got to it, was hanging by itself in Mars' barely stable leading co-orbital libration center, an immense, silver-gray wheel, turning oh-so-slowly against the motionless backdrop of faraway stars. Stars that, once upon a time, were no more than meaningless flecks painted on a black velvet canvas.

How wonderful, I remember thinking, that they one day became real.

How terrible, what they became.

I picked out bright Sirius, and had a stark memory of Porphyry's bedroom, of lying on her too-willing flesh, lying on demand, at her command.

In all my wondering about all the unknown dead, I never once wondered about her, wondered about her fate.

Sitting with Violet, waiting for her to decide, I realized I hoped Porphyry was all right, making a new life somewhere for herself.

Forgive her, after what she'd done to me, to that poor girl, to so many others, known and unknown?

Well.

Forgiveness is mine to give.

Violet said, "When I was young, it was bright chrome silver. Shining silver, like a mirror."

She reached out for her controls and slid us toward the axial docking port.

In bare minutes, we stood in a dusty, dimly lit gray corridor, looking into a room full of old, dented stainless steel vats, whisked through the almost empty, almost lightless, almost lifeless habitat by its still-functioning system of conveyors.

Over in the corner, by a splayed-open toolkit, a small, gray-furred, seallike optimod male was bent over a tangle of old plumbing, muttering softly to himself, whispering, the way a person will while trying to work his way through some complex problem.

He looked up when we stepped into the room, smiling at Violet, though not at me.

"Hello, ma'am. Come to see the old place?"

She looked around, wide-eyed, seeming bewildered. "I . . . think I was born here. In this room."

He put his tools aside and stood up slowly. "I was too. A lot of us were, back in the old days. There're pretty good records in the habitat's memory core, if you want to see which exact vat it was."

I said, "Would it still be here?"

He gave me a look. "Humans often make things and . . . just leave them to sit."

Violet put her hand on the edge of one of the vats, looking in at the connectors, which looked like nothing so much as the plumbing you'd see inside a gutted robot incubator.

This is the way Mrs. Trinket would've looked after the war got through with her.

When she turned away, expression guarded, eyes hooding some kind of pain, Violet looked at the optimod's toolkit, at the tangle of exposed tubing he'd been sorting through, and said. "What is it you're doing here?"

He cocked his head to one side, glanced briefly at me, smiled, then said, "Don't you know, ma'am? We've won the right to control our own reproduction."

One long, still moment, then Violet turned and looked at me.

We got to Earth at last, tourists with nowhere in particular to go.

It was sunset and, not far from the cosmodrome where we landed our little ship, we found a vast park, relic of an era when the only inhabitants of Earth were the richest of the rich, human men and women with wealth so immense it had no meaning.

The park wasn't a wilderness, but then we had no sense of what a real wilderness ought to be like.

The dark forests of Telemachus Major's green garden moon? Manufactured, of course. The riotous vegetation, the scummy swamplands in Audumla? Manufactured, then let grow to ruin.

We stood at the top of a long, low hill, looking down into a broad valley flooded with summery sunset light. There was a little stream down there, carefully kept grass lawn ending at a little white beach, tucked in the crook of the river.

I imagined little boys and girls playing down there, but there was no one.

This is, I remember thinking, just like the field of butterflies where I took my nameless allomorph whore. What would she think of it, were she still alive?

I imagined others in quick succession.

Ludmilla? Of course.

And Reese? Would Reese like it here?

How about Jade? Jade died in a place much like this, on a fine day not so different from this one.

Even Porphyry.

Porphyry would like it here.

I turned then and looked at Violet, who took my hand and said, "Let's go home now."

When I looked away from her, there was indeed one lone yellow butterfly, lifting off from a little blue flower.

Happily ever after.

Is that the fairy-tale ending we seek?

If so, then one day I sat by myself at the top of a long, low hill, looking downslope toward another familiar, small winding river. Beyond it, a broad, green, well-mannered forest curved up the side of one of Himera's habitat panels, growing ever smaller until it disappeared in the blue mist of distance.

Overhead, the stemshine grew dim as night began to fall, and as the blue sky beyond the panel turned dark, the stars began popping out, one by one, just as they did when I was a boy, so very long ago.

How is it that I came to be here?

Is this what I really wanted?

Was there another life I might have lived?

How does *that* story go?

Two dark shadows separated themselves from the hillside not far away, a tall black cylinder with long, spindly arms, one arm reaching out to clasp the hand of a small humanoid figure.

When they resolved themselves, it was Beebee, shiny and new again, the other figure that of a small gray optimod boy, just a few months out of the vat, growing to adulthood with astonishing speed, though nothing abnormal for his kind.

Beebee planted himself firmly on the ground beside my tree, becoming part of the silent landscape.

The boy sat down beside me, snuggling against my side as I put my arm around him.

Overhead, the sky had grown dim enough that Ygg was beginning to show through the habitat portal, like a dull red coal.

Down on the hillside there was a third shadowy figure, Violet making her way up to join us, finished with the deeds of the day, moving through blue dusk, surrounded by the moving yellow sparks of a firefly cloud, part of a set piece I must always have dreamed, dreamed so often it finally became real.

Am I happy?

You know the answer.

Even now I imagine real life can support happy endings that go on and on, while only stories must fade to black.

Don't Miss Any of These Masterpieces From

DAVID FEINTUCH'S SEAFORT SAGA

- **MIDSHIPMAN'S HOPE**
(0-446-60-096-2, $5.99 US) ($6.99 Can.)

- **CHALLENGER'S HOPE**
(0-446-60-097-0, $5.99 US) ($6.99 Can.)

- **PRISONER'S HOPE**
(0-446-60-098-9, $6.50 US) ($8.50 Can.)

- **FISHERMAN'S HOPE**
(0-446-60-099-7, $5.99 US) ($6.99 Can.)

- **VOICES OF HOPE**
(0-446-60-333-3, $6.50 US) ($8.50 Can.)

AND ALSO AVAILABLE THE FIRST FANTASY NOVEL BY DAVID FEINTUCH

THE STILL
(0-446-60-551-4, $6.50 US, $8.50 Can.)

ASPECT®

AVAILABLE AT BOOKSTORES EVERYWHERE FROM WARNER ASPECT

1004